STEEL KING

USA *TODAY* BESTSELLING AUTHOR

DEVNEY PERRY

STEEL KING

Editing & Proofreading:

Elizabeth Nover, Razor Sharp Editing

www.razorsharpediting.com

Marion Archer, Making Manuscripts

www.makingmanuscripts.com

Julie Deaton, Deaton Author Services

www.facebook.com/jdproofs

Karen Lawson, The Proof is in the Reading

Cover:

Sarah Hansen © Okay Creations

www.okaycreations.com

OTHER TITLES

Jamison Valley Series

The Coppersmith Farmhouse

The Clover Chapel

The Lucky Heart

The Outpost

The Bitterroot Inn

The Candle Palace

Maysen Jar Series

The Birthday List

Letters to Molly

Lark Cove Series

Tattered

Timid

Tragic

Tinsel

Clifton Forge Series

Steel King

Riven Knight

Stone Princess

Noble Prince

Fallen Jester

Tin Queen

Runaway Series

Runaway Road

Wild Highway

Quarter Miles

Forsaken Trail

Dotted Lines

The Edens Series

Christmas in Quincy - Prequel

Indigo Ridge

Juniper Hill

Calamity Montana Series

Writing as Willa Nash

The Bribe

The Bluff

The Brazen

The Bully

CONTENTS

CHAPTER ONE

BRYCE

"Morning, Art." I saluted him with my coffee as I walked through the glass front door.

He returned the gesture with his own mug. "Hiya, girlie. How are you today?"

At the *Clifton Forge Tribune*, I was *girlie*, *dear* and the occasional *sweetheart*, because at thirty-five, I was the youngest employee by thirteen years. Even as part owner, I was still seen as the boss's kid.

"Fantastic." I shimmied my shoulders, still feeling the dance party I'd had in my car on my way in to work. "The sun is shining. The flowers are blooming. It's going to be a great day. I can feel it."

"I hope you're right. All I can feel at the moment is heartburn." Art chuckled and his protruding belly jiggled. Even in a pair of cargo pants and a light blue button-up, he reminded me of Santa Claus.

"Is Dad here?"

He nodded. "Been here since before I showed up at six. I think he's trying to fix one of the presses."

1

"Damn. I'd better go make sure he hasn't gotten pissed and dismantled the whole thing. See ya, Art."

"See ya, Bryce."

I cruised past Art at the reception desk and pushed through the interior door that opened to the office's bullpen. The smell of fresh coffee and newspaper filled my nose. *Paradise.* I'd fallen in love with this smell as a five-year-old girl when I'd gone to work with Dad on a bring-your-daughter-to-work day, and nothing had topped it since.

I walked the length of the empty bullpen, past the desks on each side of the center aisle to the door at the back that opened to the pressroom.

"Dad?" My voice echoed in the open room, bouncing off the cinder-block walls.

"Under the Goss!"

The ceilings extended high above me, the ductwork and pipes exposed. The unique, musky smell of newspaper was stronger in here, where we kept the giant paper rolls and drums of black ink. I savored the walk across the room, inhaling the mix of paper and solvents and machinery oil as my wedge heels clicked on the cement floor.

My childhood crush hadn't been on a boy, it had been on the feel of a freshly printed newspaper in my hands. It was a mystery to my parents why I'd gone into TV and not newspaper after college. There'd been a lot of reasons, none of which mattered now.

Because here I was, working at my dad's newspaper, returning to my roots.

The Goss printer was our largest and main press. Positioned along the far wall, it extended from one side of the building to the other. Dad's jean-clad legs and brown boots were sticking out from beneath the first of four towers.

"What's wrong today?" I asked.

He scooted himself free and stood, swatting at his jeans and leaving black streaks of grease and ink on his thighs. "Damn thing. There's something wrong with the paper feed. It hitches about every tenth rotation and screws up whatever page it's on. But it all looks fine under there so I don't know what the hell I'm trying to fix."

"Sorry. Anything I can do?"

He shook his head. "Nope. We'll have to call in a specialist to get it fixed. God knows how long that will take and how much it'll cost. For right now, all we can do is print extra to make up for it."

"At least it still works and we're not using the manual press." I shot a glare at the ancient machine in the far corner. I'd only used it once, just to learn how it worked, and my arm had hurt for a week afterward from all the cranking.

"You'd better budget for a new press, or a serious mechanical overhaul on this one, in the near future."

I tapped my temple. "Got it."

Dad had been talking about future budgets and future plans since I'd moved to Clifton Forge six months ago. At the moment, we shared ownership equally—I'd bought half the business when I'd moved to town. Eventually I'd buy the rest of the *Tribune* from my parents, but we had no firm transition date in mind, which was fine by me. I wasn't ready to take over and Dad wasn't ready to let it go.

I was perfectly happy having *Bryce Ryan, Journalist* stamped after my stories. Dad could keep the *editor in chief* title for a few more years.

"What are you up to today?" he asked.

"Oh, nothing much." Besides investigating the former motorcycle gang in town.

Dad's eyes narrowed. "What are you up to?"

"Nothing." I'd forgotten how easily he could spot a lie. I held up a hand and snuck another behind my back, crossing my fingers. "I swear."

The corner of his mouth turned up. "You can fool most people, but not me. I know that smirk. You're about to cause some trouble, aren't you?"

"Trouble sounds so juvenile and malicious. I'm just going to pop down to the police station and say hello to Chief Wagner. I haven't talked to him in a couple weeks. Then I'm going to get the oil changed in my car."

Dad rolled his eyes. "First of all, Marcus is no idiot. He isn't going to buy your innocent act either. The paper can't afford to be at odds with the chief, so be nice. He'll never throw us a bone if he's pissed. And second, I know exactly why you're getting your 'oil changed.' Don't think I haven't noticed you've been digging up old articles about the Tin Gypsies."

"I, uh . . ." *Shit.* I'd asked Art to pull some from the archives, and I guess he'd told Dad, even though I'd brought him Tums and homemade cinnamon rolls to keep quiet. Traitor.

"Stay away from them, Bryce."

"But there's a story there. Don't tell me you can't feel it. This could be huge for us."

"Huge?" He shook his head. "If you want huge, you'd better go back to Seattle. I thought you came here to slow down. To enjoy life. Weren't those your words?"

"Yes, they were. And I am slowing down." I wasn't waking up at three a.m. to make it to the TV station for the morning show. I wasn't cutting my hair to appease my producer or constantly watching my diet. I wasn't reporting someone else's stories on camera. Instead, I was writing my own.

It was wonderful, but after two months of small-town Montana life, I was going a bit stir-crazy. Calling the hospital for birth announcements and the funeral home for obituaries wasn't enough of a mental challenge. I needed some excitement. I needed a decent story.

And the Clifton Forge Garage had *story* written all over it.

About a year ago, the Tin Gypsy Motorcycle Club had disbanded. They'd been one of the more prominent and lucrative gangs in Montana and had closed down without an explanation.

The former members claimed they were focusing on running the garage here in town. Their shop had become renowned in certain wealthy and celebrity circles for classic car restorations and custom motorcycle builds.

But men like them—men like Kingston "Dash" Slater with his striking good looks, cocky swagger and devilish grin —thrived on power. They craved danger and a life on the edge, without limits. As a gang, the Gypsies had power and money in spades.

So why had they given it up?

No one knew. And if they did, they weren't talking.

"Doesn't it strike you as odd that in the past year, there hasn't been any news about them? And no explanation as to why they shut down their 'club'? They went from notorious gang members to upstanding citizens overnight. I don't buy it. It's too quiet. Too clean."

"That's because they *are* clean," Dad said.

"Sure. Squeaky," I deadpanned.

"You make it sound like we're all covering things up for

them." He frowned. "Come on. Don't you think if there were a story there, I'd tell it? Or do you think so little of me as a reporter?"

"That's not what I'm saying. Of course you'd tell the story."

But would he dig for it? I didn't doubt Dad's ability to investigate. He'd been a star reporter in his prime. But since he and Mom had moved to Clifton Forge and bought the *Tribune* years ago, he'd slowed down. He wasn't as eager as he'd once been. He wasn't as hungry.

Me? I was starved.

"If there's no story, there's no story," I said. "The only thing I'm out is my time, right?"

"I'm going on the record as your father and your partner: I don't like it. They might not be a gang anymore, but those guys have an edge. I don't want you crossing them."

"Understood. I'll ask my questions and stay away." *Or away-ish.*

"Bryce," he warned.

I held up my hands, feigning innocence. "What?"

"Be. Careful."

"I'm careful. Always." Okay, sometimes. Dad's definition of careful was a little different than mine.

I stood on my toes to kiss his cheek, then I waved and hurried out of the pressroom before he assigned me something that would keep me trapped at my desk all day.

The police station was on the opposite end of town from the newspaper. It sat on the banks of the Missouri River along a busy street crowded with restaurants and offices. The river was running fast and high from the melting mountain snow. The June sun reflected off the water's rippled surface in golden flickers. The Montana air

6

was clean and fresh, a close second to my beloved newspaper scent.

It was another smell from my youth, one I'd missed in Seattle.

I parked my car and went inside the station, making small talk with the officer up front. Then I thanked my lucky stars when she waved me through without any hassle. The first three times I'd come here to visit the chief, I'd been put through the paces. Fingerprints. Background check. A photo.

Maybe it was protocol.

Or maybe they didn't like reporters.

The station was quiet this morning. A few officers sat at their desks, heads bent over keyboards and ballpoint pens as they did paperwork while the others on shift were patrolling the streets. The chief's office was along the rear wall of the building. The window behind his desk had a beautiful view of the river.

"Knock, knock." I rapped on the open door and stepped inside. "Morning, Chief."

"Morning, Bryce." He set down the document he'd been reading.

"You know, I never can tell if that's a happy smile or an irritated smile when I come here."

"That depends." His eyes narrowed on my purse, his bushy gray eyebrows coming together.

I reached inside the handbag and retrieved a pack of licorice. "How'd I do?"

He shrugged, staring at the Twizzlers as I set them on his desk and took one of the guest chairs. In my previous visits, I'd brought along Twix, Snickers and M&M's. He'd been lukewarm toward my treats at best. So today, I'd gone out on a limb at the Town Pump and picked up something fruity.

7

"It looks like a happy smile, but with the mustache, it's hard to tell."

He chuckled and ripped the package open while I did an inner fist pump. "I knew you'd figure it out eventually."

"You could have just told me."

"What's the fun in that?" Chief Wagner stuck the candy in his mouth and chomped a huge bite.

"Are you going to make me work this hard for all my information?"

"Nope," he said. "We put out a weekly press sheet. All you have to do is download it. Easy peasy."

"Ah, yes. The weekly press sheet. As truly *riveting* as those reports are, I was talking about information a bit more . . . in-depth."

The chief steepled his fingers beneath his chin. "I don't have anything for you. Just like I didn't have anything for you two weeks ago. Or the week before that. Or the week before that."

"Nothing? Not even a tiny morsel you may have forgotten to put in the press sheet?"

"I've got nothing. Clifton Forge is a fairly boring place these days. Sorry."

I frowned. "No, you're not."

He chuckled and took another piece of licorice. "You're right. I'm not sorry. I'm too busy enjoying the peace."

Chief Wagner was overjoyed that his press sheets only included infrequent 911 calls, random Saturday night drunk and disorderlies and the occasional petty theft from a misguided teenager. This town had seen more than its share of murder and mayhem over the years—thanks to the Tin Gypsies. The motorcycle club was likely responsible for the streaks of gray in Marcus's hair.

8

Yet from what I'd been able to dig up in the news archives, the former Tin Gypsy members had spent little to no time in jail cells. Either the chief had overlooked their crimes or the Gypsies were damn good at covering their tracks.

In their glory days, the Tin Gypsies had been led by Draven Slater. I'd seen him around town, and he carried himself with the same air of ruthless confidence he'd passed down to his son, Dash. And neither man struck me as a fool.

My theory was that Police Chief Marcus Wagner was a damn good cop. But Draven, Dash and their Gypsies were always one step ahead.

If I was going to get a story, I'd have to be at the top of my game. Draven had taken a backseat at the garage, which meant I'd be up against Dash. I'd seen the man—I'd been watching.

Dash rode his black motorcycle along Central Avenue like he owned Clifton Forge, flashing a straight, white smile that was blinding. He was the quintessential bad boy. His sexy smirk, chiseled jaw and day-old stubble made all the ladies swoon.

Every lady except me.

The other women in town could have fun with his amazing body. What I wanted from Dash were his secrets.

And I'd need the chief's help to get them.

In my previous visits here, I hadn't uttered a word about the Gypsies. I'd only come in to meet the chief and build a rapport. But if I was going to start my investigation, then it was time to go for broke.

"Do you know why the Tin Gypsies closed down so suddenly?"

His jaw stopped midchew and he narrowed his gaze. "No."

Wrong move. He was going to clam up.

"Okay." I held up my hands. "I was just curious."

"Why?"

"The truth? My gut says they are a story."

The chief swallowed and leaned his elbows on the desk. "Listen, Bryce. I like you. I like your dad. It's nice to have decent reporters running the paper for once. But you're new here, so let me give you a history lesson."

I scooted to the edge of my seat. "Okay."

"Our town has had more trouble over the last twenty-something years than most have in a hundred. The Gypsies brought a lot of shit here. They know it and they're trying to make up for it. They've been nothing but law-abiding men for over a year. They follow the law to the letter and the town's changing. I've got citizens who feel safe walking down the streets at night. They leave their car doors unlocked when they run into the grocery store. This is a *good* town."

"I'm not trying to impede progress."

"Great. Then leave the Gypsies alone. I've gone head-to-head with them more times than I can count. What I could punish them for, I have. And I'm watching. If they do anything illegal, I'll be the first one there to make them pay. Trust me on that."

The chief didn't sound like a fan of the former club. Good to know. But if he thought his warning was going to scare me away, he was mistaken. Now I was more curious than ever what had caused the Gypsies to shut their club-house doors.

If they were even closed. Maybe this was all a ruse.

"Uh, Chief?" A uniformed officer poked his head inside the door. "We've got an issue that needs your attention."

Chief Wagner took another licorice stick and stood. "Thanks for the candy."

"You're welcome." I stood too. "Starbursts or Skittles next time?"

"You keep bringing me licorice, and we'll get along just fine." He escorted me to the door. "Take care. And remember what I said. Some things and some people are better left alone."

"Gotcha." Probably best not to mention that my next stop was for an oil change at Dash Slater's garage.

I waved goodbye to the chief and the other officer, then headed down the hallway. The sign for the ladies' room lured me inside after too much coffee. I used the bathroom and washed my hands, my anticipation growing for my first interaction with the Tin Gypsies, but as I went to open the door, a word from two men standing in the hallway outside caught my attention.

Murder.

I froze and hovered, listening through the crack. The men were close, their voices no more than a whisper.

"Riley took the call. Said he's never seen blood like that before. The chief is debriefing him right now. Then we'll all need to be ready to roll out."

"Do you think he did it?"

"Draven? Hell yeah. Maybe we'll finally have something to pin on that slick bastard."

Oh. My. God. If my ears weren't betraying me, I'd just overheard two cops talking about a murder and Draven Slater was the key suspect. I needed to get out of this bathroom. Now.

11

I eased the door closed and took three quiet steps backward. Then I coughed, loud, and let my heels click on the tile floor. I whipped open the door in a fury and pretended to be shocked at the men right outside.

"Oh, hell." I threw a hand over my heart. "You guys scared me. I didn't think anyone was out here."

They shared a look with one another, then stepped apart.

"Sorry about that, ma'am."

"No problem." I smiled and walked by, doing my best to keep the urgency out of my footsteps.

I tucked a strand of hair behind my ear, using the gesture to sneak a glance over my shoulder at the bullpen. Three male officers were standing at the far corner desk; none had noticed me walking toward the exit. Two of the men were practically buzzing. Mouths moved fast as one talked over the other. Hand gestures flew. The third officer stood with his arms wrapped around his chest, his face pale as he shifted from foot to foot.

My heart raced as I found the nearest exit door and pushed outside. When the sunshine hit my face, I flew into motion, running for my car.

"Shit." My fingers fumbled to hit the ignition button and put the car in reverse. "I knew it!"

My hands shook as I gunned the engine for the street, checking my rearview mirror to make sure the cops weren't behind me.

"Think, Bryce. What's the plan?" I had no idea where the murder had happened so I couldn't show up at the scene of the crime. I could wait around and follow the cops, but they'd shut me out before I saw a thing. So what else was there?

Be an eyewitness to Draven's arrest. Bingo.

It was a risk, going to the garage and not waiting around to follow the cops to the murder scene. Hell, Draven might not even be at the garage. But if I was going to gamble, it was my best chance at a scoop. I could learn more about the murder itself from those blessed press sheets.

Yes, if my luck held, I'd be standing front and center when Draven got hauled off to jail. Hopefully Dash would be there too. Maybe he'd be caught by surprise just enough that I'd get a glimpse at him during a moment of weakness. I'd learn something that would help me uncover the secrets hidden behind his ridiculously handsome face.

I smiled over the steering wheel.

Time for that oil change.

CHAPTER TWO

BRYCE

My heart was pounding as the Clifton Forge Garage came into view. My fingers were shaking. This thrill —this one-of-a-kind exhilaration that only came with the hunt—was why I'd become a reporter. Not to sit in front of a camera and read someone else's story.

Regret was the driving force behind this Tin Gypsy story. Remorse was the reason it was so, *so* important.

I'd chosen a television career with such promise. I'd changed direction, moving away from the newspaper job I'd always planned to take. The job everyone had expected me to take. But after college, I hadn't wanted to follow in Dad's footsteps, at least not right away. A fresh-faced woman in her early twenties, I'd been inspired to forge a path of my own. So I'd moved to Seattle from Montana and taken up TV.

Along the way, I'd made choices. None of them had seemed wrong in the moment. Until one day, a decade later, I'd woken up in my Seattle apartment and realized the collection of those good choices had accumulated into a bad life.

My job was unfulfilling. I slept alone most nights. When I looked in the mirror, I saw a woman in her early thirties who wasn't happy.

The TV station owned my life. Every action was done to their bidding. Because my hours were so odd, I didn't even bother trying to date. What man wanted to have dinner at four and be in bed by seven? It wasn't a big deal when I was in my twenties. I'd always figured the right guy would come around eventually. Things would fall into place when it was time. I'd get married. Have a family.

Well, things hadn't fallen into place. And if I stayed in Seattle, they never would.

Clifton Forge was my fresh start. I'd rechecked my expectations for the future. The chances I'd meet a man and have kids while I was bodily able to were dwindling. So if becoming an old maid was my path, then at least I'd enjoy my damn job.

My career in Seattle had turned out to be a dud. Network executives had made me promise after promise that eventually I'd have more freedom. They'd assured me I'd get the opportunity to tell my own stories instead of interviewing other journalists and reading from approved cue cards.

Either they'd lied, or they hadn't thought I had the talent.

Regardless, I moved home feeling like a failure. Was I?

Maybe. Or maybe when I wasn't on camera, when people needed me for my brain and not my face, I'd finally stand out. I'd prove to myself I was good enough.

I'd dedicated my life to journalism. To finding hidden truths and exposing buried lies. It was more than a job, it was my passion. If there was an epic story lurking under the surface of this quaint small town, I was telling it.

A murder investigation involving Draven Slater? Sign me up.

My foot hovered over the gas pedal as I idled at the intersection across the street from the garage, checking my rearview again for red and blue lights. If the chief was coming this way to arrest Draven, I didn't have much of a lead.

That was, if I was even heading in the right direction.

There was the chance Draven wasn't at the garage but at home and the cops were headed there. I stayed the course. Whether I managed to track down Draven or not, I was heading to the garage.

Today was the day I was meeting Dash Slater. Today I'd get to size up my opponent.

I used my knee to steer as I whipped off the sweater I'd pulled on this morning. Luckily, my black tank top underneath had a plunging neckline and was free of deodorant streaks. I drove one handed, grabbing the small can of emergency-situation dry shampoo from my purse to spray and fluff my hair. Then I swiped on a coat of my dark-rose lipstick seconds before pulling into the parking lot.

The garage itself was huge. I'd driven by a few times but had never actually stopped. It was more intimidating now, being parked in front of the four open bay doors that towered above my Audi.

At the end of the long asphalt parking lot, a building was tucked next to a small grove of trees. The windows were dark and there was a thick chain looped around the front door's handle. The attached padlock glinted in the sunlight.

That had to be the Tin Gypsies' former headquarters. A

clubhouse—that's what these gangs called them, right? There were no cars or motorcycles parked by the clubhouse. The grass around it was overgrown.

At a glance, the building seemed closed down. Abandoned. But how many men had a key to that padlock? How many men went inside after the sun went down? How many men entered through a hidden back door?

I refused to take that building at face value. Sure, it looked derelict from the outside. Was it thriving behind those closed doors?

In my mirrors, there was a row of motorcycles parked against the tall chain-link fence that bordered the property of the garage. Down the fence, there were cars, some covered in tarps as they waited to be repaired or restored. All four of the garage bays in front of me were full of vehicles—three trucks and a red classic car.

The steel siding on the garage was bright in the morning sun. The office was closest to the street, the sign above its door not really a sign. The large words *Clifton Forge Garage* had been airbrushed onto the steel building with pristine strokes of red, black, green and yellow paint.

Past the vehicles in the garage, the place was immaculate. Not the greasy, dingy place I'd expected. The florescent lights illuminated what looked like a mostly spotless concrete floor. The red tool benches along the walls were clean and new. This place screamed *money*. More money than a small-town garage could make doing routine oil changes and tire rotations.

I checked my hair and lipstick in the rearview mirror one last time, then stepped outside. The moment my door slammed closed, two mechanics appeared from underneath the truck hoods where they'd been working.

"Morning." One of them waved before giving me a full-body appraisal. A grin tugged at his mouth. He liked what he saw.

Score one for the tank top.

"Good morning." I waved as both men strode my way.

Each wore denim-blue coveralls and thick-soled boots. The leaner of the two had his hair cut short, revealing a black tattoo that trailed down his neck only to disappear beneath the collar of his coveralls. The bulkier man had his dark hair tied back and his coveralls unzipped, tied around his waist. His chest was covered with a white tank, his two beefy arms bare except for the mass of colorful tattoos.

Maybe this was why the garage was raking in the cash. Single women from half the state would drive here to have their oil changed by these hot mechanics. Though neither of these handsome men was the one I was after.

Where was Draven? I hoped he was in the office drinking coffee.

"What can we do for you, ma'am?" the short-haired man asked as he cleaned his black-stained hands on a red rag.

"I'm really overdue for an oil change." I gave them an exaggerated frown. "I'm not great about making car stuff a priority. I don't suppose there's any chance you could fit me in this morning?"

The men shared a look and a nod, but before either could answer, a deep voice came from behind them. "Mornin'."

The mechanics stepped apart, revealing none other than Dash Slater stalking my way. His strides were purposeful. Potent, even. I'd expected to meet him here, hoped for it even, but I hadn't been mentally or physically prepared.

Our eyes met and my heart boomed, stealing my breath.

My mind went blank, unable to concentrate on anything except the way his dark jeans draped over his long legs and those thick, bulging thighs.

I'd never seen a man move like Dash, with confidence and charisma in every step. His hazel eyes, a vibrant swirl of green and gold and brown, threatened to lure me under his spell.

My body betrayed me, the quiver in my core irritating my rational senses. I was here for a story. I was here to steal this man's secrets one by one, then plaster them across the headlines. This raw, animalistic response was asinine.

But *damn*, he was hot.

Dash's black T-shirt strained across the muscles of his chest. It pulled tight around the swells of his biceps. The skin exposed on his arms was tan and smooth, except for the array of tattoos that snaked up both forearms.

Scorching. Smoking. There was another *s* word somewhere in my mind but as he stepped into our huddle, I lost my advanced vocabulary.

Seriously . . . *damn*.

I'd always preferred the clean-cut look. Day-old scruff wasn't my thing. *He* wasn't my thing. I liked blue eyes, not hazel. I liked short hair, and Dash's brown mop had been overdue for a cut weeks ago.

This reaction was purely chemical, likely because I hadn't been with a man since, well . . . I'd stopped counting the months when they'd hit double digits.

"What can we help you with, miss?" Dash asked, planting his legs wide as he took up the space between the other two men.

"My car." I rolled a wrist toward the Audi. "It needs an oil change."

The sun must have inched closer to Earth because it was sweltering. Sweat beaded in my cleavage as his gaze dropped momentarily to my breasts. He didn't stare at them for more than a fraction of a second, but they'd caught his attention.

Score two for the tank top.

Dash looked to the long-haired man and jerked his chin toward the garage. The man nodded, gave the short-haired man a grunt and the pair left, returning to work without a word.

Was that how they communicated around here? Chin lifts and grunts? That would make an interview difficult. And short.

Dash glanced over his shoulder to make sure we were alone, then he gave me that famous sexy smirk I'd seen from afar. In person, it was dizzying. "We'll take care of the oil change. Do a full work-up too. On the house."

"That would be great." I tried to keep my voice even and cheerful. "But I'll pay for it. Thanks."

"You're welcome." Dash stepped closer, his six-foot-something frame blocking some of the sunlight.

My natural urge was to scoot back and maintain my space, but I didn't move an inch.

Maybe he only wanted to stand closer. But I'd learned years ago that arrogant men often tested the strength of their presence over a woman. They'd make little gestures to see how far they could push her around, especially when that woman was a reporter.

They'd touch a lock of my hair to see if I'd flinch. They'd stand tall to see if I'd cower. And they'd move in too close to see if I'd step away.

Either Dash knew exactly who I was and wanted to see if I'd tuck tail and run, or he was so cocky that he thought a grin and an oil change would make me drop to my knees and undo his belt to pay for my *on the house* services.

"You new around here?" he asked.

"I am."

He hummed. "I'm surprised I haven't seen you before."

"I don't get out much." The air was heavy around us, like a brick wall had gone up in place of my personal bubble and the spring breeze couldn't get through.

"That's a shame. You feel like getting out, stop by The Betsy. Maybe I'll buy you a beer sometime."

"Maybe." *Or maybe not.*

The Betsy was Clifton Forge's infamous dive bar and definitely not my scene.

"You guys must all be into motorcycles." I turned and pointed at the row of them behind me.

"You could say that. Most of us here ride."

"I've never been on one before."

"Yeah?" He grinned. "There's nothing like it. Maybe before I buy you that beer, I'll take you for a ride first."

The way he stressed the word *ride* made my breath stutter. I locked my gaze with his, a flare of heat passing between us. Were we both picturing a very different kind of ride on that motorcycle? Because, despite my best efforts to block it out, the image of me straddling his narrow hips was now the only thing in my head. From the hungry look in his eyes, he had a similar mental picture.

"Which bike is yours?" I asked, shoving the sexual thoughts away.

He raised an arm, his wrist brushing against my elbow in a movement that seemed accidental but had definitely been done on purpose. "The black one in the middle."

"Dash." I read the name emblazoned with flames on one panel. "Is that your name?"

"Yep." He held out a hand between us. "Dash Slater."

I slipped my hand into his, refusing to let my heart flutter at the way his long fingers engulfed my own. "Dash. That's an interesting name."

"Nickname."

"And what's your real name?"

He smiled, dropping my hand. "That's a secret I only tell a woman after she's let me buy her a beer."

"Pity. I only drink beer with a man after I know his real name."

Dash chuckled. "Kingston."

"Kingston Slater. But your nickname is Dash. Does anyone ever call you King?"

"Not anyone who lived to say it twice," he teased.

"Good to know." I laughed, carefully slipping my phone from my pocket in case a photo opportunity came up. Then I fanned my face. "Is it hot out here? Do you have a waiting room or someplace cool I could sit?"

Maybe a place where your soon-to-be-incarcerated Dad is hanging out? If the cops ever showed up. What was taking them so long?

"Come on." He nodded to the office door. "You can wait in my office."

We made it three steps when a police car came racing into the parking lot, lights flashing but no siren blaring. *Yes!* I resisted the urge to victoriously throw my arms in the air.

Dash halted, holding out an arm to shield me from the police. It was a protective gesture, certainly not what I'd expect from a former criminal. Shouldn't he be using me as a shield from the authorities, not the other way around?

The two officers in the patrol car were out of their cruiser in a flash. "We're looking for Draven Slater."

Dash stood taller, crossing his arms over his chest. "What do you want with him?"

The cops didn't answer. They marched toward the office door and disappeared inside just as another police car pulled into the parking lot—this one carrying the chief.

Marcus got out of the passenger seat and walked over to Dash and me, lifting his sunglasses as he approached. "What are you doing here, Bryce?"

"Getting an oil change."

"I thought I told you to stay away."

"That car is brand-new, Chief." I smirked. "I want it to last and I've heard car care is key."

The chief's eyes narrowed, the corners of his mustache turning down. *So that's what his annoyed face looks like.* I'd never mistake it for a smile again.

"What's going on, Marcus?" Dash asked, looking between us.

"We're bringing in your dad."

"Why?"

"Can't tell you that."

Dash grumbled something under his breath. "Then what *can* you tell me?"

"With her present?" Marcus tossed a thumb my way. "Not much on the record, at the moment. I hope you didn't tell her anything you don't want in Sunday's *Tribune.*"

"What?" Dash's jaw went slack.

"She's the new reporter in town."

Dash's face whipped my way. "*You* are the new reporter? I thought they hired a man."

"Yeah, I get that sometimes. It's my name. It always

causes confusion." I shrugged. "Bryce Ryan, *Clifton Forge Tribune*."

Dash's nostrils flared. My invite to The Betsy for a beer had just been revoked.

The garage's office door flew open and the two officers came out with Draven Slater handcuffed between them.

I fought a smile, casting up a *thank you* to the journalist angels who'd blessed me today.

"Call our lawyer," Draven ordered Dash, his jaw set in an even angrier line than his son's.

Dash only nodded as Draven got shoved into the back of the cop car.

A woman with a white pixie cut came running to Dash's side, having followed the parade outside from the office. The two mechanics from the garage were jogging our direction.

I hurried to snap a picture with my phone before the cruiser reversed and sped away. We didn't keep a full-time photographer on staff at the newspaper, not that we really needed one when smartphones were so convenient.

The moment the cruiser and Draven were gone from view, Dash whirled on the chief. "What the fuck is going on?"

"Dash, I'd like you to come down to the station for questioning."

"No. Not until you tell me what this is about."

The chief shook his head. "At the station."

The pause that hung in the air was as stifling as the tension between the men. I didn't expect Dash to budge, but finally he nodded.

"The station," Marcus repeated, shooting me another one of those frowns before walking to his cruiser.

"What's going on?" The woman from the office touched Dash's arm. "Why did they arrest him?"

"Don't know." Dash stared at the chief's taillights as they disappeared down the street, then he turned his attention to me. "What the hell do you want?"

"Your father is a suspect in a murder investigation. Do you have a comment?"

"Murder?" The woman's mouth dropped as the bulky mechanic cursed, "Fuck."

But Dash only hardened at my question, his expression turning to stone. "Get off my property."

"So you don't have a comment to the fact your father might be a murderer?" The *might* was generous. "Or did you know that already?"

"Screw you, lady," the woman spat while Dash's hands fisted at his sides. His expression remained stern, but behind his icy stare, that mind was whirling.

"I'll take that as no comment." I winked and turned for my car, ignoring the angry glares that prickled my neck.

"Bryce." Dash's voice boomed across the parking lot, freezing my steps.

I looked over my shoulder, giving him only my ear.

"I'll give you one." His voice was hard and unyielding, sending chills down my spine. "One warning. Stay out of this."

Bastard. He wasn't going to scare me away. This was my story. I was telling it, whether he liked it or not. I spun around, meeting his level gaze with my own.

"See you soon, *King*."

CHAPTER THREE

DASH

What the fuck just happened?

As Bryce's white Audi streaked off the lot, I shook my head and replayed the last five minutes.

After a hot cup of coffee with Dad in the office, I'd come out to the garage, ready to get to work on the red '68 Mustang GT I'd been restoring. My morning had been shaping up pretty damn great when a hot, leggy brunette with a nice rack came in for an oil change. Got even better when she flirted back and flashed me that showstopper smile. Then I hit the jackpot because she turned out to be witty too, and the heat between us was practically blue flame.

I should have known something was up. Women too good to be true were always out for trouble. This one was only baiting me for a story.

And damn, I'd taken that bait. Hook, line and sinker.

How the hell had Bryce known Dad was going to be arrested for murder even before the cops had shown up? Better question. How the hell hadn't I?

Because I was out of touch.

Not long ago, when the club was still going strong, I would have been the first to know if the cops were moving in my or my family's direction. Sure, living on the right side of the law had its advantages. Mostly, it was nice to live a life without the gnawing, constant fear I'd wake up and be either killed or sent to prison for the rest of my life.

I'd become content. Lazy. Ignorant. I'd let my guard down.

And now Dad was headed for a jail cell. *Fuck.*

"Dash." Presley punched me in the arm, getting my attention.

I shook myself and looked down at her, squinting as her white hair reflected the sunlight. "What?"

"What?" she mimicked. "What are you going to do about your dad? Did you know about this?"

"Yeah. I let him go about drinking his morning coffee, bullshitting with you, knowing he'd get arrested soon," I barked. "No, I didn't know about this."

Presley scowled but stayed quiet.

"She said murder." Emmett swept a long strand of hair out of his face. "Did I hear that right?"

Yeah. "She said murder."

Murder, spoken in Bryce's sultry voice I'd thought was so smooth when it had first hit my ears. Dad had been arrested and I'd been bested by a goddamn nosy reporter. My lip curled. I avoided the press nearly as much as I avoided cops and lawyers. Until we got this shit figured out, I'd be stuck dealing with all three.

"Call Jim," I ordered Emmett. "Tell him what happened."

He nodded, walking to the garage with his phone pressed to his ear as he called our lawyer.

Emmett had been my vice president, and though the Tin Gypsy Motorcycle Club might be extinct, he was still by my side. Always had been.

We'd grown up in the club together. As kids, we'd played at family functions. He was three years younger, but we'd been friends all through school. Then brothers in the club, like our fathers had been.

The pair of us had broken countless laws. We'd done things that would never see the light of day. We'd joked last week over a beer at The Betsy about how quiet our lives had become.

Guess we should have knocked on wood.

"Isaiah, back to work," I ordered. "Act like it's any other day. If someone comes around and asks a question about Dad, you don't know shit."

He nodded. "Got it. Anything else?"

"You'll probably be covering for the rest of us. You good with that?"

"I'm good." Isaiah turned and went in the garage, a wrench still in his hand. We'd only hired him a couple of weeks ago, but my gut said he'd handle the extra work just fine.

Isaiah was quiet—friendly enough. He wasn't social. He didn't join us for beers after work or bullshit with me and the guys for hours in the garage. But he was a good mechanic and showed up on time. Whatever demons he was battling, he kept them to himself.

I'd taken Dad's title as manager of the garage when he'd retired years ago, but since I hated anything to do with human resources or accounting and Dad hated to sit home alone all day, he came in and helped often. When I'd tasked him with finding me another mechanic, he'd found Isaiah.

I hadn't even bothered interviewing Isaiah because when Draven Slater approved of someone, you trusted his instincts.

"What do you want me to do?" Presley asked.

"Where the fuck is Leo?"

"My guess?" She rolled her eyes. "His bed."

"Call him and wake his ass up. Go to his house if you have to. When I get back from the police station, I expect to see him working. Then we'll all talk."

She nodded and headed for the office.

"Pres," I called, stopping her. "Make some other calls too. See if anyone in town has heard anything. Discreetly."

"Okay." With another nod, she hurried to the office as I strode to my bike.

Along the way to the police station, a white car streaked past going the opposite direction, and my mind immediately jumped to Bryce.

Emmett had told me there was a new reporter in town. But *his* name was Bryce Ryan. I hadn't been expecting a woman, certainly not one with full, rosy lips and thick chocolate hair.

Any person besides Emmett would have suffered a broken nose for letting me think the reporter was a man. Though based on the shock on his own face, Emmett hadn't expected a woman either.

Served me right for disappearing any time Presley wanted to dish small-town gossip in the office. Being out of the loop, that was my fault. Not to mention Bryce . . . well, she was good.

She'd played me for the fool I'd become. Hell, I'd even

told her my real name and she'd been at the garage for all of five minutes. Isaiah didn't even know my real name, and we worked side by side every day.

One flash of her white smile, those pretty brown eyes sparkling, and I'd loosened my tongue. I'd acted like a horny teenager desperate to get into her pants instead of a thirty-five-year-old man who had plenty of women to call if he needed to get off.

Fucking reporters. I hadn't worried about the newspaper or their reporters for decades. But Bryce, she was a game changer.

The previous owners of the newspaper had been too dumb to be a nuisance. The new owner, who had to be Bryce's father, had come into Clifton Forge years ago, but Lane Ryan missed all the newsworthy stuff.

He'd come to town when the Tin Gypsies were no longer in the drug trade. When our underground fighting ring had become more of a boxing club. When all the bodies we'd buried had long since cooled.

Lane had left us alone. The times he'd brought his wife's rig in for a tune-up, he hadn't once asked about the club. He was content to let the past stay there.

But Bryce was hungry. The look on her face when she'd delivered her parting shot was fierce. She'd go for broke and never back down. On a normal day, she'd be a pain in my ass. But if Dad really was a suspect for murder, things were only going to get worse.

Who'd been killed? How had I not heard about a murder in town? Forget my old connections, murder was big news for a small town and should have spread like wildfire minutes after the body had been found. Unless . . . had

Marcus found a body from the past? Had the sins of our past caught up with us?

As a club, we'd justified murder because the men we'd killed would have done the same to us. Or our families. We'd rid the world of evil men, even though we'd been devils in our own right. We were guilty—no doubt. But that didn't mean we all wanted to spend the rest of our lives in the state penitentiary.

I raced faster down the streets of Clifton Forge, not bothering to obey traffic laws. When I pulled into the station, the chief was waiting for me at the front desk.

"Dash." He motioned for me to follow him into his office. Once the door was closed, he took a seat behind his desk, snagging a string of licorice from an open package.

"Where's my dad?"

"Take a seat," he said as he chewed.

I crossed my arms. "I'll stand. Start talking."

"There's not much I can tell you. We're investigating a crime and—"

"You mean a murder."

The chewing stopped. "Where'd you hear that?"

Marcus's shock was genuine. I guess he'd told his officers to keep it quiet, only Bryce had been one step ahead of him too. "Your new friend, the reporter, asked me if I had a comment regarding Dad's arrest for murder. What the fuck is going on?"

A vein in Marcus's forehead ticked as he swallowed the bite and ripped off another. "Do you happen to know your dad's whereabouts between the hours of five p.m. last night and six a.m. this morning?"

"Maybe." I held perfectly still, though a hint of relief slowed my racing heart. Marcus was asking about last night.

Thank fuck. The past had to stay in the past. And since Dad hadn't killed anyone last night, this had to be a mistake.

"Well? Where was he?"

"Got a feeling you already know, so why are you asking?"

"Your father has refused questioning until his attorney arrives."

"Good."

"It would help us if you *both* cooperated."

We didn't cooperate with anyone, certainly not the cops. If I opened my mouth and said the wrong thing, Marcus would mark me as an accessory and throw me into a cell next to Dad's. One Slater behind bars was enough for today.

When I remained silent, Marcus scowled. "If you're not talking, then neither am I."

"Fine." I spun for the door, slamming it so hard a picture on the wall rattled as I stormed out of the station.

I hadn't learned much, but what I'd learned was enough. For now.

Straddling my bike, I slid on my shades, then dug out my phone to call my older brother.

"Dash," Nick answered with a smile in his voice. A smile that had been there permanently over the past seven years, ever since he'd reconnected with his wife. "What's up?"

"Gotta talk. You busy?"

"Give me one sec." He put the phone into his shoulder or something, because his voice got muffled as he yelled, "Go long, bud. Longer. Last one."

There was a rush of air and Nick laughed as he came back on the phone. "This kid. He'd play catch all day if I let him. And he's getting good. I mean, he's only six but he's a natural."

"Future wide receiver." I grinned. Draven, my nephew

32

and Dad's namesake, was the spitting image of Nick. And he was Nick's constant companion. "You working today?"

"Yeah. Draven's hanging with me at the garage for a few hours. Emmy's taking Nora to get her ears pierced."

"Uh . . . isn't she a little young?" Nora had recently turned four.

"Don't get me fucking started," Nick muttered. "But I'm not arguing with Emmy at the moment."

"Why not? Did she piss you off?"

"No, she's . . ." He blew out a long breath. "We were waiting to tell everyone but Emmy's pregnant. Or, she *was* pregnant. She miscarried last week."

"Hell, brother." My hand flew to my heart. "I'm sorry."

"Yeah, me too. Emmy's having a hard time. So if she wants to get Nora's ears pierced and have a mommy-daughter day in Bozeman, I'm not going to say a damn thing."

"Can I help?"

"No, we'll get through it. What's up?"

I pinched the bridge of my nose. The last thing I wanted was to add this to Nick's burdens, but he had to know. "Got some bad news. Wish it could wait."

"Tell me."

"Someone was murdered last night. And either Dad did it, he knows who did it, or someone's trying to frame him for it. They arrested him about thirty minutes ago."

"Fuck," Nick spat. "What else do you know?"

"Nothing. The cops aren't talking." I wasn't going to admit that the only reason I knew half of what I did was because of a sexy, devious reporter. "Dad lawyered up. Once Jim meets with him, I'll learn more."

"Let me call Emmy. We'll get there as soon as we can."

"No, don't," I told him. "There's nothing you can do here. Just wanted you to be aware."

"Dash, we're talking about a murder here."

"Exactly. You, Emmeline, the kids. You don't need to be anywhere near this shit." He needed to stay in Prescott, playing catch with his son, kissing his daughter and holding tight to his wife.

"Fine." Nick blew out a long breath. "But if you need me, I'm there."

"I know. I'll keep you posted."

"It's always something," he muttered.

"Hasn't been for a while."

"True. Did he . . . do you think he did it?"

I stared at the gray siding of the police station, picturing Dad inside those walls in an interrogation room. His hands cuffed and resting on a cheap-ass table as he sat in an uncomfortable chair.

"I don't know," I admitted. "Maybe. If he did, there was a reason. And if he didn't, then Clifton Forge is definitely not a place I want you bringing those kids."

Because if someone was after Dad, they could be after us all.

"Watch your back," I said.

"You too."

I ended the call and started my bike. The feel of the engine, the vibration and noise, was a comfort as I sped through town. I'd spent long hours in this seat, driven hundreds of miles, thinking through club strategies.

Except the last year, there hadn't been club business. There were no squabbles to settle. No crimes to hide. No enemies to outsmart. My time behind the handlebars had been spent simply enjoying the open road. To think about the garage and how we could increase our custom jobs and sock away a pile of money for a rainy day.

When it came to dealing with a murder arrest, my mind felt sluggish and rusty. It surprised me how quickly I'd forgotten the old ways. Though we'd been tapering things off for years, the Tin Gypsies had only disbanded a year ago. The last arrest I'd had to deal with had been nearly four years ago, and even then, it had been for one of Leo's drunken bar fights.

I pulled into the parking lot, walking my bike back into its space. As I walked to the office, I glanced down the lot toward the clubhouse.

The yard was overgrown, and I needed to find an hour to mow. The inside was no doubt musty and covered in dust. The last time I'd been inside had been during winter when a raccoon had snuck inside and tripped the motion sensors.

On a day like today, when I needed information and answers, I'd give anything to walk inside the clubhouse, call everyone to the meeting room table and get to the bottom of this.

Instead, I'd have to settle for the garage's office and a few people who were just as loyal to us now as they had been when we'd worn the same patch.

Presley was on the phone when I opened the office door. She held up one finger for me to be quiet. "Okay, thanks. Call me back if you hear anything else."

I went to the row of chairs on the wall beneath the front window. Presley's desk was the only one in the waiting area, and though Dad and I had our two offices along the far wall, we normally congregated around hers.

Presley's official title was office manager, but she did a lot more than we'd put in her original job description. She made sure bills got paid and customers were happy. She shuffled paperwork to my desk or Dad's for signatures. She ran payroll and forced us all to talk about retirement plans once a year.

She was the heart of the garage. She set the rhythm and the rest of us followed suit.

"What'd you find out?" I asked.

"I called the salon." Her face paled. "Stacy said she saw a bunch of cop cars at the motel on her way into work this morning. There's a rumor that a woman was found dead, but she's not sure if it's true."

Goddamn it. It was probably true. "Anything else?"

She shook her head. "That's it."

What I needed was to talk to Dad, but given Marcus's attitude, that wasn't happening. So for the time being, I'd have to funnel information through the lawyer.

The door to the office opened and Emmett walked inside, followed by Leo.

"Heard I missed some stuff this morning," Leo joked.

Not in the mood for it, I shot him a scowl that wiped the grin off his face. "Where the fuck were you?"

"Overslept."

"That's been happening a lot lately."

He ran a hand through his messy blond hair, the strands still wet from his shower. "Am I not getting my work done?"

I didn't answer. Leo was the artist in the bunch, doing all the paint and design while Emmett, Isaiah and I preferred the mechanics and fabrication. His work was getting done, but he'd been drinking a lot more lately. His arrival time in the morning getting later and later. Every night he seemed to have a new woman in his bed.

He was still acting like the club's playboy.

"I think we've got more important things to worry about at the moment than Leo's degrading work quality, don't you?" Emmett asked, taking the chair next to me.

"Degrading work quality," Leo mumbled, shaking his head as he sat in the last open chair. "Assholes. I hate you all."

"Gentlemen, do me a favor," Presley interjected. "Shut. Up."

"What's the plan, Dash?" Emmett leaned his elbows on his knees.

I ran a hand over my jaw. "We need to find out whatever we can about the murder. Dad will stay quiet so the cops aren't going to get anything from him. But they have something. Need to find out what it is. Isaiah has the garage covered, but Pres, limit jobs so he doesn't get swamped. Emmett and Leo, start asking around."

They both nodded. We might not be a club anymore but we had connections.

"What are you going to do?" Presley asked.

Emmett and Leo didn't need my help, and unless the work in the garage was too much, I'd let Isaiah and Presley handle it. Because there was another person in town who had information, and she'd either give it up freely or I'd drag it out of her.

"Research."

CHAPTER FOUR

BRYCE

"I love Sundays." I smiled at the newspaper on my desk. The bold headline wasn't fancy or flowery, but it sure grabbed your attention.

WOMAN MURDERED. SUSPECT ARRESTED.

We ran an eight-page newspaper that went out twice a week on Wednesdays and Sundays. When Dad had bought the paper, he'd kept the publication days the same but had drawn a clear line between the Wednesday and Sunday editions. Wednesday was geared toward business, focused on the activities happening around town, the classifieds and announcements.

Sunday's paper had the good stuff. We ran the major headlines on Sunday, giving the townsfolk something to talk about after church. If there was a major story in town, it came on Sunday. Whenever we did a feature or multiweek piece, it was on Sunday.

I lived for the Sunday paper. And this week's was definitely going to cause a stir.

The ads George had been working on for page three and

Sue's column on the new wedding venue outside of town would likely go unnoticed behind my article.

Murder had a way of grabbing attention.

Small-town gossip traveled fast and I had no doubt that most people in and around Clifton Forge already knew about the murder. But gossip was just that, speculation and rumor, until it was printed in my newspaper. Then, it became fact.

After leaving the Clifton Forge Garage—and one pissed-off biker—behind on Friday, I'd come to the paper and immediately begun writing.

As stories go, this one didn't have a lot of detail. Chief Wagner was keeping tight-lipped about the murder as well as the victim. Before they released her name, they were tracking down next of kin.

The only details he'd divulged in his press sheet were that a woman had been murdered at the Evergreen Motel and they had a suspect in custody. Lucky for me, I knew who the suspect was and had been able to add it to my report.

Along with my well-timed photo.

Draven Slater's name was splashed across the *Tribune's* front page, not for the first time and certainly not for the last. I was going to report this story from beginning to end—the judge's gavel slamming on a wooden block as he sentenced a murderer to life in prison.

I was taking a risk that I knew the end of my story already. Journalists typically didn't assume the primary suspect was guilty, and normally, I prided myself on keeping an open mind. But my gut screamed that Draven was a criminal and while he'd been able to escape incarceration for his previous arrests, I doubted he'd be able to slip free this time.

Reporting and writing this story could be the mark I

made on this town. It could establish my career here. My name. And it could be the story that filled the hole in my life.

As the police and prosecutors worked to build a case against Draven, I'd be right along for the ride, reporting whatever tidbits they threw my way. And since the chief wasn't very forthcoming at the moment, I'd do some digging on my own.

I was buzzing at the prospect of real investigative journalism.

The door behind me opened and BK stepped out, wiping his hands on a rag. His black apron hung past his knees. "Hey, Bryce. I didn't think you were still here."

"I'm just leaving." I stood from my chair and folded the fresh paper in half before tucking it into my purse. I'd come in before dawn to help Dad and BK finish up the print run, then gotten papers bundled and ready for the delivery crew. After the paperboys and papergirls left with their parents, I snagged my own copy.

This one was a keeper.

"Are you heading home?" I asked. Dad had left thirty minutes ago.

"Soon as I get everything shut down."

"Have a good one, BK. Thanks."

"You too." He waved, disappearing back into the pressroom.

BK and I only crossed paths on Wednesday and Sunday mornings. He worked odd hours, mostly coming in at night before a print run. Sometimes he'd do maintenance on the presses, again preferring to work at night. Occasionally, he'd do some early-morning deliveries if we were short on help.

Like the other staffers here—myself included—BK

worked hard for Dad. One day, I hoped to inspire that kind of loyalty from the paper's employees too.

I smiled at the paper once more, thinking of Dad's reaction to my story. When I'd turned it in on Friday night, he'd gotten a Cheshire catlike grin on his face. Dad didn't want me digging into the Tin Gypsies, but he had no problem reporting on a murder and being the first to announce Draven Slater as the primary suspect.

He'd come in to run the presses with BK last night, making sure the paper printed without a hitch. My story had reinvigorated Dad. He knew I was going to keep digging, finding out whatever I could about the murder. He hadn't said a word to stop or slow my progress. Though he had cautioned me: Dash Slater wouldn't let his father go to prison easily.

Yawning, I walked out of the bullpen, surveying the empty desks. It was six o'clock in the morning, and once BK left, there'd be no one working today.

Except for Art, who'd been the receptionist slash security guard for nearly two decades, the staff held flexible hours. Dad didn't care. Neither did I, as long as everyone met their deadlines.

Sue was responsible for the classifieds and, like me, preferred to work in the morning. George, who ran advertising, came in before noon, just in time to clock in, grab a handful of mechanical pencils and a legal pad, then head out for whatever lunch meeting he'd booked the day before. And Willy, a fellow journalist who had an aversion to his desk, rolled in around six or seven each night, dropping off his latest story before disappearing to wherever it was Willy disappeared to.

It was a different pace, working here. A far cry from the

chaos of television. There were no makeup artists or hair stylists following me around every corner. No cameras tracking my movements. No producers barking orders.

No pressure.

Since it was quiet here, I often found myself alone. Or on the good days, alone with Dad. He worked whenever there was work to be done, which, for a newspaper with only six employees, was often. It had allowed us many hours, each working independently at our desks, but still together.

I pushed open the front door, turning to lock it up. My car waited in the first parking space, but I was too keyed up to go home. I hadn't slept for more than a few hours last night, and it would be a while before I crashed.

So I headed for the sidewalk, making my way over three blocks toward Central Avenue. I hoped the delivery drivers were fast today, getting papers into the hands of our readers.

I was sorry that today's headline was possible only because a woman's life had been cut short. While I enjoyed the thrill of a dramatic story, the sadness and tragedy beneath was heartbreaking. I wasn't sure who the victim was, if she had been a good person. If she'd been loved or if she'd been lost.

There wasn't much I could do for her but tell the facts and report the truth. I'd bring her life—along with her death —to light.

My initial impression of Chief Wagner had been positive. But I had a feeling he'd become accustomed to keeping the masses of Clifton Forge slightly in the dark.

Not anymore.

If I learned something, I was sharing.

The sun was shining bright, even this early in the morning. The cool air was refreshing on my skin and in my lungs.

I breathed deeply as I walked, the scents on the slight breeze reminding me of summers as a kid.

Montana was typically beautiful at the beginning of June, but this year, it felt especially so. Maybe because it was my first spring back after having lived in Seattle for the better part of two decades.

The trees seemed greener. The skies bluer, bigger. I hadn't spent a lot of time exploring town since I'd moved, but as I walked, I felt the urge to see it all. I was ready to make this town my own, to become a part of the community.

Clifton Forge was home.

I reached Central Avenue, turning right. Two blocks down there was a coffee shop calling my name. Nearly all the businesses and offices that crowded this street were closed at this hour, their windows dark. The only places open were the coffee shop and the café across the road.

Clifton Forge didn't get the enormous influx of tourists that other small Montana towns saw each summer. Tourism here was nothing like it was in Bozeman, where I'd grown up. Our town was too far off the interstate to get much notice. The millions of visitors who poured into the state each summer to visit Yellowstone and Glacier National Parks passed us by.

Our town's main influx of outsiders came in the fall, when hunters made Clifton Forge their home base before setting off into the wilderness with guides and horses to hunt elk, bears and deer.

Most of the locals liked it that way, forgoing added business traffic for peace and seclusion. When you walked into the café or the coffee shop, nine out of ten faces were familiar.

Except mine wasn't. Yet.

I hadn't spent enough time out and about town. Now that summer was here, that was going to change. I'd spent enough years in Seattle being recognized for my face—if I was recognized at all. For the most part, I was just another anonymous person going about their daily lives.

But here, I wanted to settle in and settle deep. I wanted people to know I was Lane and Tessa Ryan's daughter, because belonging to them made me proud. I wanted people to think of me when they thought of the newspaper, because reading my stories was a highlight of their week.

"Good morning," I said as I entered the coffee shop.

The barista sat behind a counter next to an espresso machine. Her mouth was hanging open as she stared at my newspaper between her hands. "Did you hear? A woman was murdered at the motel."

I nodded. "I heard. It's awful. At least they caught the guy."

"I can't believe it. Draven? He's such a nice guy. Leaves good tips. Always friendly. I just . . . wow." She folded up the paper and put it on the counter, the shocked look on her face remaining. "What can I get you?"

"Cappuccino, please." I smiled politely, even though I was irritated that Draven had seemed to fool so many.

"For here or to go?"

"To go. I'm just out for a morning walk."

Any other morning, I would have introduced myself, but as she made my coffee, she kept stealing glances at the paper. I doubted that if I told her my name, she'd remember it today. She seemed distraught. And not by a woman's murder, but because Draven was the primary suspect.

How does he have everyone fooled?

She made my coffee and I left her with a wave. I crossed the road, heading for the newspaper but perusing the businesses on the opposite side of the street this time. When I reached my car, I got inside but home was not my destination.

The Evergreen Motel had been swarmed with activity over the past two days, the police barricade sending a very clear *go the hell away* message to anyone driving by. But the murder was two days old and my questions would only wait so long.

It was a risk going so soon but one I was willing to take. With luck, the owners might have some information they'd be willing to share about the victim. Or Draven himself. Information they might have been too flustered to give to the cops.

The motel was on the other edge of town, away from the river. The drive took only minutes, the streets nearly empty. It was appropriately named; the tops of the evergreens that surrounded the motel on three sides seemed to brush the clouds.

The building itself was only a single story, built when the style was for each room to have an exterior door. The metal keys were no doubt attached to red oval disks with the room numbers stamped in white letters. The motel was a U shape, all twelve rooms facing the kiosk in the center that was the office.

Had the owners not taken such good care of the Evergreen, it might have reminded me of some seedier areas of Seattle where motel rooms like these were rented by the hour. But as it was, this place was clean and charming.

The siding was a freshly painted sage green. Flower baskets hung on posts outside each room, overflowing with red, white and pink petunias. The parking lot had recently been restriped.

Definitely not a place I would have expected a murder.

A man about my age sat behind the front desk in the office, the small room built solely for function. There was no waiting area for coffee in the mornings or a cookie plate in the evenings. There was just enough space to stand by the counter to collect your key—all of which hung on a pegboard on the wall. I'd guessed red oval disks. These were green.

"Morning, ma'am," he greeted.

"Good morning." I flashed my brightest, friendliest smile.

"Do you have a reservation?"

"No, I'm actually from here." I extended my hand across the counter. "Bryce Ryan. I work at the *Tribune*."

"Oh." He hesitated before taking my hand. "Cody. Cody Pruitt."

"Nice to meet you, Cody."

"You're here about what happened in 114?"

I nodded. "Yes. I'd like to ask you some questions if you don't mind."

"I don't know anything more than I already told the police."

"That's okay." I reached into my purse for a small notepad and a pen. "Would you mind if I took a few notes as we talked? You can always say no. And you can always say something is off the record if you want to keep it between you and me."

"That's fine. But like I said, I don't have much to report." His jaw was tense. His eyes narrowed. Cody was seconds away from shoving me out the door.

"Well, that's okay." I held my smile. "I'm new to town

anyway, so I'll probably just ask you a bunch of stupid questions. Are you from here?"

"Yeah. Born and raised. My grandparents bought the Evergreen. They passed it down to my parents. Now I'm taking it over from them."

"Oh, that's great. I work with family too. My dad bought the newspaper and I just moved here to work with him. Those first few months were, uh . . ." I bugged out my eyes. "It was an adjustment for us both. Kind of strange to be working for your parent. But now I think we've got a groove. He hasn't threatened to fire me in over a month, and I haven't thrown my stapler at his head in weeks."

Dad and I loved working together, but the lie was worth it when Cody chuckled.

"We had some of those days too. There were days when I was pretty frustrated with my parents. Well, maybe not so much me as my wife. She wanted to do some things to fix up the place and they were being stubborn. But eventually we worked it out. The place looks a lot better too."

"I'm guessing those beautiful flower pots were your wife's idea."

His chest swelled with pride. "They were. She's got a green thumb."

"They're beautiful."

"Yeah." Cody's smile dimmed. "My wife, she does housekeeping here. Actually, we trade off days. Friday was her day. She found . . ." He shook his head, his voice lowering. "I don't know how she'll ever get over it. My parents are heartbroken. I'm the only one who can stomach working here. Not that I have a choice. We have bills to pay and I can't turn away reservations. Hell, I'm just glad we have guests."

"I'm sorry. And I'm so sorry for your wife." Finding a dead body would leave scars for anyone.

"Thanks." He fisted his hand on the counter. "I wish I could say I was surprised."

My ears perked up. "You're not?"

"That club has never done anything but cause trouble."

My heart began to race but I did my best to hide my excitement. Cody Pruitt might be the first person in Clifton Forge who would willingly give me information about the Tin Gypsies instead of warning me away. "Have they caused you trouble here before?"

"Not lately. But I went to high school with Dash. He was an arrogant son of a bitch back then. Same as he is now. Him and some friends rented out a couple of rooms from my parents after our senior prom. Trashed them."

"You're kidding." I feigned shock when inside I was doing cartwheels. Finally I'd found someone who wasn't warning me away from Dash or a founding member of his fan club.

"Nope."

I waited, wondering if he'd say something more, but Cody's eyes drifted out the office window, toward the room marked 114. When I'd driven by yesterday, there'd been police tape over the front. Now, it was gone. Unless you knew where it had happened, you wouldn't guess a woman had been killed across the courtyard.

"Did you see Draven here on Friday?" I asked.

He shook his head. "No. My mom was working that night."

"Did she—"

I was cut off by the rumble of an engine outside. Both

Cody and I whipped our heads to the other window in time to see Dash roll into the parking lot on his Harley.

Shit. Great timing, Slater.

Dash parked next to my car and swung his leg off the motorcycle. He was wearing a black leather jacket today and a pair of faded jeans. Just the sight of his long legs and his unruly hair made my heart jump. *Damn him.* Why couldn't he have been blond? I'd never had a thing for blonds.

I did my best to keep my breaths even as he strode our way. The last thing I wanted was to have him come in here and see me panting. The flush in my cheeks was bad enough.

I turned my back to the door, keeping my attention on Cody, who was practically seething.

The bell chimed as Dash came inside. His stare burned my backside as it trailed down my spine, yet I refused to turn or acknowledge him as he came to the counter. From the corner of my eye, I saw him slip off his sunglasses.

"Cody." Dash's heat hit my shoulder as he leaned his elbows on the counter. "Bryce."

My name in his voice gave me goose bumps on my skin. I pulled my arms to the side, hiding them from his view. Did he have to be so close? He was less than an inch away and the smell of leather and wind filled my nose. And, *damn it*, I inhaled a deeper breath.

To hell with you, pheromones.

"Kingston," I drawled, daring a glance at his profile with my best unaffected stare.

A growl formed deep in his chest, but he didn't utter any other response. He held my gaze for a moment too long, and then he dismissed me, giving Cody a nod. "How are you?"

"How am I?" Cody's voice shook. "You have some nerve coming here, Slater."

"I'm not here to cause trouble."

"Then leave."

"Just want to ask you some questions."

Get in line, pal. "Cody was just telling me that he's given all the information to the police."

"That's right." Cody pointed to the door. "I have nothing else to say. So unless you want to destroy another room or two, I think it's best you leave."

"Look, I've said it a hundred times. I'm sorry about prom. My dad and I paid for that and then some. I was a stupid kid. If I could go back in time, I'd undo it. But I can't."

They'd paid for it? Interesting. I'd pegged Draven and Dash as men who wouldn't make amends for something like petty vandalism. As leaders of a dangerous motorcycle gang, they could have made some threats and gotten away with it. Taking responsibility was not something I'd expected.

And something Cody had conveniently left out of his story.

"I have nothing to say to you," Cody snapped. He was a good four inches shorter than Dash and at least thirty pounds lighter. But I got the impression this wasn't so much about the murder or prom as it was a less-popular kid taking a stand against an old nemesis.

Good for you, Cody.

"I only want to find out who killed that woman." There was vulnerability in Dash's voice. I didn't like how my heart softened.

Cody huffed. "You Slaters are all the same. Your dad takes a knife to a woman in my motel, stabs her from head to toe, and you're here to pin it on someone else. Guess it's a good thing Bryce is here. Otherwise you might try to say I killed her."

"That's not—"

"Get out," Cody snarled. "Before I call the cops."

Dash blew out a long breath, then turned his attention to me. "You put my dad's name and picture in the paper."

"Well, he was, in fact, arrested for murder. You might remember, I was there."

The corner of his lip curled up. "You make a habit of printing lies? I can't wait to shove them down your throat."

Lies? No. No one questioned my integrity as a journalist. "What I printed was the truth. A woman was murdered. Truth. She died here at the motel. Truth. Your father was arrested as a suspect. Truth. Are those the lies you're going to shove down my throat?"

He inched closer, looking down his nose at me. "Maybe. But I'd rather shove something else down that pretty throat instead."

"Weak." I rolled my eyes. "If you think threats laced with sexual innuendo will scare me away, you'll need to try harder."

"Harder. You'll beg for harder." He came closer again, the smooth leather of his jacket brushing against the thin cotton of my tee. I'd worn a sports bra to the paper last night, opting for comfort instead of lift. I'd chosen one without padding and when his eyes drifted lower, I knew he saw my nipples peeking through.

I could step away. Or I could call his bluff. Was Dash a bad-boy playboy? Absolutely. But was he a misogynistic womanizer who'd force himself on me? No. Which meant he was pushing to see how hard I'd push back.

Game on.

I took my own step forward, pressing my breasts into his chest. "I doubt that . . . *King.*"

Dash hissed as I dragged my nails up the side of his jean-clad thigh. My entire body was braced, waiting to see his reaction. If he touched me, I'd probably have to knee him in the balls. But it didn't come to that. Calling his bluff worked.

In a flash, he stepped away, his frame strung tight, and marched out the door. The bell filled the air and my breath came back in heaves, the sound drowned out by the noise of Dash's Harley as it raced away.

Cody's grin stretched ear to ear. "I like you."

"Thanks." I laughed, my heart rate settling.

"What else would you like to know?" Cody asked. "I'll tell you everything if you're out to get Dash."

Now it was my turn to grin from ear to ear. "Do you happen to know the victim's name?"

CHAPTER FIVE

DASH

"They won't let me see him." I slammed the door as I walked into the office at the garage.

"Can they do that?" Presley asked, looking between Emmett and me.

Emmett shrugged. "They're cops. At this point, they can pretty much do whatever the hell they want."

I'd been trying to see Dad for days but the chief had thrown up a steel barrier. No visitors unless it was Dad's attorney. No exceptions. So while I could glean some information from Jim, it wasn't enough. It wasn't the one-on-one conversation I needed. We trusted our lawyer but there were questions I wasn't going to let him relay. Their conversations were no doubt being recorded, which was illegal, but I didn't trust the cops to uphold Dad's constitutional rights.

Besides, depending on the situation, Dad wouldn't tell Jim everything. Because Jim wasn't a Gypsy. We might not be tied together with patches and oaths anymore, but we were still loyal to one another. Loyal until death.

"Is it normal for them to take this long to release a suspect?" Presley asked.

I shrugged. "According to Jim, the prosecutor is trying to decide whether she wants to charge Dad with first- or second-degree murder at the arraignment. We could push them to decide, set the bond hearing, but Jim worries that if we do that, they'll go for first. Thinks it's better to let Dad stay where he's at and hope for second."

"What do you think?" Emmett asked.

"I don't know," I muttered. "I don't know enough about the criminal justice system to question Jim. He's always done good by us. And Dad trusts him."

With any luck, they'd decide soon and set the bond hearing. Maybe Dad would be out by Friday. Then we'd get some answers.

"I hate being in the dark." I took a seat along the window. "Did you hear anything?"

"Nothing," Emmett said. "Leo and I asked everywhere. Not a damn word. Everyone was as surprised as we were."

"Shit." Across the room, Dad's office sat empty. Normally, we'd be in there this time of day, having a cup of coffee and talking about cars or bikes. I'd see what kind of paperwork he'd let me push from my desk to his. At the moment, I couldn't concentrate on work. The questions about the murder stole all my focus.

"I wish I could find out who she was, the woman. Find out what Dad was doing with her."

"Amina Daylee," Emmett said from his chair across from Presley's desk.

"Oh." I jerked, surprised by his answer. When had the cops released her name? Maybe they'd done it while I'd been at the station, waiting in a stiff chair for over an hour to be told I wasn't going to see Dad. Again. You'd think with the amount of taxes we paid they'd at least get a seat with a goddamn cushion.

Amina Daylee. I ran the name through my mind over and over, but it didn't sound familiar. "Doesn't ring a bell."

"She went to high school here," Presley said. "Moved away after graduation. She was recently living in Bozeman. Has a daughter who lives in Colorado."

Not a shock that Presley had already tapped into her gossip circles to find out about the victim. "Let's find out more. How old was she? Does she still have ties here? How might she have known Dad?"

Since I couldn't ask him how he knew her, maybe I could find the connection myself.

"They went to high school together," Emmett said. "She's a year younger than Draven."

"Always one step ahead of me." I chuckled, but my smile fell fast. "Wait. If the cops just released her name this morning and I came right here from the station, how did you figure all that out already? Was it on Facebook or some shit?"

Emmett and Presley shared a hesitant glance.

"What?" I demanded. "What happened?"

Presley blew out a deep breath and then slid a newspaper out from underneath her own stack of paperwork.

"Fuck." Bryce Ryan was becoming a bigger pain in my ass every fucking day.

Was I going to have to start reading the goddamn newspaper?

"They did a special piece on the victim today." Presley brought the paper over. "Amina was her name."

I ripped the newspaper from her hand, reading through

the front page quickly. Right in the center was a picture of Amina Daylee.

Her blond hair was cut just above her shoulders. Her makeup was light, not hiding a few wrinkles here and there. In the photo, she was sitting on a bench in some park, smiling as the flowers bloomed at her bare feet.

My hands crumpled the paper into a ball, the crinkling sound filling the office. I should have had that photo days ago. I should have had her name. I shouldn't have to open the paper to a bunch of new fucking information.

I'd done some digging on Bryce Ryan since Dad's arrest. Her story seemed straightforward. Grew up in Bozeman. Moved to Seattle and worked at a TV station. I'd found some old video clips of her on the internet, reading the news with that sexy voice. Then she'd quit her job, moved to Clifton Forge and bought into the paper.

Her routine was boring, at best. She was either at home, the newspaper or the gym. The only random trip she'd taken had been to the Evergreen Motel on Sunday.

When the paper was balled as tight as I could get it, I chucked it across the room. Except my aim was shit and I hit Emmett in the head.

"Hey!"

"Fucking Cody Pruitt. He probably gave her all this info the day he kicked me out of the motel. That pissant never liked me."

If I hadn't shown up, would he have told her anything? Or had he spewed it all out of spite?

"What are we going to do?" Presley asked. "Do you think he did it?"

"Draven?" Emmett asked. "No way."

According to the article, Dad was the only person seen

coming or going from Amina's motel room between the hours of eight p.m. and six a.m. the night she was murdered. Bryce was generous enough to note in her article that he hadn't been seen with blood on his hands.

But that didn't mean shit. Dad had mastered the art of washing away blood a long, long time ago.

"He didn't do it," I assured Presley.

"How do you know?"

"Because if Dad had killed Amina Daylee, they would never have found her body."

"Oh." Presley sank into the chair, her chin dropping.

She'd started working at the garage about six years ago. It had been right at the time when the Tin Gypsies were tapering off our illegal undertakings. Or at least, the *really* illegal ones.

Presley had been hired to help in the office as Dad retired. She hadn't minded overlooking some things happening at the clubhouse. The parties. The booze. The women.

The brothers who thought they might intimidate her a little. Presley was pint-sized, but her personality was full of fire, and she'd had the guts to put each man in his place when they acted like an asshole.

And her loyalty to Dad and me, to Emmett and Leo ran bone deep. She was the little sister I'd never had.

Marcus's visit to the garage last week hadn't been the first. Presley had never once hinted she'd tell the cops anything, not that we'd given her much to report. She had our backs, covering for us when we'd done stupid shit at The Betsy now and then. Leo had her on speed dial for the nights when he was too drunk to drive.

She was part of our family. We didn't tell her details of

what had happened years ago. It was best she didn't know. All of those secrets had been buried in unmarked graves.

Pres was smart. She knew what evil men we'd been.

Maybe the evil men we still were.

"What's the plan, Dash?" Emmett asked.

I shook my head. "I don't want any more surprises. I underestimated the reporter. That stops now. She's digging—deep—and we need to stop it."

"What do you want me to do?"

"Work. Is Leo in the garage?"

He nodded. "He's finishing the pinstripes on the Corvette. Isaiah is doing the routine jobs on the board."

"What about you?"

"We got a new Harley rebuild to bid."

Normally, we did those together so we could bounce ideas off one another. "Can you do it alone?"

He nodded. "Yeah."

"Good." Following Bryce to the motel hadn't ended the way I'd hoped. Guess it was time to try a different approach.

———

I WALKED into the *Clifton Forge Tribune*, taking a quick look around. I'd lived my entire life in this town yet hadn't been in this building before. Up until now, I hadn't had to bother with the press.

"Hi there. Can I help you?" The guy at the front was a dead ringer for Santa Claus. In fact, I think this guy *was* Santa during the annual Christmas stroll on Central.

"Just looking for Bryce." I pointed to the door that I assumed led deeper into the building. "Is she through here? Never mind. I'll find her."

The wheels of his chair rolled across the floor, but he was too slow to stop me. I pushed through the door. Bryce was sitting at a desk near the back, alone in the room.

Her eyes lifted from her laptop, her gaze narrowing as I strode down the aisle. She leaned deep into her chair, crossing her arms over her chest. Then she quirked an eyebrow, all but daring me to unleash hell.

"Sorry, Bryce." The man from the front caught up to me, his heavy steps thudding on the floor.

"It's okay, Art." She waved him off. "I'll deal with our guest."

The moment he was gone, she recrossed her arms, the movement pushing her breasts higher.

My eyes involuntarily dropped to her cleavage. The woman had a great rack. When I met her eyes again, that smirk was even stronger. *Busted.*

"Mind if I sit?" I slid a chair away from the empty desk in front of hers, straddling it backward.

"What can I do for you today, King?"

King. I'd hated that fucking nickname ever since kindergarten, when little Vanessa Tom had called me King every time she snuck up on me at recess and pinched me. But there was no way I'd let my annoyance show in front of this woman. She already had the upper hand.

She knew it too.

Goddamn it, she was a piece of work. Bryce sat there, looking bored as she waited for me to answer her question. I chose silence, studying her face for a few long moments.

Her full lips were irritating, mostly because I couldn't stop wondering how they'd feel when I licked them. Her beautiful eyes drove me mad because they saw too much. I hated that her dark hair was my favorite length, not too long to get in the way and blow in my face when she was behind me on my bike.

Everything about her pissed me off because of my body's reaction.

"Read your story." I plucked a copy of today's paper off the desk. "Looks like Cody was more forthcoming with you than he was with me."

"I never reveal my sources."

I tossed the paper aside and met her gaze. The silence settled and I counted to ten. Then twenty. Then thirty. Most people cracked by fifteen, but not her. Bryce kept that arrogant smirk on her face like she'd been born with it. Her eyes were bright and they held my stare without so much as a hint of fear.

Damn this woman. I liked her. That was my real problem. I *liked* her. Which was going to make threatening her a hell of a lot harder. That, and she didn't seem to be intimidated by me one bit.

"You don't scare easily, do you?"

"Nope."

"What's your game here?"

"My game?" she repeated. "I'm not playing a game. I'm doing my job."

"But it's more than that, isn't it? You're after more than just the details of this murder."

She lifted a shoulder. "Maybe."

"Why? What did we do to piss you off?"

"This isn't personal."

Yeah, right. No one worked this hard when it wasn't personal. This entire thing went deeper than her need to *do her job.* She wasn't reporting a murder investigation for the good of the populace. Everything about this was personal.

Why? What was driving her to push so hard? From what I'd found out about her, she'd been successful on TV in Seattle. Had they fired her? Was she trying to prove herself to an old employer? Or her father?

Or herself?

"What do you really want?" I asked, going for broke. Sometimes the best way to get answers to your questions was to toss them out there.

She quirked an eyebrow. "You expect me to just lay all my cards out?"

"Worth asking."

Bryce leaned forward on her desk, her eyes finally showing that addictive spark. "I want to know why the Tin Gypsies shut down."

"That's it?"

Bryce nodded. "That's it."

I'd been expecting something more. Maybe that she wanted to see all the former Gypsies rotting in prison. "Why?"

"You were the leader of one of the most powerful motorcycle gangs in the region. I'm sure that meant money. And power. Yet you shut it down without any explanation. For what? A life as a grease monkey? No way. It's too easy. It's too clean. You're hiding something."

"We're not," I lied. We were hiding so much that if she knew the truth, she'd never look at me the same way again. There'd be no more hints of attraction, no checking me out when she thought I wasn't noticing. She'd look at me like the criminal I'd been.

Like the criminals we'd all been.

"Ah, yes. The standard deflection." Bryce rolled her eyes. "Sorry. I'm not buying it."

"There's no big story here." Another lie that she wasn't going to believe.

"If that's the truth, then why did you break apart?"

"Off the record?" I asked.

"No way."

"Of course not." I chuckled. And of course, she wasn't cutting me any breaks. I'd always liked the feisty ones. "Then I guess we're at a stalemate."

"A stalemate?" She scoffed. "This is no stalemate. I'm twenty steps ahead of you and we both know it. Why exactly did you come in here today?"

"My dad is innocent. If you give the cops some time, they'll prove it too. You doing your best to prove to the world he's guilty is only going to make you look like a fool."

"I'm not scared to look like a fool." She'd called my bluff —like always—but I wasn't buying it. Something flashed in those eyes that looked a lot like the first sign of weakness.

"You sure about that? New reporter in a new town, going balls-out on a murder investigation like she's some wannabe fucking gumshoe. She sticks her neck out there to try and slime a well-known citizen. A business owner who gives back to his community. When he comes out clean, you'll be the one who looks dirty. You're part owner here, right?"

"Yes. Your point?" she asked through gritted teeth.

"My point is . . . my family has lived in Clifton Forge for generations. We're well-known. And well liked. In their day, so were the Gypsies."

"So you're saying if I don't take your side that people in town will hate me? I can live with that."

"Can you? Small-town newspaper, can't be making a ton of money. It only takes one rumor that you're printing false information for people to stop reading."

The color rose in her cheeks, the fire flaring in her eyes. "I don't like being threatened."

"And I don't like repeating myself. You had your warning. Stay out of this."

"No." She looked me dead in the eye. "Not until I get the truth."

My temper spiked and I stood, shoving the chair from out of between my legs so I could lean over the desk with my arms planted wide on its surface. "You want the truth? Here's the truth. I've seen and done things that would give you nightmares. The truth would make your stomach curl. You'd go running from this town and never look back. Be glad you don't know the truth. Back the fuck off. Now."

"Screw you." She shot out of her seat, leaning in to stand nose to nose so the only thing separating us was the desk. "I'm not backing down."

"You will."

"Never."

The sound of her teeth grinding drew my attention to her lips. The urge to kiss her was stronger than it had ever been with her, or with any other woman for that matter. With the desk between us, I probably wouldn't get kneed in the nuts.

I leaned in an inch and her breath hitched. When I tore my eyes away from her lips, her gaze was locked on my mouth. Her chest was heaving, her breasts rising and falling underneath her V-neck blouse. My threat to her livelihood hadn't done a goddamn thing except turn us both on. Was she ever going to back down? *Son of a bitch.*

I was one second away from saying to hell with it all and smashing my lips on hers when the door behind her flew open. Lane Ryan walked in, wiping his hands on a greasy rag. He took one look at me and his daughter and the smile fell from his face. "Everything okay?"

"Great." Bryce dropped into her chair, combing a lock of hair behind her ear with her fingers. "Dash and I were just discussing today's paper."

I leaned back from the desk and took a deep breath, my cock swollen and painful in my jeans. I turned away from Bryce and her father, taking a moment to let it calm down as I righted the chair I'd shoved away.

Then, I stepped up to Lane and held out my hand. "Good to see you, Lane."

"You too, Dash." He shook my hand, giving me the side-eye, no doubt worried about his infuriating daughter.

"I think we're done here," Bryce said, standing from her desk and swiping up her laptop. "If you'll excuse me, I have somewhere to be."

We were not done with this conversation, not by a long shot, but until I got my dick under control, there wasn't anything more to say. "Yeah. Same."

I nodded to Lane, shot Bryce a glare, then turned and marched out of the *Tribune*.

Goddamn it. She wasn't going to back down, no matter how often I threatened her. If anything, my visit had just spurred her on.

Which meant I was going to have to get creative.

CHAPTER SIX

BRYCE

"Smug bastard," I muttered, shuffling papers on my desk as I looked for my notepad. "How dare he come in here and threaten me? How dare he—ahh! Where is it?"

The notepad I'd been searching for was nowhere. Not in my car. Not at home in a basketful of unfolded laundry. Not on my desk, which was now a total mess.

I kept different notepads for each of my stories, a place where I could make notes so I didn't forget anything. Pink was for birth announcements. Black for obituaries. Red was for the Fourth of July rodeo and festivities. And the yellow one was for Amina Daylee's murder.

The last time I'd seen it had been yesterday morning. I remembered making a note against the steering wheel in my car that Amina's middle name was Louise. Her daughter lived in Denver. I'd written it all down so I wouldn't forget, then tucked the notepad into my purse with the others.

Retracing my steps, I'd come right into the newspaper after that. I'd dumped everything from my purse onto my desk to organize it as I worked through my various stories in progress. I'd been in the middle of wrapping up a piece for Sunday's paper. It was a no-brainer—the schedule for Clifton Forge's Independence Day weekend celebrations. I'd had all of my notepads right here by my keyboard, the red one open as I'd typed, when—

I shot out of my chair. "That asshole!"

Dash had to have taken it. The thing couldn't have just disappeared, and I'd looked everywhere. But how had he known it was the right one? *Shit.* He must have seen it at the motel when I'd been talking to Cody.

Luckily, the notebook held nothing I couldn't remember. The act of writing down my notes was usually enough to commit them to memory. And most of the information in those pages had already been printed.

Still. I was mad. "Gah. I can't believe he did this."

"Who did what?" Sue looked over her shoulder at my outburst.

I huffed and sat down. "An asshole thief stole my notepad right out from under my nose."

All because I was so distracted. Distracted by the danger that surrounded him and the allure of discovering all his secrets.

"Sorry, dear."

"It's my own fault," I muttered, giving her a nod to return to her work.

It was definitely my fault.

Dash had leaned in close and his smell . . . God, he smelled good. The spice of his cologne mixed with the summer breeze was a heady combination. Under the spell of that scent and his unwavering hazel glare, I'd feared for a split second that he'd kiss me. That I'd kiss him back.

Then I'd feared he wouldn't.

He'd probably swiped my notepad when I'd been staring at his mouth.

Damn him. I'd dropped my guard and he hadn't hesitated to take advantage. Dash must be feeling the pressure if he'd resorted to petty theft.

We both knew I was winning. I held more aces than he had kings at the moment, but the game was about to take a turn.

Tomorrow was Draven's arraignment, and unless the judge decided the sixty-year-old man was a flight risk, he'd be out on bond tomorrow. As soon as Draven was free, Dash would have an inside source.

So to keep my edge, I'd need to push harder and dig deeper. What I needed was another scoop, to find another person like Cody Pruitt who'd spill because he had a personal grudge against the Slater family.

But who?

The door from reception opened and Willy walked inside, heading straight for his desk across the aisle from Sue. He pushed his sunglasses into his thinning blond hair, revealing dark circles under his eyes. It was nearly noon but with his rumpled clothes, he looked as if he'd just rolled out of bed.

"Hi, Willy."

He lifted a hand as he sat, leaning deep into his chair. "Morning. Hey, Sue."

"Hi, Willy. Rough night?"

"Might have had one too many beers."

At that, the door opened again and George rushed through, his arms overloaded with loose papers and the briefcase trapped underneath an elbow about to slip free. He made it to his desk just in time to dump everything on top as his case crashed to the floor. "Hey, guys."

"Hi, George."

Everyone else exchanged greetings as I sat back and watched, me the newcomer to the team. For once, the room was full. Everyone was here except for Dad because, per Mom's demand that his twenty-day work streak come to an end, he was taking the day off.

"I don't think we've all been in the same room since last month's staff meeting," I joked.

Willy sat upright, his shoulders tense. "Lane said I didn't have to keep regular hours."

"That's fine by me. I was just making an observation. Work when you want."

"Oh. Okay." He slumped again. "Thanks. I don't like mornings much."

"What are you working on?" I asked.

He rifled through the shoulder bag he'd brought, hauling out a notepad. "I haven't typed it up yet but you can read it."

"Yes, please. I'd love to." I stood and went to his desk, taking the pad from his hand.

It didn't take me long to read the article, even in Willy's scratchy handwriting. The words sucked me in and by the end, I had a smile on my face.

"This series is going to be incredible," I told him, handing back his pad. "Nice work."

A blush crept up his cheeks. "Thanks, Bryce."

Willy was doing a five-week piece on the life of railroad transients. He'd spent the better part of a month this past spring getting to know a handful of individuals who'd passed through Clifton Forge courtesy of the Burlington Northern Santa Fe Railway line that ran along the edge of town.

This week's column was about a woman who'd been a railroad hitchhiker for seven years. Willy's words had painted her nomadic life in vivid detail. Hard because there were no luxuries like daily showers. Brutal at times when food became difficult to come by. Wistful with its ultimate freedom. Happy because she lived the life of her choosing.

The story was intriguing, the writing flawless. Willy's talent was the reason Dad gave him free rein when it came to pitching ideas. Whatever he wrote, our customers devoured.

Willy knew his audience well, maybe because he'd lived in Clifton Forge his entire life and there wasn't a soul in town he didn't know.

An idea slammed into my head. Maybe Willy could help me keep my lead against Dash.

"Can I ask you a question?" I perched on the edge of his desk.

"Shoot."

"I was hoping to get an early look at an autopsy report, the report for the woman who was murdered at the Evergreen. But when I stopped by the county coroner's office this morning, they had a note on the door that they were closed. If I wanted to get ahold of the medical examiner, who would that be?"

"Mike," Willy said. "Just give him a call. He'll help you out."

"Even for an ongoing investigation?"

Autopsies were public record, but when an investigation was involved, they weren't released until the prosecutor permitted it.

"He might not let you read the whole report, but he's given me rundowns before just so I could include some details in a story. Besides, never hurts to ask."

I grinned. "Exactly."

One thing Dad had taught me early on was that asking for information was free. The worst-case scenario was you'd get shot down with a no. I already knew that would be Chief Wagner's answer.

But maybe this Mike would be a bit more open to sharing.

"I'd love to ask Mike." I stood from Willy's desk. "Except I don't know Mike." Nor did I have his phone number.

Willy whipped out the phone in his pocket without a word, punched at it for a second, then held it to his ear. Five minutes later, the two of us were in my car, driving to the coroner's office.

"Thanks for coming along," I told Willy as he lazed in the passenger seat.

"It's all good. Kinda curious to see you in action. The stuff you've been writing about the murder is good. Damn good. Best work I've seen since your dad's."

"Thanks." I smiled over the steering wheel at maybe the best compliment I'd had in a decade. "Your work is impressive too."

"Glad you think so. I, uh . . . I really love my job. I can come in more . . . to the office. If I have to." His fingers fidgeted on his lap.

Willy had always been jumpy and skittish in the office. I'd just assumed he was like that all the time. Maybe he was to a degree. But he was also nervous about his job. That with me on staff, Dad wouldn't need an additional reporter.

"I don't care when you come into the office, Willy. As long as you keep writing the great stories you've been writing and handing them in on time, you'll always have a spot at the *Tribune*."

He nodded, keeping his eyes out the window on the buildings that streaked past. In the reflection, I saw a faint smile.

It didn't take us long to get to the medical examiner's office, which was located across the street from the small hospital in town. Willy led the way to a locked door, knocking on the wire mesh that covered a square glass window in its face. We waited for a few minutes, longer than I would have stood there alone, until finally the door pushed open and a man waved us inside.

"Mike." Willy shook his hand. "This is Bryce. Bryce, meet Mike."

"Nice to meet you, Mike. Thanks for doing this."

"You bet." His voice was hoarse. The dark circles under Mike's eyes matched Willy's. Despite the pungent smell of chemicals within the sterile space, the stale scent of alcohol wafting off his body nearly made me gag. "I owe Willy one after he drove my ass home last night. Had one too many after our pool tournament."

I nodded and breathed through my mouth. "That's nice."

"What can I help you with?" Mike asked.

"The coroner's office is closed and—"

"Those guys." Mike scoffed and rolled his eyes. "You know, I bust my ass getting reports done and sent over to them. They take their sweet time actually getting them processed. Whose did you want to see?"

I braced. "Amina Daylee."

"Oh." His shoulders sagged. "No can do. Active investigation. You'll have to get that one from the cops."

"Damn." I sighed. "Well, it was worth asking. I've had some examiners in the past who let me read their report or told me a little about it. Sometimes even off the record so I couldn't print anything until it was released by the police. But having an idea of the autopsy helps me ask the right questions. It might lead to other clues too."

My speech was a stretch. I expected Mike to shove us out the door at any moment, as he probably should.

"I can't show it to you," he said as I held my breath, waiting and hoping for the magic word. "But"—*bingo*—"I can give you the high level. Off the record. You'll have to wait for the details to be released to print them."

"Perfect." I glanced at Willy, who sent me a wink.

"Come on," Mike muttered, motioning for Willy and me to follow him down the hallway.

The building was deserted, the only light coming from the windows since the overhead lights were all off.

"Quiet day?" I asked.

Mike shrugged. "It's just me right now. I had an intern but she's off for the summer."

We crowded into Mike's office at the end of the hallway. The desk and floor were scattered with stacks of file folders the same teal as his unbecoming scrubs. The hallway had smelled like antiseptic and bleach, but in here, the air was perfumed with coffee and an undercurrent of hangover.

"Okay." Mike flipped open a folder as he sat behind his desk. I sat across from him in a folding chair while Willy remained standing against the doorframe. "Amina Daylee. Age fifty-nine. Cause of death, blood loss due to multiple stab wounds."

Information I'd already gleaned from the police reports and my discussion with Cody Pruitt at the motel. Cody's wife had cried as she'd told him about the scene in room 114. The entire bed had been soaked through with Amina's blood. Some had dripped to the carpet, creating nearly black puddles. Cody's wife had stepped in one when she'd rushed to Amina's side to check for a pulse.

"How many stab wounds?" I asked.

"Seven. All upper body."

I swallowed hard. "Did she suffer?"

"Yeah." Mike met my gaze and gave me a sad smile. "Not for long. He hit a major artery, so she bled out fast."

"Do you know time of death?"

"I've got a pretty tight timeline but as always, it's an estimate. Between five a.m. and seven a.m."

Which meant Draven had killed her first thing in the morning. "Anything else you can tell me?"

"She'd recently had intercourse."

My spine straightened. "Any signs of force?"

"No. It was likely consensual."

"That's something, at least." I was glad Amina hadn't had to endure a rape before her death. "Did the sperm come back as Draven's?"

"This is all off the record." Mike looked between me and Willy, a sudden look of fear crossing his face like he'd already said too much. "Right?"

"Right," I promised. "I won't use any of this in the paper until the authorities release it to the press."

Mike studied my face for a long moment, then gave me a nod. "The new preliminary quick test matched his sample. I'm still waiting on the full results. But the prelims are rarely wrong."

An interesting twist. Draven and Amina had had sex before he'd killed her. Why? Were they new lovers? Old lovers? Why the motel instead of his home? Was her death an act of passion? All questions I would have written down in my notepad.

Fucking Dash.

"Thanks so much for your time." I stood and held out my hand.

Mike stood too. "None of this gets printed until the report is released."

"You have my word. Thanks again."

Willy and I excused ourselves from the office, making our way back into the sunshine and fresh air. As we climbed into my car, Willy laughed. "You're good. I was sure he'd kick us out when you told him what report you wanted."

"I have my moments." I smiled and turned on the car. "Thanks for the help."

"Any time. What now?"

"Now?" I blew out a long breath. "Now I need to find more about our victim. Her daughter is in Colorado, but I wouldn't approach her this soon anyway. Amina grew up here but doesn't have any family left. I'm hoping to find a few people who knew her as a kid. I want to find out why she came back, and why she met up with Draven."

"I might be able to help with that," Willy said. "How about I buy my new boss a beer?"

"You're on."

———

AS IT TURNED OUT, The Betsy wasn't just a seedy bar, but a place where the town's history was as abundant as the dust mites floating from the rafters.

Thanks to three of the bar's regulars—a trio of men well past seventy who were all somehow related to each other through cousins and marriages, I'd lost track—I had more information about Amina Daylee than I'd been able to find on my trusty sources Facebook and Google.

Amina's name hadn't shown up much in the newspaper archives. The only reference was a graduation announcement decades ago. It was how I'd pieced together that she'd gone to Clifton Forge High, one year junior to Draven. But besides the same alma mater, I hadn't found much information about her family.

According to the guys at the bar, Amina's family hadn't lived in Clifton Forge long. Her stepfather had worked for the railroad and had been transferred here from New Mexico. One of the regulars recalled that the family had moved here not long before Amina had learned how to drive, because he'd sold them a car. *I was a little too old for her at the time but that girl was a head turner.*

The family was well-liked, from what the guys at The Betsy remembered, but their interactions had been limited because the winter after their daughter graduated and moved away, Amina's parents were both killed in a tragic car accident. Somehow, I'd missed that in the news archives because her mother had taken her stepfather's last name while Amina had kept Daylee.

Her parents were buried in the town cemetery. Maybe she'd come back to visit their graves.

"Another one, Bryce?" the bartender asked.

I swallowed the last gulp of my beer. "I'm good, Paul. Thanks."

About twenty minutes ago, I'd lost Willy and the three regulars to the pool table while I'd stayed in my stool, finishing up my second beer. The door behind me opened, the bright afternoon light streaking inside. The thud of heavy boots vibrated the floorboards as the new customer came toward the bar.

Glancing over my shoulder, I expected a stranger's face. Instead, I found vibrant hazel eyes and a face I'd all but memorized.

"You stole my notepad."

Dash slid into the empty stool beside me and jerked his chin at Paul, a silent order that must have meant *fetch me a beer* because Paul did just that. Dash rocked on his stool, getting comfortable. The seat was so close to mine that one of his broad shoulders came a fraction of an inch from touching the bare skin of mine.

My heart skipped—stupid organ—and I gritted my teeth. I refused to acknowledge how close his forearm was to mine. I refused to look at the black tattoo that decorated his skin in wide, black strokes. I refused to budge as he crowded me because, damn it, I was here first.

"Do you mind?" I eyed him up and down. "Move over."

He didn't budge.

"I don't like you."

The corner of Dash's mouth turned up. With his other arm, he reached behind himself and dug something out of his back pocket, slapping it onto the bar. My yellow notepad. "Here."

"Thief." I snatched it up and put it in my purse. I wouldn't give him the satisfaction of looking through it now. But the second I was alone, I was checking every single page.

"Not much of a notetaker, are you? There wasn't shit in there I didn't already know."

I scoffed. "Because I've already printed it in the newspaper."

"Here you go." Paul came over to deliver Dash's beer. "What's the word on your dad?"

"Bond hearing is tomorrow."

"You think he'll get out on bond?"

Dash shot me a wary glance, like he didn't want to answer while I was sitting here. *Tough luck, King. I was here first.* "Yeah. He'll get out."

"Good." Paul sighed. "That's real good."

Good? "Aren't you worried that a potential murderer will be out of police custody and roaming the streets?"

Paul only laughed, killing any chance at a decent tip. "Holler if you need anything, Dash. I need to head back and change a keg."

"Will do." The bastard thief had a smug grin on his face as he lifted the pint glass for a drink.

Unable to tear my eyes away—more stupid organs—I followed the bob of his Adam's apple as he swallowed. Watched with rapt attention as his tongue darted out to dry the foam on his top lip.

"I'm going to steal something else if you keep staring at my mouth like that."

I didn't look away. It was a challenge, but I didn't look away. "Has anyone ever told you that your eyebrows are rather bushy?"

Dash laughed, the low and rich sound sending a shiver down my spine. "Once or twice. How was your meeting with Mike today?"

"Informative." He was following me now? God, this man was irritating, but I kept my expression neutral. "I've learned a lot today. Sunday's paper is going to be a good one."

"Look forward to reading it." Dash set down his beer and

twisted in his seat, his knee bumping into mine. "It'll be the last time the *Tribune* prints something I don't already know."

"And why's that?"

"Dad's getting out tomorrow."

"And what, exactly? He gets out of jail and kills me too?"

His stubbled jaw ticked. "He gets out of jail and tells me what the fuck really happened. Then we end this little game."

"It's not a game." I stood from my seat, slinging my purse over a shoulder. "This is my job. The town deserves to know there's a killer in their midst. A woman was murdered and she deserves justice."

"She'll get justice when the cops find the person who killed her, not hold an innocent man."

"Innocent? I've read enough about this club of yours to know your father is far from innocent."

"Former club."

"Semantics."

"Fuck, you're difficult," he growled.

"See you later, King." I headed for the door, waving to Willy who was still engrossed in his game of pool. He'd have to find another ride to the office because I wasn't hanging around The Betsy a second longer.

Well, maybe one more second.

"Oh, and Dash?" I turned and met his glare. He'd been watching me walk away. "How long do you think it took after your dad fucked Amina Daylee for him to kill her? An hour? Maybe two? He doesn't strike me as a cuddler."

Dash's jaw barely tightened, his eyes only widening a fraction. He was good at hiding surprise, but I was better at spotting it. He'd had no idea his *innocent* father had had sex with Amina right before her murder.

I left him sitting there, his mind visibly whirling, and walked out the door. Slowly, secret by secret, I'd uncover the truth. First about Amina Daylee's murder. Then about the Tin Gypsy Motorcycle Club.

And when I did, maybe this empty feeling that I was missing something from my life would finally go away.

CHAPTER SEVEN

DASH

I waited outside the county courthouse for Dad in my truck, idly tapping my knee with my thumb. His bond hearing was over, and as soon as he checked out, we were getting the hell out of here.

It was strange to be driving the Dodge in summer. I'd bought this truck only a month before spring, so we were still adjusting to one another. It was black, like all its predecessors. It still had the new-car smell because I hadn't had much time behind the wheel. As soon as the ice thawed from the roads each spring, I only rode my bike until the snow flew in late fall. Montana winters were long and most of us who rode didn't want to miss a single decent day.

But I'd wanted to pick Dad up today. We had too much to talk about to put it off for the ten minutes it would take for us each to ride our own bikes to the garage. And I hadn't wanted to take the guys away from work at the garage to get Dad's bike over here.

He came out the front door wearing the same clothes he had been in last Friday. His silver stubble was thick, nearly a beard, and as he climbed in, his deep brown eyes were tired. Dad looked like it had been a month since he'd been arrested, not just a week.

"Hey." He clapped me on the shoulder, then buckled his seat belt. "Thanks. Appreciate you covering bail."

"No problem."

"Did you put up my house?" he asked.

"No. The garage."

The judge had determined Dad wasn't much of a flight risk, but given that he was the primary suspect for a violent murder and his past association with the club, bail had been set at half a million dollars.

"Damn." Dad sighed. "Should have put up my house instead. Wish you hadn't tied up the garage."

"They'd ask a lot of questions if I just showed up with a duffel bag of cash from my safe." I put the truck in drive and pulled away from the courthouse. "Your house. My house. The garage. Doesn't matter. It'll go away when we clear this shit up."

Half a million cash wasn't hard for either of us to come by, but considering how we'd made that money, we used it for things where it couldn't be traced. Definitely not for covering a bond.

"Could have left me in there."

"Never." I frowned. Not only because he was my dad and didn't belong there, but because I needed answers. Maybe I'd finally be able to show Bryce up. Because at the moment, in this race for information, I was losing miserably. "We gotta talk about what happened."

"I need a day." Dad laid his head back. "Then we'll talk about it all."

"We don't have a day."

"The cops aren't going to find anything they haven't already. Whoever set me up for this was thorough."

"It's not the cops I'm worried about," I told him, watching as he sat up straight. "We've got a problem with Lane Ryan's daughter at the paper."

"What kind of problem?"

"She's digging. And she's good."

"What'd she find?" Dad asked.

"At the moment, she's focused on the murder investigation. But I'm worried she's not going to stop there."

"Fuck," Dad muttered. "We don't need a damn nosy reporter digging up old Gypsy business."

"No, we don't. We've been lucky. We shut things down. We played by the rules. And people just let it go." They were happy to have peace in town for a change. "Bryce, this reporter, she's not the type to let anything go."

A trait that would have been irresistible had she been working on my side. Even as an enemy, she was damn tempting.

"Threatened to ruin her reputation. That backfired. But I'll handle her." I just had to figure out how.

The more I pushed, the more she pushed back. And Bryce was a strong-willed woman. I'd learned from my mom at an early age that most men didn't stand a chance against a strong-willed and stubborn woman.

"Just be careful," Dad said. "We both can't be in jail."

"Don't worry. I'm not going to do something to land me in jail. I just . . . I have to find something to hold over her so she'll back off."

Fear used to be my weapon. My favorite tool. In my twenties, I'd used physical violence to make people afraid. But then I'd learned that extortion and blackmail were usually more effective. None would likely work on Bryce, certainly not getting physical. I'd never harmed a woman in my life and wasn't about to start now. The idea of hurting her made my stomach turn.

"You could figure out a way to get her to work with us. Not against us," Dad suggested.

Not a bad idea. Was there a way I could get Bryce to become an ally? If she were a friend, not a foe, I'd be able to feed her information about the Gypsies, not worry about her digging behind my back. And then I could control the information she put in her precious newspaper.

"Smart. That could work."

"Maybe we should have been more open about why we shut down," Dad said, staring out his window. "I've been wondering if it was going to put a target on our backs."

"What would we have said? There was no way to explain it without bringing up a bunch of shit that needs to stay quiet."

"You're right." His shoulders sagged. "Just been a long week. Lots of thinking about the past and the wrongs I've done. I fucking hate jail."

"Most do."

I'd only been in jail once, when I was nineteen. I'd been hauled in as a suspect for an assault and battery. Guilty as the night was long, I'd beaten the hell out of a man who'd cheated me at poker and pulled a gun on me when I'd confronted him about it.

Bastard should have shot me.

I wasn't sure what Dad had done to get the guy to drop the charges, but they'd been dropped and the guy had moved out of town the next week. After that, I'd learned to be more verbal during a fight. Before I knocked anyone unconscious, they knew that if they talked to the cops, they'd pay with their life.

How many people saw my face in their nightmares?

Doubt had become a familiar feeling these past few years. Doubt. And shame. I'd been proud once. Proud of the man the club had made me. We'd lived our lives by following a set of rules not born from society, but from brotherhood. I'd been so sure of those rules, so steadfast in following them.

Then I'd begun to question them all.

That was the beginning of the end for the Tin Gypsies.

Years ago, after Emmett's father had been murdered in the parking lot of The Betsy, the club had voted in change. Too many men had been lost, too many loved ones. It had taken us almost six years to unwind the club's illegal dealings. To change the mindset of an old and outdated legacy.

We'd spent that time building up the garage so it could provide enough income to cover what we'd made illegally. No more drug protection runs. No more underground fighting ring.

Thanks to a lot of work and a little luck, the garage was more successful than any of us had imagined it would be. And when it came time to decide whether the Gypsies stayed a law-abiding club or parted ways, in the end, we were all ready to put the past to rest.

I wasn't the only brother who'd looked in the mirror and hadn't liked the man staring back.

Most of the club's members took the money they'd stashed away and moved to new towns and into new homes. They left old demons behind for a fresh start. Those of us who stayed formed a new family, this one centered around the garage. Dad, Emmett, Leo and me.

I craved this normal life.

I'd thought the norms of society would be suffocating. Turns out, life was easier on this side of the law. It was nice to have people make eye contact when they passed you on the sidewalk. Nice not to see mothers grab their child's hand when you looked their way. Nice to not be constantly looking over my shoulder.

At least, it had been until Bryce Ryan had shown up with her yellow notepad and goddamn curiosity.

I wouldn't let her ruin this new life we'd built. I wouldn't let her threaten my family. The only way I could protect us was by getting the information first.

"Tell me about Amina Daylee."

Dad blew out a long breath. "Not today."

"Dad—"

"Please. One day. Give me one day. We'll talk tomorrow."

I frowned but nodded. Then I changed direction, driving him home instead of to the garage. We didn't speak as I wound through town. When I parked in the driveway of my childhood home, I stayed in my seat. "Tomorrow."

He opened the door and nodded. "Tomorrow."

With his head hanging low, he walked to the side door of the house and went inside.

We only used the side door at Dad's place. The front door hadn't been used in years. Even the mailman knew to drop packages at the side entrance.

Because none of us would walk up the front sidewalk. Not Dad. Not Nick. Not me. None of us would set foot on the place where Mom's blood had once stained the cement. You couldn't see the stain anymore. The rain and snow and sun had worn it away.

But it was still there.

Nick and I had both tried to get Dad to move out of that house. There were too many memories there, too many reminders of what we'd lost.

But those memories had a different effect on Dad. He stayed in that house because it was where he'd lived with Mom. To him, she was in the walls. The ceiling. The floor.

He'd die in that house before letting her go.

A chill crept over my skin and I shook it off, reversing out of the driveway and heading to work. When I pulled into the parking lot of the garage, I was in a shit mood.

Why would Dad need a day? Why wouldn't he want to talk about Amina and how she'd been killed? Didn't he want to find the person who'd framed him?

Had Bryce been right? *Did he have sex with Amina?* Who was that woman besides an old high school friend? To my knowledge, Dad hadn't been with a woman since Mom had died. Maybe to punish himself. Maybe because he didn't want another woman in his life. Sleeping with Amina would have broken one hell of a streak.

It unsettled me some, the idea of Dad with anyone else. He'd been loyal to Mom. Always. He hadn't done anything wrong. So why was this bothering me?

I walked into the garage and found Emmett underneath the hood of a Chevy truck. "Hey."

He looked past me, searching for Dad. "Where is he?"

"At home."

"What?" He scowled. "We need to talk."

"I know. But he wants a day. We'll give it to him."

"Who wants a day?" Leo asked, walking up to us with a bottle of water tipped to his lips.

"Dad."

The water bottle dropped from his mouth. "Fuck that.

86

We need answers. If it's the Warriors setting him up then we need to—"

I held up a hand, my eyes cutting over to Isaiah, who was working in the next bay. "Not now."

He nodded, clamping his mouth shut.

We all trusted Isaiah as a mechanic, but we weren't going to get into old club business with him around—not just for our sake, but for his.

"Let's just . . . be patient."

Emmett scoffed. "Something the three of us excel at."

"Yeah." I took the phone from my pocket and walked over to a workbench, setting it and my keys on top. Then I looked at the workboard. The guys had the normal stuff covered, so I'd get to work on the Mustang. *Work is good.*

I could use some time with my tools and an engine. I could use some grease on my hands and time to think. Because come tonight, I needed to have a plan for dealing with Bryce Ryan.

I needed a plan for getting her onto my side.

———

"GET OFF MY PORCH."

I chuckled, tipping the beer bottle to my lips. "Hello, Bryce."

"What are you doing here?" She stood in front of me, her hands planted on her hips. "How did you know where I live?"

"Do you really want to know?" I doubted she'd want to hear that I'd been following her around for days.

"No." She'd come from the gym because her hair was up in a ponytail, a few tendrils near her temples still damp with sweat. Her black leggings molded to her lean legs. Her tank top was tight around her breasts and stomach, leaving only her graceful arms bare.

My dick jerked to life as I pictured peeling those clothes from her body, setting all her curves free. Best not to think about her naked, not when I was trying my new tactic.

"Beer?" I nodded to the six-pack by my boot, which now only had three bottles.

"I'll pass."

"More for me then." I shrugged.

"Now that you know I don't want a beer, take them and go home."

"Can't."

"Why not?" She tapped a foot on the sidewalk. "Just hop on your bike and be on your way."

"You weren't here. You made me wait for you and I got thirsty. So I had to drink three beers. Can't drive now. Someone will have to come and get me."

"I'll call you a cab."

"Can't."

"Why?" The tapping foot got faster. God, it was fun pissing her off.

"My bike. Can't leave it on the street. Have to take it home."

"So you're just going to sit on my porch until you're sober enough to drive home?"

"If you insist."

She growled at me, then bent low to take a beer from the pack. Off came the cap with a twist, but instead of putting it to that supple lower lip, she surprised me yet again.

She poured my beer onto the lawn.

"What the—" I shot off the single concrete step, reaching

for the bottle. But she put her shoulder in my way, blocking me, as my perfectly good beer soaked into the green grass. "Is there a reason you're wasting my beer?"

"Yeah. I want you off my porch." She set the empty bottle down and reached for the pack again. This time it was my turn to block her. "Relax. I'll drink the other two and maybe by the time they're gone, you will be too."

I put my finger in her face. "Pour another one out and next time I'll show up with a case."

The corner of her mouth twitched. "Fine."

"Fine."

I sat first, taking a beer out and twisting off the top. I gave her another warning stare before handing it over.

She took a small sip. "So back to my first question. What are you doing here?"

"Getting to know you better."

"And why is that?"

"Let's call it curiosity." I took a long drink. "You're kind of boring. You go in to the paper early every morning. Your dad is always there first. Then Santa Claus. Then you. Everyone else comes and goes, but you three keep a fairly regular schedule."

If I surprised her by knowing her routine, she didn't let on. She just sipped her beer, her eyes locked on the quiet street ahead of us. "That's the downside of being in charge."

"Sometimes you walk to the coffee shop on Central, though not every day. Lunch is usually at your desk unless you're running around trying to fill in one of your notepads. And then you're gone by five, straight to the gym. Except Tuesday, when you had dinner at your parents' place. Taking a guess that's a weekly thing."

Bryce took a longer swig of her beer and the color rose in

her face. It was the only sign that I was getting to her, but it was enough. "Anything else?"

I leaned an inch closer, the heat of her bare arm burning into mine. With our skin nearly touching, I bent my neck so I could talk right into her ear. "You hate doing laundry."

She turned, barely missing my nose with her own and narrowed her eyes. "How'd you know that? Did you break into my house or something too?"

"No." I ran my hand up her bare arm, from wrist to shoulder. Her breath shook and the fine hairs on her forearm rose. Her chest heaved but she didn't pull away.

At least I wasn't the only one affected by this magnetism between us. By this chemistry and this . . . want. Touching her pushed my control to the edge, so before it broke, I flicked the material on her tank top and moved away. "It says so on your shirt."

She flinched, looking down at the words on her gray tank. The color in her cheeks flushed brighter as she scooted away an inch, pretending that my touch hadn't just scorched us both.

I'd come up with a plan as I'd worked on the Mustang today.

My intimidation tactics weren't working on Bryce and never would. She didn't care that I had money. She didn't care that I had power. She didn't care that I had enough pull in this town to ruin her precious newspaper.

Because she was different. *She* wasn't going to respond in the same way as a man. So instead of treating her like I would a man, I had to treat her like the gorgeous woman she was.

I couldn't threaten her into silence, but maybe I could seduce her onto my side instead.

The plan had seemed brilliant an hour ago. Now that I'd touched her, maybe it was as goddamn stupid as it seemed.

How was I supposed to seduce a woman who made it impossible to think about anything other than stripping off those leggings?

I took another long drink of my beer and cleared my throat. "Paper comes out on Sunday. Anything you want to throw in my face before then?"

"Not at the moment," she said quietly as I studied her profile.

Her nose was straight except for a small bump at the end. Her lips were plump, the bottom slightly wet from the beer. She even had a nice chin. I don't know if I'd ever noticed the shape of a woman's chin before but hers was tapered to a soft point. I couldn't think of a nicer chin in the world.

"You're staring."

I blinked. "Yep."

She twisted her neck to meet my gaze. "At the risk of being repetitive, you haven't answered my question. Why are you on my porch? Because if it's to intimidate me by telling me you've been following me around or to threaten—"

I slammed my mouth down on hers. *Oh, hell.* I never made the first move on a woman. My seduction technique was shit. But I couldn't resist that mouth, and I had to taste it. I slid my hand up her face, my thumb resting on that perfect chin.

Bryce sat frozen. I'd already swallowed the little gasp she'd let out as my lips had crushed hers. She didn't pull away. I waited for it, mentally counting the seconds before her beer bottle would smash into my temple. I'd need stitches for sure.

Except it never came.

Instead, she melted.

My tongue darted out and licked her bottom lip, tasting her own sweetness with the bitter beer. She parted for me and angled her head, giving me permission to sink in and get wet. And God—I moaned down her throat—she tasted good.

She slid her tongue into my mouth, but before we could get serious, she yanked her face away, her cheeks flushed and her eyes full of that familiar angry fire. Bryce stood, swiping up her beer to march to the front door. The keys rattled in her hand and the door pushed open, but before she disappeared inside, she shot me a snarl over her shoulder.

"Drunk or not, get the hell off my porch."

Yeah. That was a damn good idea.

CHAPTER EIGHT

BRYCE

My fingers drifted from the steering wheel to my lips. Since Dash's kiss on Friday evening, I couldn't stop touching them. All weekend long, I'd caught myself staring blankly into space with my fingers to my lips. No matter how much I rubbed them clean, no matter the many coats of lip gloss I applied, his touch was there like an invisible tattoo.

Why had I let him kiss me? Why had I kissed him back? *Exercise, that's why.* I was blaming all of this on exercise.

I'd worked my ass off at the gym on Friday, running three miles on the treadmill followed by twenty minutes on the stair climber, then ten burpees. I'd pushed myself hard, trying to get my head on straight. Trying to get my mind off Dash and burn off some sexual frustration.

My workout had been so intense, I'd felt like a puddle as I'd driven home. Normally, *puddle* was a good state of being. Puddle meant a long, hot shower and a sound, dreamless sleep.

Fucking puddle. Exercise was no longer a sanctioned activity, not until I had my head screwed on straight where

Dash was concerned. Not when he showed up and caught me unprepared.

Forcing my fingers back to the wheel, I pulled into the parking lot at the paper. I had a busy week ahead and starting off Monday without focus was not an option. Yesterday's Sunday edition of the *Tribune* had gone out the door without a hitch, and it was time to focus on my articles for Wednesday.

I didn't have time to worry about Dash Slater. I didn't have time to think about how his tongue had tasted like cinnamon and beer. Or how close I'd been to dragging him inside my house to the bedroom on Friday.

My core quivered. *Hell.*

"Good morning, Art," I said as I came into the building, hoping my smile didn't seem as forced as it felt.

"Morning." He smiled. "How are you?"

"I'm good," I lied. "It's going to be a great day. I can feel it."

He chuckled. "You and your feelings."

Feelings. I wish I could make sense of them where a hot biker was concerned. *Why did he kiss me?* Why? I didn't have time for this kind of distraction.

I left Art hard at work adding yesterday's paper to our electronic archive system and went to my desk. Plopping down in the chair, I stowed my purse and glanced around the empty room, taking a deep inhale.

The newspaper smell wasn't bringing me much comfort today. Dash's smell was too fresh in my mind, wind and cologne and a hint of oil.

The bastard was even stealing smells from me.

Well, I wasn't going to let him take my focus from this story. Draven was going down for murder and I'd be there every step of the way. Once he was serving life in prison, I was going to find out why the Tin Gypsies had broken apart their club.

Yesterday, I'd written another feature on the murder. Timing had been on my side and the police had released some new information to the media, including a few details from Amina's autopsy. I'd printed her name along with cause of death.

I hadn't included the sexual evidence. True to my word with Mike, I'd keep that to myself until the chief deemed it newsworthy. Eventually, Draven and Amina's sexual escapade would come to light. For now, I was content having that knowledge to use as I did my own investigating.

A clang from the pressroom caught my attention and I stood, pushing through the door. Dad was at the back by the Goss.

I'd gone for a pair of Birkenstocks today with my black skinny jeans and T-shirt, wanting to feel comfortable on the outside while my insides were all twisted in a knot, so my footsteps were nearly silent as I crossed the pressroom.

"Hey, Dad."

He jumped, spinning around. "Hey, yourself. You startled me."

"Sorry." I smiled, but it fell when my eyes landed on a pair of legs hanging out from beneath the printer. "Is that BK?"

To my knowledge, BK didn't wear black motorcycle boots. BK's thighs weren't firm and the jeans he wore didn't mold around them perfectly. BK didn't have narrow hips or a flat stomach.

My heart dropped. I knew that black belt. I'd had vivid fantasies of unbuckling it all weekend.

Before I could turn tail and sprint for the door, Dash slid out from beneath the machine. He had a wrench in one hand and a screwdriver in the other. His fingers were smudged with grease.

"Got it," he told Dad, barely sparing me a glance.

"Really?" Dad asked.

"Really." Dash stood, still refusing to look at me. "I think you should be good now. There's a gear that probably needs to be replaced soon. I'll see if I can get a part and come swap it. But I managed to get the one in there working for now so it won't skip rotations."

"That's great." Dad clapped Dash on the shoulder. "I can't tell you how much I appreciate it. I was going to have to get a repairman from the press company, and bringing one out here can get expensive."

"No problem." Dash took a rag from on top of one of the towers, cleaning his hands. His eyes stayed fixed on Dad like I didn't exist.

I hated how my heart sank. Refusing to let him win, I put on my best aloof face and turned up my nose a bit. He wasn't going to ignore me. I was going to ignore him.

Hello, high school.

"How much do I owe you?" Dad asked.

"Nothing."

"No, I can't let you do all this for free."

Dash chuckled, that devilish smile going straight to my center. *Damn him.* "Tell you what, buy me a beer the next time we run into each other around town."

"All right." Dad extended his hand again. "I'll do that."

Dash tossed his rag aside and shook Dad's hand. Then, finally, he looked my way. "Bryce."

"King." I held his hazel gaze. "How are you today?"

"I had a good weekend." He smirked. "Always makes for a good Monday."

If his definition of a good weekend was invading my private life on Friday—kissing me—only to ride off and find another woman to make his weekend *good*, I was going to destroy him.

"Lucky you," I said. "I wish I could say the same. I had an unwelcome guest on Friday who put a damper on my whole weekend."

"What? Why didn't you tell me about this yesterday?" Dad asked. "What guest?"

"We were busy yesterday with the paper. But it seems that I have a pest problem on my porch. Can I borrow your shotgun?"

Dash chuckled quietly, his broad chest shaking as he smiled at the wall.

"A shotgun?" Dad's forehead furrowed. "What kind of pest? Gophers?"

"Nope." I shook my head. "A snake."

"You hate snakes."

"With a passion. Hence, the shotgun."

Dash continued to laugh under his breath. The movement making his jaw seem stronger. Sexier. *Ugh.*

"You're not using the shotgun." Dad frowned. "I'll come over tonight and see if I can find it."

"Thanks." I'd tell him later the snake was gone. "Well, I have a busy day. Glad you got the press working."

"Me too. It was a good thing Dash poked his head in when he did." Dad laughed. "I was about to light the damn thing on fire."

"I'm glad you didn't." Standing on my toes, I pressed a quick kiss to Dad's cheek, then spun around and marched for the door. Behind me, Dash's deep voice rumbled until the sound of boots echoed behind me on the floor.

Dad didn't wear boots. He was a sneaker man.

Every cell in my body wanted to tell Dash to go away. Or to ask him to kiss me again. I wasn't sure.

Fighting the urge to turn was hard but I kept my shoulders squared and my legs moving forward. When I pushed through the door, I only opened it a crack, hoping it would shut on Dash's face.

It didn't. The moment I was in my chair, Dash was perched on the edge of my desk. He crossed his arms over his chest, his biceps flexing with the movement. The definition around his muscles wasn't something you saw often on mere mortals, all tight skin covered with tattoos.

I swallowed down a wave of drool. "What do you want?"

"A snake?" The corner of that sultry mouth turned up. His eyes were shining and full of mischief.

I shrugged. "It fits."

He grinned, flashing me those white teeth. A lock of hair fell onto his forehead and I clasped my hands together so they wouldn't reach to fix it. Dash had great hair. I bet it was silky and thick, the strands like dark chocolate. It was just long enough I could get a good grip if he was on top of—

Oh, for fuck's sake. That kiss had scrambled my brain and given him the upper hand. Somehow, I had to take it back, which was going to be difficult with him sitting on the edge of my desk, smelling like sin and pure temptation.

"Was there something you needed?" I asked.

"How about a *thank you*?"

"For?"

He nodded to the pressroom door. "For fixing your press."

If not for the stress it would take off Dad and the paper's budget, I would have died a thousand deaths before uttering a word of gratitude for a job I hadn't asked him to do. But Dad's relief had been palpable. "Thanks."

"Was that so hard?"

"Would you mind getting off my desk? I have work to do today."

"Can't."

"Jesus. Here we go with the *can't*s again."

"Read your paper yesterday."

"And."

"It was . . . informative."

"Well, that is the purpose of a newspaper. To inform the people."

"You're doing a hell of a job." His compliment seemed genuine; therefore I didn't trust it for a second. "I have a proposition for you."

I arched an eyebrow, a silent *I'm listening*.

"Let's call a truce."

"A truce?" I scoffed. "Why would I agree to a truce? I'm winning."

"Maybe."

Bullshit. "Definitely."

"Fine. You're good. But we both want the same thing. We both want to find out who killed that woman."

"But I already know. It was—"

"It was *not* my dad." He held up a finger. "If it was, you can prove me wrong. But if I'm right, which I am, wouldn't it be better to print the real story? The one about the real killer, before anyone else?"

"I hate to break this to you, King, but I'm the only one in town spreading the news. I don't need your help getting the story. Hell, I can wait around and print what the cops feed me and I'll still keep my readers."

"But that's not your style."

No, it wasn't. I wanted a scoop. And not just against other news outlets. I wanted to scoop the police too. "What exactly are you suggesting we do with a truce? Work together?"

"That's right. Seems like we might be *real* good together."

Heat flushed my face as his eyes drifted to my lips. We'd only shared a single kiss, but he was right. Given the sparks that crackled when we were in the same room, we'd be incredible together. The chemistry, mixed with our mutual dislike of one other, would ignite like fireworks. We'd probably set the sheets on fire.

Innuendo dripped from his words, but Dash wasn't asking for sex, was he? He was asking for information. Slightly flattered that this request acknowledged my lead, I considered it. "You want me to hand over whatever I find about Amina Daylee's murder. What's in it for me?"

"Same. I'll share what I find with you."

"Including whatever you learn from your father?"

He thought about it, finally saying, "'Kay."

Tempting. The proposition—the man—both tempting. My eyes narrowed as I studied Dash's face. It seemed sincere. If he was lying, he was good at it, but I wasn't going to hand over all my information on a Monday-morning whim. "Maybe. I'll think about it."

"Good enough." He stood from the desk and relief rolled over my shoulders. He'd been sitting much too close.

"Bye," I said to his back.

Except Dash didn't walk to the door as I'd expected. He

crossed the aisle to Dad's desk and sat in the chair. "What are you doing?"

He waved a hand at the chair. "Sitting."

"*Why* are you sitting?"

He didn't answer. Instead, Dash scanned Dad's desk until his eyes landed on a framed photo next to a cup of pens. He picked it up, a smile spreading on his mouth. "You look different."

I tucked a lock of hair behind my ear. "I used to work in TV."

The picture he held was one Mom had had framed for Dad. It was of the three of us about a year ago. They'd come to Seattle for a visit—and to talk me into joining the paper and finally moving to Clifton Forge after hemming and hawing for years.

The day of the photo, they'd come to the TV station to see where I'd worked. My makeup had been heavy and my hair styled. I'd been dressed up in a navy suit, ready to go on camera.

"Huh." Dash put the frame back and looked me up and down. "I like this better."

"Me too." I turned to my desk, opening a drawer for my calendar. Since his last visit, I'd made it a point to put everything in a drawer or cabinet before I left for the day. I flipped to today's date, seeing that I needed to schedule a dentist appointment.

I'd do that after I got rid of Dash.

"Why'd you go into TV?"

I flipped a page in my planner. "You're still here?"

Dash chuckled, angling his chair and dropping his forearms to his knees. "Until you answer the question."

"Why? Why do you care?"

"Call it curiosity. I usually know a little more about a woman before I kiss her."

"I find that impossible to believe."

He dropped his head, his shoulders shaking as he laughed. "Yeah. You're right. I don't always ask questions first. But I am today."

"And if I answer them, you'll leave me alone?"

"Yeah." He nodded. "Scout's honor."

I frowned to hide the smile that threatened. Was this flirting? No surprise, he was good at it. God, he needed to leave. I didn't feel like talking about myself, but if discussing my history was the ticket to a Dash-free office, then I'd spill.

"I went to college at Montana State in Bozeman. I majored in English because they didn't have a journalism program. My favorite professor knew I wanted to become a journalist, so he got me an internship at the TV station. My boss at the station said I had a knack for it."

I despised the word hypnotized, but looking back, a part of me had been spellbound by the glitz and glamour of television. As an intern, I saw only the exciting events. I accompanied reporters as they went into the field, armed with microphones. I stood next to the cameramen as they filmed a crime scene with flashing blue and red police lights in the background. I shadowed the producer for the evening news. The evening anchor was a beautiful woman, smart and witty. She wore designer suits and had a makeup crew to paint on her flawless face.

It had all seemed so special. So exhilarating.

In college, I'd lived with my parents, forgoing dorm life to save them money. So I hadn't had a typical college experience. No sharing a bathroom with twenty other women. No fraternity parties or wild nights at the bars. I'd taken a heavier than normal class load and graduated a year early.

For a twenty-one-year-old who'd craved a new adventure, television was it.

"How long did you work in TV?" Dash asked.

"Too long."

I'd given the best years of my life to that job. I'd been so desperate for excitement and to climb the ladder. I'd wanted desperately to sit in that anchor's seat. I'd given up everything else, missing out on the chance to marry a good man and have children.

"Why'd you quit?" Dash asked.

"About five years ago, I interviewed a woman who left Seattle for Montana. She'd just won the Pulitzer for an undercover story about a mobster importing weapons."

"Sabrina."

"Uh . . . yes." I blinked. I guess he'd dug a lot deeper into my history than I'd suspected. "Sabrina MacKenzie."

"Holt now. I know her."

"You do?"

He nodded. "She lives in Prescott. That's where my brother lives too. Emmeline, my sister-in-law, and Sabrina are good friends."

"Small world."

"Especially in Montana."

"Anyway, I interviewed Sabrina. And I was jealous," I admitted. "I was jealous of her story. She'd put herself out there and held nothing back. Dad had just bought the paper and had been begging me to move here. But I'd stayed in Seattle, holding out for a story like hers. It never came and the years, they kept passing by. Finally, I gave up. It was time to come home."

I'd wasted five years after my interview with Sabrina busting my ass in Seattle. Every time I brought up a story idea to my producer, they'd nod and smile and tell me it was a good idea. Then they'd assign it to someone else, normally a man. Because I was needed on screen. I was the pretty face that came into people's homes to tell them news, whether good or bad.

I was tired of being the pretty face.

Here at the *Clifton Forge Tribune*, I wasn't going to win any awards. I wasn't going to save countless lives by getting illegal handguns off the streets and away from children. But I could do honest work. I could tell the truth.

And if I wasn't going to have a family, I'd have this paper. It would be my legacy instead of a family.

I wouldn't fail at another career.

"Any other questions?" I asked, vulnerability thick in my voice. Why had I told him all of that? Why couldn't I have just left it at "I worked in TV and now I don't"? Instead, I'd opened up a piece of my past and splashed it all over the room for him to scrutinize.

His stare raked over my face, seeing too much. The sadness. The failure. The regret. Even my closest friends in Seattle, not that I'd had many with my work hours, didn't know about those feelings.

"No. No more questions." The chair's wheels slid as he stood. He pushed it into Dad's desk, then returned to sit on mine again.

"Good." I bent and plucked my laptop from my tote. "I have a busy day."

"Bryce."

I met his gaze. "Kingston."

"I think I prefer King," he grumbled.

"Then go away, King. I need to get to work."

Dash stood, moving for the door, but an impulse made me call out and stop him.

"Wait." I needed my power back. I needed control. So I stood from my chair, walking right into his space without hesitation. His eyes flashed as I reached up and threaded my fingers into that hair. It was silky, like I'd expected. With a firm grip on those thick strands, I yanked his mouth down onto mine.

He froze for a split second but then he caught up to the kiss. His arms wrapped around my back, crushing me to his chest as his tongue pushed inside my mouth. The taste of cinnamon exploded on my tongue as he plundered. Not to be outdone, I made sure to meet him beat for beat, pouring everything I had into that kiss. A weekend's worth of frustration and longing, all delivered with sucking and licking and fisting his hair.

I gave as good as I could before ripping my lips away, placing a palm on his sternum and shoving him hard with all my might.

Dash staggered backward a foot. His lips were swollen, and we both breathed hard. Confusion was written all over his handsome face—along with lust. He longed for more.

And now, I had my power back.

"I'll agree to the truce after I question your dad," I said. "Set it up. I want to talk to him, tonight."

CHAPTER NINE

DASH

"Dad?" I called through the house. No answer.

The lights were off in the kitchen and living room. His bike was missing from the garage.

"Fuck," I muttered, clenching my fists.

He wouldn't skip out on bond, not when the garage was on the line. I should have pressed harder on Friday when I'd picked him up from the courthouse, but he hadn't wanted to talk then. He didn't want to talk now.

An hour after I'd left Bryce at the newspaper, my head was still spinning from that kiss. I'd gone to the garage to kill time with an oil change as I waited for Dad to come in. When I'd texted him yesterday, he'd ignored me. All damn weekend. Finally, he'd responded last night, promising to be at the garage by ten. When eleven o'clock had rolled around and he still hadn't shown, I'd come here.

When Dad didn't want to be found, he wasn't easy to track down.

What was he hiding? Why wouldn't he talk to me about

this? Murder wasn't uncommon in our past life, but this was the first time he'd been arrested for the crime.

Son of a bitch. I left through the side door, going outside to climb on my bike. There was no point continuing my search. When *he* was ready to talk about Amina Daylee, he'd show.

The return trip to the garage was fast. I spent the time wondering how I'd convince Bryce to keep this truce if Dad wasn't talking. She'd be pissed as hell, and I doubted another kiss would buy me more time. To feel her lips on mine, it would be worth a try. I'd be more than okay with a repeat of this morning if it meant I got her hand in my hair and her slim body pressed against mine.

I pulled into the parking lot, surprised to see Dad's bike in the lot and him inside talking to Presley. "When'd you get here?"

He glanced at the clock. "About five minutes ago."

"I went to the house."

"That's what Pres said. Sorry I'm late. I took a quick ride this morning to clear my head."

"You didn't go out of town, did you?"

"No, he didn't," Presley answered for him. "He promised he didn't cross the county line."

"We need to talk."

Dad nodded, not moving from his chair across from Presley's desk. "Yeah."

"I'll get Emmett and Leo. Pres, would you mind taking Isaiah and grabbing some lunch for all of us? Send Emmett and Leo in?"

"Sure thing." She stood and reached for her purse. "Sandwiches?"

"Sounds good. Here." I fished out my wallet from my back pocket and took out a fifty.

Presley took it and hurried from the office. Minutes later, Emmett and Leo came into the office from the interior door that led into the garage. The rumbling sound of the garage bay doors closing accompanied them.

I flipped the sign on the office door to *CLOSED* as the guys took a seat. Not exactly the long table in the clubhouse where we used to have meetings, but a stark reminder of just how much things had changed.

Silence stretched on long and tense as we waited for Dad to speak. The clock on the wall ticked in a mismatched rhythm to my heartbeat.

"Draven." Emmett broke first.

"We went to high school together." Dad's eyes were trained on the papers scattered on Presley's desk. "I knew her from years back."

We all knew that already, thanks to Bryce's newspapers, but I doubted Dad had read them since he'd been released. None of us interjected, though. We let him take his time. The president, current or former, deserved that respect.

"She called me out of the blue. I hadn't heard from her in ages. Met her at the motel," Dad continued. "Talked for a few hours, catching up. Spent the night."

"Did you fuck her?" I asked.

His eyes snapped to mine, a hint of remorse flashing through his gaze. Then he gave me a single nod.

So Bryce had been right about that too.

"Spent the night. Got up to go home. Shower. Came to work. You were here for the rest."

"She was stabbed," Emmett said, his fingers steepled by his chin. "Any idea if the cops have a murder weapon?"

Dad sighed. "According to Jim, they found one of my hunting knives at the motel."

"How would they know it's yours?" I asked.

"Has my name engraved on the side. Your mom gave it to me ages ago."

"Shit." Leo let his head fall back into the wall. "You're fucked."

The room went quiet again—Leo wasn't wrong. If the police had the murder weapon and could put Dad at the scene, there wasn't much else they were missing.

"Anything else?"

He shook his head. "Don't know. Jim advised me to stay quiet. I met with Marcus twice and he asked me some questions about what happened. How I knew her. Didn't tell him much other than we went to high school together. After that, they pretty much left me alone in my cell. Didn't ask anything else."

"Yeah, because they don't need to ask questions," Emmett said. "They have you at the scene during the time she was killed. It was your weapon. Unless we can prove it was someone else, they have all they'll need to put you away."

"What about motive?" I asked. "Why would you kill her?"

Dad hesitated, his eyes dropping to his feet. But then he raised them and shook his head. "No idea."

My gut twisted. I could count on three fingers the number of times Dad had lied to me. Now I'd be adding a fourth. It wasn't obvious to Emmett and Leo, but there was something he wasn't saying.

With Emmett and Leo here, I wouldn't call Dad out. I'd ask about it later, when it was only the two of us. For now, we had other things to discuss.

"So it's a setup." It had to be a setup. Right? Dad would have told us if he'd killed the woman. "Who would want you to take the fall for this?"

Dad huffed. "That's a long list, son."

"Make it anyway," Emmett ordered. "We gotta start somewhere."

"I've got some ideas," Dad said. "I need to make some calls, then we'll regroup."

"Fine. There's something else." I paused, taking a deep breath because I doubted the reaction to my announcement would be positive. "Made an agreement today with Bryce Ryan."

"Who?" Dad asked.

"The hot new reporter in town," Leo answered. "Dash has been following her around all week."

"That so?" Dad's eyes narrowed.

"It's not like that." Now it was my turn to lie. "Told you yesterday she's good. I dropped by the paper today to have a word this morning. We made an agreement. She tells us what she's got. We do the same. But first, she wants to talk to you."

"No." Dad stood and went to the door. With a flick, it was open and he was storming out.

"Where the hell are you going?" I chased after him. He moved fast, not stopping as I followed him outside. "Dad. What the fuck? We aren't done talking."

"Got nothing else to say right now, Dash. You wanted to talk. We talked. Now I need to go. Get some space."

"What for?"

"What for?" He whirled on me, anger coloring his eyes. "A woman I knew for over forty years is dead. A woman I cared about. And she's dead because of me. So is it too much to ask that you give me some fucking space and let me get my head wrapped around that?"

Fuck. I took a step away, holding up my hands. This wasn't about Amina.

This was about Mom.

This was about her murder and the guilt Dad had been carrying for decades.

The love of his life was dead because of his choices. He'd cost Nick and me our mother. And now another woman was dead because no matter how normal his life was these days, Dad would always be a target.

"Someone wants you to spend the rest of your life rotting in a prison cell, Dad. I'm just trying to see that it doesn't happen."

"I get it." He blew out a long breath. "Amina, she was . . . there's history. I can't think straight right now. Been trying to think it through for over a week. Before I can talk about it, I need to work it out in my head."

"'Kay." He might need time, but I was going to keep pushing hard to find out who'd really killed that woman. I wasn't letting the cops steal my only living parent for a crime he hadn't committed.

Dad walked to his bike, stopping three feet away to speak over his shoulder. "Stay clean on this, Kingston."

My spine straightened. Dad hadn't called me Kingston in years. It was like Mom rattling off our first, middle and last names when we were in trouble.

"I mean it," he said. "Don't do something stupid to land yourself in a cage too. Worst case, I spend the few years I have left wearing orange. I'd handle that a lot better if I knew you were free."

I nodded.

"That's what it was always about. Being free." He walked over to his bike, touching the handlebars. Though the Tin Gypsies were no longer, he still had the old motto etched on the gas tank.

Live to Ride

Wander Free

Dad and Emmett's father had started the Tin Gypsy club back in the eighties. They'd recruited some friends until it had grown and grown. In the beginning, it had been a bunch of young guys who'd wanted to ride bikes and say *fuck you* to any authority or convention. They wanted the chance to make some extra money for their families.

This was back when they restored bikes with scrap parts, the metal more like cheap tin than the steel machines we spent fortunes on now.

When Dad spoke of that time, it seemed simpler. It might have stayed that way if Mom hadn't died.

Dad blinked a few times too fast and my heart twisted. Was he crying? I hadn't seen Dad cry since Mom's funeral. Even then, it hadn't lasted for more than a few heartbreaking tears. He'd been too angry to cry. Too focused on vengeance to let his grief show for long.

Without another word, he swung his leg over the bike. He plucked his sunglasses from his hair, hiding any emotion, and raced out of the parking lot like his nickname was Dash, not mine.

I hung my head, rubbing the tension away from my neck.

"We all know who set up Draven." Emmett's voice behind me was low. I turned to find both him and Leo standing a few paces away.

"Yeah." We all knew. "Dad's got to be the one to make that call."

"You could," Leo argued.

"I could, but I'm not going to." It was the reason I hadn't made that call when Dad was in jail. "Dad approaches the Warriors. No one else."

Emmett and Leo nodded without another word.

"Let's get to work."

Maybe another afternoon working on cars would help me figure out what the hell was happening. Because at the moment, I sure as fuck didn't have a clue.

———

"SO MUCH FOR YOUR TRUCE." Bryce spun away, marching out of the garage. "I knew this was a mistake."

"Wait." I chased, grabbing her elbow. "Just wait."

"Why?" She yanked her arm free. "This is quid pro quo. I give you something. You give me something. If Draven isn't here to tell me his side of the story, then me being here is pointless. I'm leav—"

"My dad did not kill Amina Daylee."

She faced me again, planting her hands on her hips. "How do you—"

"I just know." I locked my eyes on hers. "He didn't kill her. But someone did and if you believe in truth and justice the way I suspect you do, you want to find the real killer."

"The cops—"

"—have a man pegged dead to rights. They aren't going to dig any deeper than the surface."

She huffed. "How can I trust—"

"You can—"

"Stop interrupting me."

I clamped my mouth shut.

Her face was red and her chest heaving. "How can I trust you?"

Trust? "You can't."

Bryce let out a dry laugh. "Then what are we doing?"

I took a step closer. The pull to be near her was irresistible. I wanted her to believe me, at least once. "Don't trust me. And I won't trust you. Maybe we can just not stand in each other's way and both get our answers."

"Seems complicated."

My hand drifted to her cheek, framing her face. "It is."

"Dash," she warned, putting her hand between us. It rested on my chest, firm, but she didn't shove me away.

I inched closer. The pressure on her hand gave way. "Can't stop thinking about your lips."

Bryce's eyes fell to my mouth.

My hand came up between us, covering her own and trapping it to my heart. I expected her to try and yank it away, but then it fisted in my T-shirt as she dragged my mouth to hers.

My tongue delved into her mouth, taking the time to explore the corners I'd missed on our last two kisses. With my free arm, I pinned her to me, my arm tight across her shoulders. I angled my head to get deeper and steal her breath.

She trembled, her knees wobbling, but she clung to me as fiercely. The kiss was hot and wet. Blood rushed to my cock, making it swell against her hip.

"More," she moaned into my mouth.

I growled, letting go of her hand to grab her ass, hauling her up and around my hips. Her legs wrapped around my waist and her arms looped around my neck. Walking us to the closest surface, I set her down on the hood of the Mustang I'd worked on all day.

The owner was an arrogant asshole from Hollywood and I wanted nothing more than to fuck Bryce on the hood of his car.

That was definitely where we were heading. Bryce's thighs squeezed tight around me as I laid her on the glossy hood. The metal buckled slightly as I settled my weight onto her, pressing my chest against her breasts. Our mouths broke apart, hers to gasp for air while I sucked and licked my way down her neck.

"Tell me now if you want to stop," I panted against her collarbone.

She shook her head, her hands diving into my hair. "Don't stop."

I yanked hard at the V-neck of her shirt, dragging it down over a breast. Then I did the same to the cup of her bra, so I could latch my mouth over a supple nipple.

Bryce's back arched off the car, thrusting her breast even farther into my mouth. Her fingernails dug into my scalp.

My hands tore at the other side of her shirt, seams splitting as I freed her other nipple. "Last chance."

I flattened my tongue, dragging it over the hardened bud. She hissed. "Stop."

The lust roaring through my veins turned to ice, and I froze. *Shit.* I hadn't expected that. I took my mouth from her skin, backing away a few inches.

Bryce sat up on the car, once again fisting my shirt as she pulled me close. Nose to nose, she whispered, "Stop warning me away. Haven't you figured it out? That just makes me want it even more."

Thank fuck. "Then hold on."

Slamming my mouth back onto hers, we kissed through a frenzy of fumbling fingers and flying clothes. Bryce yelped when I jerked her off the car's hood and onto her feet. I'd already tugged off her T-shirt and she'd done the same for mine. The bra was next. But as I reached for the clasp, a breeze drifted into the garage, bringing us both back to reality.

One of the bay doors was still open. It was only eight and the glow of the sunset still illuminated the parking lot. This time of year, it didn't get completely dark in Montana until well after nine. Not that it mattered. The shop's lights were blazing. Anyone driving by would see us going at it on the Mustang.

With a fast swoop, I picked Bryce up, one arm under her ass to support her as my other one dove into that soft dark hair, her legs wrapping around me again. I used my grip to tilt her head, then fused my mouth with hers, kissing her senseless as I walked us to the other wall.

The pressure in my cock made walking uncomfortable, especially when she ground her center closer. I finally reached the control panel and punched the red button to shut the door. The outside light faded, leaving only us and the florescent bars beaming overhead.

Bryce reached between us, her hand sliding down the bare skin of my stomach until it reached the waistband of my jeans. With a flick of her fingers, the button came undone. The zipper followed. Then she dove inside my boxers, fisting my shaft as I groaned down her throat.

"Fuck." I tore my mouth away, searching for a place to put her. My eyes landed on a tool bench. Two long strides and I set her down, shoving and pushing away the tools I hadn't put away.

Bryce's frantic movements matched my own as she reached behind her and unclasped her bra. "Hurry."

"Condom." I dug into my back pocket for my wallet and fished out a condom.

Shifting her weight on the bench, Bryce struggled to get out of her jeans. They were too tight, goddamn it. I'd appreciated that when she'd walked into the garage earlier. But now?

"Christ." I picked her up by the armpits, her breasts bouncing as I set her down. Then I dropped to my knees, pulling the black denim and panties off her toned legs so fast that she had to steady herself on my shoulders. The sandals on her feet clattered to the floor.

I couldn't resist. Her bare pussy was right there and I leaned in, dragging my tongue through her folds.

"Oh my God," she gasped, nearly collapsing on me.

I grinned and stood. I'd have my mouth on her again. Soon. But right now, I wanted to bury myself inside her.

My boots and jeans were gone in a flash, the condom rolled onto my pulsing cock. Then I had Bryce up in my arms. This time, I spun us for the wall, her spine colliding with the cool concrete at the same time I lined up with her center and thrust deep.

"Ahh," she cried, the sound of surprise and pleasure echoing off the walls.

I buried my face in her neck, sucking in a breath so I wouldn't embarrass myself and come after just one stroke. "Goddamn, you feel good."

She moaned, her head lolling to the side. Just the slightest tilt of her hips told me she wanted more.

I slid out, slowly, then pistoned forward again, earning myself a hitched breath and whole-body shudder. "Good?"

"Uh-huh." She nodded. "Harder."

"Fucking right, harder." I obeyed, setting a steady rhythm. The sound of her tiny moans, the feel of her wet heat, the way she moved with me, thrust after thrust. The air around us was electric. The need to get more, be deeper, sent me into a blind animal state. *Fucking this woman is incredible.*

We grappled, hands going everywhere trying to feel it all. We kissed, hard, bruising licks that didn't satisfy the craving. We rebounded from surface to surface, abandoning the wall when it wasn't enough. Discarding the tool bench when it wasn't enough. Until we ended up on the Mustang again, both of our bodies glistening with sweat and steam condensing on the hood beneath us.

"Dash." She writhed as I laced my fingers with hers, holding them flush to the red metal. "I'm—"

"Come, Bryce."

She came so hard *I* saw the white spots in her vision. As she pulsed and squeezed my cock like an iron fist, I let loose, pouring inside her and groaning to the ceiling.

Limp and wrung out, I collapsed onto the car next to Bryce, my heart thundering behind my ribs. "That was . . . fuuuuck."

There weren't words. Sex like that shouldn't exist because now I wanted it every day. Bryce was more addictive than any drug on the planet.

We heaved, coming back to reality, until our bodies cooled with the unspoken tension.

We'd fucked. Hard. We'd exposed ourselves, bringing along a weakness neither of us could afford.

"Oh my God." Bryce shot off the car like a lightning bolt. I propped up on an elbow, my legs dangling to the floor. I'd never seen a woman dress so fast.

Damn if that didn't bruise my ego.

"Thanks. I needed that." I regretted the words instantly.

Bryce's arms stilled as she zipped up her jeans. The look she shot me had the power to kill, but she schooled the fury quickly and slid on her sandals.

Maybe she should hate me. Maybe I should drive her away. It was probably better that way. So I might as well make it stick.

I flopped back on the car, tossing an arm over my forehead to hide most of my face. "Side door leads to the parking lot. Do me a favor. Flip the lock on your way out."

CHAPTER TEN

BRYCE

I should go inside. Except I was having a hell of a time getting out of my car.

I was parked in the lot of the Clifton Forge High School, inspecting my nail polish. I'd spent two hours doing a home manicure last night. It was a comfort thing. When I had a lot on my mind, painting my fingernails was my go-to stress reliever. And considering what had happened with Dash in the garage last night, there was a lot on my mind.

I'd gone straight home after he'd dismissed me. Well, not exactly dismissed. I was already leaving. His parting words had shocked me, enough that I'd obeyed and locked the side door behind me.

Even after a hot shower, the manicure and a sleepless night, I couldn't make sense of how it had happened. One moment, I was standing there, reveling in the honesty of his words when he said I couldn't trust him. I went soft at the vulnerability in his voice when he asked that we work together. When his mouth touched mine, all rational thought vanished.

Damn, what was I thinking? There was no question that Dash seduced me. And the fool I was, I'd let him. The sex, I would have been able to make sense of quickly. It was just sex. Two people coming together to scratch an itch. The tension between us was combustible, and it had only been a matter of time before we broke. The sex was not the problem.

The problem was, Dash had cast me away, and I'd never felt quite so used.

Flip the lock on your way out.

Ouch.

Hence the reason I'd gone straight for my tub of fingernail polishes at midnight.

In the dim light of my bedroom, the red I'd chosen had looked darker. Now that I was sitting in broad daylight, the color was a match for the car Dash had fucked me on last night.

Hot-sex red.

When I got home tonight, I was throwing the nearly new bottle away.

I should go inside. Twenty minutes had passed since I'd driven to the school and I wanted to get inside before the office closed for the day. School was out for the summer and according to their website, office hours ended at three. I only had fifteen minutes left, but here I was, stuck staring at my nails.

My sex nails.

It was hazy, but I was pretty sure I'd scratched Dash a time or two during our escapade. *Bastard.* I wish I'd drawn blood.

It bothered me beyond end that I felt slimy. Dash was a villain in every way, but had that stopped me from foolishly hoping he was more? *Nope.* I was ashamed of myself. Not for the sex.

For the hope.

I was no stranger to casual sex. Once, I'd gotten involved with a man from work, a junior producer who'd been as handsome as he was cocky. The two of us had started sleeping together, and weeks later, as we lay naked in bed, he asked if I'd put in a word for him with the executive producer. He was after a promotion and thought sleeping with the female anchor might improve his chances. The idiot actually thought I had some sway. He didn't realize I was merely a puppet for the network, a pretty face to deliver bad news with a smile.

I'd felt used then, but it was nothing compared to the way I felt now.

Maybe today was extreme because I'd let go of all my inhibitions. I'd given my body over entirely to Dash, letting him bring me to the edge and push me over. Maybe it stung more today because I'd never had such all-consuming sex before.

It had been raw and rough and eviscerating. From now until the end of my life, last night's orgasm would be the yardstick for all future comparisons.

Stupid, Bryce. So fucking stupid.

In all fairness, Dash had warned me not to trust him. The tenderness between my legs was a throbbing reminder of my mistake.

I never should have gone to the garage. I never should have believed Dash wanted a truce. When Draven hadn't been there last night, I should have turned tail and run.

Except I'd underestimated Dash and his ability to charm. My eagerness had been my weakness and Dash had exploited it with precision. He'd even made me doubt that Draven was guilty of Amina's murder.

Draven was guilty. Wasn't he? The man couldn't be innocent, right? Unless this was all a setup.

The doubts had been rattling around the corners of my mind all day. *Damn it, Dash.*

I took out the yellow notepad from my purse and plucked a pen from the cup holder. Flipping it to a free page, I wrote one word in big capital letters.

MOTIVE

What was Draven's reason for killing? We could place him at the scene of the crime. He'd had sex with Amina before she'd been stabbed. Chief Wagner was being extremely tight-lipped about the details of the case, but he had told me they'd found a murder weapon at the scene—a black hunting knife.

That was means and opportunity. But what was Draven's motive? Why would he kill Amina Daylee, a woman he'd gone to high school with and, from what I could tell, hadn't seen much of since?

Was it a crime of passion? Maybe Draven had used Amina like Dash had used me. But instead of leaving through the side door like I had, Amina had gotten angry. Maybe she'd ignited his rage and he'd killed her in the heat of the moment.

As tempting as it was to go with that theory, it didn't jive.

I hadn't spent much time around Draven, but I did have carnal knowledge of his son. Dash had the talent to rile me up. We stabbed at one another's buttons and flared each other's tempers. But he wasn't a hothead. Dash was calculated and precise, traits he'd likely learned from his father.

My eyes went back to the word on my notepad, spinning it around, looking at it sideways, backward and upside down.

What was Draven's motive?

I'd hoped to ask him last night. Instead I'd let Dash get me naked in the garage. *Truce, my ass.*

He'd seemed sincere. There was no way he'd faked that level of satisfaction with the sex. So why dismiss me? Surely he knew that would be counterproductive to the alleged *truce.*

One thing was certain—Kingston Slater confounded me. Using him to glean Draven's motive wasn't an option now.

So I'd have to find another way.

There'd been two people in that motel room when Amina had been murdered: the killer and Amina herself. She was the key. If Draven was innocent, then her past might lead me to the truth.

I donned a smile for the first time all day, slung my purse over my shoulder and headed for the school. Inside, the lobby was empty and quiet. My shoes echoed as I walked to the office, waving at the secretary stationed up front—Samantha, according to the nameplate on her desk. "Hello."

"Hi. How can I help you?" she asked.

"I'm Bryce Ryan." I extended my hand over the counter. "I work at the newspaper and I was hoping you could help me."

"I'll try." Her cheerful smile eased my nerves.

The secretary at my high school had been more terrifying than the principal, but based on the number of thank-you cards pinned to a corkboard on the wall beside her chair, I was guessing the students here adored Samantha.

"I'm looking for any information I can find on a former student."

Samantha's face fell. "Shoot. The principal is gone and she's who you'd have to talk to about student records. She knows all the rules about granting permission and all that."

"Dang." I drummed my hot-sex red nails on the counter. "Will she be in tomorrow?"

"No, sorry. She's gone for two weeks on vacation. We try to take advantage during the summer."

"I can imagine you've all earned it." I scanned the hallway past the office. It was empty, all of the classrooms closed with the exception of one. The door beneath the *Library* placard was open. I pointed to the door. "I don't suppose you have any old yearbooks in the library I could look at?"

Samantha glanced at the clock. "There might be, but I'd have to look. And I was hoping to get out of here early today to get to the salon for a hair appointment. I'm the only one here. Would you mind coming back tomorrow? I can dig them up for you."

Shit. I'd wasted too much time in the parking lot staring at my nails and thinking about Dash.

Infuriating, womanizing, sex-magician Dash.

"Sure." I nodded, forcing a wider smile. "Thank you."

Samantha waved. "See you tomorrow then."

"Tomorrow." Except I really didn't want to wait until tomorrow.

With one more longing look at the library, I turned and retreated to the front doors. On my left was a wide entrance to the bathrooms, boys on one side and girls on the other.

An idea hit and my steps slowed.

The bathroom.

Behind me, Samantha was out of her chair, pulling a tote bag from a cabinet in the office. Her back was to me.

Screw it. I ducked into the girls' room and slipped into the second stall.

Was I really doing this? I didn't answer that question for myself. Instead I held my breath and didn't move other than to blink. Maybe my ambition for the story had gotten out of hand. Maybe I was delirious from lack of sleep. Maybe I was desperate not to return to my car where I'd undoubtedly think of Dash. Whatever the reason, it was a stupid idea.

But I stood there, unmoving and taking shallow breaths.

Worst case, Samantha would find me and I'd lie about an overactive bladder. Best case, she'd walk out the door and I'd be locked inside the high school alone. Okay, that wasn't great, but I'd find a way out eventually. Maybe.

Hiding in bathrooms had worked for me at the police station. I might as well roll with it.

The sound of flip-flops echoed from the hallway outside. I remained frozen in my stall, my heart racing and palms sweating. When the light that seeped into the bathroom from the lobby went out, my shoulders fell and I blew out a breath.

I waited another five minutes before making a move. Then I tiptoed my way out of the bathroom.

"My car." I slapped my palm to my forehead. If Samantha noticed it in the lot, she might come back. But she hadn't so far, so maybe I was safe. I spun in a slow circle, spotting small black orbs in the upper corners of the lobby. Should I wave at the cameras? Give them a smile?

My commitment to the act was solid, so I walked to the front door, pretending to open it. Then I faked a dramatic sigh, pulling at the strands of my hair. I was kidding no one here, but it made me feel better. With a fast turn, I marched through the lobby, looking down all the hallways and mouthing a silent *Hello?* It felt as awkward as I assumed it looked—an actress I was not.

Pretense over, I went right for the library. The room was dark, the only light coming from the windows along the wall. It was bright enough that I wouldn't bump into a bookshelf but not enough to do any serious exploring, so I dug my phone from my purse and flipped on the flashlight.

"Yearbooks," I muttered, scanning shelves as I inched deeper into the room. "Where are the yearbooks?"

I passed shelf after shelf of nonfiction books, followed by a few rows of young adult fiction. Five rows along the back wall held an ancient *Encyclopedia Britannica*. My parents had bought a set of those when I was a kid twenty-something years ago and these looked to be about that old.

It was a waste of perfectly good library space, in my opinion. Wouldn't those rows be better suited, for let's say, *yearbooks?*

"Damn it." Time to give up and attempt to get myself out of this building. Samantha was expecting me tomorrow, so I'd wait. It's what I probably should have done in the first place.

I rounded the last corner of the room, passing the librarian's desk. Behind it, the shelves were white, whereas the others in the room were wood. With a quick whip of my flashlight, I expected to find dictionaries and thesauruses. I did a double take when my light landed on tall, thin books, most with foil-pressed letters on the spines. All with a year and *Clifton Forge High*.

"Bingo." My smile felt borderline insane.

I rushed to the shelves, my purse getting tossed to the

floor as I dropped to my knees. I scanned the rows of year-books for the years when Amina would have been in school. I dragged a six-year span off the shelves and got comfortable on the carpet.

The year Amina would have been a freshman had no pictures of her, so I moved on to her sophomore year and found her immediately. My light shone on her dim school photo, picking out shoulder-length blond hair. True to the style at the time, it was feathered away from her face.

I touched the page. Amina had been beautiful. Her smile was natural and bright, even in black and white. On the page, hers was the best photo by far. Somehow, she didn't have the awkwardness her classmates couldn't hide.

My heart pinched. She was gone now, her light smothered by a vicious murderer. It wasn't fair. Unless she proved to be a horrible person, I was making it my personal mission to memorialize Amina Daylee in my newspaper. It wasn't much, but it was something I could do for the young woman in the photo.

And something I could do for her daughter.

I flipped the page, searching the photos carefully, hoping to find pictures of her involved with clubs or sports or—

"Breaking and entering? Didn't expect that from you."

I shrieked as the deep voice carried through the room. Every muscle in my body tightened, holding stiff, as Dash emerged from the dark corner where he'd been lurking.

"Asshole." I slapped a hand over my heart. It pounded so hard and fast that I felt its beat in the split ends of my hair. "You scared the shit out of me."

"Sorry." He held up his hands, though his smirk betrayed his apology.

"No, you're not," I muttered. "God, I don't like you."

He stalked my way, those long legs eating up the distance between us. Dash moved like he wasn't scared of getting caught, the thud of his boots loud in the muted space. He took up a spot next to me on the floor, his thigh nearly touching my own.

"What are you doing here?" I inched away. "How did you get in?"

"Used a window in the girls' locker room in the gym." He wagged his eyebrows. "I used to sneak in there a lot in high school."

"No surprise." I frowned, ignoring the pang of jealousy.

Those high school girls had probably *loved* Dash. No doubt he'd had some tattoos back then and ridden into the parking lot on a Harley. He'd probably fucked the head cheerleader in the girls' locker room while her boyfriend, the hottest kid on the football team, was on the other side of the wall in the boys'.

"Why are you here?" I asked.

"Followed you."

"Of course you did." I rolled my eyes. Given his knowledge of my routine, the man must have been following me for weeks.

He leaned closer to eye the yearbook I'd been studying. I scooched away another inch, then I gathered up the yearbooks in front of me and placed them to my other side, using my body as a blockade. These were *my* yearbooks, not his. But before I could grab the last, he snatched it away.

The only way I was going to get there was by reaching into his lap. My brain screamed *danger zone* and I shied away even farther.

"What are we looking for?" he asked, picking up his yearbook and thumbing through the first couple of pages.

"Pictures of you," I deadpanned. "To frame and put on my nightstand."

"Really?"

"No."

He chuckled, flipping through more pages. "Glad to see sex hasn't dulled your spirit."

"On the contrary, I hate you even more now."

"Ouch." He clutched at his heart. "Harsh."

"No harsher than you sending me on my way last night like I was a five-dollar hooker." I flipped through my own book, the pages turning too fast to really see what was on them. But I kept my eyes glued to the page so he wouldn't see how much he'd hurt me.

"Bryce." His hand came to my arm, stilling my movements. I stared at his long fingers on my wrist but refused to look at his face. "I'm a dick. The whole thing . . . it caught me off guard. And then you acted like you couldn't get away from me fast enough. I'm sorry."

"It's fine." I shook off his hold. "It was only sex."

"Only sex? Woman, that was out-of-this-world fucking."

I shrugged, not trusting myself with words. I mean . . . he wasn't wrong. And I should have hated him after last night.

It irritated me to no end that I didn't.

Returning to the yearbook, I found the section for club photos. I studied the small faces in the abundance of group photos, doing my best to ignore the intoxicating scent coming from Dash's T-shirt. Whatever laundry soap he used, it added a fresh smell to his naturally rich aroma. The combination was tempting. Even after last night, this man still tempted.

Damn him.

I raised my flashlight to the page, squinting at the tiny

photos until I spotted Amina's face in the sophomore class's group photo. Her hair had grown since the previous picture, but the smile and carefree look remained.

"That's her?"

His breath ghosted across my cheek and my face turned up to his profile. Dash was an inch away, right within kissing distance. I leaned away, not trusting myself in his proximity.

"That's her." I twisted to give him my shoulder and force him away.

He went back to his own yearbook but didn't move away. The heat from his arm radiated against me, distracting me from the photos. *Focus, Bryce.* I narrowed my eyes at the yearbook. *Focus.*

I was here to find information on Amina. Dash was a nuisance and nothing more. Except for the fact that he was responsible for the dull ache in my center.

The sound of flipping pages was the only noise in the room. Dash turned his pages in rhythm with my own, until he stilled.

"What?" I leaned over to look at the page he had open.

"Nothing." He turned the page. "Just saw a picture of my old neighbor. He hasn't aged well."

"Oh." I went back to my book, scooting even farther away.

Dash flew through the rest of his yearbook, setting it on the floor when he was done. Then he reached for the shelf behind us and pulled out a different book. This one newer and thicker.

"What are you doing?"

He grinned and thumbed through the pages until he found what he was looking for. Then, with the book split open, he handed it over. "That's me my senior year."

I found Dash quickly on the colorful page. He looked younger—and cockier, if that was even possible. I hated myself for it, but teenage Kingston Slater was total jailbait.

His jaw was more defined now, his shoulders broader. Dash's eyes had more crinkles at the sides when he grinned. Lost in his young face, comparing its differences to the man I'd been with last night, I jumped at a rustle of pages and the whoosh of a book slamming closed. I tore my eyes from the photo just as Dash stood from the floor in a flash, the yearbook he'd been looking at left discarded on the floor.

"You're leaving?"

He raised a hand, waving without a word as he walked out of the room.

What the hell? Should I leave too? I looked around, trying to find out if there was a reason for Dash's sudden disappearance, but the library was still. Maybe he'd gone to the bathroom. Maybe he didn't want to be sitting so close to me either.

I dismissed it all, focusing on what I'd come here to do. Besides, given his recent behavior, Dash would show up again soon.

I made it through the rest of Amina's sophomore year and then scanned through her junior. I'd just opened the hardcover to start on her senior year, the book Dash had been looking at, when the screech of tires sent a chill up my spine.

Setting the yearbook aside, I stood, creeping around one of the bookshelves to look out the window. A police car was parked right out front.

In the distance, I spotted Dash on his Harley. Watching. Waiting.

Either he'd known that the cops were on their way and that was why he'd left. Or . . .

"He wouldn't," I told myself.

He wouldn't have called the cops on me, would he?

As the cops rushed to the front doors, I answered my own question. *Of course he would.*

I gritted my teeth. "That son of a bitch."

CHAPTER ELEVEN

DASH

I refolded the page I'd torn from the yearbook and stuffed it into my back pocket. There was no need to stare at it anymore—I'd memorized the picture.

As I'd been sitting next to Bryce and flipping through that yearbook, it hadn't been Amina's face that caught my attention.

It had been Mom's.

Amina Daylee and Mom were smiling side by side. Mom's arm was around Amina's shoulders. Amina's was around Mom's waist. The caption below the photo read *Inseparable.*

They'd been friends. From the look of it, best friends. And yet I'd never heard the name Amina Daylee before. Dad knew, yet he hadn't mentioned that Amina was once Mom's friend. He'd chalked it all up to vague *history.* Why?

Why hadn't he mentioned Amina had been Mom's friend? I'd been twelve when Mom died. I didn't remember her mentioning a friend named Amina either. Had there been a falling out? Or had they just drifted apart? Until I knew, I was keeping this photo to myself.

Dad had summed it up with a single word.

History.

Fucking history.

Our history was going to ruin us all.

If Bryce wasn't the one asking questions, it would eventually be someone else. We'd been stupid to think we could walk away from the Gypsies without suspicion. We'd been stupid to think the crimes and bodies we'd buried would stay six feet under.

Maybe hiding our history had been a mistake. Maybe the right thing to do would be to tell the story—the legal parts, at least—and ride it out. Except, did I even know the right story to tell? The picture in my back pocket said otherwise. It said I didn't know a goddamn thing about history.

"Dash?" Presley's voice filled the garage. "I thought you'd left."

"Came back." I turned from the tool bench where I'd been lost in thought. "Didn't feel like going home."

"I was just locking up." She walked deeper into the garage from the adjoining office door.

The guys had left about twenty minutes ago, their jobs done for the day. But Presley never left before five. Even when we told her to go home early, she always made sure the office was open according to the hours on the door.

"You okay?" she asked.

I sighed and leaned against the bench. "No."

"Want to talk about it?" She took up the space next to me, bumping me with her shoulder. "I'm a good listener."

"Hell, Pres." I slung an arm around her, pulling her into my side.

She hugged me right back.

Mom had been a hugger. She'd always hugged Nick and me growing up. After she'd died, the hugs had stopped. But then Presley had started at the garage and she didn't believe in handshakes.

She hugged everyone with those thin arms. Her head only came to the middle of my chest, but she could give a tight hug like no one's business.

Presley was beautiful and her body was trim and lean, but the hug wasn't sexual. None of us saw her like that, never had. From the day she'd started here, she'd fit right in as family. And these hugs were her way to give us comfort. Comfort from a close friend who had a heart of gold.

"I did something." I blew out a deep breath. "Fuck, I'm a prick."

"What did you do?"

"You know I've been following Bryce around, hoping I could get her to back off this story. I threatened her. That didn't work. I offered to work with her. That didn't work."

I left out the part about my plan to seduce her because, from my standpoint, she'd been the one to seduce me by simply breathing. And I wasn't going to talk about the sex, and not because I felt ashamed. It was the other way around. It felt special. For the moment, I wanted to keep it all to myself.

"Okay," Presley said, urging me to continue. "So . . ."

"So I, uh . . ." I blew out a deep breath. "I got her arrested today. She broke into the high school to look at some old yearbooks. I followed her in, left her there and called the cops. They hauled her in for trespassing."

"Whoa." Presley flinched. "I don't particularly like the

woman, especially since she seems determined to prove that Draven is a murderer. But damn, Dash. That's cutthroat."

It was cutthroat. And years ago, it had been my norm. I'd treated women as objects. Usable. Disposable. Replaceable. Presley hadn't been around during the years when I'd gone through women like water. She'd come along later, when I'd slowed down and done my best to become a decent man. When I hadn't been as cutthroat.

Presley had started at the garage, brought along her hugs, and she'd softened us.

We'd let her soften us.

"You like her, don't you?" she asked. "And that's why you feel like a prick."

Not a question I was going to answer.

Taking my arm away, I turned to the bench and busied my hands with putting some tools back on the pegs hanging on the wall. "Isaiah said his landlord is jacking up the price of his rent."

"Yeah." She went along with my change of topic. "His lease is month to month. I think the landlord realized fast that Isaiah was a good tenant. Add to that the fact that he's working here and the whole town knows we pay well. The landlord is taking advantage."

"Take him up to the apartment above the office tomorrow. Let him look around. If he wants to stay there for a while, it's his."

"Okay." Presley nodded. "It's a mess, but I'll ask. How much for rent?"

"He cleans it up, he can stay there for free."

"That's nice of you."

I shrugged. "Guy needs a break."

Isaiah was an ex-con. Finding an apartment was never

going to be easy, something the landlord probably also knew. It wasn't fair and definitely not something Isaiah deserved. He wasn't an evil man. I knew what evil men looked like—I had a mirror. Isaiah had gone to prison for a much lesser crime than many I'd committed.

"What are you doing tonight?" I asked.

"Nothing much. Jeremiah has to work late so I'm eating dinner by myself. Then I'll probably watch TV or read until he gets home."

"Hmm." My face soured and I ducked my chin to hide it from her. Not well, because she saw my grimace.

"Don't," she snapped.

"Didn't say a word."

"You didn't have to." Presley scowled. "At some point, you're all going to have to accept that I'm marrying him."

"Maybe when he buys you a ring."

She fisted her hands on her hips. "He's saving up for it. He doesn't want to start our marriage in debt because of a diamond."

"He's got the money, Pres."

"How do you know?" she shot back.

"A hunch."

I wasn't going to tell her that we'd looked into Jeremiah. Extensively. Presley had come into the office one morning about a year ago and announced they were getting married. They'd been dating for a month at that point and had just moved in together.

But the rush to tie the knot had stopped the minute Jeremiah had earned the title fiancé. He'd started working late. He spent less and less time around Presley. We all saw the writing on the wall. The man was never going to marry her. The promise of a life together was how he kept her on the hook and how he lived off her dime.

None of us thought he was cheating on her, and we'd been watching.

We were worried about her. But any time we spelled it out, expressed our concerns, she'd shut down. She'd get mad. So we'd had a meeting—Dad, Emmett, Leo and I. We'd all agreed to keep our mouths shut until they set a wedding date. Then we'd jump in, because there was no way in hell was she marrying the dumbass. And after he broke her heart, we'd take turns breaking his nose.

I cracked my knuckles. The anticipation of a long overdue fight brought back a familiar feeling I'd locked away when we'd shut down the fights at the clubhouse. Sometimes I really missed the fight. The aggression. The win. To step in the ring and leave it all behind.

"I'll take you to dinner," I offered.

"That's okay. I have leftovers that need to be finished. See you tomorrow."

With a parting hug, she crossed the garage for the office door. But before she disappeared, I stopped her. "Pres?"

"Yeah?"

"About Bryce."

She gave me a small smile. "You like her."

"Yeah," I admitted. *I like her.*

And I felt guilty for getting her arrested. I felt guilty for kicking her out of the garage the way I had last night. I'd told myself it was the best thing.

Sure as fuck didn't feel that way.

Pres waved, giving me a small smile. "Night."

"Night."

I stayed in the garage for a while after I heard Presley's

car drive away. There was plenty of work to be done, but the gnawing in my gut kept stealing my focus. Finally, I gave up and left.

I wasn't sure how, but I knew I wouldn't be able to sleep tonight until I made this right with Bryce. Or at least tried.

My first stop was her house. All the lights were off so I picked the lock to her garage, only to find it empty. Next, I hit up the newspaper. That woman was so damn driven, it wouldn't surprise me if she'd gotten out of jail and gone straight to work to write a story about the experience. But the newspaper's windows were dark too and the parking lot was empty. I checked the gym. The grocery store. The coffee shop.

Nothing.

It had been a few hours since she'd been arrested at the school, giving me plenty of time to get out of there before she'd realized I'd ripped that page out of the yearbook. The cops should have let her go by now. She'd get a slap on the wrist and a lecture from Marcus. Nothing more. That should have taken an hour, tops. So where was she?

My stomach rolled as I drove past the high school and spotted her car. It was in the same place it had been earlier.

Meaning Bryce was still in jail.

"Shit." I raced for the police station.

I pictured her sitting on a cot in a cell, fuming mad. She'd probably plotted my murder ten times over.

The station's parking lot was dead. A few patrol cars were parked along one side of the building as I pulled up along the front curb, shutting off my bike to wait.

And wait.

An hour and a half passed while I messed around on my phone. I'm sure the surveillance cameras and the officer watching them were wondering what I was doing, but no one came out. And no one went in.

Shit. Was she here? I hadn't checked her parents' place. Maybe they'd come to pick her up and she'd gone there. I checked the hour on my phone for the hundredth time as the sun began to set, the evening light dimming. I huffed and swore under my breath just as a familiar yellow cab pulled into the space behind me.

"Hey, Rick." I waved and walked up to his driver's side window.

"Dash. What are you doing here?"

"Waiting to pick someone up. You?"

"Same."

Rick was likely starting his shift. He ran his own cab company—Uber wasn't a thing here yet—and he made a decent living hauling drunk people home. Hell, he'd collected me on more than a few occasions.

What were the chances that there was more than one person needing to be picked up from the police station in Clifton Forge on a Tuesday well before the fun stuff began at the bars? *Slim.*

"You here for Bryce Ryan?"

"Uh, yeah. I think that was the name dispatch called in for me."

"Here." I dug into my pocket, getting my wallet, and pulled out two twenties to hand over. "I've got her."

He nodded and smiled as he took the cash. "Great. Thanks, Dash."

"See you around." I knocked on the hood before getting out of his way. His taillights were barely off the lot when the front door to the police station opened and Bryce came rushing out.

"Hey, wait!" She waved for the cab but Rick was already gone. "Damn it."

Bryce ran a hand through her hair, her shoulders slumping. They straightened when her eyes landed on me waiting at the base of the steps.

"I'll give you a ride."

"No." She started down the steps, her footfalls heavy. "I'll walk."

"Come on." I met her as she reached the last step, her angry eyes level with mine. "I'll take you home."

"Stay away from me. You got me arrested for trespassing. I was handcuffed. I had to have my mug shot and fingerprints taken. I've been in *jail*."

"Sorry."

"No, you're not." She tried to sidestep me, but I moved too fast, blocking her escape.

"Bryce," I said gently. "I'm sorry."

"Are you really that afraid I'll find something?"

"Yes."

My answer—and the truth in that single word—caught her off guard.

She recovered quickly. "I don't understand you. You come to my house and kiss me. Then you fix my dad's press and ask for a truce. We have sex. You kick me out. You follow me to the school and break in yourself. Then you call the cops on me. It's inferno or ice. I'm done."

"Look, it doesn't make sense to me either." From the day she'd come to the garage, my brain and emotions had been all twisted. "All I know is I can't seem to stay away from you even though I know I should."

She crossed her arms over her chest. "Try harder."

"Let me take you to your car."

"On that?" She pointed to my motorcycle. "No."

"Scared?" I asked, baiting her.

Her eyes narrowed. "Never."

"Please. I fucked up earlier. I'm sorry. Let me at least get you to your car."

"No." She wasn't going to budge, so I decided to appeal to her logic.

"There's no one else. You'll have to walk miles and it's getting dark. Rick's probably on his next call already. I'm guessing you didn't call your parents for a reason. Come on. It's just a ride."

A growl came from her throat. It sounded a lot like *fine*.

This time when she attempted to stomp past me, I let her past. She went to the bike, her eyes taking in the gleaming chrome and shiny black paint.

I met her there and swung a leg over. "Hop on."

If she was unsure, she didn't let it show. She climbed on behind me, shifting back and forth until she was steady. Then she wrapped her arms around my waist, trying not to hold on too tight.

The way her arms felt around me, the way the inside of her thighs hugged my hips, squeezing around every turn, was nearly as good as it had felt lying on top of her in the garage. The drive to the high school wasn't long enough.

My cock swelled as we rode. Another few miles and it would have been impossible to ignore, but we pulled into the school's lot and the second I stopped, she swung off the bike. The spell broke.

She went right for the door of her car, digging the keys from her purse and refusing all eye contact.

"Bryce." I shut off the bike's engine so she could hear me, so she could hear the sincerity in my words. "I'm sorry."

"You told me not to trust you, and I should have listened."

"Here's the thing. I want you to trust me."

"So you can fuck me over?" She spun around, her eyes blazing. "Or just fuck me, period?"

"So we can find out the truth. So we can learn who really killed Amina."

"I. Don't. Need. Your. Help."

"No, you don't." I ran a hand through my hair. "But maybe . . . maybe I need yours."

That made her pause. Bryce was no pushover. She was tough and dynamic. Unique. She saw through bullshit like a pro, and the truth was, I trusted her. Why? I couldn't articulate it. But I trusted her.

Never, not once, had I told a woman I needed help. Yet here I was, offering that to her.

I kicked the stand on my bike and sat on the seat to face her. I couldn't go to Dad for information; he was hiding too much. Having Bryce's fresh eyes might be the only chance for his freedom.

That meant it was time to lay it all out there. To be real with her. To try and win her trust. So she knew what she was getting into with me.

"Let's talk. No bullshit. No ulterior motives. Just talk."

She leaned against her door. "Everything you say is fair game for my paper."

"Not everything."

"Then we're done here." She reached for the door's handle.

"It could ruin the lives of people who deserve a second chance. You want to destroy me when this is all over? Fine. But for them, I can't let that happen."

Emmett and Leo had risked their lives to stand beside us when we'd closed down the club. They were building good lives. Honest lives. I'd give mine up, but I wouldn't betray them.

Bryce planted her hands on her hips. "So where does that put us?"

"I'll answer your questions. Some things are on the record. Some are off."

"And I'm just supposed to believe you?"

I nodded. "Yeah."

"How can I know you'll be honest?"

"Because I feel like shit," I admitted. "Not many people can get under my skin, but you have. And I feel guilty. For what I said last night. For calling the cops today. This is me saying I fucked up. Asking for one more chance."

She cast me a wary glance. "You have to know that I think this is all crap. Just another one of your tricks."

"I get it." I sighed. "Ask me your questions anyway. Just don't print the stuff that will hurt other people. Agreed?"

The offer hung in the air, until finally, she gave me a single nod. "Agreed. I want to know why you closed down your club."

"On the record, our members decided to go different directions. Dad and I stayed in Clifton Forge with Emmett and Leo. Most of the other Gypsies moved away." When she frowned, I held up my hands. "I know you probably think of it as this big event, but it wasn't. It happened slowly. One guy would leave for one reason or another. We wouldn't bring on anyone new."

"Attrition. You're saying you shut down your club because of attrition?"

"It's the truth."

Jet had prospected the club the same year as I had. He'd moved to Las Vegas after he'd met his girlfriend there and now ran his own garage. Gunner had moved to Washington to live by the ocean with the money he'd stashed away over the years. Big Louie, who was a few years younger than Dad, had bought the bowling alley here in town and met Dad for drinks at The Betsy every Thursday.

The others had scattered to the wind. Some had even left to join other clubs. Those had stung, but we didn't fault the men who wanted to keep living the club life.

"The club changed," I told Bryce. "We all made that choice together. Unanimously." I'd always been proud to put on my leather cut with the Tin Gypsy patch on the back. Then one day, I pulled on that vest and there was no pride. That was the day I began to question everything. "What it was, what kind of men we'd become, didn't hold the same appeal."

"And what was it? What kind of men were you?"

"Men who did whatever the fuck we wanted." If someone pissed me off, I'd knock out some of their teeth. If someone hurt a member of our family, they paid with their life. "We were fearless. Intimidating. Didn't care much about the law. And we had money."

"How'd you make your money?"

"The garage."

She frowned. "Don't forget who you're talking to. Fifteen years ago, it was rumored you had at least thirty members. Your garage might be nice, but it wasn't supporting that many people."

No surprise Bryce had done her research. The woman who'd completely thrown me off guard, who'd seized my attention, was sharper than the knife tucked into my boot.

We'd actually had more like forty members back then. About fifteen had been guys Dad's age and nearly all of them were dead now. Life expectancy with the club didn't exactly fit a standard bell curve.

Even though we'd been small compared to other clubs around the nation, we'd been powerful. Dad had wanted to grow and expand all the way through the Northwest. He would have done it had we not decided to disband. But his ambition had made us targets.

Made our families targets.

"Off the record?" I waited for her to nod before I continued. "Money came from drug protection. Sometimes we smuggled the drugs ourselves, but mostly we made sure mules made it to their destination safely. Kept trucks from getting hijacked from either the cops or another dealer."

"What kind of drugs?"

"Meth mostly. We ran whatever the suppliers cooked in Canada. Some pot. Some cocaine and heroin. I don't know what else there was, but does it matter?"

"No." The disappointment in her eyes made my stomach fall. "I guess it doesn't."

For her, I wanted to be better. Do better. Why? It was the question I'd wrestled with since the beginning. But there was something about her, *this woman*, that made me want to make her proud. And I'd give all the money in my safe not to see that look on her face again.

"That was how we made most of our money," I said. "It was easier years ago before border patrol started cracking down. We could slip through the cracks because Montana has a big border and they can't watch it all."

"So you worked for drug dealers?"

I nodded. "Among other things."

"What other things? Be specific."

"Protection. A business in town could hire us and we made sure they didn't have any trouble. We made sure their competitors *did*. We had an underground fight circuit too. Got to be pretty big. We'd have fighters come from all over the Northwest. We'd organize it, some of us would fight, and the club would take a rake off all the bets. Made damn good money too."

Had Emmett and I had our way against Dad, we'd still be running the fights. But Dad had insisted it all had to stop. He'd been right. It was better this way.

"It doesn't make sense. If you made good money, why quit?"

"Can't spend money in prison, Bryce. And turns out, we make damn good money on custom cars too."

She studied my face. "That's it?"

"That's it. Sorry to disappoint you, but we closed down the club for noble reasons. It wasn't worth putting members or their families in danger anymore."

"In danger from whom?"

"Rival clubs. Old enemies. And my guess is one of those enemies is Amina's murderer."

CHAPTER TWELVE

BRYCE

The urge to pinch myself was overwhelming. Part of my brain was sure I'd fallen asleep on the rock-hard cot in the jail cell and this was all a dream. I couldn't believe I was standing across from Dash in his high school's empty parking lot as the sun faded from yellow to tangerine in the distance. The cool Montana evening breeze blew a strand of hair across Dash's forehead. The green treetops that bordered the school rustled in the distance.

It was almost too serene. It was nearly too pretty to be real. But if this was a dream, I wasn't ready to wake up.

Hungry for more, I stood still, watching as he sat propped against his motorcycle and told me about his former club.

This might all be a lie and another betrayal. While I was still livid at Dash for the past twenty-four hours, I wanted the story badly enough to listen and pretend that, as his eyes brightened, it was from honesty.

God, I was stupid. But did I leave? No. True or false, I

licked up every one of his words. Questions popped into my head faster than a string of exploding Black Cat fireworks.

"So you think one of your club's former enemies killed Amina?"

He nodded. "They're the most likely. Someone is looking to take revenge against Dad. They waited until we let down our guard. Got comfortable. Took a chance to set him up for murder."

"Who?"

"Probably another club."

"But there is no such thing as the Tin Gypsies anymore. Unless that's a lie."

"No, the club is over."

"Then without a club, you aren't a threat anymore."

He shrugged. "Doesn't matter. Vengeance doesn't care if we're wearing patches or not. Someone wants it bad enough, they'll wait."

This was true. When revenge consumed people, it was amazing the incredible patience they could summon. If Draven was being set up, the person responsible was smart. They'd waited, like Dash assumed, until the Slaters were unprepared to face a threat.

"So you suspect it was another club. Which one?" I'd caught some names in my research. There were a surprising number of motorcycle gangs, or members at least, who were in Montana.

"Our biggest rivalry in recent years was with the Arrowhead Warriors. They weren't as big as us but their president was and still is ambitious. Not afraid to pull a trigger. For a while, he made it a habit to go after our prospects, promising them money and power. He'd manipulate the weaker ones. He convinced younger guys to join his club instead of ours."

"You probably didn't want them anyway."

He chuckled. "No skin off our nose to lose guys who weren't loyal."

"What else?"

"The Warriors ran their own drug routes but we had relationships with the bigger dealers. They did whatever they could to ambush us, hoping the dealers would see us as weak and change business partners. We'd retaliate. They would too. By the end, it was hard to know exactly what one thing had started it all."

The hair on the back of my neck stood up. "Do I want to know what retaliation means?"

"No." The hint of malice in his voice made me shiver. "But the turning point was when they went after my sister-in-law."

"What?" I gasped. "Is she okay?"

"She's fine. They tried to kidnap her but we got lucky. Local law enforcement stopped it before things turned bad. But it was a line they never should have crossed. Members were fair game. They knew the risks from day one. So did their wives and girlfriends. When shit got bad, we'd lock everyone down. But Nick, my brother, has never been in the club. Emmeline should never have been in danger."

It was interesting how these men, these criminals, lived by a code. They had boundaries. Though I guess since Emmeline had been threatened, those boundaries weren't exactly solid. Would this attempted kidnapping have hit the news? I made a mental note to check the archives when I went to work tomorrow.

Dash's eyes lowered to the asphalt. "Dad was the president then. Something about Emmeline's kidnapping flipped a switch in him. I think because he saw how much Nick loved her. He didn't want to cost his son his wife. Not after he'd already cost us our mother."

"Your mom?" My heart stopped. In all the news articles I'd read about the club, Draven and Dash, only a few had mentioned Dash's mother. According to the stories, she'd been killed in a tragic accident at home. There had been no mention of the club's involvement or the details around her death. "How?"

Dash gave me a sad smile. "That's a story for another day."

"Okay." I wouldn't push this one. Not now when it would clearly bring him pain. Or when it would risk the conversation ending.

"Timing was everything," Dash said. "Dad approached the club after Emmeline's threat and asked all of us if we'd consider getting out of the drug business. The year before, every person at the table would have said *fuck no*. But border patrol had tightened. A handful of guys had been busted and were either serving time or had just gotten out. And at the same time Emmeline was kidnapped, one of our oldest members, Emmett's dad, was murdered."

I tensed. "Murdered? By who?"

"The Warriors. We'd been fighting for over ten years. This wasn't the first death, on our side or theirs. But it was the final straw. They came to The Betsy where we were drinking a beer, watching some playoff game. Stone, that was his name, got up to take a piss. A couple of Warriors were waiting. Hauled him outside and before any of us even knew he was gone, they shoved him on his knees and put a bullet between his eyes."

I flinched, the mental image impossible to ignore. And, my God, poor Emmett. My stomach twisted into a tight knot.

Did I want to know more? I knew this violence Dash spoke of wasn't confined to only the Arrowhead Warriors. I was sure it extended to the Gypsies as well—and Dash.

Was he a killer too? I definitely didn't want the answer to that one.

"Stone had been with the club since the beginning." Dash spoke to the ground but there was sorrow in his gaze. "He and Dad both joined about the same time. He was like an uncle. Stone helped me fix up my first bike. Gave me condoms when I turned fourteen and told me to always keep one in my pocket. Neal Stone. He hated his first name. He was balder than a baby's ass so he grew out a big white beard to compensate, then braided the damn thing." Dash shook with a silent laugh. "Shit, I miss that guy. Emmett went off the deep end for a while. It wasn't good. But he came back to the club. Made peace with it, or tried to at least."

"I'm sorry."

"Me too." Dash blinked a few times before he looked at me again. "Anyway. Timing was on Dad's side. Enough fucked-up things were happening to our members, our families, that we all hit pause. Saw the writing on the wall. It was time to change."

"You disbanded."

"Not right away, but we got the wheels moving in that direction. The first thing we did was come to an agreement with the Warriors. Their president knew they'd crossed a line. He knew if family was fair game, they'd risk losing some of their loved ones. So we agreed to a truce."

"You and your truces," I muttered.

He chuckled, the corner of his mouth turning up. "We sold them our drug routes. Made sure our dealers were good with it and wouldn't retaliate. Got out of drugs all together."

"Just like that?"

"Yep. I smile every time I spend that money."

And I was guessing there was a lot of it. Probably stacks of cash he'd hidden under his mattress or buried in his backyard.

"After that, we unraveled the rest of the illegal activities too," he said. "The fights. The payouts from businesses in town. All of it. Just wasn't worth the risk we'd end up in jail. Wound it all down in about six years."

"And then you disbanded."

He nodded. "Then we called it quits. We could have stayed a legal club but too much had changed. And the Gypsies would always have a reputation. No matter what we did, people would have been afraid. Expected the worst."

It made sense. Though I couldn't imagine how hard it had been to say goodbye to something that had been his life. The club had been ingrained in every aspect of his world, his career. His family. It must have been like cutting off a limb, but he'd done it.

They all had.

We stood across from one another, the only sound coming from the breeze and a few birds flying overhead. I processed everything he'd told me, hoping it was true.

It seemed true. Was it? Had he trusted me with his story? It was hard not to be moved with his gesture of faith.

My gut was telling me Dash hadn't lied. And for now, that was good enough, especially because nearly everything had been off the record. I could see it now, why he'd want to keep his secrets. If all this got out, it would ruin the reputations they'd been trying to repair. It could mean a deeper investigation from the police.

"Hold on." My head cocked to the side. "If you came to a

truce, why would the Warriors set up Draven for Amina's murder?"

"Good question. Could be one of their members is acting without permission of the president. Could be one of our old members who joined the Warriors."

Wait, what? "You had members who left the Gypsies and joined the Warriors even after they killed your"—what did they call each other?—"brothers?"

He scoffed. "Yeah. The life of an honest, hardworking mechanic isn't for everyone. These guys were all in their early twenties. Drawn to the club life. It wasn't that big a surprise."

"You think a former member is framing Draven?"

"At this point, anything is possible. But there are five men who went to the Warriors. Right now, they're my top suspects."

If I were in his position, I'd be wary of them too. I wanted their names, but I doubted Dash would give them to me. I had a feeling I wouldn't get invited to a club-to-club meeting.

The silence returned, the birds having found a tree in the distance to land and sing. The information rolled over and over in my mind but I was out of questions for the moment.

"What now?" I asked.

"Now?" He stood from the bike and walked closer. "Now you make a decision. You take all this and decide how deep you want to go. You believe me or you don't. You trust me or you don't. You keep it quiet or you don't. But now you know what kind of men you're dealing with. Ones who hold grudges for years. Ones who have no boundaries. Ones who aren't afraid to come after a woman just because she's fucking a man with the last name Slater."

"Fucked. Singular. Past tense."

Dash stepped closer, the heat from his body chasing away the chill from the breeze. Goose bumps broke out on my forearms and I clutched them tight around my waist.

He raised an eyebrow. "Past tense?"

"You got me arrested. I have to go to court tomorrow. Definitely past tense."

"Hmm." He brought a hand up to my face but didn't touch my cheek. Instead, he took the end of an errant lock of hair and tucked it behind my ear. His fingers skimmed the shell, but the slight brush was enough to send shivers all the way to my toes.

I was pathetic. I'd spent hours in a jail cell, yet here I was, panting over him again.

"Is that why you told me all of this?" I asked. "So I'd fuck you again?"

Dash shook his head, taking a step back. "You want the truth?"

"You know I do."

"Then help me. Help me find it."

Was I really going to do this? Was I going to trust him? There was no doubt if we worked together, whatever story I told would be better. Deeper. Fuller. And damn it, we both knew how badly I wanted *that* story.

"If you hide something from me, something that makes a difference or puts me in danger, I'll print it," I warned. "All of it. Whether or not it's on the record. Whether or not it ruins your life and those of your friends, I'll tell the world."

It could cost me my newspaper. I would have to violate my journalistic ethics and no source would likely trust me again. And it might even cost me my life if this former motorcycle club decided to retaliate. I was putting myself, my integrity and my job on the line. But it was the only leverage I had over Dash.

In the meantime, I'd print the superficial. I'd print the things he gave me on the record. And I'd hold the rest.

"I mean it." I shoved a finger in his face. "No hiding things. I won't do this if I can't trust you."

He hesitated, his hand going to his pocket, but then he nodded. With a turn, Dash walked over to his motorcycle, throwing a long leg over to straddle the machine.

"Do we have a deal?" I called before he started up the engine.

He shot me a sexy grin. "Deal."

———

GOING through old newspaper articles was not exciting on a normal day, but today, it was akin to torture. Not only was the Clifton Forge news from decades ago exceptionally boring, it was also incredibly incomplete.

I'd gone back thirty years in search of information on Dash's mother. When I'd done my previous digging into the Tin Gypsies, I'd been focused on club references and those associated with the prominent members, like Draven and Dash. I hadn't kept an eye out for Chrissy Slater's name.

When I'd come across the obituary stating she'd died in a tragic accident, I'd read it and moved on. But last night's conversation had stirred my curiosity.

How had she died? What exactly was the tragedy? Dash had said it was a story for another day, and given the look on his face, it wasn't a happy tale.

So I'd gone looking this morning. Maybe I'd save him from having to relive her death if I could read about it instead. Except all I'd found during that time was her obituary, which I'd already seen, and a picture of Draven and his two young boys at the funeral.

Draven's grief consumed the photo, his hands resting on the shoulders of his sons. Draven looked nothing like the confident man I'd watched be arrested. His frame bore the weight of a thousand boulders, his face ashen. The photo was black and white but I swore his eyes were red from crying.

Dash and Nick had looked so alike as kids. I wasn't sure how old Dash was, maybe middle school, but he looked lost. Nick was the opposite. While his little brother and father wore their grief outwardly, his face gave away nothing. Nick wasn't only lost, he was angry. And now it made sense why he hadn't joined the club.

Nick's punishment for Draven was turning his back on his father's lifestyle, but how had his relationship been with Dash? I pushed that thought away, drawing a firm line there. Dash's family dynamics were none of my business. That was too personal. Too intimate. That was his problem, not mine.

Was I curious? Absolutely. But if I let myself cross over, if I cared too much, the person who'd suffer most would be me.

I don't care. I don't care. I don't care.

I can't care.

My task was to obtain information to write the best story possible. I'd fail if I allowed myself to get wrapped up in feelings.

This wasn't about Dash. This was about facts. This was about Amina and finding her killer.

Dash was so certain of his father's innocence. Me? I wasn't sure. Not yet. But Dash's conviction was hard to ignore. He'd planted doubts in my mind that popped up constantly.

How would Dash react if Draven was, in truth, the murderer? My stomach knotted at the idea of Dash's heart breaking.

Damn it.

I cared.

Logging out of our archive system, I jotted down a few more notes in my notepad. As I'd been searching for information on Chrissy Slater, I'd come across most of the articles I'd read before on the Tin Gypsies.

It was interesting reading them again, this time knowing more about their history. The stories were all superficial, which hadn't come as a shock. Unless one of the club members betrayed their secrecy, no one from the outside would ever know the truth.

But I knew.

Even shallow news articles fell into place with what Dash had told me last night. Maybe he really had told me the truth.

Maybe it was a test to see if I'd betray him. I wouldn't. He'd get to keep his secrets. I'd take them all to the grave because I'd given him my word.

Unless.

Unless he deceived me. Then I would do exactly as promised. I'd tell the world every sordid detail and he could rot.

Last night when I'd arrived home, I'd spent hours writing up everything he'd told me. All of the information was safe on my computer and backed up to an encrypted cloud file.

If anything happened to me, Dad would get access to that cloud drive per my will.

My brain was overloaded with information and I dropped my head into my hands, massaging my temples. I couldn't stop thinking about everything Dash had told me.

Was it strange that I believed him? That I believed every word?

Why? Because we'd had sex? I should have been able to maintain my distance. But the arrogant bastard had snuck his way under my skin. I couldn't write him off completely, even after the stunt he'd pulled at the high school.

I groaned. God, I was pathetic.

"What's wrong?"

I sat up straight, spinning around at Dad's voice as he came through the pressroom door and took a seat at his desk. "Nothing."

"Hmm. I thought you might be upset because you have to go to court in an hour."

"You heard?" I winced. I hadn't planned on telling my parents about my arrest, but I should have known they'd find out. This was Clifton Forge, not Seattle. "How?"

"You're not the only one who talks to Marcus Wagner on a regular basis." Dad shook his head, the same slow shake he'd given me growing up whenever I'd disappointed him. That disappointment was ten times worse than any spanking I'd ever received from Mom's wooden spoon. "What were you thinking?"

"I wasn't," I admitted. "It was stupid."

"Yes, it was."

"Does Mom know?"

He shot me a look that said *what do you think?* My

parents didn't believe in keeping things from one another, especially when it came to their only daughter.

"Damn it."

"Be ready for an ass chewing." While Dad was the one to give me the disappointed look—it was his specialty—he'd always left the lectures to Mom because those were hers. "What's happening on the murder investigation? What can I expect for the paper on Sunday?"

"Right now, it won't be much. The police haven't released anything new."

"And what have you found?"

"Nothing solid. Yet." As soon as I had a story to tell, Dad would be the first to know. "I'd better get to the courthouse. I don't want to be late."

He chuckled. "Tell Judge Harvey I said hello."

I did not tell the judge hello. Instead, I stood in front of him and received a lecture that put thirty-five years' worth of Mom's lectures to utter shame.

Luckily, the lecture about my responsibility as an adult and member of the press was the worst of it. Judge Harvey made me swear to always obey school hours and ask for permission before entering a library, to which I promptly agreed. My punishment for trespassing at the high school was time served—plus the lecture. It was arguably the worse of the two.

Wiped and ready for an evening alone, I didn't go back to work after leaving the courthouse. I swung by the grocery store and bought ingredients to make homemade enchiladas. Then I skipped the gym and went home.

I'd just convinced myself to double the cheese in my enchilada recipe—screw the calories, I needed cheese—when I turned onto my street. All thoughts of dinner went out the window. A gleaming black Harley was parked in front of my house.

Its owner was sitting on my porch.

I pulled into the driveway and got out of my car. Then I loaded up my arms with the grocery bags and walked to the front door. "What are you doing here?"

"What's in the bags?"

"Dinner."

"Enough for two?" Dash stood and took the plastic sacks from my hands, his biceps flexing. The bags weren't heavy but a lickable vein popped on his forearm, making my mouth water.

Pathetic. I was pathetic.

Sex with him two nights ago had turned me into a hormonal mess. I was achy. Squirmy. I couldn't stop thinking about those long fingers digging into my curves. Those soft lips on my bare skin. And his eyes, those vibrant hazel eyes that saw way beneath the surface. I couldn't be around him and not think about what had happened in the garage. Had I not been so furious with him last night, that ride on his motorcycle would have brought me close to an orgasm.

"Did you just invite yourself over for dinner?" I slid the key into the lock, hoping to hide my flushed cheeks.

"What are you making?"

"Enchiladas with extra cheese."

"Then yes, I did." He trailed behind me into the kitchen, depositing the bags on the counter. As I put the groceries away, he showed himself around my living room. "Nice place."

"Thanks. What are you doing here? Besides encroaching on my meal."

"You said something I didn't like last night."

"Really?" I tossed a bag of shredded cheese onto the counter. "And what was that?"

"You said, 'Fucked. Singular. Past tense.'"

"I did." Impressive he remembered it word for word. "Your point?"

"I didn't like it."

"Too bad. I don't like you."

"Huh." He stared out the window from the living room for a long moment, his hands planted on his hips. Then he gave the glass a single nod, turned and stalked my way. The temperature in the kitchen went up twenty degrees as he approached. He didn't stop walking until he was right there, the heat from his chest hitting mine like a wave. His hands framed my face with those rough, calloused palms. "Grammar isn't my thing."

"No?" My breath hitched as his mouth dropped to hover above mine. "I love grammar."

Dash's breath whispered against my lips. "Did you mean it?"

"Mean what?" The proximity to him made my brain short-circuit.

"Singular." He placed a soft kiss to the corner of my mouth. "Because we were explosive in that garage. Aren't you a little curious what we'd be like in a bedroom?"

"No," I lied.

I wanted to say yes, but my pride was on the line here. My heart. He'd treated me horribly after the hookup in the garage. But it was only sex, right? Casual sex. It didn't need to mean anything. Because I didn't care.

I don't care.

My body, on the other hand, cared a lot about having a decent, *non*-self-induced orgasm.

Screw it. Yes, I wanted to know what sex would be like in a bed. My hand stretched for the counter's edge, bracing for Dash to take a deeper kiss. To let him. But a whoosh of air forced my eyes open as Dash spun away and sauntered out of the kitchen.

He reached behind his head, tearing off his black T-shirt as he headed for the hallway that led to my bedroom.

He knew I'd follow.

Bastard.

CHAPTER THIRTEEN

DASH

"Dash." Tucker Talbot shook my hand. "Take it easy."

"Have a good one, Tucker." I waved at the Arrowhead Warrior president and climbed on my bike.

Dad gave Tucker one last nod goodbye, followed by the same for the five men he'd brought along to this meeting.

All the men who'd once been in the Tin Gypsy MC.

The six of them stood next to their own bikes, each wearing their cut. On the back of the vests, the patch for the Warriors was stitched into the black leather. The design was an arrowhead framed by their club's name and year they were founded. It was all in white, simple and plain compared to the artwork of the Tin Gypsy patch.

It had taken me almost a year to stop looking for my cut to pull on before walking out the door. That leather vest had been the most important article of clothing I'd ever owned. It was strange to come to a meeting with another club and not have it on my back.

I missed its power. Its status.

Instead, I was wearing a black leather jacket I'd bought

the first month after we'd put our cuts away for good. It was too hot for a jacket, but I'd needed something to cover the Glock holstered at my side.

Dad and I rode away from the Warriors and down the highway. About fifty miles away from the bar where we'd met with Tucker and his crew, Dad pulled off the road at a little turnout next to an open meadow. We got off our bikes and walked where asphalt met grass, staring at the trees and mountains in the distance.

"Do you think Tucker's telling the truth?" I asked.

Dad sighed. "Don't know."

"Smart of him to bring the guys." I'd expected Tucker to show up with his vice president and sergeant at arms. Instead, he'd brought the men previously loyal to the Gypsies.

Tucker had let us ask them point-blank if they'd had anything to do with Amina's murder. We knew them. Spent time riding alongside them. And when each had promised they had nothing to do with setting up Dad, we believed them.

Those five were off the list.

Tucker still had a question mark behind his name.

Since the Warriors were at the top of the list of people who'd want revenge against Dad for past crimes, he'd arranged this meeting with Tucker.

The Warriors were located in Ashton, a town about three hours away from Clifton Forge. Dad couldn't go there without violating his bond, so we'd all met at a country bar on the edge of our county. It was far enough away from town that the Warriors saw it as neutral ground.

All Dad had asked for was a meeting. No explanation.

No reason. Not that Tucker needed one. He'd been keeping better tabs on us than we had on him.

"Tough to say if Tucker was lying," Dad said. "But he made a good point. What reason would they have to set me up?"

The Warriors were making more money now with our former drug connections than they ever had before. We weren't killing one another off anymore. They were happy the Gypsies were gone. Tucker had said so himself today.

"I don't think he'd risk pissing us off, having us start the club back up again," I told Dad.

"Me neither."

"How tight a hold do you think he's got on his members these days?"

Dad scoffed. "Considering how much control he had back in the day? Not much."

If Tucker wasn't the one to set Dad up, it could have been one of his members. It wouldn't be the first time one of them had gone against orders.

The Warriors who'd tried to kidnap Emmeline had been acting of their own stupid fucking accord. They'd hoped to get some attention from their president by walking back into their clubhouse as heroes, dragging Emmeline behind them. Except they'd failed to get her. And instead of patting them on their backs, Tucker had sent a message to his members.

No one went against his orders.

Tucker delivered the men who'd tried to kidnap Emmeline to Dad's front door. The Gypsies had dealt with them for good. Those two were buried in the mountains where their bodies would never be found.

We didn't know if Tucker's message had been received.

Maybe another idiot looking to make a name for himself had gone rogue too.

"If it was a Warrior, we'll probably never know," Dad said. "Tucker won't admit one of his brothers disobeyed his orders. Not again."

"Then where does that leave us?"

"Hell if I know." Dad stared out at the meadow's grass rolling in easy waves under the gentle wind. "What's going on with the reporter? She still a problem?"

Yeah, she was a problem. I couldn't get the woman off my damn mind.

"Yes and no," I answered. "Think I've got her convinced to work with us and not against. But it cost me."

"How much?" Dad had paid off the previous newspaper owners for years to only print the minimum.

"Not money. A story. She wanted to know more about the club. Why we quit. What we did. Some was on the record. Most was off."

Dad turned from the view and planted his hands on his hips. "And you trust her to keep quiet?"

"She'll stay quiet. She's honest."

It was the best way to describe Bryce. When she said something was off the record, it wouldn't make the print. It was part of her code as a journalist. As long as I held up my end of the bargain and told her the truth, our relationship would stay mutually beneficial.

It wouldn't be hard to do. Those deep brown eyes looked at me and the truth was easy to see. Besides, if I tried to lie, she'd see through my bullshit. Those eyes were beautiful. And cunning.

After I'd fucked her twice last night, Bryce had fallen asleep exhausted and spent, naked under her sheets, her silky hair spilled over her white pillows. The corners of her mouth turned up slightly when she slept, and that little grin had made it nearly impossible to leave.

But I didn't spend the night with women. Waking up with them gave them ideas about commitment. Rings. Babies. None of which was for me.

I left Bryce smiling on her pillow, even though there was temptation there. The urge to pull her into my arms and hold her until sunrise.

It was a damn good thing I went home. Fuck temptation. I rode home, fell into my own bed and stared at the ceiling for a few hours wondering when exactly I'd been cast under her spell. The hell of it was, it always came back to the first day.

To her in the sunshine, walking up to me at the garage.

"How long have you been fucking her?" Dad asked.

"Not long." *Am I that obvious?* "How'd you know?"

"I didn't. But I do now. Is that smart?"

"Probably not," I admitted.

It would be much safer to keep my hookups with easy women who stopped into The Betsy searching for a one-night distraction. Bryce was not easy by any stretch. She was tough. She made me laugh with her wit and sass. She challenged me. And when she wasn't pissing me off, she was turning me on.

"Truth. She caught my eye and I'm having a hard time turning away."

"Your mom was like that," Dad said quietly. A small smile tugged at his cheek. "We were little kids when we met in grade school. I didn't think anything of her. She was just another girl on the playground. But then she walked into high school her first day of freshman year. She was smiling and wearing this yellow dress—she loved yellow. Wore it all the time."

"I remember."

"One look at her and I never looked away." The smile faded. "Should have let her go. Let her find someone worthy."

I put my hand on his shoulder. "If Mom were here, she'd kick your ass for saying that."

Dad huffed a laugh. "She had so much fire. I forget that sometimes. God, I miss her. Every day. I miss fighting with her. I miss her telling me to put my socks in the hamper. I miss those chocolate chip cookies she made every Sunday. I miss the yellow."

"Me too."

Dad's face got hard as he swallowed. Behind his sunglasses, he blinked furiously to clear away the emotion. This was more from him than I'd seen in years. He didn't talk all that often about Mom.

More since Amina Daylee.

"I found a picture in her senior yearbook." I reached for my wallet and pulled out the page I'd folded and shoved in next to a stack of twenties.

This picture was something I'd been keeping from Bryce. I'd nearly told her about it when we'd been talking the other night, but I'd kept it in my pocket. Soon, I'd tell her and keep my promise to share. But this one was too close to home. Before I handed it to Bryce, I had to get some answers from Dad.

Maybe he wouldn't shut me out this time around.

"Here." I handed over the picture. If he was surprised, he didn't show it. "Mom and Amina. They were friends?"

"Best friends," he corrected. "You could barely separate the two."

"Did they have a falling out?"

"Amina moved away after high school." He shrugged. "I guess they lost touch."

"You guess?" Even if they'd lost touch, you'd think Amina would have at least come to Mom's funeral.

"Yep." Dad folded up the page and handed it back, that topic over.

Seriously? He was infuriating. Dad had fucked this woman. He had to have some kind of feelings for her. As far as I knew, Amina had been the only woman he'd been with since Mom. I could badger him for more, but it was pointless.

He was already on to the next topic.

"Called a couple of guys around town to see if they've heard word of anyone who'd want to set me up. No one has a clue. Their first guess was the Warriors too."

"What about the Travelers?" Saying that club's name soured my stomach. The hatred I had for them would last a lifetime.

"They're all dead."

"Are you sure?"

Dad slid the sunglasses off his nose and into his hair. His brown eyes met mine to reinforce his declaration. "They are dead. All of them. I made sure of it."

"All right." I believed him. "Who else?"

"No damn clue. I think all we can do now is wait. Hope someone starts talking."

"That's it?" I couldn't believe I was hearing this. "You're giving up that easily? This is your life we're talking about, Dad. Your freedom."

"Maybe this is for the best. Maybe my sins have finally caught up with me and it's time to pay. We both know I deserve a lifetime behind bars. If it happens, I'm not fighting it."

Who was this man? This was not the same man who'd vowed revenge against the Travelers after they'd killed my mother. This was not the man who'd taken his vengeance with horrific violence. This was not the man who refused to quit.

"You're serious?"

"Dead." He was done fighting.

I shook my head, waving him off as I walked to my bike. Dad might be giving up, but I wasn't.

The trip to Clifton Forge was fast. I let the roar of the engine, the wind whipping my face and the tires beating on the pavement soak up some of my frustration with Dad. When I hit Central Avenue, I didn't turn to go home or to the garage. I kept on straight, making my way into the quiet neighborhood where Bryce lived.

She had a way of looking at things with fresh eyes—a different perspective—and I wanted her take on my meeting with the Warriors.

When I pulled up, she was in the kitchen. I spotted her through the large window over the sink. I rang the doorbell, raking a hand through my hair as her footsteps came my way.

There was no surprise on her face as she opened the door. "You again? Is this going to become a regular thing?"

The smell from the kitchen drifted outside and I looked past her. "What are you making?"

"A roast. It's been in the Crock-Pot all day."

I hadn't eaten anything since breakfast and my stomach rumbled. Loud.

She took pity on me, opening the door wider and stepping out of the way. "Come on in. Beer's in the fridge."

I kicked off my boots and followed her into the kitchen. Grabbing a beer, I twisted off the top, then went to stand behind Bryce at the stove, peering over her shoulder. "Mashed potatoes?"

"I hope you like salty gravy." She was whisking it in a saucepan. "I only make salty gravy."

"You won't hear me complain." I dropped a kiss to her shoulder, enjoying the shiver that rolled down her spine. Last night, we'd had some fun learning each other's tender spots. That was one of hers.

Bryce turned at the stove, running her hand down my pecs to tweak her thumb over my nipple. I grinned. And that was one of mine.

My stomach growled again, insisting on dinner first. Last night, we'd had enchiladas near midnight. But tonight, even as much as I wanted her naked, I was too hungry to deliver any kind of decent performance.

"Plates are in the cupboard next to the fridge. Silverware is in that drawer." She pointed to the one beside the sink. "We'll eat at the island."

"'Kay." I set the dishes out as she finished cooking and heaped my plate full. Taking a first bite, I nearly came in my jeans. It wasn't better than her enchiladas but it was definitely equal. "Damn, that's good."

"Glad you approve."

"Keep feeding me food like this and I'll never leave."

"Then consider this your last meal." She smirked. "What are you doing here?"

"Dad and I met with the Warriors today."

"You did?" Her fork froze in midair. "What happened?"

"Their president assured us it wasn't them. He brought along the five guys who left the Gypsies for the Warriors. They gave their word they had nothing to do with it. I'm inclined to believe them. Still, it could have been someone acting on their own, but unless we catch the guy, no one will admit it."

"Interesting." She twirled her fork in the air as she thought it over. "So what now?"

I shrugged. "I don't know. That's why I'm here. What do you think?"

"Hmm." She took another bite, thinking as she chewed. "If you don't have a lead into who might be setting Draven up, then I think we should continue looking into Amina. At least find out why she was here in Clifton Forge. That might give us a clue as to who would have known she was in town. It could narrow down the possibilities."

"Except my hunch is that the guy who killed her was following Dad around. Waiting for an opportunity to set him up."

"True. But don't you think that the way she was killed was sort of personal? I mean, she was stabbed *seven* times. Like he knew her."

"Maybe. Or maybe it was meant to seem personal since it was supposed to look like Dad did it after they had sex." Still not something I liked to picture.

"Also true. But if you don't have any leads on who could be out to get your dad, then we don't have any other option than to look into the victim."

"Yeah. Guess it's worth a shot." I scooped up a bite of potatoes and gravy—salted just right.

If we didn't find clues to prove Dad was innocent,

digging into Amina's life might at least get me more information about her relationship with Mom.

Because the superficial answer from Dad was not going to stand. Mom had been the type of person who pulled others into her life. She wouldn't have let a best friend drift away. Something had to have happened, and whatever it was, Dad wasn't telling.

"Anything else?" Bryce asked.

This was probably the point in time for me to tell her about that yearbook picture. I should confess I'd stolen it and had her arrested before she'd noticed, but that would mean a fight. Tonight, I didn't have it in me to battle Bryce. Not when she'd win.

So I shoved another bite into my mouth and hoped like hell she didn't find out before I told her. "Nope. This is really good."

"You already said that." She smiled.

"Worth repeating. I'm not much of a cook. Never learned. Mom loved cooking for us, and after she died, Dad didn't take her place in the kitchen. We ate out a lot and Nick got sick of it, so he taught himself. He got pretty good. When he graduated and moved out, Dad and I went back to eating out."

"I learned to cook from my mom. Have you met her?" When I shook my head, she said, "I'm not surprised. You don't exactly run in the same circles. She's more Bunko on Friday nights than beers at The Betsy."

I chuckled, demolishing the rest of my meal. "Thanks for dinner. Again."

"You're welcome."

We both stood at the same time to take our plates, but I stopped her and took hers from her hand. "I got dishes."

"I don't mind."

"Take a load off. I got these." I went to the sink and turned on the water. "Nick learned to cook. I learned to clean."

"How did the Gypsies get started?" Bryce asked behind me.

I smiled at a plate as I rinsed it clean. She always had a question, this one. In a lifetime, I doubted she'd be able to ask them all. "My granddad was part of a small club in town. Mostly it was guys who loved to ride. He owned the garage. Built it from the ground up and it was the focal point for the club. Dad always knew he'd take it over but had planned to go to college and get out of Clifton Forge for a while first. But then Granddad died a week after Dad graduated, so he stayed to run the garage. Joined the club too."

Dad was never bitter about not getting the chance to move away. Because he'd had Mom who was more than happy to stay here, close to her family. She only ever wanted to be where Dad was.

"One of Dad's friends from high school left for California. Stone, that guy I told you about, Emmett's Dad. Anyway, Stone got hooked up with a big club down there. Didn't join, but it gave him ideas. So he came home to Montana and talked to Dad about joining the club here. Making some changes. The Clifton Forge Motorcycle Club became the Tin Gypsies. The rest is history."

"So your grandfather started the Tin Gypsies?"

"Technically. Though most give credit to Dad and Stone. And really, Stone never wanted to be the leader, so it fell to Dad."

"He was the president?"

I nodded. "For all but the five years that the position

belonged to me. Stone was his vice president, like Emmett was mine."

Dad had told me once he and Stone hadn't meant for the Gypsies to get so big. Things had spiraled deeper than they'd ever expected. But the garage hadn't always made good money. Stone worked as a mechanic too, and they'd both had families to feed. Their brothers in the club all needed money too, so he'd made decisions, right and wrong, for the better of all the men.

To my knowledge, Dad hadn't regretted any of it until Mom had been murdered.

And then, it was too late. He lost himself in rage and revenge.

"Where'd you get the nickname Dash?"

I loaded a plate into the dishwasher. "Mom. She called me Dash as far back as I can remember because I never stopped running. I only got Kingston when I was in big fucking trouble. As a kid, nothing was fast enough. I broke an arm racing my bike around the block when I was seven. Nick built me a soapbox go-cart when I was ten and I disabled the brakes. Shit like that all the time. All she could do about it was make me wear a helmet."

"I didn't realize I was sleeping with an adrenaline junkie." She giggled. "Want another beer?"

"Depends. Am I driving home anytime soon?"

"Before I answer that, I have one more question."

"Of course, you do." I loaded the last of the dishes, then faced her. "Fire away."

"What's this thing with us?"

"Sex." I grinned. "Really great sex."

"Do you think we should set some, uh . . . limits?"

"Limits." I arched an eyebrow. "Like anal?"

"No. Oh my God. You're such a man." She laughed, rolling her eyes. "Not sexual limits, though I do have some. I mean limits on this tryst we're having. I'm assuming you're not looking for anything serious."

"Nope."

"Okay then. Limits."

"How about we go at it until we're sick of each other? Then we're done." Though depending on those sexual limits of hers and whether the sex got hotter—if that was even possible—I wouldn't get sick of Bryce anytime soon. "Agreed?"

"Agreed." She slid off her stool, slowly coming my way. "You should know, watching you do the dishes is really sexy."

My cock twitched as she came into my space, running her hands up my chest. "Maybe I'll stick around tonight. Let you cook me breakfast. Then I'll do your dishes again."

"I don't cook breakfast."

I dropped a kiss to her mouth and ran my tongue along the seam. "I wasn't really talking about doing more dishes."

She smiled against my mouth. "Then I guess you can stay."

CHAPTER FOURTEEN

BRYCE

"Ugh. Where is it?" I dug through the laundry basket at the base of the dryer, searching for the green shirt I wanted to wear. It wasn't under five towels or my impressive collection of unfolded socks that never seemed to get paired.

Abandoning that basket for the one next to the washing machine, I searched but came back empty-handed. It wasn't on one of the many empty hangers in my closet. I'd checked all three baskets here in the laundry room. The only other place it could be was the dryer itself. Wearing only my bra and jeans, I knelt in front of the machine and began digging.

"What are you doing?"

"Shit." I jumped at Dash's voice, clutching my heart. "You scared me."

"Sorry."

"Whatever." I kept digging, still irritated at him for keeping me up all night. And not in a good way. "You snore."

His chest shook with a silent laugh. "Again, sorry."

Dash yawned as he leaned against the doorframe,

wearing only a pair of black boxer briefs. His eyes were sleepy and his hair a mess. My mouth watered at that delectable skin on display.

It was really hard to be mad at him when he looked like that in the morning. Maybe a sleepless night had been worth it for the morning view.

His washboard abs deserved daily applause along with that V of his hips. His thighs bulged beneath the seam of those boxers, straining the elastic around sculpted muscle. His arms were roped with the same strength and smooth veins snaked down his forearms. Add the tattoos and I wasn't all that annoyed by the snoring anymore.

On one arm was a skull, artfully adorned—half of the face was detailed with bohemian jewelry while the other gave the illusion of metal. Both of his forearms had different black ink bands. And on the other arm, a black and white portrait of a woman smiling.

We hadn't talked about his tattoos, but I knew the portrait was of his mother.

That one wasn't sexy but it melted my heart. This man had slept in my bed. When was the last time I'd literally slept—or attempted to sleep—with another person? It had been ages since my mattress had felt the weight of two people.

Dash had slept like the dead too. Minus the snoring. This morning, I'd tossed his arm off my naked back and slid out of bed—and he hadn't budged.

I'd only had a minor freak-out in the shower. It was expected since I was basically sleeping with the enemy and Dash wasn't exactly long-term relationship material.

I refused to let myself get attached.

Sex. Only.

I'd been reminding myself over and over and over, because if I didn't keep that thought circulating in my brain, I'd forget Dash couldn't be trusted. Worse, I'd develop feelings more dangerous than the ones already brewing.

I couldn't afford deep feelings or connections. Yes, it had been comforting to wake up with his long fingers splayed on my skin. He'd touched me all night. When I'd shift or move, his hand always found me. But I didn't need that from Dash. If I needed some comfort, I'd go get a hug from Mom.

Dash and I were working together to find information. We were enjoying each other's bodies at night. That was where I drew the line. When we found Amina's killer—or if the evidence pointed to Draven, and Dash accepted his father was a murderer—then this fling would be over.

I wasn't getting used to Dash snoring in my bed. I wasn't counting on that delicious body and tanned skin to be around for long. I wasn't admitting how adorable it was that he'd practically fallen back asleep as he stood in the entrance to my laundry room, watching me find a shirt.

I dug deeper into the dryer, my eye catching the shade of green I was after. "Bingo." I yanked it out with a smile and tugged the top over my head. The front was a V-neck, the shape loose but not drapey. And the cute little pocket over one of my boobs gave it some added detail.

When I looked up, Dash's eyes were open and locked on that pocket.

"What are we doing today?" he asked, rubbing a hand over his face. The stubble on his jaw was thick, nearly a beard. I liked beards.

"We?"

He nodded. "It's Friday."

"Yes. It will be all day. So?"

"So, it's Friday. I don't have to be at the garage. Let's do something."

"Something," I drew out the word. *Did he just ask me out on a date?* What happened to sex only during the investigation? A Friday spent together was something a couple would do. We were not a couple, though I wouldn't say no to a day reserved for sex with Dash.

"Yeah." He shrugged a shoulder. "What were you going to do next to look into Amina?"

"Oh. Right." *Amina.* This wasn't about sex or spending time with me on his day off. Silly me. Time to get back on track. "I want to know why she left town after high school. Where she'd been. Why she came back to Clifton Forge and why she called your dad."

"'Kay."

I stood and breezed by him as I left the laundry room. "I was going to go back to the high school and finish checking yearbooks. You know, the ones I was looking at when you called the cops to the library."

"How long are you going to throw that at me?" He followed me to the kitchen, his bare feet padding on the floor.

"Forever. Remember? I don't like you."

"Good to know." Dash chuckled and nodded at my coffee mug. "Got any more of that coffee?"

"Sure." I took out a mug and set it under my single cup brewer. With a pod brewing, I faced him. The island was between us, keeping me from reaching for those tattooed arms. They were so . . . *ugh.* Tempting. He was so annoyingly tempting. And he *really* needed to get dressed.

"Do you want to come with me to the school?" I asked, handing him his full mug. Maybe if I brought Dash along, it would be easier to face Samantha at the school's front desk. I was thoroughly embarrassed to face her again after being arrested. A sidekick, especially one as distracting as Dash, might take away some of the focus on me.

"Um . . . maybe." The crease between his eyebrows deepened as he sipped the coffee. "Do you know where she's been living? Bozeman, right? That's what your article said."

"Yep." I'd gotten that information from Chief Wagner when he'd given me the preliminary report on Amina along with her name.

"Let's skip the school. Take a road trip instead."

I'd been contemplating a trip to Bozeman anyway. It was two hours one way, and depending on what we found, it would take up the entire day. I'd already delivered my content for this Sunday's paper and I was ahead on Wednesday's. If I was going to write something about Amina in next week's edition, I'd need to get new information soon.

"All right." I nodded. "But I'd still like to drop by the school."

"Why? We're probably not going to find much there anyway."

We'd likely find a few more old pictures, and while they might shed light on teenaged Amina, it was more important to know the person she'd grown into as an adult. "Yeah, you're probably right. We can skip the school and get on the road. I need to text my dad and tell him I won't be in today. Then we can go."

"Good." He grinned. "Mind if I use the shower?"

"Go for it. Towels are in the tall cabinet."

"Want to join me?" He winked.

183

I ignored the rush of heat between my legs. "We don't have time."

"Babe." He set down the cup on the island and sauntered my way, his slow, steady strides raising my heart rate with every step. I gripped the edge of the island and prayed my body didn't melt at his feet. When he spoke, his voice was rough, like the fingertips he shifted into my hair. "There's all the time in the world."

"We should go." There was no conviction behind that statement.

"Tomorrow, don't shower without me."

I suddenly wished it was tomorrow.

With a playful tug on my ear, Dash dropped his hand from my hair and walked out of the kitchen. This time, his steps were sure and swift. Those of a man ready to get to work.

I closed my eyes and let my heart rate settle to normal, then made us travel cups of coffee while the water ran in the bathroom.

Dash was mere feet away, naked and wet. I unloaded the dishwasher so I wouldn't go anywhere near the bathroom. Then I readied my purse for the trip, taking out the extra notepads I wouldn't need for this story. I sat at the island, drinking my coffee until Dash came out wearing yesterday's clothes and his signature, cocky grin.

"Here." I held out a travel mug.

"No cup holders on the bike."

I blinked. "Huh?"

"Cup holders." He went to the front door to pull on a boot. "My bike doesn't have them."

"Well, then it's a good thing I'm driving. My car comes equipped with cup holders."

Dash straightened. "We're taking the bike."

"No, I'll dri—"

"Babe, the bike is fun. Trust me."

"You told me not to trust you."

He grinned. "Make an exception. Riding through Montana in the summer is unbeatable."

"Fine." I shoved his coffee mug into his belly and tipped mine to my lips, guzzling because I didn't want to risk falling asleep on the motorcycle.

"That was easier than I thought it would be." He took a long drink from his own cup.

"Shut up." Did I secretly want to ride on his Harley? Yes. But I'd die before admitting that to him.

I set my cup down on the island and began digging the essentials out of my purse and wallet. Cash. Credit cards. Driver's license. Lip gloss. Hair tie. Gum. Phone. The jeans I was wearing were tight and the pockets wouldn't keep it all, so the hair tie went on a wrist. The gum, money and cards into my jeans. But the other items still needed a new home.

I looked at Dash and smiled. Then I moved into his space, nice and close. My fingers hooked in his jeans pocket, pulling it open as his breath hitched. With my things dropped into his pocket, I patted his thigh before backing away. "All set."

"Careful." Dash palmed his zipper, making a blatant adjustment to his cock. "I might make you go in there to get them back."

My core tightened. "I might insist."

Outside, the morning air was fresh and clean. We walked to Dash's bike and he sat on the dewy seat first. "Climb on."

"Helmets?" I hadn't minded when it was just a slow ride through town. But the highway? I was insisting on a helmet.

Dash opened his mouth to protest but stopped when he saw the look on my face. I was guessing it was part fear, part excitement.

"Please?"

He sighed. "We'll stop by the garage and pick them up."

"Thank you." I settled into the seat behind him, wrapping my arms around his waist. Then he started the motorcycle, roaring away from the curb and down the street.

To my relief, the garage wasn't open when we arrived. I wasn't ready to show up on Dash's bike and get questioning looks from his employees about why I was wrapped around their boss. With the way Dash jogged inside to retrieve a helmet, I guessed he wasn't ready to address our relationship with his employees either.

After Dash insisted I wear his leather jacket and buckled the matte-black helmet on my head—he refused one for himself—we rode out of town. The crisp morning did more to keep me awake than coffee ever could, and it was a thrill to be behind Dash as he navigated the curved highway.

I felt the shift in his muscles as he leaned us to one side or the other. The power of him and the machine between my legs. A couple of times, he'd let go of the handlebar with one hand to grip my thigh, those long fingers giving it a squeeze to make sure I was okay. I'd tightened my arms around his ribs in a silent *yes*.

The familiarity of my hometown wrapped around me as we arrived in Bozeman. These were the streets where I'd learned to drive. We passed my high school and the restaurant where we'd always celebrated Dad's birthdays. We rode by stores and buildings that hadn't been there during my youth, the changes I'd missed living in the city.

I'd always pictured coming back here and having a family. I'd hoped one day to return to Bozeman and go house hunting with my husband. I'd wanted to send my kids to the same school where I'd gone.

Being here was bittersweet. The memories swirled together with dreams now gone. A pang of sorrow hit and I pushed it away, not wanting to think about my lack of husband and children.

I didn't need them to be happy.

But I wanted them all the same.

When we reached an intersection, I pointed for Dash to take a left. Then I navigated us through town and toward Amina's address. I'd pulled it from public records one day and had jotted it in my yellow notepad in preparation for this trip.

Dash slowed down on the residential streets as my eyes scanned house fronts for numbers.

"There." I pointed to a pale peach two-story home.

We parked and I climbed off the motorcycle first, removing my helmet. Dash simply stood and raked a hand through his hair to tame the windblown mess. Two swipes and it looked perfectly disheveled. I pulled my hair tie off my wrist, twisting my mane up into a knot.

"This was her house?" Dash pointed to her place.

"It's cute." Her home was located on a pocket park. Bordered by five nearly identical homes, the park had two picnic tables and a playground for kids. The block formed a horseshoe around the park. In front of Amina's home, there was a *For Sale* sign freshly staked into the green grass. "I hadn't expected it to be listed already."

"Now what?" Dash asked.

"Now"—I held out my hand—"you give me my phone and we go house hunting."

One call to the realtor and she was on her way to show us into the house.

"Didn't waste any time getting it on the market," Dash said as we sat at the picnic table, waiting for the realtor.

"It's not like she's coming back. I'm sure her daughter or whoever is settling the estate wanted to get it up this summer so it would sell before winter."

"Yeah. Nice place."

"It sure is. All this is new from when I grew up here. This all used to be farmland."

This subdivision would have been on my short list as a mother. It was exactly the kind of place I would have wanted to have my kids grow up in, where we'd know the neighbors and the children would all play together on Saturday afternoons.

My place in Clifton Forge was a single-story home, like all the others on the street. There was minimal yard area. The HOA took care of shoveling snow from the sidewalks. I'd moved in and learned that I was the youngest person on the block, surrounded by elderly couples and a retired widower.

As the street's new spinster, I fit right in.

A car door slammed. The realtor from the sign smiled and waved as she came our way. "Hello."

"Hi." I smiled. Dash and I both stood, and when we were on our feet, I slipped my hand into his. The arm attached stiffened.

Good to know how he feels about hand-holding. There

was no time to let that irritate me because the realtor was speed walking our way, her hand held out the entire time.

After introductions, she led us into the house. "Your timing is perfect. We just put this on the market yesterday afternoon. This neighborhood is so desirable right now. It will go quick."

"It's adorable." I smiled up at Dash, pretending to be the happy couple. When the realtor stepped up to the door, I squeezed his fingers. "Don't you just love this porch, honey?"

"Uh . . ."

This guy. I'd held his hand and his brain had short-circuited. I rolled my eyes and mouthed *pretend*.

"Right." Dash's tense arm relaxed. "It's perfect, baby."

The realtor stood and pushed the door open to let us inside first. Then she flipped on lights behind us as we let ourselves wander.

"This is three bedrooms, two and a half baths. Open concept, as you can see. It was built six years ago and has only had one owner. She took incredible care of the place, and the seller is interested in selling it furnished."

"That might be great, wouldn't it, sweetie?" I asked Dash.

He threw an arm around my shoulders. "Sure would be. We've been wanting new furniture. That couch looks a hell of a lot nicer than ours."

I faked a laugh, stepping out of his hold to look around. My eyes searched for pictures, any clues to Amina's life. It wasn't easy with the realtor hovering, but luckily, her phone rang.

"Would you mind if I stepped out onto the porch to take this?" she asked, already moving that way. "Feel free to show yourselves around. I'll catch up."

Dash closed the door behind her and we both watched as she walked toward the park, her phone pressed to her ear.

I hustled over to an end table and opened the drawer. Empty. Then I hurried to the next, doing the same. It only had the remote for the television. The kitchen was my next stop and I started with the drawers in there too.

Dash followed, glancing over his shoulder to the front door. "What are you looking for?" he whispered.

"Anything that might tell us about Amina."

"'Kay." He went to a drawer, but I stopped him with a glare.

"No. You stand guard." I waved him away. "If she comes back, distract her."

He scowled. "How?"

"I don't know. Smile at her. That seems to make most women fall at your feet."

"Except for you," he muttered.

I stayed focus on my search, not bothering to correct him. Dash didn't need to know that his smile was just as lethal on me too.

The kitchen didn't have anything other than typical kitchen stuff. There wasn't even a junk drawer with old mail. Maybe the daughter had come and cleaned things out already? Maybe Amina was a neat freak?

I bolted up the stairs, glancing left and right to get my bearings. Then I went right for the master bedroom. Downstairs, there had been no pictures. Nothing framed on end tables or above the fireplace mantel. And the same was true here.

There wasn't a hint of the life lived inside these walls. I wasn't completely surprised, but I had hoped for a photo here and there.

I checked the drawers in the master bedroom and bathroom for good measure, but all were empty, as I'd expected. I was finishing up my loop through the guest bedroom when I heard Dash's voice carry up the stairs.

"Nope. No kids. Thank God."

Really? Was that last part necessary? It was a good thing I was only using him for sex. Even pretending to be a couple was exhausting. First the hand-holding. Now the aversion to kids. Yes, it was a very good thing this was sex only.

I put on a smile and brushed a fallen lock of hair off my face as I came into the hallway. I went right to Dash's side, wrapping my arms around him. "It's such a beautiful home. I can see us living here. Having babies here. Lots and lots of babies."

A visible grimace crossed his face.

"If you two would like some time to talk over an offer, I'd be happy to meet you back at my office." The realtor beamed with dollar signs in her eyes. "You don't have a buyer's agent, correct?"

"That's right," I said. "But I think we'll need a little more time to discuss. Maybe over lunch. Could we call you later?"

"Absolutely." Her card came flying out of her hand, faster than a poker cheat with an ace up her sleeve.

We followed her out of the house, lingering on the sidewalk as she got into her car. She was on the phone again before she even slid into the driver's seat. The moment her car was gone, I took a healthy step away from Dash.

"That was unproductive." I frowned. "I hadn't expected it to be listed so soon. And for all the personal touches to be erased. Amina's family must have cleared it out fast. I didn't see a picture or anything."

"Me neither."

"Damn," I muttered, pacing the sidewalk just as a woman pushed a stroller around the corner. I didn't think much of her until she walked up to the house beside Amina's.

"Excuse me, miss?" I waved as I approached. "Did you happen to know your neighbor?"

"Amina? Well, sure." Her shoulders fell. "I was so sad to hear what happened to her."

"Me too." I held out my hand. "My name is Bryce. I'm a journalist and I'm writing a piece about her. A memorial of sorts." Not entirely a lie.

"Oh." She shook my hand. "That's nice."

"We just came by to see where she lived and get a glimpse into her life. It seems like this place fits her. It's charming and beautiful."

"She was both those things," the young woman replied. "We loved having her as our neighbor."

"Was it just Amina? She lived alone, right?"

She nodded. "Her daughter visited occasionally. She came last week to clear out her mom's stuff. Poor thing. She looked heartbroken doing it all by herself."

"Oh, that's awful. There was no other family?"

"No." She shook her head. "Amina didn't have many visitors. Just her daughter a couple of times a year and the boyfriend who'd visit on the occasional weekend. But it was normally just her. She made me enough meals for two weeks when the baby was born."

"That's lovely," I said, though my mind was still stuck on one word. "I didn't realize Amina had a boyfriend."

"Oh, yes. Except maybe boyfriend isn't the right term. I don't know how serious they were. But he was here every now and then."

"Do you happen to know his name?"

"Sorry. Amina didn't talk about him much. And when he came, they kind of kept to themselves, if you know what I mean. He'd get here late on a Friday night. Leave Sunday morning before church."

"I see." Sounded like Amina had had a booty call, not a boyfriend. Was it Draven? Had they been sleeping together for a while? "Well, thank you. And I'm sorry for your loss."

"Thank you. Good luck with your memorial. Amina was the best."

I waved, stepping away but paused. "Can I ask you one more question?"

"Of course."

"Do you know what he looked like? The boyfriend?"

"He was probably her age. Older. About the same height as him." She pointed a finger at Dash, who still stood in front of Amina's house. "I only saw him two or three times and always as he was leaving. Like I said, Amina didn't talk about him much and I didn't want to pry. I have a feeling that he was from her past and came with some memories."

"Why do you say that?"

She shrugged. "I don't know. Maybe because she never talked about him. Like never. I even asked her once if she'd had a nice weekend with her company and she just smiled without answering me. It was almost like they were hiding something. I always wondered if maybe he was married."

"Maybe."

The neighbor's eyes got wide as she realized what she'd just said. "Oh, God. No. That's not what I mean. Please don't put that in your story. Amina was so kind and sweet and generous. I don't want you to think she's some kind of home-wrecker or mistress. I was just talking out loud. I'm sure he wasn't married. She wasn't like that."

"Don't worry." I smiled. "I won't write anything that isn't true. Speculation is just that."

Her face paled. "Really. I'm sure he wasn't married. And she was wonderful. Truly."

"I'm sure you're right. Thanks again."

She went to her door, quickly disappearing inside with the stroller. Probably scared she'd stick her foot in her mouth again.

Dash and I didn't stay longer. We both walked silently to the bike, not talking until my helmet was on.

"Well, that was interesting," I said quietly. "Turns out Amina had a regular visitor on the weekends."

"I heard that."

"Do you know where your dad has been most weekends?"

Dash's jaw ticked. "He didn't kill her."

"I'm not saying that." I frowned. "But I think we'd better find out exactly how long your dad has been having sex with Amina Daylee. And if it wasn't him, then she did have a boyfriend. I wonder how he'd react to learning she'd gone to Clifton Forge and hooked up with your dad."

"Sounds like we need to track down a boyfriend."

"Yes, we do."

Dash straddled the bike. "Good thing the neighbor showed. Otherwise this would have been a wasted trip."

"We got lucky." I settled behind him. "And we were lucky the house was listed too so we could get inside."

"What were you going to do if it hadn't been listed?" he asked over his shoulder.

I shrugged. "Pick the lock on the front door or break in through a window."

Dash's eyes crinkled at the sides as a slow grin spread across his lips. Then he burst out laughing, the sound echoing across the block as his shoulders shook. "God, you're fucking amazing. Too bad you don't like me."

"That's right. I don't like you." *Not at all.*

CHAPTER FIFTEEN

DASH

Bryce and I stopped by a taco joint to grab lunch before riding home to Clifton Forge. The return trip was quiet, not as intimate and exciting as the trip to Bozeman had been. Her arms didn't grip me quite as fiercely. Her legs didn't hug the outside of my thighs.

Maybe she'd gotten used to the bike and how to shift her weight. But that featherlight touch felt more like her pulling away.

I hadn't expected the whole *act like a married couple* bit. It made sense why Bryce had done it, but dumbass that I was, it had taken me too long to catch on.

I just . . . wasn't that guy. I wasn't the wife-and-kids type. Being a family man was Nick's priority, not mine. My niece and nephew were amazing kids. I liked having a sister-in-law who gave me shit and loved my brother as eternally as my mother had loved my father.

But I had never imagined that in my life, and even if I could picture it, I didn't want it.

Fucking no, thank you.

I'd witnessed firsthand the destruction it had brought to Dad's life when Mom had died. I saw Nick's fear when he'd learned Emmeline had almost been kidnapped.

I'd had numerous black eyes, a fractured ulna and collar-bone, two broken noses and a few concussions thanks to the boxing ring and a few fights. Physical pain I could handle. A broken heart?

Nope. No point in even putting myself in that position.

Bryce being pissed at me wasn't going to change my mind. She didn't get to judge the way I lived my life—past, present or future. She wasn't my wife or girlfriend, so she didn't get to be angry that I wasn't a hand-holder or cringed at the idea of *babies*.

By the time we pulled into Clifton Forge, it was my turn to be mad. Bryce and I were casual. We were having sex, temporarily. I guess I shouldn't have spent the night.

When I pulled up to her house, she was off the bike in a flash, stripping off the helmet. "We need to talk to your dad and see if it was him visiting Amina."

"Yeah."

"I want to be there."

"Fine." I narrowed my eyes and studied her face. It didn't look angry. She didn't seem hurt. She just seemed tired.

Maybe I'd been reading way too much into her reaction to me at Amina's house. Maybe she was just preoccupied with what we'd learned from the neighbor. Had I gotten worked up for nothing?

I sure hoped so. This would be a lot easier if I didn't have to worry about Bryce pressuring me for a commitment.

"Meet me at the garage at ten tomorrow," I told her, returning her items from my pocket.

"I'll be there." Without another word, she turned and walked up the sidewalk to her front door.

I waited only long enough to see that she made it inside, then I raced away. I didn't want to stay another night anyway. Her bed was uncomfortable, her pillows too firm. And she woke up so damn early, I couldn't even enjoy sleeping in on my day off.

The ride home took ten minutes. My house was on the edge of town, surrounded by some open property I owned, ensuring I'd always have space. When I walked inside, I went right for my walk-in shower, wanting to rinse away the smell of Bryce's sweet coconut soap. I didn't need the reminder of her on my skin all evening.

Water dripped off the ends of my hair as I toweled off. I walked to my bedroom naked and, though it was still after-noon, collapsed on my king-sized bed. Sprawling out, I took a pillow and punched it into a ball under my head.

Much better.

Except I tossed and turned during my nap. And all night, my hand kept searching for something that wasn't there.

———

"MORNING." Emmett walked through the open garage bay door the next day.

"Hey," I said from the floor where I was lying beside the Mustang. The bumper I'd installed this morning was on and I was double-checking that everything was exactly right.

He came over as I shoved off the floor, handing me the extra cup of coffee he'd brought along.

I tipped the white lid to my lips, surprised when I tasted cream and chocolate. "What is this?"

"A double mocha something. I don't know. I hooked up with the blond working at the coffee hut last night and she gave me these for free when I dropped her off this morning."

I chuckled. "Nice."

"What's up?"

"I'll tell you when everyone else gets here."

I'd called Emmett and Leo this morning, waking them up at six a.m. on a Saturday. Both were annoyed I'd woken them up on their day off. They were lucky I hadn't called at four—that's when I'd called Dad.

He'd been up that early too.

I'd asked everyone to meet me at the garage by ten.

The clock on the wall showed nine forty-five. And a white Audi was turning into the lot.

Emmett looked at the car, then to me. "Did you know she was coming?"

"I invited her. She's part of this now."

"Part of what?" His forehead furrowed.

"Finding the truth. Better to have her on our side than against."

Emmett studied my face. "You got something going with her?"

"Something like that." There was no point denying it. When she was around, she had my focus. Emmett wouldn't miss it when she walked into the garage.

"Is that smart?"

I blew out a long breath. "No, but it's too late now."

"She's under your skin."

And soaking deeper, down to the bone, every day.

Walking outside, I took Bryce in as she stepped out of her car. Gorgeous, as always. Her hair was straight and sleek, draping down her back. I instantly regretted not staying at her place last night.

Her sunglasses were on, shielding her eyes. But the way she held her shoulders, the upward tilt of her chin, said she was prepared for a fight.

She'd probably get one.

Bryce walked my way, wearing a pair of loose jeans cuffed at the ankle. They left her curves to the imagination, but I knew what she looked like underneath. Her black tee fit tight across her breasts and stomach. With her heeled sandals, it was impossible to look away. Though she could be wearing a potato sack and she'd still have my undivided attention.

She was classy and gorgeous no matter what she wore. It came from the way she carried herself, with tenacity and strength. Not many people, let alone women, questioned me. But this woman was a fighter. She wouldn't be pushed around, and she wouldn't take things at face value.

Which was why she had to be here today.

Bryce would see something I might miss.

The roar of a familiar engine echoed off the steel walls of the garage as Leo sped into the parking lot. He drove right up next to Bryce, slowing to match her strides. When he parked and slid off his shades, he gave her the smile that often landed him in the bathroom of The Betsy, fucking whoever had fallen for it.

My hands fisted. I'd be informing Leo that Bryce was off-limits. For good. Even when the two of us called it off, she wasn't to be anywhere near his bed. Emmett's too for that matter.

"Garage is closed, beautiful," he said, still astride his

bike. "But I'll take a look at your car on Monday. Give you the special service. I'd even stay late, just for you."

"Wow." Bryce stopped beside Leo. She brought her hand to her heart. "Really?"

"This oughta be good," Emmett muttered. I hadn't noticed him standing by my side.

"Really." Leo winked and ran a hand through his hair. "Maybe when we're done with your car, I can take you for a ride. Teach you how to have a real good time."

"I do like a good time." Bryce used that same voice she'd used on me the first day she'd come here, pure sugar and sex. She was luring Leo into her trap, the same damn thing she'd done to me. God, I was a fucking idiot. She'd baited me. And watching her do it to Leo, I could see why I'd fallen for it.

"Damn, she's good." The way she held her body was confident and poised. She didn't flaunt her looks the way some women did to hold you captive. She didn't push out her chest or give him a shy smile. There wasn't a damn thing shy about her smile, and that's why it was so devastating.

She stood there like the goddess she was and let Leo look her up and down, knowing that he liked what he saw. And knowing she was in complete control.

My dick stirred. I'd screwed up by not staying at her place last night. We were a short-term thing and I wanted to savor it while it lasted. I wouldn't make the same mistake tonight.

"What do you say?" Leo licked his lips.

Bryce took a step closer. "I'd eat you alive, pretty boy. Save the special service for someone who'll take your orders in bed."

Leo's jaw dropped.

Bryce spun on a heel and marched my way. "Do you

guys all deliver the same line to get women into bed? Offering them a *ride?* Does it actually work?"

I grinned. "Every time."

"Not every time." She smirked.

"True." I'd acted the same way as Leo that first day she'd come to the garage. And she'd shot me down. "We only use that line in the summer. We can't ride in the winter so we come up with something new."

"Given your reputation, it's got to be better."

I shrugged. "Not always. Sometimes all it takes is *hello*."

"Let's be done talking about this." A flare of annoyance—*and jealousy?*—laced her voice. Whatever she was feeling, she shoved it away and extended her hand to Emmett. "I'm Bryce Ryan."

"Emmett Stone." He held her gaze, as if assessing a potential enemy.

"Who's this?" Leo glared at Bryce as he came to stand by Emmett.

"Bryce Ryan," she spoke at the same time I said, "She's the new reporter in town."

"Ahh. The pain in our ass."

"Or the woman who might actually be able to help clear your boss's name," she shot back.

"Cool it. She's on our team, Leo." I sent him a warning glare. "We're working together."

His scowl deepened as another engine's thunder signaled its approach.

Dad pulled into the garage, parking by Leo, and wasted no time coming right up to Bryce and holding out his hand. "Bryce. I'm Draven. Didn't get to meet you the last time we were both here."

"Yes." She shook his hand. "You were a bit busy that day."

Did she have to remind him of the arrest? I got that it was her way of exerting some control over the situation, sending a message that Dad wouldn't intimidate her either. But she risked pissing him off. He was tight-lipped about this whole thing enough as it was.

Christ. I was going to end up playing mediator between the guys and Bryce.

"Let's talk inside." I waved everyone into the garage.

We all assumed places in the garage. Leo and Emmett both hopped up onto a tool bench. I stood against a wall. Dad stood in the center of the room, his legs planted wide and arms over his chest.

And Bryce, to torture me, went and leaned against the Mustang.

"How much does she know?" Dad asked, staring right at Bryce.

"Enough to bury you if you betray me," she answered.

"Enough that she knows the risks involved," I corrected. "We have an arrangement. It's between me and her. And not the point of this meet."

"She's an outsider. And not part of—"

I held up a hand, silencing Leo's protest. "It's done."

The garage went still. Bryce looked around the room, waiting to see if anyone would object. But Leo's would be the last. At least, the last objection while she was in the room. Emmett would corner me later and voice his concerns. Dad wouldn't object; he knew it was too late. His criticism would only come if I'd made a mistake and we were dealing with the fallout of Bryce writing a story that condemned us all.

"Emmett and Leo"—I looked to them— "any word around town about who might have it out for Dad?"

Both shook their heads as Emmett spoke up. "There's nothing. Not a hint. I even met with a couple of old members who'd gone to the Warriors. They could be lying, but I don't think it's them."

"That goes with the story they gave us when we met with them and Tucker."

"It's quiet because everyone thinks Draven did it," Leo said.

My gaze met Bryce's, silently reinforcing my message. *He didn't kill her.* "Listen. Yesterday, Bryce and I went to—"

"How long were you sleeping with Amina?" Bryce fired the question at Dad.

"Jesus Christ," I mumbled. So much for giving Dad a little background about our trip yesterday before springing it on him.

"I spent the night with her," Dad answered, the tension in the garage spiking. "Though, you already knew that."

"Not the night before she was killed." Bryce shook her head. "Before. How many times did you go visit her?"

His eyebrows came together. "Visit her?"

"We went to her house in Bozeman yesterday," I explained. "Looked around. Her neighbor said she had a guy about my height and your age visit every few weekends. Was it you?"

"No. The first time I saw Amina in over twenty years was the day she came here."

"Why'd she come?" Bryce asked. "Did she tell you?"

"Said she wanted to visit. See how things had changed. Called me here at the garage and asked if I'd meet with her for a drink. I told her I'd pick her up from her room. Got there. We started talking. Never had that drink."

I looked to Bryce. "That means there is a boyfriend out there. Maybe one who'd get jealous and kill her after he left."

"Crime of passion makes sense," Emmett said. "Given the number of times she was stabbed. But how'd he get your knife, Draven?"

"Hell if I know. I haven't been hunting in years. I can't even remember where I kept it. Somewhere at home, probably."

"A boyfriend wouldn't have known that." I ran a hand through my hair. "Or who you were to go and steal it. No boyfriend acting in a jealous rage would take the time to set you up."

"Unless." Bryce began swaying, shifting her weight from foot to foot as a crease formed between her eyebrows. "What if Amina was dating someone from Clifton Forge? Maybe she had come back here. Maybe she'd lied about not being here for decades. If her boyfriend was from town, it would be plausible he could have set you up. Especially if he knew you, Draven."

"She didn't lie," Dad said. "Amina had no reason to deceive me."

"But what if she was part of the setup?" Bryce countered, talking with her hands moving. "Maybe she and this boyfriend came to town. She called you to the motel while he went to your place to steal your knife. Except something goes wrong. Maybe they'd planned to plant the knife at another crime. But he comes back to the motel and gets enraged that you two had sex. Kills her. Frames you."

It was possible. Thin, but possible.

"Amina wasn't out to get me," Dad insisted. "She . . . she wasn't like that."

"You said there was history, Dad. Are you sure she wouldn't want to see you in prison?"

"I'm sure."

"How can—"

"Kingston." One word and there was no room for argument. "I'm sure. Someone set me up to take the fall for murdering an innocent woman. She just wanted to visit a town she hadn't been in for years. And to see me, an old friend from high school. That's it."

Bryce opened her mouth but took one look at my gaze and clamped it shut again. There would be no debating this with Dad. She didn't know him well enough to hear the conviction in his voice.

"So where are we?" Emmett asked, taking his hair in his hands to tie it up.

"We're in the same place we were." Dad sighed. "Whoever did this has me dead to rights. The cops know I was there. They have my fingerprints on my weapon. There's nothing we can do but wait and hope someone gets stupid and starts talking."

"That's not happening." I fisted my hands. "No one is talking. Whoever did this is patient. Really fucking patient. They've made no move against the rest of us."

"They probably won't," Emmett said. "At least not yet. They're waiting to see what happens with Draven."

"Exactly," Leo muttered. "Meanwhile, we're stuck. And we all gotta keep looking over our shoulders until we can make some headway."

"Or," Bryce said quietly, "we use the one lead we have. We make sure this boyfriend didn't start dating Amina to get to Draven. If the killer knew there was a connection between Draven and Amina, he could have been playing her from the beginning."

"Agreed," I said. "We need to track this guy down."

"How?" Leo asked.

"We could ask her daughter," Bryce suggested.

"No." Dad's bark echoed off the walls.

"Why not?" I pushed off the wall. Was Dad really that set on life in prison? "She might know who her mother was seeing."

"No." He pointed at my face. "The daughter is off-limits. She just lost her mother. She doesn't need to be bothered by a goddamn reporter and the son of the man who is suspected of killing her mom. Leave her alone. That's an order."

It had been a long time since he'd issued an order. Not since the days when he'd worn the president patch for the Gypsies rather than me.

"Am I understood?" Dad asked Emmett and Leo.

"Understood," they answered in unison.

Dad looked to me, his gaze hard and unwavering. "Dash?"

Fuck. Bryce was seething but I was pinned in the corner. I wouldn't go against Dad. Not when he'd gone this far to make his point. "Understood."

"We're with you, Prez," Emmett said as Leo's head bobbed in agreement.

"Good," Dad said. "And that goes for her too. She bothers the daughter, I'll see to it that she'll never write another story again. Hard to write when you're missing your hands."

Hell. Did he have to keep making it worse? That was over the top. If his intent was to scare Bryce, he had failed.

She was livid. I could feel the heat of her anger from across the room. She'd probably melt the paint on the Mustang.

But I didn't say a word as Dad marched out the door.

"Guess this meeting is over." Leo hopped down from the bench as Dad rode away from the garage. He jerked his chin up at Bryce as he walked backward toward his bike. "Change your mind about that ride—"

"I'll call Dash."

Leo looked between us, realization dawning, then laughed. "Ah. Good luck, brother."

Emmett followed him out, waving as he walked to his bike. "I'll keep an ear open."

"Do that," I said. "Have a good weekend."

"I will." He grinned. "Think I might need another coffee."

When the noise from their bikes was gone and the garage was quiet, I turned to Bryce.

"He threatened me."

"Yes, he did."

She lifted her chin. "Will you take his side?"

My immediate response was *yes*. I'd always support Dad and he'd made it clear where he stood. But if it came down to that, to hurting her, I knew the answer was no. "No. But it doesn't matter because you're not going to bother the daughter. You're more compassionate than that."

"We have to talk to the daughter," she said immediately. "Maybe the boyfriend is nothing, but it's the only new information we have."

"Dad has a point. She just lost her mother. If she's living in Denver, the chances that she even knows her mom's weekend hookup are small anyway. It's not worth stirring up a bunch of hurt."

"Even if it means your dad spends the rest of his life in prison? Do you still think he's innocent after threatening to cut. Off. My. Hands?"

I raked a hand through my hair. "He wouldn't do it." Maybe he would have years ago, but not now. "He's just trying to scare you. And yes, he's innocent. If he wants to spend his life in prison for a murder he didn't commit, then I guess that's the reality of the situation."

"It doesn't have to be."

No, it didn't. *Why won't Dad fight? What is he hiding?*

Draven Slater's secrets were going to land him in the state penitentiary for the rest of his life. *Son of a bitch.* I clenched my teeth, resisting the urge to pick up a wrench and throw it across the shop. Why was he backing down? That wasn't like him.

And why should I fight for his freedom when he wasn't fighting himself?

"Don't know what to do here, babe," I confessed, shaking my head. "I'm pissed, for sure. But Dad's right. I honestly don't think the daughter is going to give us any information. And I'm at a dead end until Dad decides how hard he wants to push. All I can do is respect my father's wishes while defending him because I *know* he's innocent. What would you do if it was your father?"

"I don't know." Bryce's anger vanished. Her voice softened. She crossed the room and put her delicate hand on my arm. "We both want the truth, but I have a story. I can print exactly what happens with his trial. With his conviction. We both know it will come down to that. And I can accept that he's the killer. That justice is served. I can accept that as the truth. Can you?"

"He's my dad," I whispered. "It's his choice."

"Okay. Then I guess we're done here."

"Yeah, I guess so."

She dropped her hand and stepped away. "See you around, King."

"Take care, Bryce." My heart twisted. I was losing on both sides. Emmett had gotten one thing right: she was more than just under my skin. She was *in* there. Deeper than I wanted to admit to myself.

Her heels clipped on the floor as she made her way outside. But before disappearing, she paused and looked over her shoulder. "How about dinner, one last time?"

One last time.

"I'll bring the beer."

CHAPTER SIXTEEN

BRYCE

S itting alone at my kitchen island, I picked at my chicken salad sandwich.

Two weeks had gone by since the meeting in the garage and my last night with Dash. Dinners since had been eaten in this spot so I could watch out the front kitchen window, hoping to hear the thunder of his motorcycle before it pulled up to my curb.

I missed having an uninvited dinner guest. More and more each day, I missed Dash, and not only for the sex. I missed talking to him and hearing his voice. I missed the easy way he moved around my house. I even missed the snoring.

But I hadn't heard a word from him. Our final parting had been, well . . . final.

My foolish heart had hoped I'd left a lasting impression. One that would make him yearn to see me again—the way I yearned. Clearly the sex I'd thought unforgettable was actually the opposite.

He'd probably found a new replacement at The Betsy to keep himself company. An easy feat for Dash Slater, finding

211

a woman willing to take him to her bed. *Sometimes all it takes is hello.* The thought of him saying those words to another woman made my stomach roll.

I tossed down my sandwich, most of it uneaten. I hadn't had much of an appetite over the last week. The gnawing feeling that I was quitting on Amina Daylee's story had frayed my nerves.

How could Draven not want to find Amina's killer? How could Dash be okay leaving a lead unfollowed? Especially given how strongly he believed his father was innocent.

It didn't make sense. It felt like giving up.

I hadn't written anything about her murder or the Tin Gypsies in the past two weeks. My stories had been focused on summer activities around town, particularly the upcoming Independence Day parade and the holiday's various celebrations.

Because I wasn't sure what to write yet. Without new information on Amina's murder case or knowing when Draven would be brought to trial, there was nothing to print. And I wasn't ready to write a story on the former Tin Gypsy MC.

The information Dash had told me on the record would suffice for an easy Sunday feature. A popular one too. But for me, that story was dull. Lifeless. The good stuff was all the things he'd told me off the record. Since he'd kept his end of the bargain not to hide things from me, I'd be keeping mine too.

Or had he?

The meeting at the garage played over and over in my mind. Draven's insistence we not talk to the daughter had been nagging at me. I didn't know the man from Adam, but he'd been so firm.

Was he always like that? Was he just trying to intimidate me? I believed his threat, more so than I'd believed any Dash had given me. If I went to Amina's daughter, he'd retaliate. He might even cause me physical harm.

And that was why I had to go.

Draven's insistence was more than sparing the feelings of a grieving child. He was hiding something. Was I the only one who saw it?

Either Dash didn't care, blinded by his loyalty to his father, or Dash knew Draven's secret and was lying to me— which meant my story would include every word he'd spoken about the Gypsies.

I'd been waiting to see if something came up—it wouldn't. Murderers with a lick of sense didn't go around talking about said murder. They certainly didn't brag about framing a notorious criminal. And Amina's murderer was smarter than your average gummy bear.

Screw Draven's threat. And screw Dash for making me miss him. Besides, Draven would never know I was leaving. Not unless he was following me too.

Picking up my phone, I opened my United Airlines app and checked into my flight leaving tomorrow morning for Denver.

Then I flipped open the yellow notepad sitting next to me, reading Genevieve Daylee's address for the hundredth time.

———

"THANKS," I said to my Uber driver as I got out of the car.

The late-morning air was fresh and warm in Colorado. The sunshine beat down bright. I'd gotten up long before dawn to drive to Bozeman and catch my flight, watching the sun rise from my tiny window on the airplane. Then I'd ordered a ride to Genevieve's.

The condos on this street were all the same, a row of tan siding with white grid windows. Genevieve had a planter full of purple and pink petunias by her door, brightening up her stoop.

I took a deep breath, pinned my shoulders back and walked up the sidewalk. After a sure knock, I waited.

Maybe I should have called first, but not wanting to raise any questions or have word get back to Draven that I'd contacted her, I'd risked a surprise visit. It was a gamble that she'd even be home, but it was a Saturday and hopefully I'd get lucky. If not, my return flight would be delayed until I could find some time to see her.

Light footsteps, a quick flip of the lock and the door opened.

"Hello." She smiled.

"H-hi." I did a double take. She looked so much like Amina. Familiar, but there was something else there too. Something I couldn't put my finger on.

Her hair was dark and long, curled into thick spirals. Her face was heart shaped with flawless skin. Her eyes were a deep brown that I was sure I'd seen somewhere before. And she had her mother's chin and mouth.

"Can I help you?"

I snapped myself out of my stupor, smiling and holding out my hand. "Hi. I'm Bryce Ryan. Are you Genevieve Daylee?"

"Yes." She hesitantly took my hand. "Do I know you?"

"No. We've never met. I'm a reporter from the *Clifton Forge Tribune*."

"Oh." She inched away, lifting a hand to the door.

"I was hoping you might be willing to help me," I said before she could shut me out. "I'm writing a special piece on your mom. A story to show who she was and what her life was like before."

Her eyes narrowed. "Why?"

"Because her death was awful and tragic. Because people killed in that way are so often remembered for the way they died, not the way they lived."

Genevieve let my words linger. I was sure she'd slam the door in my face, but then the hesitancy in her face vanished and she opened it wider. "Come on in."

"Thank you." I stepped in behind her, letting out the breath I'd been holding. When I inhaled, the scent of chocolate and brown sugar filled my nose. My stomach growled, starved from only eating the small bag of airplane pretzels. "It smells incredible in here."

"I made chocolate chip cookies. Mom's recipe. I was missing her today."

"I'm so sorry for your loss."

She gave me a sad smile, leading me through the clean and cozy living room and into the breakfast nook off the kitchen. "Some days it doesn't feel like it's real. That I'll call her and she'll pick up the phone."

"Were you close?" I asked as she waved me into a chair.

"We were. Growing up, it was just the two of us. She was my best friend. We had our struggles when I was a teenager, normal mom-daughter fights. But she was always there for me. She always put me first."

"Sounds like a great mom."

Her eyes welled with tears. "Why would he do this to her?"

He meaning Draven. Genevieve thought Draven had killed her mother. Dash had planted enough doubts in my mind that I'd been operating under the possibility he was innocent.

But as far as the world was concerned, as far as Genevieve knew, Draven Slater was Amina's murderer.

"I don't know. I wish things were different."

"Me too." She pushed away from the table in a flurry, going to the kitchen and getting two glasses from a hickory cupboard. Then she filled them both with milk from the fridge and brought them to the table. Next came a heaping plate of freshly baked cookies. "I'm grief eating. If you leave here and this plate has any cookies left, I'll be disappointed in both of us."

I laughed, taking a cookie. "We can't have that."

The first cookie was inhaled, followed quickly by a second. After the third, we each gulped some milk, then looked at one another and smiled.

Maybe she seemed familiar because she was so welcoming. So friendly. She'd brought me into her home, shared a piece of her mother and trusted me to take care of it. Naïve? Yes, slightly. Or she wasn't jaded to the world. She didn't expect people to lie, cheat and steal.

I envied her.

"God, these are good." I took a fourth cookie.

"Right? I don't know where she got this recipe but it's the only one I'll ever use."

"I might have to steal it from you."

"If I give it to you, will you put it in your story? I think Mom would have liked sharing that one with the world."

My hand went to my heart. "It would be my pleasure."

Genevieve's eyes drifted past my shoulder, staring

blankly into her living room behind us. "Mom and I didn't get to see each other much. Not after she took that job in Bozeman and moved to Montana."

"Did you grow up in Denver?"

"I did. We lived about five miles from here. I went to the high school you probably passed on your way in."

A sprawling red brick building five times the size of my high school. "Is that why she moved to Bozeman? Her job?"

"Yeah. Mom worked for a plumbing supply company. They were expanding and started an office in Bozeman. She volunteered to go. But you probably already knew all of that."

"Only the name." The internet could tell me all about the company, its branch offices and its products. But it didn't tell me about Amina. The internet couldn't tell me about the person she'd been. "Was she good at her job?"

"She was," Genevieve said with pride. "She worked for that company from the beginning and they really loved her. It was like a family. I knew all her coworkers growing up. A few of them would hire me in the summers to mow their lawns. They all came to my college graduation." Her voice hitched. "Her boss helped me plan her funeral."

My heart squeezed. I couldn't imagine having to plan my mother's funeral. "Sounds like she was the type of person who made close, lifetime friendships."

"She loved. People were drawn to her for it. It was hard being a single mom. My grandparents passed before I was born so she did it all by herself. She never complained. She never treated me like a burden. She just built this life for us. A happy one."

Genevieve dropped her chin, sniffling. I stayed quiet, the

emotion clogging my throat, as she wiped her eyes dry. When she looked up, she forced a smile.

"I should have called," I said. "I'm sorry. I'm here, surprising you. I should have called first." *Goddamn it.* Draven had been right about that, hadn't he?

I'd let the weeks of silence from Dash irritate me. And now I was here bothering a young woman who'd lost the most important person in her life.

"No, I'm glad you're here." Genevieve took another cookie. "I haven't talked about Mom in a couple of weeks. It was a flurry after she was . . . you know. Everyone was so shocked and I was so busy getting her memorial arranged. People talked about her then. But after it was over, it got quiet. People went back to their lives."

"And you're here."

"I'm here. Heartbroken." She took a bite and chewed it with a quivering chin. "But it's nice to talk about how wonderful she was. And not about how she died. The only person who's talked to me about her this week is the prosecutor in Clifton Forge and that's only because I want to keep tabs on the trial."

"It's not scheduled yet."

"I know. I want him locked up. I want him off the streets and away from the world. Maybe then I can forget. I get so angry and . . ." As she trailed off, her free hand fisted on the table, her knuckles white. "I want to see her grave. Did you know we buried Mom in Montana?"

"Um, no. I didn't." I hadn't kept up on Amina's funeral arrangements. The obituary I'd included in the paper had been vague on the topic, stating the family was having private services in Denver. I'd assumed those services had included the burial.

"She wanted to be buried in Clifton Forge. Let me tell you, that was a shock to learn from her will. But I think she wanted to be by her parents again."

"So you were in Clifton Forge?"

"No." She shook her head. "I couldn't go. I wasn't ready to face it yet. I went to Montana to pack up her personal items and get her house on the market. But that was as close as I could get. I wasn't ready to be in that town where she was . . . you know. But I'm going there next week."

"You're coming to Clifton Forge?" My eyes widened.

She nodded. "I want to see it for myself. The funeral home sent me a picture of her gravesite and the mockup of her tombstone but it's not the same. So I'm making a fast trip out of it next Sunday. Get in and get out. I don't want to risk running into *him*."

Yes, seeing Draven would be bad. "If you need company, I'd be happy to go with you."

"Thanks, Bryce." She looked at me with her kind, brown eyes and that pang of familiarity hit again. "I might take you up on that."

"Please do." In our short time together, I'd become strangely loyal to Genevieve. If I could help by standing at her side while she visited her mother's grave, I would.

Not for my story. For this woman who already felt like a friend.

I'd meant what I'd told Genevieve. I'd write something special for Amina. I'd include the cookie recipe. Maybe that would appease some guilt for unexpectedly showing up at her doorstep.

Genevieve took her empty glass to the sink to rinse it out. I stood and brought mine over too, handing it to her. "Can I ask you another question?"

"Sure." She laughed. "For a reporter, you haven't asked many."

"I was just warming up." I winked. "Did your mom have anyone else she was close to? A best friend? Or a boyfriend? Others who'd want to talk about her for the story."

She blew out a long breath. "Mom was dating a guy. Lee."

I froze, ready to soak up every word about the boyfriend. "Lee."

"Lee." She said his name with a curled lip. "In all my life, Mom didn't date. Not once. But she was different lately. Quieter. And I can't help but think it was because of him."

"Were they serious?"

She shrugged. "I don't know. That's the crazy part. She acted differently but never talked about him. The only reason I even knew about him was because I flew to Bozeman to surprise her one weekend and she had to call Lee and cancel plans. Whenever I'd ask about him, she'd brush it off. Say it was casual. But if you knew Mom, you'd know nothing about her was casual. She held people tight. Her friendships lasted decades."

"So you didn't know him?"

She shook her head. "No, we never met. I didn't even know his last name."

And there went my lead. "Maybe she was worried you wouldn't like him."

"Yeah. That's what I think too. It was weird for me, her having another person in her life. Mom was good at sensing when I was uncomfortable. I just couldn't picture her with a boyfriend." She looked over her shoulder from the sink. The light from the window caught in her eyes, making them glow.

Gah! What was it about her eyes?

"What else can you tell me about her?" I asked. "Something nice you'd like to have other people know."

"Her smile was always full on. All wide, white teeth. It was like she didn't know how to give a half smile." The pain in Genevieve's smile came back along with a sheen of tears. "She was beautiful."

"I'd be honored to write that about her. Do you have any pictures? I'd love to include some of your favorites."

"I'd like that."

For the next hour, I sat beside Genevieve on her couch as she went through plastic tubs of old pictures and mementos from her childhood. They'd all been at Amina's house, and though she'd packed them up and brought them to Colorado, she confessed to not having the courage to have gone through them yet.

"Thanks for sitting with me." She fit the lid on the last box. "I'm sure this was more crazy than you were expecting when you came here. Sorry."

"Don't be." I put my hand over hers. "I'm glad I could be here."

The truth was, the longer I sat with Genevieve, the more I liked her. She told story after story about her mother as we looked at old pictures. Ones from road trips the two of them had taken. Photos of a few special camping trips in the Colorado mountains.

Genevieve had told me about how Amina would always give a few dollars to a homeless man begging on a corner, even though as a single mother, she hadn't had much extra to spare. She'd taught Genevieve to be strong, never quit and to live an honest life.

After hearing it all, I knew my accusations in the garage

that Amina could have been in on the setup with Draven were off base. Amina hadn't been a deceiver.

And she'd raised a lovely daughter.

In every photo, Amina's bright, smiling face was present. When she stood by her daughter, the two were always touching—a hand hold, an arm over the shoulder, one leaning on the other. Their bond was special and seeing it through the pictures made me more determined to tell Amina's story.

For mother.

And daughter.

Amina deserved to be remembered for more than her death.

"This was actually perfect," I told Genevieve. "I feel like I know your mom now. I hope my story can do her memory justice. May I ask one more question, off the record?"

"Sure." She pivoted on the couch, giving me her attention.

"In all these photos, it was mostly just the two of you." Even as a baby, the photos had been of only Amina and Genevieve. There'd been the occasional friend or neighbor included, but the vast majority of the photos were of mother and daughter. "What about your father?"

"Mom never talked about him. Never." Her shoulders fell. "I'd ask. She'd say he was a nice man but not a part of my life. She always said *he* was a mistake but that he gave her the best gift in the world. And you know, I didn't push. I was good with that answer because I had her. She was enough."

"I can see that."

"Except now that she's gone, I wish I knew who he was. If he's even still alive. It would be nice to know if I had another parent out there."

My gut was screaming that Amina's secrecy about her daughter's lineage and the secret boyfriend were not a coincidence. Could this mystery boyfriend be Genevieve's father?

"Did she ever tell you his name?" I asked.

She shook her head. "No."

If Genevieve's father was the boyfriend, it would explain everything. Why Amina didn't want Genevieve to meet *Lee*. Why she hid him from everyone. Because she wasn't ready to introduce father and daughter.

My mind was racing, wondering how this man fit into the picture. Was he the killer? Would he try and contact Genevieve now? Did he even know he had a daughter?

More questions flew through my mind when Genevieve destroyed my theories with a single sentence. "Mom didn't tell me his name, only that people called him Prez."

Prez. Where had I heard that name before? No, not a name. A nickname.

Prez.

My racing mind screeched to a halt.

We're with you, Prez.

In our meeting in the garage, Emmett had said that to Draven. He'd called Draven *Prez*.

I looked at Genevieve, focusing on her eyes. I knew those eyes. Like Draven had given his brown hair to his son.

He'd given those brown eyes to his daughter.

CHAPTER SEVENTEEN

DASH

"Another one, Dash?"

I swirled the last swallow of beer around the bottom of my pint glass. "Yeah. Thanks, Paul."

As he went to get my Guinness—dark, like my mood—I looked around the crowded bar. It was a busy night at The Betsy with locals out enjoying a hot summer Saturday night. People bumped into each other as they milled around the room and shouted out conversations over the loud music. Emmett and Leo were at the pool table. They each had a woman hanging off their elbow.

Emmett caught my eye and motioned me over to play. There was a third woman roaming by the pool table who'd been eye-fucking me all night.

I shook my head and faced forward, staring at the wall of liquor bottles across from me as Paul set down my fresh beer. One gulp and it was half gone because drunk was good. The only way I was going to enjoy tonight was if I got hammered.

Goddamn it, Bryce. This was her fault. She'd ruined Saturdays for me.

She'd been on my mind often over the past couple of weeks. At the garage, I'd be working on an oil change and wonder what she was doing. I'd fall asleep at night, missing the touch of her skin. I came to town early on Sundays and Wednesdays to grab a paper from the grocery store the minute they opened.

Her articles were the only ones I read. Each time, I expected to see something about me, Dad or the Gypsies on the front page, but I guess we weren't big news anymore. Still, I'd read every word she'd written, needing that connection.

Last night, I'd been so hungry after work, I'd almost gone to her house. I'd been tempted to wait on her porch until she got home. Flash her a smile and beg her to cook me dinner. Except we'd ended things, so I'd gone home to peanut butter and jelly instead.

I'd forget about her soon enough, right? It was better for us to go our separate ways.

Or it should have been.

Until she'd ruined Saturdays. Until she'd ruined The Betsy.

The only comfortable stool in the bar was *this* stool, the same one she'd been on the day I'd found her here. The Betsy was normally a place I'd come to hang out with other people. Be social. Only everyone here irritated me. They weren't as much fun to talk to as I'd remembered, not when compared to talking with Bryce. And there wasn't a woman in the room who held any allure.

I chugged the rest of my beer and waved at Paul for a refill. One swift nod and thirty seconds later, I had a fresh Guinness. His fast service *almost* made up for the fact that I'd caught him eyeing Bryce's tits.

"What are you doing over here?" Leo slapped his hand over my shoulder, pushing himself between me and the guy sitting on my right. He turned backward, a smile on his face as he scanned the bar. He winked at a woman walking by. Gave a table in the corner a chin jerk.

That used to be me. The king of this bar. This was my happy place.

Then Bryce ruined it all with her sexy smile and shiny hair. She'd ruined me.

I slugged down my entire beer with three huge gulps and let out a burp. "Paul." I smacked my hand on the bar. "Whiskey this time."

"You're in a shit mood," Leo muttered. "Come on over and play a game. I'll let you beat me."

"Pass."

"Brother." Leo angled his shoulder into me to speak low. "Cheer up. Take home the blond in the corner. She'll make you feel better. Or at least let her suck you off in the bathroom."

"Not interested." The only woman whose lips belonged wrapped around my cock was a beautiful reporter.

"I give up on you." Leo frowned, then waved Paul over. "Don't cut him off. I'll make sure he gets home."

The beer was going right to my head, thank fuck, and I nodded to Leo. "Thanks."

"Hey, Dash." A delicate hand slid up my thigh and I spun away from Leo to see the blond who'd been in the corner. "How's it going? Haven't seen you around for a couple weeks."

"It's good." I dropped a hand over hers before it could reach my zipper. "You?"

The blond didn't get a chance to answer.

A hand fisted the back of my T-shirt, pulling it tight across my neck. Before I could turn and see who it was, that hand gave a hard yank and I flew backward off the stool. If not for Leo's quick reflexes, I'd be sprawled on my ass on the dirty bar floor.

I found my balance, righting myself, and stood to face the person who was about to get his ass kicked. But the face I met was not one I'd be punching. "Bryce, what—"

"Goddamn you." Her hands slammed into my chest, shoving me back against the stool.

Leo kept his grip on my arm so I wouldn't fall. Or maybe he'd thought I'd go after her.

I wasn't a fan of being pushed around, but damn, I was glad to see her. Bryce's face was full of rage, her cheeks red and eyes blazing. She was a furious knockout.

Surging forward, I ignored the anger rolling off her in waves and wrapped my arms around her, crushing her to my chest.

"Get your damn hands off me." She pushed and squirmed, trying to break free.

But I held her tighter, burying my nose in her hair. It smelled like sugar, overpowering the stale beer on the floor and secondhand smoke wafting in from the front door.

"Dash," she snapped, the sound muffled in my chest. "Let me go, you asshole."

"Miss me?" I chuckled. The smile on my face hurt from not using it lately. "I gotta say, babe, I really like that you're jealous."

"Jealous?" She froze in my arms. "You think I care about the blond? Fuck her brains out for all I care."

227

"Huh?" I let her go. "Fuck her brains out?"

I'd given her just enough space for her to wind up and slap me across the face. *Smack.*

What the fuck was happening right now?

"You're a lying bastard," she seethed. "You might have fooled me twice but it will *never* happen again. I'm not playing your game anymore. No matter what it takes, I'm going to do everything in my power to bring you all to your knees." With that, she spun and stormed out of the bar.

I blinked twice, dazed as the eyes around the room all landed on me. Bringing a hand up, I rubbed at the cheek she'd likely turned red. Then I looked over my shoulder at Leo. "Did that just happen?"

"Damn." He was staring at the door, a huge grin spread over his face. "She's a firecracker, that one. If you don't marry her, I will."

"Go to hell." I flipped him off, then bolted for the door. "Bryce!"

The parking lot was packed. There were cars and bikes everywhere. And no sign of Bryce, until the flash of head-lights caught my eye in the distance.

I took off, sprinting for the one and only exit from the lot. It wasn't easy after the beer, but I pushed my legs hard, my boots pounding on the cracked asphalt. I made it just in time to stand in the middle of the road as Bryce's Audi came skid-ding to a halt inches from my knees.

She rolled down her window. "Move."

"No." I planted both hands on the hood. "What was that about?"

"Seriously? Don't play dumb."

"Help me out here, babe. I'm drunk. You came in there

and I was just so happy to see you. Then you tossed out a bunch of shit that made my head spin. I just did a dead sprint and I'm pretty sure my heart might explode. If I collapse, don't run me over."

"This isn't a joke!" she screamed. Her frustration filled the night air. When she swiped at a tear, my heart clenched. "You lied to me. Again. And I fucking fell for it."

My stomach knotted. Something bad had happened. Something serious. And I hadn't a clue what it could be other than the yearbook picture. But that wasn't a big enough deal for this reaction, was it?

"Come out and talk to me." I held up my hands, retreating from the car. "Please."

She kept her hands on the wheel, her eyes drifting to her rearview mirror. Ten seconds passed and I was certain she was debating running me over. But finally, she dropped her chin and put the car in park.

She stepped out, wearing a pair of tight jeans and heels. Her gray blouse was wrinkled, like she'd slept in it or been wearing it since dawn.

I stayed back as she leaned on the car, crossing her arms. "Why did you lie?"

"I didn't lie to you." Unless. *Shit.* The yearbook photo. Had Bryce figured out that Mom and Amina had been best friends?

"There's another one right there." She rolled her eyes. "Drop the act."

"Woman, what are you on?"

"She looks like you. It took me a minute to figure it out, but you have the same hair and the same nose."

"Who?" How many drinks had Paul given me? Because

she wasn't making any sense. Was she talking about Mom? I didn't have Mom's hair. I had Dad's. "Who are you talking about?"

"Your sister."

My sister? "I don't have a sister."

"This is a waste of time." She spun away from the car, going for the handle. "All I'm going to get are more lies."

With a burst of speed, I ran to her side, trapping her against the car before she could open the door. Any buzz I'd had inside was gone. The truth in her voice sobered me right up.

What the hell had she found?

"I don't have a sister," I repeated.

She twisted and I let her have enough room to turn. Her face was hard, pure stone one second. Then the anger disappeared. It fell away as her eyes got wide and a hand came up to her mouth. "Oh my God," she whispered. "You didn't know."

"Know what?" I demanded. "What did you do?"

She gulped. "I went to see Amina's daughter in Denver. I flew out this morning and just got back. I talked to her for hours. About her mom and her childhood. And . . ."

"Keep going," I growled when she paused.

"I asked about her father, but she didn't know anything about him. All Amina had told her was that he was called *Prez.* I think . . . I'm fairly certain that Draven is her father. She's your sister."

No. I staggered away, shaking my head. "No. It's not possible."

"Maybe that was why Amina came here to meet with Draven. To discuss their daughter. It makes sense."

"No way. If I had a sister, I'd know." I balled my hands

into fists, pacing in front of her. Could I have a sister? Dad had been a different man after Mom had died. Maybe he'd gotten Amina knocked up sometime after the funeral.

"How old is she?"

"Twenty-six."

All the air escaped my lungs and I couldn't breathe. Dropping my hands to my knees, I struggled to stay off the ground. Mom had died when I was twelve. I'd been a middle-school kid riding home in my older brother's car to find my mother dead. To find her blood soaking the front sidewalk next to a plastic tray of yellow flowers.

If this sister was twenty-six, then she was nine years younger than me. Three years old when my mother had been ripped away from us. *Three.*

"No. Impossible." Mom and Dad were hopelessly in love. Always. I couldn't remember a time that they'd fought. I couldn't remember a night when Dad had slept on the couch because he'd pissed her off.

"Dash, she could—"

"No!" I roared. "Dad wouldn't have cheated on Mom. It's. Fucking. Impossible."

Bryce kept her mouth shut, but there was judgment in her eyes. She was sure Dad was a murdering cheat. And I'd defend him to the end.

"Get in the car." I walked around the front of her car, ripping the passenger door open. When Bryce didn't move, I bellowed across the roof, "Get in the car!"

Her body jerked into action. She spun around, getting in and strapping on her seat belt. I climbed in too, not bothering with a belt.

"Drive."

She nodded, putting the car in gear. But before she let off the brake, she looked at me. "I'm sorry. I thought you knew."

"There's nothing to know." I stared out the window, my hands gripping my thighs. Every ounce of my willpower went to not putting my fist through the glass.

Bryce's hand stretched across the console. "Dash—"

"Don't. Touch. Me."

Her hand snapped back to the wheel.

I didn't want comfort. I didn't want the smooth heat of her skin on mine. I didn't want to believe a word that had come out of her mouth.

She was wrong. She was dead wrong. And I'd prove it to her. Tonight.

"Drive," I ordered again.

"Where?"

"Right."

Bryce silently followed my one-word directions through town until we turned onto the quiet street of my childhood. I pointed to the curb in front of Dad's house and she pulled over. Without a word, we got out of the car and she trailed behind me to the side door.

Five punishing knocks and a light flipped on inside.

Dad made his way to the door to unlock it. "Dash?"

I pushed past him inside, marching into the kitchen.

Mom's kitchen.

The one where she'd cooked us meals every day. Where she'd packed our lunches into aluminum boxes with cartoons on the front and filled our thermoses with chocolate milk. Where she'd kissed Dad every evening and asked him about his day.

Impossible. Dad had loved Mom with every ounce of his being. He'd never cheat on her. Bryce was wrong and I wanted her to stand witness, to hear the truth in his voice when he denied having a daughter.

Dad came into the kitchen, his eyes squinting as they adjusted to the light. He was shirtless, wearing only a pair of plaid pajama pants.

Bryce slipped in behind him, choosing to stand against the refrigerator. If she was scared, she didn't show it. If she was doubting herself, she didn't show that either.

Fuck her. She didn't know. She didn't know that I'd grown up with two people who loved one another more than life. That Dad had almost died of a broken heart when Mom had been killed.

"What's going on?" Dad asked.

"I want the truth." My chest heaved and I fought to keep my voice steady. "And you're going to give it to me."

He stood motionless. Calm. "The truth about what, son?"

"Bryce went to see Amina's daughter."

Dad's eyes closed and his chin dropped.

No.

Dad always hung his head whenever he disappointed his sons.

"It's true then? She's your daughter?" A slight nod and I flew across the room, my fist colliding with his cheek. A crack filled the kitchen and Bryce let out a small scream as she jumped. "You're dead to me."

Without another word, I marched out of the room. The walls were closing in on me. I flew through the mudroom and burst outside, gasping for breath in the night air.

A hand, gentle and light, landed on my spine. "I'm sorry."

"She loved him. And he . . ." My throat closed on the

words. I couldn't say it. I couldn't believe Dad had cheated on Mom.

My mother had put up with so much shit from him. And it had cost her her life. Meanwhile, the man I'd loved, the man I'd looked up to, had gotten her best friend from high school pregnant.

Mom and Amina's fallout made sense now. They hadn't drifted apart. Did Mom know? Or had Dad kept Amina and his daughter from all of us?

"Fuck." I stood and walked to Bryce's car, her footsteps echoing behind.

Inside her car, she didn't utter a word as she drove away.

I dropped my head, shoving my hands in my hair. "I have to tell Nick."

After years, my brother and Dad finally had a decent relationship. One phone call and I'd destroy it all over again.

"I'm sorry. I'm so sorry," Bryce chanted over the steering wheel. Her eyes were glued to the road ahead. "I thought you knew. I thought you were lying to me and covering up for your dad. I would have handled it differently. I *should* have handled it differently."

"You're not the one who cheated on his wife and just lost the respect of his son."

Her shoulders fell. "I'm still sorry."

"Not your fault." My hand drifted to her shoulder and she tensed. *Shit.* Was she scared of me? I was angry, but not at her. "Sorry. For earlier."

"Don't worry about it." Bryce relaxed. "I always figured you had a temper. And I'm a big girl. I can handle a man yelling at me. Just don't make it a habit."

"I won't." I didn't want Bryce to ever fear me. I watched the road as she drove toward The Betsy, but when we got there, she didn't slow. She blew right past the bar. "Where are we going?"

Bryce gave me a small smile as she turned into the parking lot of Stockyard's, a bar two blocks down from The Betsy known for its greasy food. "Are you hungry? I'm starving. All I had for lunch were cookies."

CHAPTER EIGHTEEN

BRYCE

"I like it here." Dash looked around the dim bar, holding a huge cheeseburger in his hands. "I haven't been here in ages. It's so much quieter than The Betsy. Food's damn good too."

"So good." I took another enormous bite of my burger and moaned.

My parents loved Stockyard's. It was more their speed than a seedy ruckus bar like The Betsy. It catered to the low-key crowd in Clifton Forge with its subtle music and an abundance of tables for people to sit and visit. It was no surprise that, at nearly midnight, the place was mostly empty.

I figured the only reason they stayed open late was because it was the only place in town to serve food this late. They'd probably get a rush from The Betsy soon, drunks looking for a heavy meal to combat the alcohol. And then, of course, they were open to serve the poker players at the table along the back. Seven men sat hunched over their chips as a young redhead with a pretty smile dealt their cards.

Dash's back was to them, but every ten minutes, he'd glance over his shoulder, throwing a glare across the distance of the room.

"Not a fan of poker?" I asked after another one of his scowls.

"The one in the gray hoodie is Presley's fiancé, Jeremiah." He frowned. "She's probably sittin' at home alone while he's here losing money and getting loaded. Guy's a tool but she puts up with his shit."

"And I'm guessing she doesn't like it when you express that opinion."

"Not much." He shook his head. "We've all tried to talk to her but it always ends in a fight. So now we keep quiet. At least, we will until they actually decide to get married. Then we'll all gang up on her."

"An intervention?" I laughed. "Good luck with that. You'll have to tell me how it goes."

From my brief encounter with Presley at the garage, I imagined she was the type who'd make up her own mind. Telling her *no* would probably work about as well as it did on me.

Dash and I didn't speak as we finished our meals. Since we'd come in and ordered, neither of us had spoken about what had happened at Draven's house. But with every bite swallowed, it was coming. What had happened couldn't be ignored forever.

With rumpled and grease-stained napkins tossed over the few remaining french fries on our plates, Dash's gaze met mine. "So . . ."

"So. Want to talk about it?"

He ran a hand over the stubble of his jaw. "Can't believe he'd do that to Mom. She was amazing. This carefree, loving woman. She didn't deserve a cheating husband. God, I hope she never knew. That she died thinking he was faithful."

"Can I ask how she died?"

"She was killed outside the house." He leaned his elbows on the table, speaking in a low voice full of pain. "We found her, me and Nick."

My hand came to my sternum. It was unimaginable. Heartbreaking. I wanted to hold Dash, but for now, I settled for a whispered, "I'm sorry."

"Nick was sixteen and had a car. I begged him to give me a ride home from school that day so I didn't have to ride the bus. He was pissed because there was this girl he was chasing and she wanted him to drive her around. But he took me home instead. He always put me first, our family first. Even as a teenager. We got home and saw Mom lying on her side on the sidewalk. She'd been gardening, wearing the gloves I bought her for Mother's Day."

I put my hand over Dash's, holding tight.

He turned his over, threading his fingers with mine. "There was another club in Montana who'd been causing the Gypsies some trouble. They were called the Travelers. Dad and the club had plenty of petty beefs with them over the years, but it had been nothing too serious. Nothing dangerous. Then Dad and the club got aggressive about expanding. They took on more drug routes to up the club's income, even poached some from other clubs. The Travelers didn't like losing and made some threats. Dad dismissed them, not taking them seriously. Until they took it further."

"They came after your mom."

He nodded. "Drove up to our home. Shot her in the back of the head while she was planting yellow flowers. You couldn't even recognize her face. The bullet just tore through her."

My hand tightened around his and I closed my eyes. The cheeseburger wasn't sitting well, not when I imagined myself in Dash's shoes. Finding your mother's dead body was a horror no child should have to see.

"Dash, I'm . . . I'm so sorry."

"Me too." He stayed quiet for a few minutes, his eyes on the table. Even when the bartender came by to take our plates and refill our waters, he didn't move. He just held my hand until it was the two of us alone. "Dad and the Gypsies killed all of their members. Every last one."

I opened my mouth to respond but I didn't have the words. It was hard to fathom that kind of murder and violence. Hard to see Dash in that life. And at the same time, I was glad he, Nick and even Draven, had gotten their vengeance. It wasn't black and white, this world he'd pulled me into. There wasn't a clear-cut line between right and wrong, not like I'd believed before.

He looked up from the table and adjusted his grip on my hand, wrapping it up completely. "We aren't good men, Bryce."

"Maybe. But you're a good man to me."

"You sure about that? I got you thrown in jail. Haven't always treated you right. Yelled at you tonight."

I locked my eyes with his. "I'm sure."

Dash loved the people in his life. He was loyal and kind. He enjoyed pushing my buttons, but he'd never once pushed too hard. When he had crossed a line, they'd all been forgivable acts. And an apology hadn't been long to follow.

Even the whole jail thing.

Because had our roles been reversed, I probably would

have done the same to him. I wouldn't admit it anytime soon, but I'd pardoned him for it all.

After paying the check, Dash and I made our way out into the dark night.

"Where to?" I asked as we walked to my car.

"Mind if I crash at your place?"

I fished the keys from my purse. "I'm punching you in the ribs if you snore."

He chuckled. "I don't snore."

————

MY ALARM BLARED me awake at four in the morning. I scurried to shut it off and not wake Dash.

The man was sprawled on his stomach, his face turned away from me. But his hand was on the small of my back. His thumb moved, rubbing a tiny circle. "It's early."

"I have to go to the paper and make sure everything gets out for delivery," I said, sliding out of bed.

Dad was probably already at the newspaper, bright-eyed and smiling. I was anxious to join him. Sunday and Wednesday mornings were the two days I didn't want to linger in bed.

Though today, with Dash here, I was tempted.

I took an efficient shower and swiped on the minimum makeup to hide the dark circles under my eyes. Staying up past midnight on a Saturday wasn't something I'd normally do. But last night had been an exception. To a lot of things.

Dressed in a pair of jeans, tennis shoes and a T-shirt, I walked toward the bedroom door, ready for coffee, but hesitated when I glimpsed Dash. Should I say goodbye? Or just leave?

He was probably asleep. Not snoring now that I was on my way out.

"Bryce."

"Yeah?" I whispered.

"Come here."

I tiptoed around the bed, bending low. "What?"

"Kiss," he ordered with his eyes closed. Those dark lashes were lying perfectly on his cheek.

I smiled, putting my hand on his forehead to push his mussed hair away before dropping my lips to his temple. "Bye."

It was impossible to keep the smile off my face as I drove to the newspaper. Even with only a few hours of sleep, I was rested and fresh.

Dash and I had fallen into my bed last night, emotionally exhausted and full. He hadn't made a move for sex. Neither of us had. He'd slept in his boxers. I'd pulled on a tank top and shorts. Then, with his hand slipped underneath the hem of my shirt, we'd fallen asleep.

His palm had stayed warm on my skin all night.

He'd probably be gone when I returned home. Dash had been hit by an emotional steamroller last night and needed time to work it all out. I only hoped he knew he could turn to me if he needed a sympathetic ear.

Last night, things had moved way past my story. This wasn't about me anymore. Or Amina Daylee. Or Genevieve. Or even Draven. This was about Dash.

My feelings for him could no longer be ignored. When Dad asked me for a story on the Tin Gypsies, I'd tell him a lie. There wasn't one worth printing.

A story wasn't worth breaking Dash's heart. He'd had enough of that in his life. He wouldn't get more from me.

Coming through the rear entrance to the pressroom, I found Dad standing by the Goss. "Hi, Dad."

"How's my girl?" he asked as I kissed his cheek.

"Good. How's it looking?"

He handed over the sample paper in his hands. "We're about done. I've got one last run here. BK is working on the bundles."

Scanning the front page, I smiled at the last of Willy's articles about the railroad travelers. People had loved his segment, me included.

"It couldn't have turned out better," I told Dad. "I'll go help out BK."

After an hour of bundling papers and organizing them into stacks, we greeted the delivery drivers in the loading dock. Five parents with their five kids pulled into the parking lot about the same time. They'd be driving papers through town and the surrounding areas this morning.

Most of our subscribers would have their news before seven.

"What are you up to for the rest of the day?" Dad asked as he shut off a row of lights in the pressroom. BK had left already, making a few of his own deliveries before going home.

"Not much. I need to do laundry," I grumbled. "What about you?"

"A nap. Then your mom wants to go out to Stockyard's for dinner. You're welcome to come along."

"Thanks. We'll see." Which we both knew meant *no*.

I was cheeseburgered out. The thought of another made my stomach roll. The coffee I'd guzzled while bundling papers wasn't sitting well either, probably from all the heavy food right before bed.

When I got home, I was going to make myself a piece of dry toast and hoped that it would soak up some of the residual grease.

"I have a couple new story ideas I want to run by you. Will you be in tomorrow?"

"Of course. By eight at the latest. We can talk about them then." He hugged me and I waved as I walked for the door. "Bryce."

"Yeah?" I turned.

"You've been quiet about the Tin Gypsies. Did you really give that up?"

"Turns out, there isn't much to tell." It was a relief. Dad wouldn't pressure me to write the story, but by telling him I was letting it go, it gave me permission to do just that.

"All right. And the murder investigation? Has Marcus released anything new?"

"Not lately. I doubt there will be much until the trial. I'd like to do a memorial piece about Amina Daylee, but I think it's too soon after the murder." Too much was up in the air. "I'd like to give it some time."

"Okay. Then I guess we'll print happy news for a while. Not a bad thing."

I smiled. "No, it's not."

"See you tomorrow."

"Bye, Dad." I waved again, then emerged outside, savoring the heat from the morning sun on my face. It was a strange time for a nap, but as I drove home, a wave of exhaustion crashed into me hard and I knew the second I made it home, I was going back to bed.

Toast would have to wait until I was fully awake.

With my car parked in the garage, I walked into the house, half asleep.

"Ahh!" I screamed. I clutched my heart, hoping it would stop trying to break free. "What are you doing?"

Dash dropped the towel he'd folded on top of the stack of others. "Laundry."

"I thought you'd be gone."

"Took a shower but couldn't find a towel in the bathroom. So I went searching and got one from a laundry basket. Decided to fold that one. Then I found another. And another."

"What can I say. I loathe folding laundry."

He grinned. "Figured that out two baskets ago, baby."

I walked deeper into the room, plopping down on the arm of the couch as Dash folded another towel. "What are you really doing here? Because it's not folding my laundry."

"Hiding."

"Hiding," I repeated.

"Yeah." He picked up the basket, now full of folded clothes, and set it aside. "Can I hide here?"

The vulnerability in his voice twisted my heart. "Of course."

"Thanks." Dash came to stand in front of me, his feet bare on the rug, and lifted his hands to frame my face. "Kiss."

"You're demanding today."

He dropped his lips to mine. "You like it."

As his tongue swept across my lips, the swell of heat in my core proved his point. I opened my mouth, letting him sweep inside. His taste consumed my mouth and my hands reached for his hips, pulling him closer.

He stepped between my legs, using his own to push them wide. Then he leaned down and forced me back on my perch, keeping his grip firm on my face.

Our mouths twisted and turned, battling one another for

more. The temperature in the room spiked and I ached to feel my bare skin against his. The weeks since I'd had him inside me had been far too long, and the need to feel him was overwhelming. Panting and searching for more to stoke the fire burning, I gripped at his T-shirt and pulled him on top of me.

He ripped his lips away, grabbing me by the hips and spinning us both, so he was sitting on the couch and I straddled his lap. Dash's erection, thick and hard beneath his zipper rubbed against my core.

"Off." I yanked at his shirt, dragging it up his body as he worked the button and zipper free on my jeans.

"Are you wet for me?" He slipped his hand into my panties, finding my slippery folds with his middle finger. A grin spread across his face as I gasped at that finger curving inside.

"Yes," I moaned, closing my eyes and letting my head lull sideways. "I missed you."

I'd missed more than just his body, but I kept that thought to myself.

Dash's lips sucked at my neck, kissing and licking as his free hand tugged at the collar of my tee. "Missed you too."

He was most definitely talking about sex. But in the corners of my heart, I pretended it was something more.

His hand between my legs tormented, teased, until I was nearly breathless. But I didn't want to come around his fingers. Digging for the strength in my wobbling knees to stand, I climbed off his lap, shoving my jeans and panties to the floor.

I whipped off my shirt and by the time I looked back at Dash, he'd pulled his own jeans down his hips and his shirt was off. Those ripped abs were bunched and his hand was fisted around his pulsing shaft, a condom in place.

I straddled his waist, taking his face in my hands. "Damn, you're sexy."

"I know." He grinned as I kissed the corner of his mouth.

That arrogance should have been a turnoff, but the man had a mirror. And he knew what he did to me.

Dash positioned himself beneath my entrance, and as I slowly sank down, I sheathed him. The stretch, that incredible fill, sent a shudder down my spine and I nearly orgasmed right then.

"Fuck," Dash groaned, the cords of his neck straining as I lifted up before sinking down again. "You've ruined me."

The laundry he'd folded tumbled from the couch as we got lost in the frenzy. I rode him hard until my muscles weakened and my pace slowed. Dash took over, smashing our chests together as he repositioned us, me on my back with my legs spread wide. Him between me, powerful and in control.

The sheer masculinity of his arms and legs amazed me as he braced himself, thrusting his hips over and over until I came undone. My orgasm washed over me in hard, long waves until I was limp.

Dash came not long after, pouring himself free as the ridges of his chest and abs flexed. I had definitely gone too long without that view. It was mine. All mine. For just a little bit longer.

"It just gets better," he panted into my hair as he collapsed on top of me. Then he dropped a swift kiss on my neck and stood, sliding out. "Be right back."

While he went to deal with the condom, I worked to catch my breath. There was a charged feeling under my skin.

An electricity. I'd been so tired when I'd come home, but now I wanted more.

Dash came back into the living room, holding out a hand to help me from the couch. The moment I was on my feet, I reached between us for his cock. Maybe he'd be up for round two.

"Not yet." He grinned, taking my hand away. "I'm out of condoms."

"Oh." My spirits fell. "I don't have any."

"I'll run out and get some later. Like to have my own anyway."

He liked to have his own? I blinked, unsure I'd heard him correctly. "What exactly does that mean? Because it kind of sounded like you need condoms to use with someone other than me."

And that was absolutely not going to work.

"What? No, babe." He took my face in his hands and kissed my forehead. "You're it. But I watched one of my brothers in the club get a girl pregnant because she'd fucked with the condom. I've always made it a habit to provide them myself."

"I'm not some lying, manipulative—"

"Stop." He kissed me again. "Know that's not you. But I still buy the condoms."

"Fine." I huffed, stepping out of his hold and walking down the hallway to my bedroom. It hurt that he didn't trust me enough to provide protection, that I was no different than any other woman he'd slept with.

"Don't be mad." Dash caught me in the hall, wrapping me in his arms. "Not saying any of this to hurt you. I just don't want kids. Don't see myself as a father. Never have."

Why was I drawn to such an emotionally unavailable

man? This wasn't the first time I'd been with a man who was terrified of commitment. Why did I seem to find men who thought the idea of a family was a death sentence?

"It's fine," I muttered, unable to hide the irritation in my voice. It wasn't his fault. He was only being honest. The problem wasn't Dash. It was me. "I'm just tired."

Emotionally and physically.

He let me go. "Let's crash for a while."

And forget this conversation ever happened. What did it matter if he didn't want kids? We weren't on that path, so it was best to forget this whole thing. Maybe this was more than just sex. But that didn't mean we were a couple. I might be his temporary hiding place—that didn't mean we had a future.

Dash followed me to the bedroom, and I climbed under the sheets, facing away from him. But instead of giving me my space, he took me in his arms, positioned me on his chest and stroked my hair until, bruised hearts and all, we both fell asleep.

———

WE WOKE hours later as the sun streamed into the room, though neither of us made a move to get up. I stayed draped over his chest as his fingers drew patterns on the small of my back.

"I don't know how I'm going to tell Nick," Dash said into my hair.

"About . . ." *Genevieve.* I left her name unspoken, suspecting it would only irritate him. Dash wasn't ready to learn about his half sister, wonderful as she was.

"Yeah. About . . . her." He sighed. "Nick and Dad had

this falling out after Mom died. Took years for them to work it out. The shit that happened, with Emmeline almost getting kidnapped, brought them back together. This will destroy them all over again. Dad'll lose his son and his grandkids this time too. Nick won't forgive him."

I lifted up to see his eyes. They were golden in the dim light. Captivating. Sad. "Maybe before you call Nick, you should get the whole story."

"No." He frowned. "I can't talk to Dad."

"You will have to at some point." Unless Draven went to prison for killing Amina. Then Dash might be able to avoid his father. But in the end, he'd regret it. "Don't do it for him. Do it to get answers. And then you can decide what to do about Nick."

He blew out a long breath. I expected him to take some time to think over my suggestion, but one moment I was sinking on his exhale, and the next I was being toppled to the side as he flew off the bed. "Let's go."

"Now?"

"Now. And you're coming with me."

"Me? Why? I think it would be better if this was just you and your dad." I'd already intruded on last night's kitchen scene.

"You need to be there to stop me if I try to kill him."

I shot him a glare. "Not funny, Dash."

"Then . . . will you be there for me?" He held out a hand. "Please?"

249

CHAPTER NINETEEN

DASH

"I s this the house where you grew up?" Bryce pulled into Dad's driveway.

It wasn't really the question she was asking. She wanted to know if this was where Mom had died.

I glanced at the sidewalk. "Yeah."

"Oh." She put the car in park. "I thought maybe you would have moved. After . . ."

"No. Dad thought it would show weakness."

Her mouth fell open. "What?"

"That's what he told us anyway. But really, I think he stayed because he couldn't fathom the idea of living somewhere else. He bought this house for Mom a few years after they were married."

This was the house where they had loved. Where they'd brought Nick and me home from the hospital. Where they'd made our family.

The house was painted a soft green. The trim was maroon and matched the front door. Dad had had it repainted a few years ago because it was starting to chip.

He'd told the painters to pick the exact same colors because those were the colors Mom had picked four decades prior.

"She's in the walls," I told Bryce. "The floors and rooms and hallways. That's why he couldn't leave. It's not *her* house. The house *is* her."

"He loves her."

I nodded. "Above anything else, she was precious to him. At least, I thought so. Now . . . I'm not sure."

Maybe I didn't know Dad at all. The father I'd admired wouldn't have cheated on his wife.

Why? It didn't make sense. When Dad loved Mom so much, why would he take another woman? How could he do that to her?

We sat for a few moments because I couldn't bring myself to reach for the handle on the door. I was so angry on behalf of my mother, who I missed every damn day.

How could he?

"Dash." Bryce placed her hand on my knee. "I can hear the questions popping into your mind. Ask him. Get your answers."

She looked at the house and I followed her gaze. Dad was standing in the front window, watching as I debated whether or not to get out of the car. Even from a distance and through the glass, I could see a gash on his cheek. I'd hit him harder than I'd thought. Made sense because my knuckles were killing me today.

I'd never hit my father before. Never would have dreamed of it.

Or, I had.

I blew out a deep breath. Bryce was right. I had to get some answers. "Let's go."

We exited the car in unison, and I took her hand,

marching us to the side door. I didn't knock. We found Dad waiting on the leather couch in the living room.

Without a word, I sat in a chair across from him. Bryce took the other in the room. The pair used to match the couch, but Mom had had them reupholstered a few months before she'd died to a deep green. They were ugly as sin, but the second Dad was ready to get replacements, I was taking these two chairs home.

Dad's eyes were red rimmed and his skin pale. That gash was a lot worse up close and could probably use a couple of stitches. His salt and pepper hair was a mess, oily and in need of a good shampoo.

While I'd somehow managed to fall asleep in Bryce's bed last night, Dad looked like he hadn't slept a wink.

"I want to know why." I broke the silence, wanting to talk first. This visit wasn't for Dad; he didn't deserve to run the show. "I want to know why you did this to her."

"It was a mistake." Dad's voice cracked. "Your mother and Amina were friends. Best friends."

Bryce stiffened, her face snapping my way. "Did you know that?"

Yes. I stayed quiet. If I told her about that stupid yearbook picture, she'd get pissed and leave. I *needed* Bryce for this today. Having her here provided a buffer. I'd keep my temper in check with her in the room. I couldn't risk her finding out and leaving me to deal with Dad alone.

Dad's gaze held mine. He knew I was lying by omission, but there was no way he'd speak up, not when he knew my white lie was nothing compared to the sins he'd committed.

"Keep going," I ordered.

"We spent a lot of time together, the three of us. Your mom never left Amina out. She loved Amina."

That love was apparently one-sided if her best friend had slept with her husband.

"I didn't know." Dad hung his head. "I didn't see it. I think maybe your mom did and that was why she began to put some distance between her and Amina their senior year. But I didn't see it."

"See what?" I asked.

"Amina was in love with you," Bryce guessed.

Dad nodded. "She was my friend. That's all it ever was for me. I've never loved another woman other than Chrissy."

"Then how could you fuck her friend and get her pregnant?" My fists pounded on my knees.

Bryce's hand stretched across the space between our chairs, covering one of my fists. Thank fuck, she'd come with me today. I already wanted to leave. But her hand held firm, keeping me in my seat.

"Amina left Clifton Forge after high school. Didn't think much of it when she and your mom stopped talking for a couple of years. Figured they'd drifted apart. But then Amina called her one random afternoon. Came to visit and spent the weekend in town. They came to party at the clubhouse one night."

"And that was when—"

"No." Dad shook his head. "Not then. Amina went back to Denver. But after that first trip, she came back every year. Always in the summer. Always for a weekend. She'd come party at the clubhouse, get drunk, hook up. You boys were young and the clubhouse wasn't really your mom's scene anymore. Wasn't really mine either, truthfully. But Amina was single so we didn't think much of it."

The story was progressing, and my skin was crawling. But I kept my jaw screwed shut.

"Chrissy and I hit a rough patch. You and Nick were boys then. My God, we fought. All the time. Every day."

"When? I don't remember you ever fighting."

"She hid it." He dragged a hand through his hair. "She put a smile on when you both were home because she didn't want you to know. We'd tolerate one another and then duke it out when you and Nick were asleep. She didn't like how things were going with the club, we were taking risks and I was keeping stuff from her. It got so bad, she kicked me out."

"But you always lived here." I would have remembered if he'd moved out.

"You were only eight. Nick was twelve. We told you both I was going on a run. A long one. And I spent three weeks living at the clubhouse."

Now that trip, I remembered. Dad had never been gone so long before and Mom was sad. Because she missed him. Guess there was more to it.

"You missed my go-cart race. I was mad at you for being gone because I won and you didn't see me win." I scoffed. "But you were in town the whole time."

"I watched you win that race from behind a pair of binoculars about a hundred yards away."

"You lied to us."

He nodded. "Because your mom asked me to."

"You don't get to blame *anything* on her," I snapped. "Ever."

Dad held up a hand. "I'm not. This is on me. All of it."

"So while you were living at the clubhouse, Amina came up for a visit," Bryce said.

"Yeah. We had a party. The pair of us got drunk and high. Things are hazy but I took her to bed. The next morning, I woke up and knew I'd made a horrible mistake. Told her the same. She started crying and confessed to being in love with me. Amina hated herself for it. She loved Chrissy too."

Who the fuck cared about Amina? She didn't get to love Dad. He wasn't hers to love. And she sure as hell didn't love Mom, not if she'd fuck her friend's husband. For the first time, I couldn't find it in myself to feel sorry that Amina had been stabbed to death.

And I'd never forgive Dad for doing this to Mom.

"I hate you for this."

Dad let out a dry laugh. "Son, I've hated myself for twenty-six years."

"And Mom? Did she hate you too? Because you came home. You seemed happy. Or was that all bullshit?"

"I came back. Got on my knees and begged your mom to let me come home."

"She forgave you?" My eyes bulged. "No way."

Dad's face paled as his eyes filled with tears.

"You never told her," Bryce whispered. "She never knew."

"She never knew." His voice was hoarse. Thick. "Amina and I both promised to keep it quiet. She knew it would crush Chrissy, so she went home to Denver and didn't come back. It ate at me. I'd finally decided to confess. To come clean. But then . . ."

"She was murdered." My voice was flat and lifeless, like my mother's body alone in her grave.

"I let your mother down in every way possible." A tear fell down his face. "I've wished for years I'd had the courage to tell her about Amina because then she would have left me. She should have left me, then she wouldn't have been planting flowers that day. But I was a coward, scared to lose her."

"You lost her anyway."

Another tear fell, dripping down his cheek and into the beard he'd grown since the arrest. "My silence was the biggest mistake of my life."

My throat burned and my heart broke. What would have happened if he'd told her the truth? Would Mom still be alive?

"What about your daughter?" Bryce asked. "She doesn't know about you."

"Because I didn't know about her. Not until Amina called me last month and asked me to meet her at the Evergreen Motel."

I closed my eyes, not wanting to hear any more. But I couldn't find the strength to stand. So I sat there, thinking of my beautiful mother and how unfair this was. All she'd done was love a selfish, cowardly man. And he'd destroyed her. He'd had a child with another woman.

"We talked about Genevieve that night," Dad said. "It took me a few hours to get my head wrapped around it, that I had a daughter. And I was furious that she'd kept it from me."

"But you fucked her?" *Again.* He'd fucked that bitch again.

He lowered his eyes as I fumed. It was like he'd spit on Mom's grave.

Bryce's hand on mine squeezed tight. "Did you do it, Draven? Did you kill her?"

I opened my eyes, locking my gaze on him. It would be so much easier if he said yes. Then he'd rot in a prison cell and I'd never think about my father again.

"No. I didn't kill her." It was the truth. "I calmed down and we talked for hours. Amina was sorry about keeping Genevieve away, but she was scared. She knew Chrissy had been killed. She knew being in my life could put her daughter at risk. So she stayed away."

"Why did she come back now?" Bryce asked.

"She said it was time her daughter knew her father. I think she got word the Gypsies had shut down and waited to make sure it was safe."

Safe. I surged from my chair and walked to the window. "Has it ever been safe?"

Both of the women who'd loved my father had died violent deaths. He hadn't stabbed Amina, but he'd killed her all the same. Like he'd killed Mom.

"You deserve to spend the rest of your life in prison," I said to the glass.

"No question," Dad replied instantly. "I do."

No matter how angry I was at him, I wouldn't let that happen. Not for Dad, but the rest of us. If someone was out to get Draven Slater, there was a very real possibility the rest of us were up next.

Besides, Dad should have to live in this house for the rest of his life. It was the prison of his own making. He could live out his years alone here, surrounded by the ghost of his dead wife. And no judge or jury would ever punish him the way he'd been punishing himself.

"Anything else?" I asked.

"No."

"Okay." I turned and walked away from the window, straight out of the room.

Bryce hesitated, but when I didn't pause, she hurried to catch up.

I was nearly to her car when Dad called my name. It wasn't from behind at the side door. He'd walked through the front door to stand on the porch.

Dad didn't utter another word. Instead, he fisted his hands and took the porch steps one at a time.

How long had it been since he'd walked those steps? On the last one, his foot hovered over the cement of the sidewalk, reluctant to put it down. When it landed, his boot was heavy and sluggish.

Slowly, painfully, Dad walked down the path toward the place where Mom had been. The last time I'd seen him on that sidewalk had been the worst day of my life.

Nick had rushed inside to call him. My brother's screams had been so loud and frantic, they'd carried outside to the street. I'd knelt by Mom's body, a scared boy crying and begging it to be a nightmare.

Dad had raced home from the garage. When he'd jumped off his bike, he'd come right to Mom, pushing me aside. Then he'd scooped her up into his arms and wailed, his heart broken.

Our lives broken.

The memory snuck up on me. The pain in my chest was unbearable, making my legs weak and my head dizzy. My arm shot out, searching for something to grab.

I found Bryce. She came right to my side, standing straight. She was my rock as Dad took one last step and dropped his head.

"I'm sorry," he whispered to the ground, then he looked at me. "I'm sorry."

"You never should have started the club." Words I never thought I'd say.

I hadn't blamed the club for Mom's death. Nick had. But

I hadn't. I'd blamed the man who'd pulled the trigger, the one Dad had promised me had been dealt a cruel, slow death.

Now? Now I wished I'd never been a Tin Gypsy.

"You're right." Dad nodded. "I never should have started the club."

At least it's gone now.

I let go of Bryce, turning my back on my father for the car.

She didn't make me wait. She jogged to the driver's side and got in, reversing out of the driveway and speeding down the street. Dad just stood in the same place on the sidewalk, staring at his feet like he could still see Mom's body there.

I leaned forward, dropping my head into my hands as I squeezed my eyes shut. My stomach churned. The pressure in my head was overpowering. White spots popped in my vision. The sharp sting in my head was like a dull dagger being pushed slowly into my temple.

Was this a panic attack? Anxiety? I'd never had either, but I was three seconds from puking in Bryce's car.

"Want me to pull over?" she asked.

"No. Drive." I swallowed hard. "Keep driving."

"Okay." Her hand came to my spine, rubbing up and down before returning it to the wheel.

I focused on the hum of the wheels against the blacktop, breathing deep to fight the emotions. Miles later, when I wasn't afraid I'd puke or cry or scream, I opened my mouth. "I miss Mom. She was so happy, and damn, she loved us. All of us. Even him."

Fuck. One tear slipped free and I swiped it away, refusing to let more fall.

"I wish he had told her."

"Yeah," I choked out.

"But since he didn't, I'm glad she never knew about Amina," Bryce said gently.

Part of me would have liked to see her kick Dad's ass for it. To leave him and punish him for being unfaithful. But it would have broken her heart. "Me too."

Bryce drove through town, going nowhere as she turned down one road, then the next. Finally, when I had pulled myself together, I asked, "Would you take me to my bike?"

"Sure. Are you feeling okay to ride?"

"Yeah. I'm not sure what that was. Strange feeling though."

She gave me a sad smile. "Grief, if I had to guess."

"Never goes away."

Bryce drove a few blocks until we were on Central Avenue and headed for The Betsy. "Genevieve didn't have a last name for Amina's boyfriend. We'll have to keep digging to find out who he is. If you even want to."

"You're assuming I don't want Dad to go to prison."

"I know you don't," she said. "You want the truth just as much as I do. Someone killed Amina, and that person deserves to be brought to justice."

"Agreed." I wouldn't let that person threaten my family. Nick and Emmeline. Their kids. Emmett and Leo. Presley. They were the only family that mattered now. "How do you want to go about finding the boyfriend?"

"Genevieve didn't have any pictures because I doubt Amina ever took them. Apparently, she didn't talk about him much. All Genevieve knew was his name, Lee."

"Genevieve." Her name tasted bitter.

I hated her already.

It wasn't logical, but emotions were gripping the handlebars today. Genevieve was no sister of mine. She was someone I'd do my best to forget was breathing.

"Yes, that's her name." Bryce frowned. "Before you condemn her for the actions of her parents, remember that she just lost her mother too. She's a sweet person. Kind and genuine."

"She means nothing."

"*She* is your half sister, like it or not. Before this is over, she's going to learn about Draven. About you. Right now, she thinks he's responsible for killing her only parent. How do you think she's going to feel when the man who she thinks murdered her mother is actually her father? Take it easy on Genevieve. She doesn't deserve your anger. She didn't do anything wrong."

"Jesus," I grumbled. "Do you always have to be so reasonable?"

"Yes."

I fought a grin. "So now what? The daughter—"

"Genevieve," she corrected.

"*Genevieve* is a dead end. What's next?"

"I don't know." She sighed. "Honestly, with everything that's happened over the last couple of days, I need some time to think. To let it breathe until it comes to me."

Breathing and time sounded good to me too.

The parking lot at The Betsy was nearly empty when we arrived. My bike was parked beside the building where I'd left it last night. No one who went to The Betsy would dare touch it.

Bryce stayed in her seat as she waited for me to get out of the car. "Bye."

"Call you later."

"You don't have my number."

I raised an eyebrow. "You sure about that?"

I'd had her phone number memorized since the day she'd come to the garage for a fake oil change. Willy had given it to me when I'd called him. I doubted Bryce knew her employee had once been a frequent guest at our underground fights. He'd always bet on me and I'd made him a lot of money, so there wasn't much he kept to himself whenever I called.

"Fine. Whatever. Call me later."

She left me at my bike and I watched her drive away.

I waited a whole five minutes before digging my phone out of my pocket.

"Seriously?" she answered, a smile in her voice. "Do I need to be worried that you're turning into a clinger?"

Yes. There was no keeping my boundaries with her. She'd stood by me these past twenty-four hours and things were different. From the beginning, everything about her had been different.

"Got a deal for you," I said, straddling my bike. "I'll fold the rest of your laundry if you cook me dinner."

"I'm making breakfast for dinner. I feel like biscuits and gravy."

My mouth watered. "I could eat breakfast."

"I'm making the biscuits from scratch. It's a pain in the ass and makes a mess. Toss in cleanup with the laundry and you can come over at six."

How was it this woman could make me smile after the afternoon we'd had?

Sorcery.

"I'll be there."

CHAPTER TWENTY

BRYCE

"Good morning," I said as I walked into the Clifton Forge Garage. One of the men I'd seen the first day I came here was working on a motorcycle in the first stall.

"Hey there." He glanced over his shoulder from his crouched position on the floor.

This one wasn't Emmett. Emmett was the bigger guy with long hair. "You're Isaiah, right?"

"Yep." He finished tightening something—*a bolt?*—with a something tool—*a wrench?* I'd have to work on my car terms if I was going to hang around here. He put the tool down, then stood. "You're Bryce."

"I am. Nice to see you again." I walked over, my hand outstretched.

"Sorry, I'm greasy." He held up his hands, making me drop my own. "What can I do for you?"

"I was looking for Dash."

"Haven't seen him yet this morning. Still a little early for him to get here."

It was only seven thirty, but I'd woken Dash up at six. I'd

263

left for the newspaper early to spend some time with Dad. Dash had gone home to shower and change, then I assumed he'd be on his way to work. The garage opened at eight and I didn't feel like leaving just to come back again.

"Would you mind if I waited?" I asked Isaiah.

"Not at all. Would you mind if I kept working?"

"Go for it." There was a black stool on wheels a few feet away. I took it, letting Isaiah return to the motorcycle as I took in the space.

For a garage, it was bright and clean. The smell of oil and metal hung in the air, mixing with the crisp morning air flowing in from the open bay door. Car signs were hung on some of the walls, tools on others. It was nearly pristine.

That Mustang was still in its stall. Ever since Dash and I had gone at it like wild animals on that car, I'd kept my nails painted hot-sex red. I smiled to myself, thinking it was my own dirty, little secret that the owner of that car would never know.

"Dash told me that some celebrities get their bikes and cars redone here. Is that a famous person's motorcycle you're fixing up?"

"No celebrity." Isaiah chuckled. "This is mine."

"Ah. Were you in the club?"

"Nah." He shook his head. "I just moved here. But this one was cheap so I thought I'd get it. Fix it up."

That explained why it looked more like a dull mishmash of scrap metal than Dash's gleaming Harley. Isaiah's motorcycle had a lot to improve upon if it was going to fit in here.

"Where did you move from?" I asked, but before he could answer, I waved my hand like I was erasing the question. "Sorry. That's the reporter in me coming out. You're trying to work and I'm distracting you. Forget I'm here."

"It's okay." He shrugged, still not answering my question as he went back to work.

What was his story? He was handsome. Isaiah had dark hair cut close to his scalp. A strong jaw. If he smiled, I bet he'd be devastating. Except Isaiah never smiled. And there wasn't much light in his eyes. Had it always been like that? There were so many questions to ask, but I held my tongue. I doubted he'd answer them anyway. Isaiah had this gentle way about shutting people out. It wasn't rude or combative. But his entire demeanor said he was a closed book.

The rumble of an approaching engine grew louder. I stood from the chair, assuming it was Dash.

"Have a good day, Isaiah."

"Thanks, Bryce." He waved. "You too."

Those eyes made me want to wrap my arms around him and never let go. They were so lonely. So heartbreaking. My heart twisted. Did everyone else know about Isaiah's past? Did Dash?

In the parking lot, I spotted a black motorcycle, but no Dash. So I walked to the office, finding the wrong Slater.

Damn it. I should have looked more closely at the motorcycle along the fence before coming in here—in my defense, except for Isaiah's, they all looked alike from behind.

Draven stood in the doorway to what I assumed was his office. He wore a blank expression on his face.

"Uh, sorry." I took a step backward. "I was—"

"Dash isn't here."

"Right." My choices were to wait here or run back to Isaiah. *Easy choice.* I was halfway to the door when Draven stopped me.

"Come on in."

Assuming a polite smile, I walked into his office, taking

the chair across from his behind the desk. Next time I came here in the morning, I'd wait until nine.

"So . . ." Draven clicked a pen four times. "You met her."

"Her?"

"Genevieve."

"Oh. Yes."

Draven kept his eyes on the pen. "What's she like? Is she okay? Healthy and all that?"

Well, shit. He made it hard to dislike him entirely. Especially with the guilt that laced his voice. He wasn't making any excuses, not anymore. And there was a hint of desperation there. My heart softened. There was no questioning Draven had been an unfaithful husband. But he loved his sons.

And wanted to know his daughter.

"I only spent a few hours with her, but she seems healthy. She's devastated about her mother. But she was sweet. Very kind. She looks a bit like you. She has your eyes and hair."

"Amina showed me pictures." He swallowed hard. "She . . . she's beautiful."

"From what I can tell, that beauty is inside and out."

"I want to meet her but I don't know if that's such a good idea," he said quietly. "I failed all my children, even the one I didn't know."

"Yeah, you probably shouldn't try to meet her. She, um, thinks you killed Amina."

He flinched, his knuckles turning white as he strangled the pen. "Oh. Right."

"If you want a relationship with her, we have to prove you're innocent."

"We?"

"Yes, we. I want the truth." I'd asked him point-blank yesterday if he'd killed Amina. I believed now that he hadn't. He'd cared for her. "I want to find Amina's killer."

"For your story."

Was this for the story? That's how this had all started, with my drive to prove myself as a journalist. To show the executives in Seattle I wasn't a flop.

Except I wasn't a failure. When I looked at Dad's career, he'd written countless stories and there wasn't one that stood out above the others. There wasn't one crown jewel he touted. Yet he was my hero. He wrote because he loved to write and spread the news.

So did I.

I didn't need an exposé on a former motorcycle gang to prove my worth. I needed the truth.

This was for me. And . . .

"For Dash."

This was about saving his father from a life in prison. It was about identifying a murderer. It was about finding the person who might come after Dash one day too.

Somewhere between the time he'd fixed the Goss printer and folded my towels, Dash had slipped into my heart.

Could I get over his criminal past? Could I forget that he'd done violent, vicious things I could barely fathom? *Yes.*

Because he wasn't that man anymore. Not to me.

Last night, as I'd watched him scrub my cast-iron pan and wipe down the counters from the biscuit mess, I'd realized how well we fit together. He'd held my heart in his soap-suds-covered hands.

If only he wanted kids.

Did that have to be a deal breaker? Maybe we didn't have to face that looming end.

I'd already given up on having children, so why make it a requirement to stay with Dash? Besides, I wasn't sure if I could even bear children at this point. Maybe we'd be like the Caseys, my seventy-six-year-old neighbors who lived across the street. Mr. and Mrs. Casey didn't have children, and every time I saw them, they seemed hopelessly happy.

Hopelessly happy sounded like a dream.

A new dream.

The office door pushed open and Dash entered, followed closely by Emmett.

"Hey." Dash walked into Draven's office, casting his father a brief glance before pretending he wasn't there. Dash had shaved and showered after he'd left my house. His hair was still damp at the ends where it curled at his neck. It was a good look. A very good look. "What are you doing here? Everything okay?"

I nodded. "I'm good."

Emmett crowded into the office, not looking at Draven either. Clearly in the time that Dash had left my house, he'd caught up Emmett on Draven's adultery.

From the corner of my eye, I saw Draven's shoulders fall. What had he expected? That after a day, all would be forgiven?

Dash was crushed. His mother's memory was sacred. Chrissy wasn't here to punish Draven, so Dash was doing it for her.

The only problem was, if we were going to find a killer, we needed to put feelings aside.

"The reason I came here this morning was because I've been thinking about something and wanted to run it by you," I told Dash.

"Shoot." He leaned against the wall, Emmett beside him.

"The police found a murder weapon at the scene and identified it as Draven's. We've been operating under the assumption that the knife was Draven's. But we also think this was a premeditated setup. Could the knife have been a fake? You said that it had your name engraved on the side. What if someone copied it to set you up?"

Draven shook his head. "They have my prints on it."

"Can't prints be faked?" I'd seen it on a murder-mystery movie, so the question wasn't entirely farfetched. Maybe they'd stolen prints from the handlebars on Draven's motorcycle.

Emmett nodded. "Possibly. Wouldn't be easy."

Dash rubbed a hand over his jaw. "What knife was it again?"

"Just a Buck knife," Draven said.

"With the cherry handle," Emmett added. "I borrowed it once a few years ago when I went hunting."

Cherry? That wasn't right. I dove into my purse for my yellow notepad, flipping to the page where I'd made a note about the knife's description. It was the one thing Chief Wagner had told me weeks ago that hadn't been in the press sheets.

"Not cherry. Black. The knife found at the scene had a black handle."

"Your knife was cherry." Emmett shook his head. "I'd bet my life on it."

My heart was racing. Maybe if there was another knife, we'd find a trail that led to the person who'd faked it. How many people engraved knives in Montana? We were grasping at straws, but it was something.

Dash's brow furrowed. "No, wait. You had a black knife, Dad."

Before Draven could respond, the office door opened again.

"Morning." What I assumed was Presley's cheerful voice preceded her as she came into Draven's office. The smile on her face fell when she spotted me in the guest chair.

"Hey, Pres? Remember that knife you had engraved for Dad?" Dash asked. "The one you got him for Christmas a few years ago?"

"Yeah. He said his other one was getting old and the engraving was wearing away. Why?"

Dash pushed off the wall. "What color was it?"

"Black, of course. You all love black."

All eyes shot to Draven.

"Where'd that knife go, Dad?" Dash asked.

"I, um . . . I think I left it in the office at the clubhouse after Presley gave it to me. Might still be in the box too."

"Seriously?" Presley put her hands on her hips. "That was four years ago. You never even used it?"

"Sorry, Pres, but I liked the old one. It fit my hand."

Without a word, Dash stalked out of the office, Emmett close on his heels. I shot out of my chair, following too. Draven's bootsteps thudded behind me.

As we walked outside, I squinted at the bright morning sunlight. Dash picked up his pace, storming for the clubhouse. His long strides required me to skip a few steps to keep up.

I hadn't taken more than a few curious glances at the clubhouse in my trips to the garage. The building had always loomed, dangerous, shadowed by the surrounding trees. But as we got closer, details jumped out.

The wood siding was stained a brown so dark it was nearly black. It had grayed in some places where the sun had faded the boards. The charcoal tin roof had a few droplets of dew that hadn't burned off yet. A spider's web grew in one corner under the eaves, thankfully far away from the door.

There weren't many windows, only two on the building's face. They'd always been dark when I'd come here and now I saw why. Behind the dirty glass, there were plywood boards. The green stamp from the lumberyard showing in a few places.

Dash marched up the two wide steps to the concrete platform that ran the entire length of the building. It was shaded by a small overhang of the roof. He fished out his keys from his jeans pocket and we all crowded at his back as he unlocked the padlock on the door.

The smell of must and stale air wafted outside, followed by the lingering scent of booze, smoke and sweat. I gagged. Desperate for information, I shoved it aside and stepped inside behind Dash.

We'd walked into a large, open room. Draven pushed past us, flipping on a row of florescent lights before disappearing down a hallway to the left.

On my right was a long bar. The dusty shelves behind it were empty. The mirror behind the shelves was cracked in a few places. There were some tin beer signs and an old neon light. Only one stool was tucked under the bar. On my left, there was a pool table, the cues hung on a wall rack. Two flags were pinned behind the table: an American flag and the Montana state flag.

"What is this place?" I asked.

"Common area," Dash answered at the same time Emmett said, "Party room."

I'd take The Betsy over the Tin Gypsy party room any day.

"Knife's gone." Draven's voice echoed in the room as he came rushing down the hall. "Given the fresh smudges in the dust on my desk, it was taken recently."

"Cameras." Emmett snapped his fingers, already moving for a door behind the bar. "Let me see if they picked anything up."

Draven followed Emmett, leaving Dash and me alone.

I'd been so busy inspecting the room, I hadn't noticed him. He stood frozen, staring blankly at a pair of double doors directly in front of us.

"Hey." I walked to his side, slipping my hand in his. "Are you okay?"

"Haven't been here in a year. It's strange." He squeezed my fingers tight. "It was easier to stay away. To shut it out."

"Do you want to wait outside?"

"Had to face it sometime." He pulled me to a hallway on the right of the party room, different than the one Draven had taken when he'd gone in search of his knife. "Come on."

The hall was dim, with closed doors on both sides. From the outside, the building didn't seem all that large, but it was deceiving. Though not as tall, it had to be at least double the size of the garage.

Dash kept hold of my hand but jerked his chin at one of the doors. "This was where some of the guys would stay if they didn't have a house. Or if they just needed to crash."

These were their rooms. "Did you have one?"

He stopped at the last door down the hallway, using a different key from his chain to unlock the deadbolt. Then he pushed the door aside.

The smell in here was different, still dusty but there was a hint of Dash's natural spice clinging to the air. There was a window, boarded up like the others. And a bed covered with a simple khaki quilt stood in the middle of the room.

No pillows. No end table. No lamp. Only the bed and an old wooden dresser in the corner.

"This was your room?" I stepped in farther, letting go of his hand to flick on the light. Then I walked to the dresser, swiping my finger through the coat of dust on top.

"This was my room." Dash leaned on the doorframe. "I thought maybe it would look different. Feel different. Thought I'd miss it."

"You don't?"

He shook his head. "Maybe I would have two days ago. But not now."

Oh, Dash. I hated standing by, watching as his heart broke. I hated that something he'd held dear, something he'd once loved—the club—had been tainted.

"What's this?" I walked over to the bed, picking up the leather square folded neatly on top of the quilt.

"My cut."

"That's what you call your vests, right?"

He nodded, stepping up behind me. "When you prospect the club, you get a cut. It has the club's patch on the back and a prospect patch on the front."

"How long did you have to prospect?"

"Six months. But Emmett and I were exceptions. Normally it's about a year. Long enough we knew the guy was serious. That he'd fit in."

"Then what happened?" I unfolded the vest, laying it carefully on the bed. My fingers ran over the white patch below the left shoulder, the word *President* stitched in black thread.

"Then you're in the club. You're family."

I turned the vest over, staring at the patch on the back as Dash looked on. "This is beautiful."

The few pictures I'd seen of the Tin Gypsy emblem had been in black and white from old newspapers. But in color, the design was stunning. Artful and menacing at the same time.

The club name was written at the top in Old English lettering. Beneath it was a detailed and carefully stitched skull.

A skull, exactly the same as the tattoo on Dash's arm.

One half of the face was made entirely of silver thread, giving it a metallic feel. Behind it was a riot of orange, yellow and red-tipped flames. The other half of the skull was white. Simple. Except for the colorful head wrap over the skull and delicate, almost feminine stitching around the eye, mouth and nose. It was like a sugar skull with a harsh, violent edge.

Live to Ride

Wander Free

Below the skull, the words were stitched in threads grayed from years of wear.

How long had Dash worn this cut? How many days had he put it on? How hard had it been to fold it up and leave it here, collecting dust in a forsaken room?

Dash put a hand on my shoulder, turning me into his chest. His hands came to my face. His mouth dropped to mine. And he kissed me soft and sweet, like a thank-you.

When he broke away, he dropped his forehead to mine.

"I bet you've kissed a lot of women in this room," I whispered.

"Some," he admitted. "But none were you."

My eyes drifted closed. This was not the right place or the right time for this conversation, but questions hung between us, begging to be asked. "What's going on, Dash? With us?"

"I don't know. It's more than I thought it would be." He tucked a lock of hair behind my ear. "You kind of snuck up on me."

I smiled. "You snuck up on me too."

The next kiss wasn't soft or sweet. Dash crushed his lips to mine, his hands leaving my face to band around my back, pulling me tight into his firm body. He needed this, like he'd needed me last night. He'd gotten lost in my body, seeking comfort.

I looped my arms around his neck, angling my mouth so I could get a deeper taste. I'd gotten lost in him too. He made everything an adventure. Even watching him fold my laundry or do the dishes was exciting. How was I ever going to let him go? I knew right there, in that moment, I wouldn't be able to walk away from Dash.

He'd ruined me. He'd changed the game.

We were seconds away from ripping at each other's clothes when a throat cleared from the doorway, forcing us apart. With swollen lips, we both turned to see Emmett.

"Dash." He nodded down the hallway. "Better come and see this."

CHAPTER TWENTY-ONE

DASH

B ryce and I followed Emmett through the clubhouse party room and to the basement. This wasn't a place I wanted Bryce, but there was no keeping her away.

As we descended the steps, I took a look around. It was cleaner than upstairs. That, or the dust was less noticeable on the concrete floors and walls.

Dad had built this clubhouse alongside the original members. They'd made the basement into a bunker of sorts. It was a concrete labyrinth of rooms, all varying in size, but each with a drain in the center. Rivers of blood had been washed down those drains. The bleach smell still lingered in the air, even though it had been over a year since we'd cleaned up the main room from our last underground fight.

The smaller rooms had seen far worse than boxing.

It was strange being in the clubhouse, especially when it was so quiet. The nights I'd stayed here in my twenties, I'd learned to sleep with a party raging beyond my door—if I hadn't been in the middle of the party myself.

There were good memories here. As a kid, we'd come

here for family barbeques with Dad's brothers, men who'd been like uncles until they'd become brothers of my own. Nick and I would light off fireworks in the parking lot on Independence Day. We'd each had our first beer in this clubhouse and many more after.

I'd always wanted to be a Gypsy. Other kids in school would talk about college. Fancy jobs. I'd just wanted to be in Dad's club. Nick had been the same until Mom died. But even after he'd shunned the Gypsies and moved away after high school, my feelings hadn't changed.

I had been a Gypsy long before earning my cut.

Yesterday, I'd told Dad that I wished he hadn't started the club. I was angry. Hurt. A part of me did want to reject this place. It would be easy to put Mom's death on the club and walk away for good. Burn it down and, with it, the havoc it had wreaked on my life.

Except then I'd have to forget the good memories too.

There had been good memories.

One thing was certain, I was glad Bryce moved to Clifton Forge *after* we'd disbanded. I wouldn't have had a shot with her had I been leading the club. She was too good to get mixed up with a criminal. Hell, it was a stretch for me to chase after her now.

But I couldn't look into the future and not see her face.

She dared me, called me out on my bullshit. She shared her heart, her loyalty, her honesty—all things I'd had with the club, with my brothers. She filled that hole and then some.

"In here." Emmett ducked into one of the smaller rooms where he'd set up a surveillance station a few years back. Security and hacking had become Emmett's specialty. He called it a hobby. I called it a gift.

Dad was leaning over a monitor, staring at a frozen image on the screen.

"What'd you find?" I asked, taking Dad's place.

Emmett sat in the chair, clicking to rewind the video. "I guess we should have kept the sensors on after that raccoon incident. Look at this."

He pressed play on the video and rolled out of the way to make room for Bryce. She came right up beside me, my hand immediately finding hers. Together, we watched footage from one of the cameras hidden above each window in the clubhouse as a man approached the building.

The color on the screen was a mix of green and white and black from the night vision setting. The man's face was covered in a black ski mask, his shirt and pants a matching shade.

He walked up to the building, taking a utility tool from his pocket. And then he jimmied open the glass window.

"Fuck. We should have boarded up the basement windows." They were so small, not even eighteen inches wide, that we hadn't bothered. Plus the drop from the window was at least ten feet. Our concrete bunker was not small. And up until this winter, we'd had sensors on all the windows.

The man was probably close to my size, but he managed to shimmy his way into the basement. He turned on his stomach, his legs going inside first, and that's when we saw it.

A patch on his back.

"Fucking lying bastards." My booming voice echoed off the walls.

I dropped Bryce's hand, pacing the room as I rubbed my jaw. Now I understood why Dad was against the wall, fuming in a silent rage.

"What am I missing?" Bryce asked.

"That's an Arrowhead Warrior patch," Emmett answered, tapping the screen. He'd frozen it before the man had dropped inside.

"Oh." Her eyes widened. "When was this taken?"

"The night before Amina was murdered," Dad answered. "He must have come here, broken in while I was with her in the motel, stolen my knife, and then waited until I left to kill her."

"Any idea who he is? How he'd know you'd be with Amina?" I asked Dad, getting a headshake in return. "Emmett, can we print that out?"

He nodded, ripping a sheet from the printer below his desk. "Already did."

"When we leave today, turn all the sensors back on," I ordered Emmett. "And ask Leo to come over and board up the basement windows."

"Will do."

"You need to call Tucker," I told Dad.

"Yeah. Let's talk in the chapel. Bryce looks like she needs to sit."

My attention immediately shifted. Her face had lost all its color, and I rushed to her side. "What's wrong?"

"Nothing." She waved me off, her face souring. "It smells funny down here."

"Come on." I gripped her elbow, leading her upstairs. It didn't smell great in the party room either, but once we reached the chapel, the rotten beer smell was gone.

The chapel was the heart of the clubhouse, located directly in the center. You got in through two double doors off the party room. It was one long, open room with a table running its length. The table had been built to accommodate about twenty members, but there had been years when it was standing room only. The officers and senior members would sit. I'd spent plenty of years against the wall, listening as decisions were made.

The black high-backed chairs were all pushed into the table. The room had been left in pristine condition except for the dust. The walls were lined with pictures, mostly of members standing together in front of a row of bikes. The Gypsy patch had been made into a flag that hung on the wall behind the head chair at the table.

The president's chair.

Dad had given up his seat, passing it to me. He went for it, but then realized his mistake. Had it not been for Bryce, I would have sat there to put him in his place. He didn't deserve that seat.

But instead, I pulled out one of the middle chairs for Bryce, sitting at her side.

"What's the raccoon incident?" Bryce leaned over to ask.

"This winter, Emmett and I got an alert from the motion sensors. They went off at three in the morning on the coldest night we'd had in months. We hurried down, nearly froze our dicks off, and found three raccoons in the kitchen. They'd crawled in through this old vent hood."

"They were making a goddamn mess, shitting every-where," Emmett grumbled. "It was cold as hell so it took us forever to get them out. I don't know why they'd leave their dens in the first place. Maybe to find something warmer."

"After that, we closed off the vent hood and decided to leave the sensors off," I told her. "The place was empty. There wasn't anything in here to steal."

"Or so you thought," she murmured.

"Yeah." I nodded. "So we thought."

Dad pulled out the chair next to Emmett. He wasn't in the president's seat but a shift came over the room as he sat down. Like a meeting coming to order. When he sat, no one else dared to talk until he gave them permission.

Even though I'd sat in the head chair for years, I'd never had that kind of commanding presence. I'd worried about it for a while, wondered if I'd be revered like Dad. Maybe it would have come, in time. But we'd already begun to shut things down when I'd been voted in as president. My job hadn't been to lead the Gypsies into the future. I was the president who'd made sure we'd covered all our asses so we could live a normal life.

"What are we going to do about the Warriors?" I asked, leaning my elbows on the table. "Tucker lied to us."

"Or he didn't know," Dad countered. "Yeah, there's a chance he ordered this. Or he's as clueless as we are and it's someone's personal vendetta. Someone who's been following me around, saw me with a woman for the first time in decades and used it as their opening to strike."

"For what?" Bryce asked.

Dad scoffed. "Hell. A million things."

"A million and a half," I muttered.

We'd burned down their clubhouse once. It had likely cost them a fortune to rebuild. The two Warriors who'd tried to kidnap Emmeline had been Dad's guests in the basement, their last breaths taken inside those concrete walls.

"What do we do?" Emmett sighed. "Go after them? Start up another war?"

"We'll lose," I said. "There's no chance at winning."

"I don't want a war. Not this time." Dad shook his head. "First, I'll go to Tucker, show him the photo and see what he does. Maybe he'll give us a name and it can end. But if it comes down to it, if he covers for his men—which I suspect he will—then I'll take the fall for Amina."

"They'll put you away for life." Yesterday, I was okay with it—when I was furious and in a rage. Today, now that I'd calmed down, the idea of him in prison didn't sit as well.

"I'll go if that's what it takes to keep you and Nick free of this."

"Except they could be after any of us," Emmett said. "This might have started with you, but I bet it goes deeper. I'm not looking over my shoulder for the rest of my life. I know we're up against bad odds, but we have to fight back."

"Why not do it legally?" Bryce suggested. "Let's get the evidence to prove there's reasonable doubt. We can use the paper to print it, create a circus around town. Get rumors started that Draven is innocent. The chief won't have any choice but to dig deeper."

"You're talking about following the rules." Dad barked a laugh. "We're not great at working with the cops."

"You're also not great at keeping the people in your life alive by *breaking* the rules, so maybe it's time to try a different approach."

Damn, woman. She wasn't pulling any punches. I flinched at her words. Emmett did too. Because no one talked to Dad like that, especially in this room.

But she was fearless. The fire in her eyes, that blaze, made my chest swell. Was it with pride? Or love? Both?

I think I'd fallen for her the night she'd kicked me off her front porch. Or maybe it was the day she'd shown up at the garage, bursting with attitude and determination.

"She's right," I told Dad. "Not just because it's legal, but because the Warriors will never expect it. Let's use the cops to our favor for once."

Emmett nodded. "If Tucker did know about this, then he's waiting and watching for us to retaliate. The cops showing up at his door might be a surprise."

"We need to find evidence, solid evidence, and fast," I said. "The state's attorney will set a trial date soon, and once that starts, it's going to be even harder to get people to consider another suspect. We need them to delay."

"What do we do?" Dad asked.

I looked to Bryce. "You need to write a story. Marcus is a good cop, but he's not going to believe me if I walk in there with new evidence. Not when his mind's made up that Dad is guilty. We need to plant the seed that Dad's knife was stolen. Show the picture of someone breaking into the club-house. Marcus won't be able to ignore it if you print it."

"I'll start on it today. We can feature it on Sunday. But . . ." She locked eyes with Dad across the table. "It would mean more if I could print the reason you and Amina were in the motel. It makes you more human if people know you were there to discuss your daughter."

Dad blew out a deep breath but shook his head. "Not until I meet her. I owe her that much. She shouldn't learn I'm her father from a newspaper. Like you said, she thinks I killed her mother."

"I might be able to help with that." Bryce raised her hand, like she was volunteering to go into battle. "We're going to get lucky on timing. When I went to visit Genevieve last weekend, she said she was coming up Sunday to see Amina's grave. I'll call her and double-check she's coming. And I guess . . . tell her when she gets here. Hope she doesn't pick up a newspaper that morning. I don't know. But maybe I can smooth it over."

"Do it," I said. "We need the story to shed more light on

283

the relationship between Dad and Amina. To give it some context and show Dad wouldn't kill her. I think *my sister* would be a good way to do that."

"I feel like I'm about to blindside her, Dash." Bryce's worried eyes met mine. "I feel terrible already."

"Be gentle," Dad murmured. "Please."

"I will," she promised.

"And we'll keep searching for more." Emmett knocked his knuckles on the table. "Draven, you call Tucker."

He nodded. "I'll go meet with him. Alone."

"Keep us posted." I pushed away from the chair, helping pull Bryce's away so she could stand. Then we all walked out of the clubhouse, the plan in place. I escorted Bryce to her car. Her eagerness to get to the newspaper was palpable, but before she left, I wanted to make sure she was all right. "Feeling better?"

"Not really, but I'll be fine. It's just a stomach ache. That smell in the clubhouse was"—she gagged—"potent. I'm going to get to work. Call me later?"

I nodded. "I need to get caught up on some jobs here. We've been leaning pretty heavy on Isaiah and Presley to run the garage while we've had this extra shit happening. Time for me to get my hands dirty and finish some cars."

"Be sure to wash those hands before dinner." She winked, standing on her toes for a kiss. It was a short good-bye. Nothing out of the ordinary for most couples. But we weren't a couple.

We hadn't made a commitment. We hadn't made promises. Except as I stood and watched her leave, I realized that no other woman would kiss me again.

Bryce was it for me. The one.

Dad's shadow crossed mine. "You love her."

I didn't respond. Bryce would be the first to hear the words. I took a step toward the garage. "Need to get to work."

"Dash." Dad's hand flew out, stopping me. "I'm sorry."

"I don't want you to go to prison, not when you didn't kill Amina. But you and me? We're done."

His shoulders fell. "I understand."

"I need some time without you here at the garage. Some space to think. You're not the man I thought you were."

"I've never been a hero, son."

I met his brown gaze. "But you were to me."

The blow hit Dad hard. His face tightened like he'd been sucker punched and was fighting to breathe.

Leaving him alone on the asphalt, I walked toward the garage, then paused and looked back while Dad was still in earshot. "Nick deserves to know. Either you tell him, or I will."

He simply nodded.

And two hours later, as I was flat on my back underneath the Mustang, the engine of Dad's motorcycle revved as he left the garage. My phone rang thirty seconds later.

Pushing out from the car, I dug my phone from my pocket. Nick's name flashed on the screen. "Hey."

"Guess you expected this call."

"Was hoping for it. I take it Dad called you?"

"Yep. Sounds like we have a sister." The calm tone in Nick's voice surprised me. I figured, given his past relationship with Dad, he'd be furious.

"You don't sound upset."

"I'm surprised. It wasn't easy to hear and maybe I haven't wrapped my head around it all. But mostly, I'm disappointed. Sad for Mom. Glad she never knew. But no, I'm not angry. Far as I'm concerned, Dad got knocked off his pedestal a long time ago. He's a flawed man, Dash. Always has been."

"I don't know what to do about it."

"Nothing to do. Move on."

"Yeah, I guess so." I walked over to the open garage door, looking outside. There was a car lined up in front of each bay. Emmett, Isaiah and Leo were all working fast to get them through the queue.

It was a good business, this garage. Provided us with decent livings. Just like the garage Nick ran in Prescott.

Move on. That didn't seem all that bad now that I had Bryce. We each had decent jobs, nice homes, and there were a lot of people who didn't even have that.

"I met someone."

There was so much to talk about—things to say about Dad and the murder. But none of it mattered. Right now, I just wanted to tell my brother about Bryce. To share her with my family.

"Is it serious?" he asked.

"She's my Emmy." It was the best way to describe my feelings for Bryce. Nick loved Emmeline with every molecule in his body. "But it hasn't been long."

He chuckled. "I fell for Emmy the first night I met her. Time doesn't matter."

Nick and Emmeline had married the first night they'd met. Things had been rocky for them, but they'd found their way back together.

"I'm happy for you. Want a piece of free advice from your older, wiser and more handsome brother?"

I grinned. "Sure."

"Now that you've found her, don't let her go."

CHAPTER TWENTY-TWO

BRYCE

I clicked save on my story and uploaded the final version to the drive where Dad would pull it into the layout for tomorrow's paper. He'd already staged the photos and formatted the headline. Now all he'd have to do was input the text.

I'd waited to finalize the details until the very last minute, hoping Dash or Emmett would find more to include. But in the past five days, nothing new had come to light about the man who'd broken into the Tin Gypsy clubhouse and stolen Draven's knife. The man who was likely responsible for Amina Daylee's death.

Draven had found his original knife—the one with the cherry handle. It had been in his home, as he'd expected, tucked away safely in a bag of hunting gear.

The picture Emmett had printed from the surveillance cameras would be on Sunday's front page, along with speculation about the murder weapon's theft. Our newspaper was all about printing the facts, so my personal conjecture had been pushed to the wayside. But there were hints between those facts, enough to plant seeds of doubt. Add to that my *exclusive* interview with Draven Slater and his confession of a secret daughter, this plan might just work.

Now all I had to do was pray that when Genevieve came to Clifton Forge tomorrow, she didn't read my article before I could tell her about Draven. I could call her and ask her not to pick up a local paper—I doubted she would anyway. But if she was anything like me, that call would only make her curious. I was hedging my bet that she didn't care about the latest *Clifton Forge Tribune*.

"It's all yours." I spun in my chair to face Dad, who was seated at his desk.

"Thanks." He smiled. "I'll put it in after lunch. Did you give Marcus a heads-up?"

"No. He can read it with everyone else."

"Oh." His eyebrows came together. "Uh, okay."

"What? Do you think it's a mistake?"

"I think a lot has changed in the last month. You were on Chief Wagner's team not long ago, wanting to be in his good graces. And now"—he pointed to the computer—"the story you drafted is not the one I expected."

"No, it's not." It wasn't the one I'd expected to write either. "But this is the right story to tell. Draven didn't kill Amina Daylee. The real killer is out there, and if that means lighting a fire under the chief's ass to get him to dig deeper, then that's what I need to do."

"Still might be worth giving him a heads-up. Tip your hat. You don't want to ruin that relationship, Bryce."

I sighed. "I don't think he'll like me much after this anyway."

No amount of licorice would make him trust me once this story came out.

"One phone call will smooth things over," Dad suggested. "Just make him feel like you haven't completely switched teams."

"Why don't you call him? It might be better coming from you." Because the truth was, I had switched teams. My loyalty wasn't to Marcus Wagner anymore. June had come and gone. The July weather had engulfed Clifton Forge in sunshine and heat. And as the calendar had ticked by, my priorities had changed.

I'd fallen in love with the man I'd once hoped to expose as a criminal.

Technically, he was a criminal—or a former criminal. Mostly, he was mine. Flawed and mine.

"Do you need anything else from me?" I yawned. "If not, I'm going to head home."

"Still tired?"

"Yeah." I gave Dad a weak smile. "It's been a long week. I'm out of energy."

"You need a nap. Get some rest. Would you like to come over for dinner tonight? I'm sure your mom would love to cook for you."

It had been weeks since I'd gone over to Mom and Dad's house. Mom had been begging me constantly for a visit and had apparently enlisted Dad to help too. "No plans. I'd love to. I'll call Mom and ask what I can bring."

The door into the bullpen pushed open. "Hey, you two."

"Speak of the devil." Dad stood from his chair, meeting Mom in the middle of the room for a kiss.

"Hi, Mom." I waved but didn't get up from my chair. "You look pretty today."

"Thanks." Her hair was the same rich brown as mine but carried a few gray streaks. Mom refused to get them covered up anymore because on one of their trips to Seattle, a waiter had accused us of being sisters. Where most women would have been flattered, doubling the young man's tip, she'd taken offense. She'd corrected him gently, informing him of our relationship. She'd told him that being my mother was the greatest source of pride in her life.

Like Dad always said, it was easy to love Tessa Ryan.

Mom came over and bent low to give me a hug while I stayed in my chair, then she sat on the edge of my desk. "Want to come over for dinner tonight?"

I laughed. "Dad just asked me the same question. And yes. I'd love to. What would you like me to bring?"

"Oh, nothing. I'll take care of it. In fact, I have extra if you want to bring the boyfriend along."

The boyfriend. Was Dash my boyfriend? He'd probably cringe at the term. Much too juvenile for someone like him. It wasn't edgy enough. What was the MC terminology? Was he my *man*? Or *old man*? If—and that was a big if, considering his commitment phobia—we got married one day, would that make me his old lady?

I cringed. If he ever called me his old lady, I'd deny him sex for a month.

"I've been missing you guys," I said. "Ryans only tonight. I'll invite Dash next time."

"Fine." Mom pouted. "But I expect to meet him sooner than later."

"You will." Assuming we were at the point where we introduced each other to our families. We were, right?

Dash and I needed to continue the conversation we'd started in the clubhouse. Our relationship needed some definition, but neither of us had brought it up over the past five days. I was too nervous to ask. And I suspected Dash was in uncharted waters.

Covering another yawn, I collected my things from my desk and shoved them into my tote. "So, six tonight?"

Mom nodded. "Are you feeling all right?"

"Just tired."

She leaned forward, taking my cheeks in her hands, then pressed her palm to my forehead. She'd been testing my temperature that way since I was a toddler. I closed my eyes and smiled. No matter my age, she was always Mom, there to comfort and care. "You don't have a temperature."

"I'm not sick," I promised. "It's been one of those weeks. I'm drained."

"Ahh. I used to get tired when it was that week of the month too. I don't miss the tampons but"—she fanned her face—"these hot flashes every ten damn minutes are a pain in the ass."

I giggled. "I'm not on my per—"

My heart dropped. When was the last time I had my period?

Mom said something else, but my mind was whirling, counting the weeks of June and calculating when I'd last bought tampons at the grocery store. The last time I could remember had been sometime in May. I remembered because we'd gotten a heavy and wet spring snow. I'd gotten all weepy and hormonal because a bunch of trees in town had begun to bloom but the weight of the snow had broken their branches.

Oh. Fuck. I shot out of my chair, grabbing my purse.

"What's wrong?" Mom asked.

"Nothing," I lied, not making eye contact with her or Dad. "I just realized I need to run a quick errand and want to

291

make sure I get there before they close. See you guys at dinner."

Without another word, I left the newspaper, driving immediately to the grocery store.

I bought things I didn't need—toothpicks, limes, Cheez Whiz—filling my basket as I passed the entrance to the feminine products aisle over and over. Each time, I'd stared down the shelves only to chicken out and walk away. Finally, after grabbing a gallon of orange juice, my basket was getting heavy and my purpose for this trip couldn't be avoided any longer.

I sucked in a deep breath and marched down the aisle. When I got to the pregnancy tests, I quickly scanned for brands I recognized and shoved three different types into my basket. Then I practically ran to checkout, hoping no one spotted me.

The cashier made no comment as she scanned my items, *thank God*, and when all my things were safely hidden in paper bags, I hefted them to my car and drove home.

The sinking feeling in my stomach was unbearable. The anxiety, crushing. Was I pregnant? I'd been in such a rush to buy the tests, I hadn't really thought of what would happen after I took them. But as my house, and toilet, drew nearer, a panicked chill settled into my bones.

A month ago, the idea of being pregnant would have sent me into joyful hysterics. But now? If I had a baby, would I lose Dash? Was I enough to raise a child on my own? Would I be heartbroken if the tests were negative?

Three positive pregnancy tests later, I didn't have to worry about that last question.

"HEY, BABE." Dash walked through my front door without knocking.

I was in the kitchen, sitting at the island, staring blankly at the striations and granules in my gray granite counter. I'd canceled dinner with my parents and texted Dash to come over. "Hey."

"Got some news." He took the stool by my side, leaning over to kiss my temple. "Dad met with Tucker today."

"Yeah?" I faked some excitement about the meeting with the Warriors' president. "What did he say?"

"Dad says Tucker swears it wasn't the Warriors. He took a look at the photo and get this." Dash leaned to the side to fish out his wallet. Then he slipped out a copy of the photo Emmett had printed from the surveillance video, flattening it on the counter.

I leaned in close. "What am I looking at?"

"See this right here?" He pointed to the stitched Warriors logo on the man's cut. "See at the bottom of the arrowhead, where it flares?"

"Yeah."

"Tucker said they changed the patch a few years ago, cleaned up some of the edges and got rid of that flare. Everyone in the club got new cuts."

"Did they confiscate the old ones?"

"Nope. Which means whoever has an old cut has been a Warrior for a while. And that confirms it wasn't one of the former Gypsies who joined them this past year."

So a Warrior was trying to restart an old war. "Can we get a list of names?"

"Not from Tucker. He'll never give up his men. But Dad is going to start putting names on paper. He's with Emmett and Leo at the garage, doing it now. Told them I'd be over soon. Thought you might want to come along."

"No, thanks." I wasn't feeling up to a trip to the garage. And I had a feeling after I told Dash I was pregnant, he wouldn't want me along either.

"You sure?"

"I'm sure."

"And, um . . . Genevieve?" He struggled to say her name. Dash hadn't thawed to the notion of his sister.

"Her flight gets in late tonight. She's staying in Bozeman and will drive over tomorrow. She thinks she'll be in town midmorning. She promised to call and I'll go meet her at the cemetery."

"Call me when she leaves. Tell me how she takes it."

"I will."

I didn't have a clue how I was going to tell Genevieve that she was Draven's daughter. And as if that weren't hard enough, I was also going to try and convince her that he hadn't killed her mother. That fledgling friendship we'd forged over chocolate chip cookies was guaranteed a crushing.

Dash stood and went to the cupboards for a glass, filling it with water from the fridge. He was itching to get to the garage.

"So, before you go . . ." God, how did I say this? I busied my hands by folding up the photo and reaching for his wallet to put it away. I opened the bifold, ready to stuff it inside, but another folded page caught my attention.

I lifted it out, recognizing a black and white photo. The trophy case behind the kids was familiar. It had been the backdrop for numerous pictures in the Clifton Forge High yearbooks.

"What is this?"

Dash lowered the water glass from his lips and closed his eyes. "I, uh . . . shit."

Unfolding the page, I scanned the photos, only seeing school photos with no one recognizable. But I turned it over and spotted Amina's youthful face. She stood smiling with another girl.

It was the younger version of a face I'd seen in an obituary.

Chrissy Slater.

"Dash. What's this?"

He had the decency to look guilty. "A page I found at the high school when we were looking at yearbooks."

"You found this and never showed me." I fought the urge to crumple the photo into a ball and throw it at his face.

"I was going to. Swear. But then it didn't seem that important after you learned Mom and Amina were friends."

"It didn't seem important?" I gaped at him, sliding off my stool. "You promised that you'd tell me everything. You pretended not to know your mom and Amina were friends. I asked you, straight up, if you knew and you lied to me. What else have you lied about?"

"Nothing."

"I trusted you. How could you do this to me? After everything? I *trusted* you." Against my better judgment, I'd believed Dash. I'd believed in him.

"Bryce, come on." Dash took a step toward me. "It's not that big of a deal."

"No. It is a big deal." I backed away. "Is this why you called the cops that day? So I wouldn't find out you tore the page from the yearbook?"

"Yes. And I'm sorry. But we were in a different place then. We weren't together."

"No, we were only fucking, right? I was just another woman to use until you had your fill. Do you still feel like that?"

His jaw clenched as it tightened. "You know I don't."

I closed my eyes, fighting the urge to cry. How could I trust him? After all our time together, he could have told me, but he'd kept the secret.

It was a nothing secret too. Nothing. Something so small that, by keeping it from me, he'd actually made it worse. Bigger than it had to be.

Or maybe I was blowing this out of proportion. Maybe this pregnancy was making me overthink everything. How were we ever going to be together if he didn't confide in me? How were we going to have a child?

He crossed the distance between us. "Baby, you're over-reacting."

"Maybe I am," I whispered. "But something about this feels . . . off. Like we have a fundamental problem here."

"A fundamental problem? It's a goddamn picture. Yeah, I should have told you, but it stopped being important."

"You promised no secrets. You wouldn't hide anything from me. Otherwise I'd write it all."

"Wait." His eyes narrowed. "Is that what this is about? Your story?"

My story? What was he talking about? "Huh?"

"It is, isn't it? Fuck. I'm so fucking stupid. I actually thought we had something here. But you've just been playing me from the start. Waiting until I did something that would justify you writing the tell-all you've been dying to write."

"That's not true."

"You've already got it written, haven't you?" He pointed to my laptop still in the tote on the counter. "It's all done, isn't it?"

"Yes, I wrote it," I admitted. "In case you betrayed me. But it was only for backup. I'm not going to print it."

"How do I know that?"

I threw up my hands. "Because I'm telling you this isn't about the story. And I haven't made it a habit of lying to you."

"It's always been the story. From the beginning. And I was stupid enough to think you didn't want it anymore because you wanted me instead."

"I do want—wait. How am I now the villain? You're the one who held something back. You're the one who lied about that stupid picture." Why did I feel guilty?

"That picture means nothing. We both know that. You have a story written that could ruin the lives of people I love. Not an apples-to-apples deal here, babe."

I opened my mouth to argue but closed it shut. My shoulders fell, weighed down by a hopelessness that might topple me to the floor.

"It's not about the photo or the story," I whispered. "We don't trust each other. How can this work if we don't trust each other?"

Dash's anger evaporated and he shook his head. "Hell if I know. When you figure it out, do me a favor and clue me in. Because right now, it's looking to me like this is over before it really got started. I'm gonna take off."

He swiped up his wallet, shoving it into his jeans. And then without another word, he stalked out of the kitchen.

"Wait." While we were dealing with the heavy stuff, I

had to add on one more thing. He deserved to know before he walked out the door. "I have to tell you something."

Dash turned, putting his hands on his hips. "Can it wait?"

"No." I swallowed the burn in my throat. *Tell him.* "I'm pregnant."

A terrifying silence filled the room. Seconds ticked by like hours. A minute felt like a day. Dash stood so still, it looked like he wasn't even breathing.

It was how I knew he'd heard me.

My heart thudded, painfully so, as I waited and waited and waited. Until finally, he blinked, shaking his head just slightly. "Not possible. I always use a condom."

His precious condoms.

"One of them didn't work."

It was hard to tell when, but the timing suggested it was soon after we got together. Maybe on the Mustang. But guessing was futile. Other than our two-week hiatus after Draven had threatened me, Dash and I had been having sex constantly.

The silence returned. Tears welled in my eyes and no amount of blinking could keep my vision from turning glassy.

I'd had a friend at the TV station in Seattle who'd made a big deal out of telling her husband she was pregnant by staging baby foods at home next to a onesie with *Daddy* stamped on the front. The morning after her announcement, she'd come to work and reported that he'd been overjoyed.

And I'd been jealous. I wanted the laughter. The excitement. The kiss after my husband learned we were making a family.

"Say something," I whispered. The silence was breaking

my heart. At this point, I'd take yelling if that meant he'd speak.

His eyes drifted up from the floor, and it was then that I saw true fear.

Dash spun on his boot. He ripped open the door, not bothering to close it behind him as he rushed to his bike. The sound of his motorcycle engine didn't linger because he was gone in a flash.

"Goddamn it." I walked to the door, blinking away the tears as I closed it and flipped the lock. If he did come back, he'd have to ring the doorbell.

Eventually, he had to come back. Didn't he? He wouldn't leave me forever. Right? The idea of doing this alone, of not having Dash to lean on, made my entire body ache. Would we get through this? Together?

We had to. We were better together. Didn't he see that? Sure, I could do this alone. But I didn't want to. I wanted Dash.

He couldn't avoid me forever. *Us* forever. We lived in the same town. We were having this baby whether he was ready for it or not. Because maybe he'd pegged himself as the fun uncle, but I'd be damned if I let my kid grow up not knowing his or her father.

I wouldn't let Dash turn into Draven, missing out on his child's life until it was too late.

Walking to the counter, I pounded a fist on the granite. "Damn him."

We'd have words. And soon. Before this baby came, Dash was going to man up.

I'd make sure of it.

Determined not to sit here and wallow, I picked up my phone and sent Mom a text, telling her I'd be over for dinner after all; I was feeling better. She replied with a string of happy-face emojis and confetti.

I shut off the lights in my house, taking my purse and a bottle of wine for Mom—I wouldn't need it for a solid year. Then I went to my parents' house, enjoying some time with them alone and doing my best not to think about Dash and the baby.

When I got home, I was exhausted and ready to collapse. I was so tired, I barely had my eyes open as I shuffled inside.

The house was dark, but I didn't need the lights on to find my way to the bedroom. I liked the dark because it hid the basket of laundry on the couch. It hid the glass Dash had left by the sink.

It also hid the figure, cloaked in black, who'd been waiting for me to get home.

CHAPTER TWENTY-THREE

DASH

"**M**orning." Isaiah came into the garage, running a hand through his short hair. "You've been at it for a while. Stay all night?"

"Yep." I slammed the door of the Mustang, a cleaning cloth in my hand.

After leaving Bryce's place yesterday evening, I'd taken a long ride. Miles and miles had flown by as I'd tried to wrap my head around the bomb she'd dropped. She'd changed my world with one word. Turned the whole damn thing upside down.

Pregnant.

I couldn't make that idea stick. We'd been careful. Condoms were required when I was with a woman, no exceptions. And though I would have loved to go bare with Bryce, there was a reason I'd kept us safe.

Some men were designed to be good fathers. Nick was one. But I'd done too many things, violent and vile things, to be a decent dad. No matter what Bryce said, how much I wanted to believe her, I wasn't good.

I'd fuck up a kid of my own.

All my precautions, my strict rules for condoms, were pointless now.

Within months, I was going to be a father.

And it scared me to death. I didn't know how to be a father. Look at the example I had to go by. A man who'd led murderers to his wife's doorstep and kidnappers to his daughter-in-law's bedroom.

I didn't want to become my father. Which was a mind-fuck since I'd spent thirty-five years following in his footsteps.

I'd joined his club. I'd sat in his chair. I'd taken over his garage when he'd retired. In thirty-five years, would my own kid look at me and wish he or she had forged their own path too?

After the long ride, I'd come back to the garage. It was dark, but Dad and Emmett had still been here, talking over Warrior names. I'd come in, not saying a word, and gotten to work on the Mustang.

Eventually, they'd realized I wasn't here for talk and they'd left me alone.

The hours flew by as I'd finished the final tasks on the car. Then I'd detailed the inside. I'd do the same to the exterior next and call the client to arrange for pickup.

I needed this car out of my garage. I had this gut feeling that the night I'd fucked Bryce on this Mustang, I'd also gotten her pregnant.

"Got it finished?" Isaiah asked, running his hand over the hood.

"Almost. Sorry if I kept you up last night." I hadn't really thought much about Isaiah in his apartment above the garage as I'd been working. The guy had probably heard me crashing around down here all night.

"No worries. I don't sleep much anyway."

"Insomnia?"

He shook his head. "Prison."

Isaiah hadn't told me much about why he'd been locked up, only that he'd been convicted of manslaughter and spent three years in prison. I hadn't asked for details. That was how it went here because that was how it had been in the club.

We asked enough to know what kind of man we were dealing with. Then we judged based on character, not past mistakes.

This garage was its own sort of brotherhood—though brother wasn't the right word, considering Presley was as much a part of this family as Emmett or Leo or Isaiah.

"So, are you, uh . . . you doing all right?" Isaiah asked.

I cleared my throat, ready to brush it off, but the truth came out instead. "Bryce is pregnant."

His eyes widened. "How do you feel about that?"

I let out a dry laugh. "I have no goddamn clue."

"And Bryce?"

"I didn't stick around long enough to ask," I admitted. I'd fucked up as boyfriend last night. And as expected, I was already fucking up the fatherhood gig too. Tossing my rag to the floor, I leaned against the car. "I don't know what to do. How to deal with a kid or a pregnant woman."

"I've only known one pregnant woman." Isaiah paused. "She was . . . special."

Was. Maybe it was someone he'd known once. But I had a feeling it was someone he'd lost.

"It terrified her," he said. "The idea of being responsible

for another life. She was excited too, but scared. And brave enough to admit it."

"Terrified seems about the right word."

"I bet Bryce is too."

"Yeah." I hung my head. I'm sure Bryce was scared too. Especially home and alone, dealing with this thing by herself.

What was I doing here? There was one person who held the power to ease my fears. And I wouldn't find her in the garage.

"I gotta go." I pushed off the tool bench, waving to Isaiah as I walked out the door. When my phone vibrated in my pocket, I fished it out. An unknown number had sent a text, so I slowed my steps, opening it up to see the picture attached.

That's when my heart stopped.

Bryce was on her knees. Needles and leaves were scattered on the dirt beneath her jeans, thick tree trunks crowded behind her. The photo was dark but there was enough light to see the terror on her face. Her mouth was gagged with a filthy rag tied around her head. Her eyes were red and her cheeks tearstained.

There was a gun pressed against her temple.

"Oh, Christ." I stumbled, losing my balance and collapsing on the cement. *No.*

I took a long breath, trying to focus. Then I turned again to the photo, my eyes narrowing at the person holding the gun. *It was a woman.* She was in profile, her arm held tight.

Who was she? Why did she have Bryce?

I went back to the text, looking for any kind of message, but there was nothing. Only the picture.

"Dash?" Dad was running my way. I hadn't heard him

drive up. "What's wrong?"

I blinked, snapping myself out of the haze as he helped me to my feet. Then I shoved the phone into his face. "Who the fuck is that woman?"

"What woman?"

"Her." I pointed to the picture. "With the gun to Bryce's head."

Fear turned to rage. My hands fisted and my heart rate slowed. The murderous feeling I hadn't had in years came roaring home with a vengeance, settling into my bones. Fury boiled my blood.

That woman was dead, whoever she was. And the person holding the camera. Dead.

"That's . . ." Dad slid the sunglasses off his face, squinting at the phone. Then his jaw dropped. "Fuck."

"What?"

"It can't be." He shook his head.

"What?" I roared, directly into his ear, making him flinch. "Who the fuck is that woman?"

"Genevieve." He gulped. "I think—Amina showed me pictures—I think it's Genevieve."

"Your daughter?" I seethed. "Your fucking daughter took my woman and held a gun to her head?"

"No, it can't be. It doesn't make sense." Dad ran a hand over his face.

Sense or not, she was dead.

"What's going on?" Isaiah rushed to my side.

"This." I showed him the picture. He hadn't been part of the club, but this was not the time for secrets. Not when I needed to get to Bryce. Isaiah let out a string of curses as I pulled back the phone, calling Emmett. He answered on the second ring. "Get here."

"Ten minutes."

I hung up, making the same call to Leo, then turned to Dad. "Why would she take Bryce?"

"I don't know," he answered.

"She must know about you. She thinks you killed her mother. Could she have taken Bryce for revenge?"

"No," he insisted. "She doesn't know I'm her father. Amina swore she never told her."

"She lied. This woman fucked her best friend's husband and stayed quiet about his kid for twenty-something years. I'm not taking her word for gold."

"Unless Bryce told her already."

"Doubtful," I told him. "They weren't supposed to meet until midmorning. And it's dark in this picture."

I risked another glance at the photo, ignoring my rolling stomach. I clung to the fact that Bryce was alive. Or she had been. Was the next text going to be Bryce's lifeless body?

No. I squeezed my eyes shut, forcing the mental image away until all that was left was black. Bryce had to live. We had things to work out. Things to talk about. A pregnancy to survive.

A kid to raise.

Together.

The roar of an engine came racing to the garage, Leo barreling in and skidding to a halt. Emmett's ten minutes was less than five as he pulled in moments later.

It didn't take long to catch them up.

"She must have come in from Denver early," Leo said. "Waited for Bryce to be alone."

Alone because I hadn't been there to protect her. I'd been too busy here, brooding about shit that was just as much my doing as it was hers.

If she survived this, I'd beg for forgiveness.

But maybe we'd all be better off if she didn't give it to me.

"Fuck!" I roared. Beside me, Isaiah flinched.

This wasn't happening. Not now. Not to Bryce. She was it for me. She was the woman I hadn't known I'd needed. My partner in crime. My confidant. My heart. Whoever did this to her would pay. I'd have my vengeance and it would be bloody.

If she didn't come out of this—no, I couldn't think like that. She had to come out of this unharmed. And for every scratch, every bruise, I'd deliver the same punishment tenfold.

"It doesn't make sense." Dad had been saying that over and over.

"What doesn't make sense?" I snapped. His muttering was grating on my last nerve.

"Why would she do this? How does she even know about us? If she wanted revenge on me for Amina, why go after Bryce?"

"We're missing something important," Emmett said. "She's mixed up in this somehow. Has probably been since the beginning."

"And she what, killed her own mother?" Dad huffed. "Doesn't figure right."

"What if she was angry at her mom? Maybe Amina and her had a falling out. Someone is holding that camera." I shook my phone. "She might not have been the one to hold the knife, but we all saw a Warrior break into the clubhouse. My guess is that same Warrior is the one behind this photo. And my *sister* is calling the shots."

"What do we do?" Emmett asked. "We can't sit here and wait. Bryce could be—"

"Don't." I held up a hand. "Don't say it."

The thoughts in my head were bad enough. I didn't need him adding horrors to my ears.

"We need to find her. She's alive." She had to be alive. I wasn't living the rest of my life miserable and alone.

I was going to find Bryce, lock her in my house and never leave her side again.

"Dad, call Tucker. Let's hope he's got more information than he was letting on."

He nodded, the phone already out from his pocket.

"Emmett, find out what you can about Genevieve. When she got to Montana. Where she's been hiding out."

With one short nod, he ran for the clubhouse.

"There's something—ahh." Leo dragged a hand through his hair. "I can't place it."

"What?"

"Something's familiar about that place."

"What place?"

"Let me see that picture again." He walked over and took the phone from my hand. Then he narrowed his eyes, his fingers zooming in on the far edge. "There. See it?"

"What am I looking for?"

"That building in the distance. See it?"

I'd been so focused on Bryce and the gun, I hadn't studied other parts of the photo. But there it was. In the distance, an old log building was nearly invisible within the trees.

"Do you know that place?" I asked Leo.

"It's familiar." He closed his eyes, thinking for a few aching seconds. Then his eyes popped open and he snapped his fingers. "It's up off Castle Creek Road, about an hour from here. Way the fuck up in the mountains on a steep old trail. I haven't been there in ten years but that building looks like the old Warrior hideaway a couple guys and I staked out back in the day."

"You're sure?" We couldn't afford to drive an hour into the mountains on a hunch. Bryce might not have any extra time, and if a call came in for ransom money, I wanted cell service.

"Yeah, brother. I'm sure."

Dad came over, his jaw clenched. "Tucker swears it's not the Warriors."

"Did he know anything about Genevieve?"

"Nothing."

"He's fucking lying," Leo bit out, ripping the phone out of my hand to show Dad the cabin. "Remember that cabin you had me, Jet and Gunner stake out? This is it."

"Fucking Tucker," he cursed.

"I'm going." I pointed to Leo. "Lead the way."

"Wait." Dad grabbed my arm, stopping me. "Could be a trap. Tucker knows we think a Warrior is behind this. He could have taken Bryce. Genevieve. Set it all up."

"Or Genevieve's a fucking psycho. Maybe she's not even your kid. Maybe this has all been one clusterfuck setup because you couldn't keep your dick behind your zipper. Who knows? What I do know is that Bryce is in danger and I'm going to do whatever it takes to keep her alive. If she's by that cabin, then that's where I'm going."

He blew out a long breath. "I'm coming too."

"We all just believed Amina's story, but it might not be true. We've been sloppy. We're all over the damn place and missing something major." I looked between Dad and Leo. "We've been on the defense from the start, and it's time to remember who we are. No one fucks with us, whether the club is gone or not. Someone's going to pay for this. Shoot first. Bury later."

Leo's face hardened. "Damn straight. Fuck this bitch."

Dad wasn't as quick to condemn Genevieve. "I'd like to talk to her."

"If she hurt Bryce, you'll have to live with the disappointment."

This was his chance to pick a side and it had sure as hell better be mine.

"Okay, son." He slid his sunglasses on his face. "Leo, lead the way."

Our boots pounded on the pavement as we went to our bikes. As I walked, I called Emmett, telling him to leave the clubhouse and catch up. As I shoved my phone in my pocket, movement at my side caught my eye.

"I'll come too." Isaiah was running toward his motorcycle.

Shit. This could get ugly and probably wasn't the place for him. "No, you stay."

"Please. Let me help."

I didn't have time to argue. "Your bike ready?"

"It'll keep up."

"Good. Because we're riding hard." I got to my bike and unlocked the storage compartment under the seat. I took out my Glock, tucking it into the waistband of my jeans. Then I took out another pistol, handing it to Isaiah. "You know how to use this?"

"Yeah."

"You get a clear shot, you take it."

I didn't care how much blood was spilled today.

As long as it didn't belong to Bryce.

CHAPTER TWENTY-FOUR

BRYCE

"**D**ash will come for me." I clenched my fists, pulling on the duct tape that bound them behind my back.

"I'm counting on it." The man standing before me, dressed in black, crossed his arms over his chest. "Now shut up."

I clamped my teeth together—my molars grinding so hard they could have pulverized diamonds. I wasn't obeying his order. I was freezing cold and wanted to keep them from chattering. My toes and fingers had gone numb hours ago. At least, I think it had been hours. I had no idea what time it was. The sun was up but not high enough to burn the chill that clung to the misty forest air.

Beside me, Genevieve sniffled. Her arm was pressed against mine, trembling. She was shaking head to toe, the body-racking kind of shakes that were pure fear.

Hours ago, I'd been scared too. When I'd been taken from my home and shoved in the trunk of a car, I'd been terrified. I'd cried until there were no more tears.

Then, lying in the dark trunk, my hands and ankles

bound, the fear had vanished. I couldn't afford to be afraid. I had another life counting on me to get my shit together.

My anger was keeping me alive. It kept my blood from turning to ice, fueling the fire in my heart. Because I had to hang on. To fight. I was finally getting a piece of the future I'd hoped for, a child I would love unconditionally. This asshole wasn't going to take that away from me.

Fuck this guy. He was the same man who'd broken into the Tin Gypsy clubhouse. I assumed as much based on his clothing. He wore black jeans and a black long-sleeved thermal. His ski mask covered his hair and his face. Black leather gloves stretched tight across his hands. And he wore a cut with the outdated Warrior logo on the back.

His eyes were covered with sunglasses, even in the dim light, the lenses and frames black. He showed no skin except for plain lips poking through the mask.

He was of average build, meaning even if we managed to get out of this situation—unlikely—there'd be no providing the police any identifying information. His dedication to keeping himself hidden actually gave me hope. If he was just going to kill us, why hide?

Maybe I was grasping for hope.

Around us, the forest was shadowed and eerie. The smell of pine and earth was heavy. This place he'd brought us to was so thick with evergreens, I doubted it ever got bright.

It was creepy as hell, but the low light might work to our advantage if we could figure out an escape. Maybe we could hide under some bushes or something. I grimaced at the thought of curling up with decaying leaves and needles.

Behind us, there was an old cabin tucked into the trees. I'd spotted it when he'd pulled us out of the trunk. It was menacing and the windows were blacked out like someone had boarded it up a decade ago and forgotten it existed. It was straight out of a horror movie, the type of place where human bodies were butchered in the basement. If I did get free, I'd be heading in the opposite direction of that cabin.

A phone chimed in the man's pocket. He turned away from Genevieve and me, disappearing deeper into the trees where we couldn't see him anymore.

But he was there. Waiting. Watching.

"What's he going to do to us?" Genevieve asked through chattering teeth.

"I don't know," I whispered. "But just hang tight."

Dash would find us. This guy had set it up that way. He wanted Dash to find me. But why? And why Genevieve? How had he known about her? Why was she here?

After the man had taken me from my house, he'd loaded me in the trunk, and I'd been jostled around as he took turn after turn, probably navigating through town. Then the whirl of tires against the asphalt became high-pitched as he sped down a smooth stretch of road.

Exhausted and emotionally wrecked, I fell asleep. Maybe for ten minutes, maybe an hour, I wasn't sure. I jolted awake when we stopped. I waited, barely breathing as his car door slammed, but he didn't come for me.

I waited, my heart hammering in my chest, until finally, the trunk opened. I squinted against the parking lot light above the car, adjusting my vision just in time to see the man heft another struggling body into the trunk.

Genevieve, gagged and bound, took one look at my face and stilled. We had only enough time to recognize each other before he slammed the trunk closed and the light was gone. We were sandwiched in tight with no room to move even though the trunk was larger than that of any car I'd owned.

With the gags, neither of us could talk. Instead, we both cried silent tears for hours until the car slowed and we were bounced around on a road so bumpy it couldn't have been paved.

It was still dark when he hauled us both from the car, threatening to slit our throats if we tried to run. With the enormous knife sheathed on his belt, I believed him.

Then he made us walk uphill for what felt like a mile, bringing us to this spot and shoving me to my knees. He untied Genevieve and put a gun in her hand, promising it was unloaded so she shouldn't try anything. Then he pushed her into position so the gun touched my temple in her shaky grip.

Her gag was stripped. The tape was removed from her wrists and ankles. And he told her to hold still. *Stop fucking crying.*

After all, Genevieve was supposed to look like my murderer.

He took a few pictures, then taped her up again, setting us both next to this tree. Thankfully, he pulled off my gag too. It wasn't like we needed them. Out here, no one would hear us if we screamed.

He disappeared for a while, but I knew he hadn't gone far. If we tried to run for it, he'd see. If we tried to get our hands free, he'd see.

So we sat, both of us in shock, until he returned and stood over us, watching silently.

I kept my head down, not wanting to provoke him. Every minute, we got colder. I was in flip-flops from dinner at my parents' place. Genevieve was barefoot and in a pair of black silk pajama pants. He must have taken her from the hotel where she'd been staying in Bozeman. Her white top was thin but at least it had long sleeves. The back was open, showing her strappy green sports bra. When she leaned forward, there were angry red scratches from the tree's bark on her skin.

Her feet were practically raw from the long walk through the forest.

She sniffled. "Why is this happening?"

I leaned toward her, letting my temple rest on top of her head. It was the best hug I could give her at the moment. "I need to tell you something."

"What?" Her body tensed even as she trembled.

"When I came to Denver, you told me something. You said your mom always called your father *Prez*. Well, that nickname was familiar and I . . . well, I sort of figured out who your father is."

Her head pulled away from mine. Her eyes got impossibly wide. "You did? Who?"

"Before I tell you, please keep an open mind. I know you don't have any reason to trust me, but I'm begging you to trust me."

She gave me a slight nod. "Tell me."

I took a deep breath, then blurted, "Draven Slater did not kill your mother. I'm sure of it. I don't have proof, but from the bottom of my soul, I think he genuinely cared for your mother and would not have harmed her."

Her eyes narrowed. "The police have evidence. He killed her. He lured her to that motel and stabbed her to death."

"She asked him to come to the motel because she had something to tell him. He's your fa—"

"No." She closed her eyes, shaking her head.

"I'm sorry. It's true. He's your father. Your mother asked him to come to the motel to tell him about you."

"*No*," she hissed, the word a combination of anger and despair.

"Draven was the president of a motorcycle club. They called him Prez."

"That nickname could be for anything."

"Genevieve." I gave her a sad smile. "You have his eyes and his hair. You even look a little bit like Dash."

"Who's Dash?"

"My boyfriend. And your half brother."

She leaned away from me, twisting to look the other direction. Either I'd done the right thing by telling her the truth, or I'd pushed her too far. I only hoped that she'd inherited some of Draven's strength because when I made a run for it, she was coming with me.

"I think this guy, the one who took us, is the one who killed your mom."

She shook her head, her eyes still squeezed shut. When she opened them, a new wash of tears fell. "Why?"

"I think it has something to do with Draven's motorcycle club. Some old grudge that never got settled. Somehow, we landed right in the middle of it."

She swallowed hard, sucking the tears back. "I just wanted to see Mom's grave."

"You will." I scooted into her side. "We'll get out of here. Dash will come for us."

I only hoped it wouldn't be too late.

We sat quietly, Genevieve's head probably spinning and mine frantic for some way to escape. I could run with my hands bound but not my ankles.

"Do you think he can see us?" I whispered.

"Maybe. But I can't see him."

"We have to get our legs free. He used duct tape. We can probably unwind it or cut it or something. But if he can see us, I don't want to try."

"Let's go pee."

"Right here?" *Gross.*

"Let's tell him we have to pee. Maybe he'll untie our legs."

"Oh." I relaxed. "Good idea."

My leg was falling asleep and tingling, but changing position seemed to make the cold seep deeper into my bones. We waited until the man emerged from behind a tree about fifty feet away. I hadn't seen him duck behind it. He walked toward us with sure strides, a man confident his infallible plan was coming together.

Chances were, it probably was. We were probably going to die today, but not without a fight.

"I need to pee," I said as he got closer.

"Then pee."

"Here?" I gaped. "And sit in it?"

He shrugged. Minus a few words here and there, he'd been mostly mute.

"No, thank you." I gritted my teeth again, the anger roaring to new life. I wasn't a violent person, but damn, I wanted to steal this guy's knife and stab him in the eyeball. I squirmed. "Please? Call it a last request. Don't make me die covered in urine."

"Fine." He took that enormous knife from its leather sleeve and brought it over. The metal seemed to find the only flicker of sunlight, glinting as it came toward my legs. One fast swipe and my ankles were free.

"Can I go too?" Genevieve looked at him with those big

eyes, weepy and seemingly pathetic. She put on quite the act.

He swiped the tape at her legs too, then motioned for us to stand.

My legs were wobbly and stiff, my arms tingling with sleep. Walking would have been hard on a flat surface, let alone the uneven ground of the forest floor. Running would be disastrous. *Shit.* Even if we could catch a break and slip free, it wouldn't take much for him to catch us again.

Was this hopeless? Were we going to die soon?

The man took his gun from his holster and pointed it at my nose as I found my balance. "Go."

I nodded, shuffling two steps away. "What about my hands? I can't get my jeans undone."

He frowned and came over, but instead of releasing my hands, he jerked the button and zipper on my jeans free and dragged them down to my knees. He did the same for Genevieve.

It was humiliating, having this man see me squat, my bare ass freezing in the cold air. Genevieve took her steps in the opposite direction. Her eyes squeezed shut as she squatted.

I did the same, pretending I was hovering over a toilet in The Betsy, not a pinecone. When we were done and he'd yanked our pants back in place, he pushed us back into the tree.

Please don't tape us again.

He reached for the backpack he'd brought, likely going for the tape.

"You sent that picture to Dash, didn't you?" I hoped the question would distract him. Maybe if I could keep him talking, he'd forget the tape.

"I did. Left him enough clues to find your body."

My heart jumped into my throat. "You're going to kill us and leave us here?"

"Just you." He pointed to Genevieve with the gun. "Dash will kill her for killing you."

I didn't need to ask why. This asshole was clearly good at framing others for murder, and he was banking on the fact that Dash would take his revenge, that no matter how much Genevieve pleaded and begged for her life, he'd kill her.

"But why her? She didn't do anything."

He stared at her and the muscles in his face behind the mask seemed to tense. "I have my reasons."

This had to be about Amina, right? Her murder had started this whole thing. I'd thought all along she was the key, but I was missing the connecting piece.

How had this man known when Genevieve was going to be in Montana? Did he know she was Draven's daughter? The paper hadn't gone out yet. If he did know, it meant someone in the garage had been talking.

But I couldn't believe that Emmett or Leo would let it slip. Had Draven told anyone? Maybe he'd confided in an old friend that he was a father to an unknown daughter.

Dad's face popped into my mind. Did he wonder why I hadn't shown up at the paper for delivery prep this morning? Was he worried? Whatever happened, I hoped Mom and Dad knew I loved them. If I did die today, I was glad we'd had dinner last night. A few hours, just the three of us.

I pushed away the thought of never seeing them again and focused on keeping this guy talking. He hadn't gotten out the tape yet. "Are you doing all this to start up an old war between clubs?"

"Not start. Win."

Then what was he waiting for? Why not kill us now and disappear? I wasn't sure how much time had passed since he'd sent Dash the picture, but it had to have been at least an hour.

He shoved his gun in his jeans and took out his phone. "Think we've waited long enough."

"For what?" I asked.

He nodded to Genevieve. "For them to find her and kill her. Can't have her get too far away."

Genevieve flinched, leaning closer to my side.

"Stand up." He reached for Genevieve, dragging her to her feet.

Then he did the same to me, hauling me up so fast I was dizzy. My heart raced. We needed more time.

Hot streaks raced down my cheeks. Tears streamed down Genevieve's too.

"Get on your knees," he ordered, taking out his pistol.

I was too scared to defy him. I dropped onto my knees but kept my eyes on Genevieve. She was going to see the worst, wasn't she? He'd make her pull the trigger. He'd make her see the blood and watch me die.

I gave her a sad smile. "It's okay."

A sob escaped her lips and her shoulders shook violently as he cut the tape to free her hands.

The man wrapped his arms around her, making her cry out. She fought him, twisting and turning, but he was too strong. With a tight squeeze, he held her to his body until she gave up the fight. One by one, he put her fragile hands on the gun. She shook her head, over and over, her hair falling into her face.

I was glad for it. I didn't want her to see.

I closed my eyes, challenging my thoughts to my lower belly. *I'm sorry, tiny one. I'm so sorry.*

In my mind, I pictured a little girl. She had hazel eyes and unruly hair. She had a wide smile and soft cheeks. She'd squeal when Dash threw her into the air and giggle on the way down.

I blew out a deep breath, holding my chin high. I was here because I'd wanted a story. The story of my lifetime. Everyone had warned me away from the Tin Gypsies, and I hadn't listened. I could be safe and home, right now. I could be at the newspaper, working alongside Dad.

But I wouldn't regret my choices. I'd do it all over again for the chance to fall in love with Dash Slater.

Another sob broke from Genevieve's mouth and I blocked it out. I stayed in my happy place, imagining his face. How it felt to fall asleep in his arms. I was there, curled against him in my bed, when the trigger squeezed and a bullet ripped through the gun.

The boom made my entire body seize. I'd expected nothingness. Death.

But as a fresh wave of cold crept up my skin, I opened my eyes to find the world moving in slow motion.

Genevieve slumped in the man's grasp, sliding her hands free of the gun. Her knees landed hard on the dirt.

The man kept hold of the gun, cursing as he swung the barrel toward the trees. He fired, the blast making me flinch.

"Bryce!" Genevieve reached for me, taking my arm as I struggled to stand.

"Go." I nudged her with my shoulder. "Run!"

Another gun fired. The shot whizzed by us and the bullet slammed into the tree at my back. The bark flew, sticking into my hair.

"Go, Genevieve," I said as we both rushed for the trees.

She kept a grip on my arm, lending me her balance. One second, her hand was there, the next she was flying backward. The man had grabbed her by the hair, pulling her to his front as a human shield.

"No!" I spun to go back for her, but more bullets went flying. Two from the man's gun, another from the distance. It slammed into his shoulder, making him stagger.

"Dash!" I screamed, knowing he was out there.

"Get out of there, Bryce." His voice came from deep in the trees.

Genevieve ripped herself away from the man and took off in the other direction, sprinting toward the old cabin.

I couldn't follow her, not if I wanted to get free.

Another bullet went flying and I wasted no more time. I ran, tripping on branches and doing my best to stay upright with my hands behind my back. My hair snagged in my mouth as I kept looking forward at my path and backward for the man.

He was moving my way, his gun outstretched as he ducked behind a tree.

I did the same, hoping he'd lose sight of me. When I looked back again, he was gone. *Where is he?* I checked to my left, then my right. I looked over my shoulder again but there were only trees.

But he was out there.

Too busy looking for my kidnapper, I didn't watch where I was running. My flip-flop caught on a rock and the forest became a blur. *This is going to hurt.* I braced for impact, except I didn't fall.

Dash caught me.

A sob broke free from my chest as his arms wrapped around me, pulling me to my feet.

"Are you hurt?" His hands touched me from head to toe. The touch was almost too hot against my frozen skin.

"No," I croaked, collapsing into his warmth. "No, I'm okay."

He pulled me in closer, his hands running up and down my back to create some friction. "You're freezing."

I nodded, huddling into his body and letting my knees give way.

He held me tight, speaking over my head. "Find them and kill them."

Them? Had there been two kidnappers? I'd only seen the one man. Had someone else helped him take me and Gen—

"No. Stop." My teeth chattered so loud they rattled in my ears. I found the strength to stand, pushing away from Dash. Isaiah and Leo were only a few feet away. "It's not her."

"She tried to kill you," Dash snapped.

"No." I shook my head. "It's not her. He took her. He posed it all. It's *him*. Find him."

"You're sure?"

"I'm sure. Don't hurt her. Please, *help* her."

Draven and Emmett came running over from the trees at our other side.

"Find him," Dash ordered when they reached our huddle. "Whatever it takes."

Draven put one hand on my shoulder. The other was holding a gun. They were all holding guns. Dash had one behind my back, in the hand of the arm holding me up.

"Genevieve ran toward the cabin." I spotted it in the distance. "Don't let him get her again."

"I'll find her," Isaiah said.

Dash nodded. "I need to get Bryce out of here."

"Go." Draven jerked his chin toward Leo and Emmett and the three of them began creeping through the trees, their guns extended and ready to fire.

I lost sight of them in seconds.

Dash ducked behind me, bringing his teeth to my wrist and tearing a slit in the tape. He ripped it all free, probably taking some hair along with it, but I was so cold, I didn't feel the sting. Then he scooped me into his arms and carried me away.

I curled into his warm chest. "H-how did you find us?"

I knew the man had left enough clues for him to get to us, but he must have come faster than expected. Otherwise, I'd be dead and they'd be hunting Genevieve.

"Talk later."

"Okay," I whispered, closing my eyes as he walked.

He stopped only once to shift my weight in his arms on the long walk to where he'd parked his bike. It was no wonder we hadn't heard their engines. And now it made sense why Dash was so warm and his T-shirt slightly damp. They must have sprinted through the woods.

"Here." He set me down next to his bike, running his hands up and down my bare arms. Then he dug into a compartment on the bike, pulling out a sweatshirt and yanking it over my head.

"Thanks." My muscles were convulsing from the cold, adrenaline leaving my system.

"Kick off your flip-flops."

"Huh?" I asked as he began toeing off his boots. "W-what are you doing?"

Dash didn't answer. He took off his socks and guided me to the bike's seat. Then he put his socks on my feet, stowing my flip-flops away. "Just an hour. Hold on for an hour, baby, and we'll be home. Can you make it?"

"Yeah."

He kissed my forehead. "Goddamn, you're tough. Strongest woman I've ever known."

I had a lot to live for.

I settled behind him on the bike's seat, wrapping myself around his broad back and pressing my cheek to his shoulder. The smell of his shirt—the fabric softener, the wind, the spice of his sweat—filled my nose and chased away the forest stink.

"You found me," I whispered in a voice I didn't think he'd hear over the engine.

Dash twisted, taking my face in his hands and dropping his forehead to mine. "And I'm never letting you go."

CHAPTER TWENTY-FIVE

DASH

"Hold on, baby." I pinned Bryce's hand to my chest, driving whenever I could with one hand. "We're almost there."

Bryce nodded against my shoulder. Her entire body was shaking. It had been like that for the last thirty miles into Clifton Forge and I was worried that she might be on the edge of getting hypothermia. Or worse, that the stress that bastard had put her through had hurt the baby.

Damn it. The bike was a habit and had been faster, but I should have stopped and taken my truck.

We were close to my house, so close that I wanted to gun it and just get there. But I was nervous she'd fall. Except for the few times when I'd had to use both hands to get us around a tight corner or a rough patch on the mountain, I'd been holding her to me for most of the ride. A few times, her weight had gotten so heavy on my back, I'd looked over my shoulder to see she was nearly asleep, so I'd woken her up.

She was exhausted.

When my house came into view, I exhaled. *Finally.* I

pulled into the driveway and onto the grass, parking next to the front porch. I shut off the bike and slowly unwrapped Bryce's arms from around me, then I stood, making sure to keep a grip on her hand.

"Where are we?" Her gaze was slow and heavy as she took in the house.

"My place." I scooped her up and walked to the door. Her forehead felt like ice when she burrowed it into my neck.

Walking straight for the master bathroom, I didn't set her down as I turned on the shower to lukewarm. We'd slowly crank the temperature until the steam seeped into her bones and chased away the cold.

Should I have taken her to the hospital?

Carefully, I set her on the vanity between the double sinks. As she glanced around, her lips nearly blue, I began to pull off her clothing.

The chattering in her teeth was gone. Either she had warmed up a little or things were much worse.

"This is nice," she whispered. "Not what I expected."

I was too focused on getting off her clothes to respond.

She'd probably expected a bachelor's bathroom with towels tossed on the floor and toothpaste splatters on the sinks and mirrors. But I'd spent a lot of time and money designing this place. I had a heated marble tile floor and coordinating countertops. The tiled, walk-in shower could hold five people with room to spare. There were double spouts and a rainfall head in the center.

The socks I'd put on her were on the floor, the sweatshirt gone. When I stripped off her shirt and bra, she pulled her arms in tight. Her skin wasn't its normal smooth, creamy color. It was dotted with purple and covered in tight, angry goose bumps.

"Can you stand?" When she nodded, I picked her up and set her gently on her feet. Then I went to work on her jeans, unzipping them and pulling them down her legs, taking her panties along with them.

She stood there naked and shivering while I stepped back and whipped off my own clothes.

Bryce pressed a hand to my bare chest as I undid my jeans. "You're cold too."

Was I? I didn't feel cold. From the moment that picture had hit my phone, fear had made me numb.

"Slowly." I took her hand, helping her into the shower and under the spray. She winced when the water hit her skin. It felt room temperature to me, not even warm enough to create steam. "Too hot?"

"It'll be okay." She squeezed her eyes shut and the pain on her face nearly broke me.

"I'm sorry." I wrapped her into my arms, pulling her into my body as the water ran over her shoulders. "I'm so sorry."

"It's not your fault," she said into my chest, giving me her weight.

We stood there, holding on to one another until she began to relax. Then I turned up the hot water, making adjustments every few minutes until we were cloaked in a box of steam and it was hard to even see her face.

Only when my fingers and toes began to loosen did I realize how cold I'd been too. The morning air had been cool on the race to the mountain, but adrenaline, my temper and worst-case scenarios had kept me from freezing. Then I'd been running. Literally. The guys and I had parked nearly a mile away from the cabin, hoping we'd be able to hide the sound of our bikes. Then we'd made a sprint for it.

I'd never run a mile faster in my life. And each time I'd checked, Emmett, Leo and Isaiah were right on pace, keeping up as we'd dodged trees and fallen limbs. Even Dad had kept up, showing that his daily workout wasn't for nothing.

Christ, we'd gotten lucky. We'd gotten a jump on the guy, though as I'd dashed through the forest, my gun drawn, I'd been hunting for Genevieve, not a man cloaked in black.

What the hell had happened? When Bryce was warm, we'd talk. But for now, I was simply glad my heart was climbing down from my throat.

When the hot air filled my lungs, they loosened. The muscles in my arms relaxed. And as the color came back to Bryce's face, some of my fears washed down the drain.

I kept her in the shower until we'd nearly run the hot water heater through. "Warmer?"

She nodded. "Much."

"Good." I tipped her head under the spray, then took some shampoo, massaging it in her hair and rinsing it out.

She'd smell like me today, but soon we'd get her stuff. I'd clear one of the built-in ledges for her. She could have all the space she wanted because she was here now.

Bryce was home.

She was my home.

When she was clean, I quickly scrubbed my hair, washing away the smell of panic and wind from the ride. Then I stepped out first, grabbing a towel to dry off.

"Give me your hand." I extended my own, helping her onto the bathmat as she turned off the water.

"I can do it," she said as I kneeled to towel off her legs.

"Let me." I looked up at her from my knees. "Please."

She ran a hand through my damp hair. "Okay."

I closed my eyes, savoring that light touch. A few hours ago, I was sure I wouldn't feel it ever again. My throat burned; a sting hit my chest. It was too much. Emotion. Fear. *Love.* How the hell did I process it all?

Clearing my throat, forcing it all down, I focused on my task, making sure every drop of water was gone from her skin. I squeezed the water from her hair until it was as dry as I could get with only a towel.

"Do you have a comb or br—Dash," she gasped as I scooped her into my arms. "I can walk."

"I need this, baby."

"Okay." She burrowed in close like she had earlier, this time not for the heat but for the touch.

I took her to my bed, ripping back the white down comforter I'd made flat yesterday morning. The morning before I'd known Bryce was pregnant. Before I'd spent the night working in the garage. Before she'd been taken.

That was on me. Forever, this whole thing was on me. And I'd spend forever making it up to her.

Settling Bryce under my sheet, I tucked us both in tight, turning her so I could press my chest against her back.

"Do you know . . . did they find Genevieve?" Her voice was scared and quiet.

"Don't know yet, babe. Emmett will let me know, but in this case, no news is good news. Okay?"

Bryce clutched my arms as I wrapped them around her. She threaded her legs into mine. And there, when I could kiss the skin on her shoulder, I let one of my hands slide down and splay my fingers over her belly.

"Do you think it's okay? The baby?"

Her breath hitched. "I hope so."

"Me too."

"Do you?" she whispered. "You said—"

"I know. I said I didn't want to be a father. When you told me last night, I didn't know what to say. How to react. The truth is . . . I'm fucking scared, babe."

"So am I."

I hugged her tighter. "You are?"

"Yeah. This wasn't something I planned. I thought— hoped—maybe one day, when the timing was right. When I was married and settled. This was unexpected but . . . but I can't say I don't want to be a mother."

Bryce would be a wonderful mother. She'd fight for her child—our child—like a warrior. She'd hold a firm hand. She'd give her love unconditionally. And I wanted her to have that chance.

I wanted to be along for the ride.

"What if—the stress of all this—" She sighed. "What if something happened?"

It was on our minds and neither of us would stop worrying. We might lie here, warm and quiet, but our minds were racing. Screaming *what if*.

Fuck it. I whipped off the covers, bouncing out of bed.

"What are you doing?" Bryce asked as I opened up a drawer in the walnut dresser in the bedroom.

"Let's go to the doctor."

"Now?"

"Now." I took out a pair of jeans. "We gotta know."

She was out of bed in a flash. "I don't know if the hospital here will have the right equipment. It's so early."

"Then we'll drive to Bozeman." I crossed the room and pulled her into my arms. "Before the day is over, we'll know."

Rather than make her pull on the clothes she'd been wearing, I found a pair of sweats. The waistband was rolled to cinch them around her waist, the legs folded up so she wouldn't walk on the hems. And then I pulled a T-shirt and my favorite Harley-Davidson black hoodie over her head.

"You're beautiful." Dressed in my clothes, her hair damp and limp, her eyes red and tired, she'd never looked better.

"I'm a wreck."

I kissed her forehead. "Gorgeous. Ready?"

"No," she confessed. "I don't want bad news."

"Me neither." With our hands linked, I led her into the garage and to my truck.

She took one look at it and her shoulders relaxed. "Thank God. I need a break from your bike."

I chuckled and loaded her into the passenger seat. She rolled her eyes as I buckled her seat belt but let me help her all the same. With the heat cranked up, I drove through town to the hospital. We marched right to the emergency room, and two hours later, Bryce and I were back in the truck.

I took her hand, pulling it across the console to kiss her knuckles. Then I stretched to cup her cheek, using my thumb to dry a tear falling from her beautiful eyes. "You good?"

"Yeah." She sniffed, the tears still falling. Then she smiled, the relief and joy hitting me square in the chest. *Sweet relief.* "I mean, a lot could still go wrong but—"

"It won't."

They'd called in the OB/GYN for us, the doctor who delivered all the babies in Clifton Forge. First, he'd ordered a blood test. Then he had wheeled in a cart, covered a wand with a condom and done an ultrasound of her womb. From everything the doctor could see, there weren't any risks to the pregnancy at the moment. We stuck around, waiting for the blood test. When he confirmed hormone levels were where they needed to be and they'd picked up a heartbeat on the ultrasound, we were sent home.

And yeah, shit could still go wrong. But I wasn't going to think like that.

"I need to call my parents. I'm sure my dad is worried since I didn't show up for Sunday delivery."

"Want to just go to their house?"

"Not like this. I'm a mess and they'll worry. Can I borrow your phone?"

"Sure, babe." I handed it over and let her call as we sat in the parking lot. She assured them she was fine and that she'd explain everything later. When the call ended, I pulled away from the hospital, driving to my house again.

"Should we go to the garage?" she asked. "I want to make sure Genevieve is okay."

"Dad will come to my place. Let's start there."

"Okay." She was so tired, her eyes drooped as we drove. But when we arrived home and there were three bikes in the driveway, she sat up straight.

I pulled into the garage and helped her inside where Dad, Leo and Emmett were already waiting in my living room. Leading Bryce to a couch, I sat down and put her right at my side.

"Did you get him?" Bryce asked before anyone else could speak.

Dad's jaw clenched as he shook his head.

"Fucking bastard," Leo hissed from the leather chair across from us. "We were close. Followed his trail right up past the cabin, but then he just disappeared. He had to know that area."

"Goddamn it," I growled as Bryce tensed. The last thing we needed was this guy still breathing. If he came after Bryce again, he wouldn't find her alone.

"We split up and searched the area," Emmett said. "Then hightailed it back to the road in case he got around us but then had to leave."

"Why?"

"Fire." Dad shook his head. "Fucker must have torched the cabin to cover his tracks. We saw smoke billowing up from the trees, knew we had to report it. We called it in to the forest service, then got the hell out of there before the authorities showed up."

"And Genevieve?" Bryce asked. "Where is she?"

"We don't know." Dad shook his head. "When we got back to our bikes, Isaiah's was already gone. Figured we'd find him at the garage but it's empty. Tried calling him but he's not answering."

"What if the guy got her?" Bryce clutched my hand. "We have to find her."

"Isaiah wouldn't leave the mountain if he didn't have her with him. He ran right after her."

Except they should have been here already. With the time it had taken me to get Bryce home and shower, then for us to go to the doctor, Isaiah should have had Genevieve back in town by now.

I shot Dad a look, silently conveying my worry. With one nod, I knew he felt the same. But I didn't want to worry Bryce even more.

"He probably took her someplace to get warm," I assured her. "We'll give them thirty minutes to call back. Then we'll go looking."

"Okay." She nodded.

"All right. Since we've got thirty minutes"—Dad faced Bryce—"what happened?"

"I went to my parents' house for dinner last night. It was almost dark when I got home. I was tired and didn't bother turning on the lights because . . . I was tired. I just wanted to go to bed." She sucked in a ragged breath. "Then he was there. I tried to fight him off but he was too strong. He taped my hands and ankles together, gagged me so tight I could barely swallow. Then he hauled me out the back door to the alley. No one would have seen us out there, not in my neighborhood. Everyone's asleep after seven. He stuffed me in the back of a car. In the trunk."

My stomach pitched. She'd been in a trunk? This fucker was dead. He'd put my woman in a trunk. If I had just been there, if I hadn't left after she'd told me she was pregnant, none of this would have happened.

"It's not your fault," she whispered, lacing her fingers with mine as she read my thoughts.

"Should have been there."

"He would have found another way. This was planned. He wanted you to think Genevieve had taken me so you'd go after her."

"Why?" Emmett asked. "Did he say why?"

Bryce shook her head. "Just that he wanted to win an old war."

"The Warriors," Leo bit out. "Tucker lied to us."

"You're right," I said. "It has to be the Warriors, but Tucker isn't the kind of man who would hide his intentions. If he had a beef with us, he'd own it. Hell, he'd brag about fucking us over. So why hide behind a ruse? Why try to frame Genevieve? How did he even know about her?"

"My gut says it's not the Warriors." Dad stood, moving to

stand in front of the fireplace. "That Tucker's been telling the truth from the beginning. This is someone else. Someone knows I went to meet with Amina that night. He knows she —we—had a daughter and went after Genevieve too. Bottom line, this is all about me. Making me pay."

"Who?" Emmett asked. "We've been trying to come up with a target for a damn month and we're no closer now than we were the day you got arrested."

"What else happened?" I asked Bryce. "After he loaded you into the trunk, what else happened?"

"We drove," she said. "For a long time. Then he parked and got out. It was a while later that he came back with Genevieve."

"Bozeman. Bet he took you to Bozeman to grab Genevieve after her flight got in. Probably took her from the hotel. Which meant he had to know she was coming. Do you know who else she told about coming here?"

Bryce shook her head. "As far as I know, it was just me. But if he was watching—I don't know, can you hack someone's credit card transactions?"

"Yeah," Emmett told her. "It doesn't take much."

"That makes me feel safe," she muttered.

I'd wait until a different day to tell her Emmett had broken into her accounts the day after she'd shown up at the garage.

"Let's find out what hotel Genevieve was at. Maybe they have video footage of him taking her." Though I wouldn't hold my breath. This guy was smart. He'd taken precautions. Even in the mountains, he'd been covered head to toe. "Did he show his face?"

"No." Bryce's shoulders fell. "Not once."

"Then he took you up to the mountains, right?" Dad asked.

"Yep. He made us pose for the picture. He said he wanted you guys to find me dead because then you'd kill Genevieve. He had me on my knees. The gun . . ." She swallowed hard. "The gun was to my head. I really thought that was it. Thank God, it wasn't. I guess you got there faster than he'd expected."

"Did he . . ." I swallowed hard. "Did he hurt you?"

"No." She gave me a sad smile. "He pushed me and Genevieve around, but nothing more."

Other than trying to kill her.

He'd die for that. Except we'd missed our shot. "Fuck, I wish I hadn't missed."

When was the last time I'd missed a target? *Years.* But I hadn't shot a gun in a year either. I needed to fit in time at the range. I'd been so close with my shot, but after sprinting up the mountain, my heart had been racing. Then to see the guy holding Genevieve, I'd made a split-second decision to shoot at him instead of Genevieve.

"I'm just glad you didn't shoot Genevieve," Bryce said. "Where are they? Can you call them again?"

Dad took out his phone and made the call. He didn't leave the room as he pressed it to his ear. The rings were loud enough for us to hear until they ended and he dropped the phone. "No answer."

Shit. Something had gone wrong. Maybe this guy had caught up to Isaiah? I didn't want to drag Bryce along to go find them, but it might come to that. I wasn't leaving her alone or in anyone else's care.

"After he got Genevieve, did you go anywhere else?" Emmett asked her.

"No, we drove right to the mountain. He made us walk to the spot where you found us."

"Any trace of a car up there?" I asked Leo.

"None. Wherever he parked, it was far. Probably a trail we don't know about."

"Did you get a look at the car? Maybe a license plate?"

Bryce shook her head. "He took us out, faced us away, and I didn't even think to look at the plates. The car was nothing special. It was a typical black sedan. Sorry."

"It's okay, babe." I put my arm around her shoulders. "You did good."

She'd lived. That was all she'd had to do. She'd fought. And when it was time, she'd run.

"He seemed so determined. Angry. This is . . . personal. It has to be someone you know," she told us. "I could feel it, when we were up there. He hates you."

Dad's eyes met mine. *Who?*

We'd been asking that question for a month.

"If we haven't figured it out by now, we're not going to today." I stood from the couch, pulling Bryce to her feet. "We need to find Isaiah. Let's check the garage first."

"Wait." She tugged on my hand. "Don't you think we should go to the cops and tell them about the kidnapping?"

I looked to Emmett and Leo, both shaking their heads. I sighed, turning to Bryce. "Babe, I know you trust Marcus. But I think this would be better kept between us."

"Why? We're trying to prove that Draven is innocent here. To show reasonable doubt that someone is out to frame him. If me being kidnapped makes them investigate, then shouldn't we try?"

"They won't find anything. If we didn't, they won't."

And if the cops were involved, I wouldn't get the vengeance I wanted against the man who'd taken her.

She narrowed her gaze. "You don't know that."

"I do," I said gently. "I'm not saying they aren't good at their jobs, but no matter how hard they tried, they never pinned much on the Gypsies. We're just . . . better than they are. We don't have to follow the same rules."

"What if we don't find who took me? He can't get away with it, Dash."

"He won't," I promised. "But we'll have an easier time finding him if we're not worried about Marcus in the middle of everything. If we bring in the cops, we'll be constantly worried they'll stumble onto something they shouldn't. Some secrets need to stay secret. If they're hovering over us, it'll cripple us. Trust me. Please?"

Her face softened. "Okay."

"Come on." I put my arm around her shoulders. "Let's go to the garage and find Isaiah."

Except when we got there, it was deserted. Open and empty, the way we'd left it this morning. It seemed like years, not hours, since I'd been working on the Mustang.

"Where are they?" Bryce asked as we stood together in the office. Emmett had gone to the clubhouse to make sure nothing had happened there while we'd been gone. Leo and Dad had just run upstairs to check Isaiah's apartment.

"I don't know." I hugged her to my chest. "We'll find them."

I took out my phone, calling Isaiah's number and not expecting him to answer—and he didn't. Boots thudded down the metal stairs at the side of the building, preceding Dad and Leo as they came into the office.

"Nothing," Dad said. "Leo and I are going to head back up to the mountain. You guys wait here. Stay safe."

"Call as soon as you can." There was plenty of light this time of year. They had until almost nine before the dark would creep in and make a search impossible.

"Will do. Lock down tight. Everything. Call Presley and make sure she's home. Tell her to stay there and lock the doors."

"You think he'd go after her?"

Dad's gaze drifted to Presley's desk. "Don't know what to think anymore."

When the door closed behind them, I took Bryce's face in my hands. She leaned her cheek into my palm. "You're dead on your feet. Let's go home. Get some rest."

"I want to be here in case they show up. Can we wait in the office?"

I wouldn't tell her no. Not today. "I'll call in for some food. What do you want?"

"Whatever. I'm not all that hungry."

"Well, you have to eat." It had been twenty-four hours since she'd eaten.

I led her into my office, where I had a couch. I made sure she was comfortable, then called for pizza. She did her best to eat two slices while I inhaled the rest. Then we sat in the silence. Waiting.

Other than Emmett stopping in to tell us he'd found the hotel and was trying to get security camera footage, no word came. Eventually, Bryce fell asleep on my lap. I kept one hand on her hip. The other ready to grab my gun from its holster.

The light behind the window blinds in my office faded slowly. It got dark, enough for the timed lights outside to flicker to life. And that was when the buzz of a motorcycle caught my ear. The sound didn't belong to Dad's bike.

"Babe." I gently shook Bryce awake. "Someone's coming."

She roused from sleep, rubbing her eyes. "Do you think it's them?"

"Don't know. Come on." I held her hand, keeping her hidden behind me as I went to the office door. I cracked it an inch, taking out my gun. When the machine came into view, I put it away. "It's Isaiah."

"Finally." She opened the door wider, pushing past me as he pulled into the parking lot.

His face was haggard as he shut off his bike. His shoulders slumped. When he spotted us outside the office, at the base of the stairs that led to his apartment, his frame fell even further.

"Where's Genevieve?" Bryce asked after he climbed off his motorcycle and walked our way. "Is she okay?"

"She wanted to leave. I drove her to Bozeman."

"And you left her there?" Bryce's jaw dropped. "We don't know who took us. What if he got to her again? He took her from that hotel once, he could have—"

Isaiah held up a hand. "I took her to the hotel and went in and got her stuff. Then I drove her to the airport, waited until her plane took off. She's on her way to Colorado if she's not there already."

"Okay." Bryce relaxed. "But she's all right?"

"She's fine."

"What happened? Why didn't you answer?" I asked. "We've been calling."

Isaiah dropped his eyes to the ground, his jaw set tight. He looked awful. More haunted than the first day he'd shown up here, desperate for a job and to get on with his life.

I put my hand on his shoulder. "What happened?"

He didn't answer. He brushed past us to the stairs, taking each one with heavy footfalls.

"Isaiah," I called his name.

He paused and glanced over his shoulder. "I got her out of there. Just like I said I would."

Something else had happened, but before I could ask for more, he was up the stairs and out of sight.

Bryce and I shared an anxious look.

We weren't going to get any more answers tonight.

CHAPTER TWENTY-SIX

BRYCE

After Isaiah left Dash and I standing with our mouths hanging open, we went back to his place for the night. I wanted my own pajamas, a brush and clean panties, but I wasn't sure when I'd be ready to go home, especially in the dark.

As we drove, Dash called his dad to tell him Isaiah had returned. And it was unlikely Genevieve would ever set foot in Montana again.

"Dad said they're already on their way back," he told me after hanging up. "They couldn't get close to the cabin anyway."

"Because of the fire?"

Dash nodded. "Forest service had a whole crew up there, making sure it doesn't spread to the trees."

"Why do you think he burned it?"

"Don't know. But like Dad said, it was probably to cover his tracks."

Something in that cabin could have identified my

kidnapper, but we'd never find it now. "I wish I had my phone to text Genevieve. Just to make sure she's all right."

Genevieve and I had been through so much in a short period of time. But given what had happened, what I'd told her about Draven and her mother's murder, I didn't blame her for running.

I probably would have done the same.

"Tomorrow." Dash took my hand from my lap, threading our fingers together. "Tomorrow I'll get your phone and whatever else you want from your house."

"That'd be great." I'd have to go back eventually, but for now, I was content to spend some time at his place. I had a feeling not many women could claim they'd spent time at Dash Slater's home. I was too tired tonight, but tomorrow, I wanted to explore. Relax in his space.

After I made sure Genevieve was home safely.

"Do you think Genevieve will be safe in Denver?"

"Might be the safest place for her. Or she'll be an easy target."

"She has to be okay, Dash. None of this was her fault. I can't help but think if I'd only stayed here, stayed away, that—"

"This is not your fault, babe." He tightened his grip on my hand. "If not for you, we wouldn't know the truth. Dad would have died keeping it a secret. And it needed to come out. It's for the best."

Except it had cost him his relationship with his father. I wasn't sure what was best now.

"What do we do now?"

"Sleep." Dash sighed. "Regroup in the morning."

If my mind kept racing, sleep would not come easily.

Dash led me straight to his bedroom when we got to his

house. The room overlooked a large backyard. Was that a hot tub? Before I could get a look at it on the patio, Dash pulled the blinds over the windows shut.

"Bed. Sleep. You can have free rein of the place tomorrow."

"Fine." I pouted, stripping off my clothes.

We met in the middle of Dash's enormous bed, our naked bodies molding to one another as we lay face-to-face.

"I don't know if I can sleep," I whispered.

My mind raced over everything Isaiah didn't say. Why would he stay quiet? What had happened on that mountain? Was it really as simple as he'd taken Genevieve to Bozeman and then come back? But why had it taken so long? Why did he seem more broken than ever?

"Isaiah looked—"

"Sleep, babe."

"But—"

"Bryce. You need to sleep. Tomorrow, 'kay?"

I huffed. "Okay."

Closing my eyes tight, I breathed in and out in a steady rhythm. It was odd, remembering that only last night I'd been at home, wondering if I would be raising this baby alone. If Dash and I were over.

"You rescued me," I whispered, bringing a hand up to push a lock of his hair off his forehead.

His lashes lifted, and even in the dark, his eyes were shining bright. "We've got a lot to talk about. You and me. The baby. And we will."

"Are we going to be okay?"

He pulled me tighter into his arms, holding me safe. "Swear it on my life."

————

TOMORROW CAME and went without the answers we'd hoped for.

Because when we went to find Isaiah at the garage the next morning, he was gone.

CHAPTER TWENTY-SEVEN

BRYCE

"I need to go to work." I pulled a tank top over my head. "Can you wait a few hours? Please? I need to get to the garage first thing and make sure we have everything covered for the day in case Isaiah doesn't show again. Then I can drive you to the paper."

"I could go alone. Other people will be there."

"Not an option." Dash pulled on a pair of jeans. "Until we find out what the hell is happening and who took you, you're not going anywhere without me."

This was not an argument I was going to win. "Fine."

It had been two days since he'd rescued me from that mountain and he'd only left my side once. And that was to go to my house yesterday and pick up some things so I could stay at his place for a bit. Even then, he'd called Emmett to stay with me while he was gone.

"How you feeling?" Dash, dressed in jeans and a gray T-shirt, came over and ran his hands up and down my arms.

"Meh." I'd been sick this morning. Yesterday morning too. I hoped it had passed because if we were going to the garage, I was nervous about getting up close and personal with the shop's toilet. "Will you grab me some crackers?"

"Sure." He kissed my forehead, walking out as I finished getting dressed. When I found him in the kitchen, he had a box of saltines on the counter and a travel mug of decaf ready for me. It wouldn't be until noon that I'd be able to stomach anything else.

Picking up my laptop from his dining room table, I loaded it into my purse, then followed Dash to the garage. He looked longingly at his bike, parked next to his truck, but knew I wasn't ready to get on it yet.

Soon. But not yet.

When we got to the garage, three bikes were already lined up against the fence in the parking lot.

"Since when does everyone beat you here in the morning?" I asked Dash. The clock on the dash said seven thirty.

"Since never." He pursed his lips. If Draven, Emmett and Leo were here already, it meant trouble.

All three men were waiting inside Draven's office when we got inside, Emmett and Leo across from his desk, Draven behind it. The moment he spotted me, Draven leapt up and offered me his seat.

"Thanks."

He nodded, standing against the wall next to Dash. He didn't get a *good morning* or *hello* from his son.

"What's up?" Dash asked.

"Got some news from the DA," Draven announced.

"And?" My article had been printed on Sunday, showing a man breaking into the clubhouse and exposing Genevieve and the reason Draven and Amina had been at the Evergreen Motel in the first place. Had it worked? Had we planted a seed of doubt that might make the prosecutor delay?

"It's not enough." Draven gave me a sad smile. "The photo of the guy. The speculation that the knife was stolen. It's not enough. They're going to proceed with the trial. Starts within sixty days."

"No." My heart sank. If only I could have told them about being kidnapped. I trusted Dash and his reasons. The last thing I wanted was for Marcus to find something that might land Dash in prison alongside Draven. But I couldn't help feeling that had we reported the kidnapping, Draven might have an easier time being acquitted.

"We've got time," Emmett said. "Two months to prove you're innocent."

"More than that," Dash said. "Trial will take a while."

Except we were at yet another dead end. Unless we could find my kidnapper, we had nothing to go on.

"I have some news too," Leo said. "Cops are releasing it today. My source says they found a burned body in the cabin."

"No," I gasped. "Who?"

"Could it be our guy?" Dash asked.

Leo shrugged. "No idea. Body was burned to a crisp. They're going to have to do dental records to identify him, but I'm guessing it was our guy. Maybe he ran up there, circled back and holed up inside. Started the fire, who the fuck knows. But if he was our guy, the chances of proving he murdered Amina without a confession are dust."

Draven's frame slumped against the wall. "Shit."

The room went quiet.

"It might not be him. The guy who took me. Maybe he had another friend up there. Maybe someone he'd already killed. Who knows? I think he's probably dead but we don't know for sure."

"Bryce is right." Dash pushed off the wall. "Everyone watch their back. Something about this doesn't sit well. It's too clean. He was smart enough to take Bryce *and* Genevieve but then killed himself in a fire? Doesn't fit."

"Agreed." Emmett stood from his chair. "We'll keep looking. Keep thinking. Something will come to light."

Leo stood too. "Fuck, I hope so."

"Until then, let's get back to work," Dash said. "Show whoever this fucker is that we're moving forward."

He nodded for me to follow him into his office. The desk was cluttered and he gathered the paperwork up, making one large stack in the corner. "It's all yours, babe. Unless you want to come hang out in the garage with me. I can set you up on a tool bench."

I grinned. "We did that before, remember? Pretty sure that's how you knocked me up."

He chuckled, sitting on the edge of the desk. Then he motioned me into his arms, into the only place I felt safe at the moment.

"Eventually, all this will end, right? Life will return to normal?" Or a new normal. I didn't want to go back to the days when he wasn't in my life.

"One way or another. Either we find out who killed Amina or . . ."

Or Draven lost his freedom.

———

ONE WEEK LATER, Dash and I were already finding a new normal.

We were at the garage, working. That was how we functioned now. In shifts. We'd come to the garage when he had to work. I'd sit at his desk, writing at my laptop. And whenever I needed to work at the newspaper or go somewhere in town for an interview, he'd be my silent sidekick.

Dash wouldn't let me out of his sight, and oddly enough, I didn't feel smothered. I felt protected. Cherished.

Loved.

If my new schedule bothered Dad, he didn't comment. He and Mom were so happy they were getting a grandchild, he didn't care what I did all day as long as I was *growing his future reporter*.

After a long talk, Dash and I decided not to tell my parents about the kidnapping mostly because it would terrify them. They'd worry it might happen again, and we didn't need any extra attention. Which included deleting my story about the Tin Gypsies.

My backup file—the one I wrote in case Dash betrayed me—had been trashed for good. The ghosts of the former Tin Gypsy Motorcycle Club would rest in peace.

And I was going to print fun stories for a while. I'd let Willy tackle the weekly police press sheets for a couple months. At the moment, I was working on a story about one of Clifton Forge's high school graduates who was off to Harvard in the fall. Exciting news for our small town. The boy's face on the front page was full of hope and wonder.

I clicked save on the final draft, uploading it to the shared drive, as my phone rang. When Genevieve's name flashed on the screen, I blinked twice, not believing it was really her.

"Hey," I answered, standing from the desk because I couldn't keep still. "Are you okay? I've been so worried."

Not a day had gone by when I hadn't sent her a few texts and called at least twice. All had gone unanswered.

"Yeah. Sorry." She sighed. "I'm okay. I just had to get out of there."

"I can certainly understand that." *Except you could be in danger.* I held back the lecture I really wanted to give her. "I'm really glad to hear from you."

"Yeah. Listen." She paused. "I-I was wondering if you could do me a favor."

"Of course."

"I'm here, in Clifton Forge."

"What? You are?"

"There are some things happening. Some, uh . . . changes. Anyway, before it gets crazy, would you meet me somewhere?"

"Sure." I didn't have a car but I'd figure it out. "Where?"

"The cemetery. I'm sitting here in my car and I can't seem to get out."

"Oh, Genevieve." My hand flew to my heart. "I'll be there. Just wait."

"Thanks, Bryce."

I ended the call and groaned.

Dash is going to love this.

———

TWENTY MINUTES LATER, my heart was racing as Dash and I pulled into the cemetery.

After my call with Genevieve, I'd gone to the shop and told Dash about it, knowing full well he'd never let me go alone.

We parked behind a gray sedan with Colorado plates. I

sucked in a deep breath as I got off his bike. Ten seconds later, the rumble of another motorcycle filled the air.

"Damn it," I muttered as Draven pulled into the cemetery. "How'd he know we were coming here?"

"Emmett must have overheard us talking and told him after we left."

This was a good lesson to remember to keep my voice low in the garage.

"It's bad enough that you're here."

He pouted. "Gee. Thanks."

"Oh, you know what I mean." I waved him off. "She needs a friend. Not a crowd."

Not to mention Dash still hadn't warmed to the idea of Genevieve. He still didn't trust her motives completely. Even though he believed she was innocent and hadn't played a part in my kidnapping, I think the picture of her holding a gun to my head was permanently burned into his brain.

"Can you watch from here?" I asked. "I won't be far."

"I'm coming." He moved to stand, but I put my hands on his shoulders, forcing him down.

"She came here to see her mother's grave, Dash. You of all people should be able to understand losing a mother. Let me go with her. Let me help her do this. Please?"

He blew out a deep breath. "Fine."

"Thanks." I leaned in and kissed his cheek.

Behind him, Draven had parked and turned off his motorcycle. I could feel his anticipation from feet away. He wanted to meet his daughter, but I shook my head.

He'd have to wait.

Leaving them on their bikes, I walked over to the sedan. As I got closer, the door opened and Genevieve stepped out.

"Hey. It's good to see you." Warm and dressed, not in the forest where I saw her in my nightmares.

"Thanks for coming."

We hugged hard, like friends who'd known each other for decades, not days. The hug of two people who'd survived the unthinkable together.

When we released each other, she shot a glance at Dash and Draven.

"I have an escort. Sorry. Dash is a little overprotective at the moment."

Her face, if surprised or irritated, gave nothing away. She leveled them with a cool, apprehensive look, like she was bracing herself to be hurt.

I wished I could promise her that Draven wouldn't hurt her. But I wouldn't.

"Ignore them." I took her hand in mine. "This is about you."

Genevieve nodded and we walked onto the grass, dodging tombstones until we came to a granite slab situated under a towering cottonwood tree. A vase of yellow roses had been placed by the tombstone.

"This is a pretty spot," I said.

Genevieve simply nodded, wiping at her eyes before the tears could fall. "She shouldn't be here. She should be smiling with a friend, laughing at a movie or talking to me on the phone. She should be in her kitchen, making Chrissy's cookies."

"Chrissy's cookies?" *As in Chrissy Slater?*

"Yeah." She wiped another tear away. "Those chocolate chip cookies I made the day you came to Denver. That's what Mom always called them. Chrissy's cookies. I guess she got the recipe from a friend named Chrissy once. I didn't know the friend but the cookies are good. Doesn't matter now."

So Amina had used Chrissy's cookie recipe. Maybe someday, those cookies would be something Dash and Genevieve could bond over, something to bridge the gap. Or would it drive them apart? For now, I'd keep the origins of that recipe to myself.

I squeezed her hand. "They are good cookies. The best. And I bet once we publish the recipe with your mom's memorial, the whole town will love them too."

"I hope so," she whispered.

We stood there, staring at the tombstone and Amina's name written in the white-and-gray-swirled rock, until a flash of movement caught my eye. Draven was hovering about twenty feet away. When he met my gaze, he held up a hand.

The movement got Genevieve's attention too and her frame tightened. The grip on my hand turned punishing.

I leaned in close. "You have to meet him eventually."

"Do I?"

"Do you believe what I told you? That he didn't kill your mother? That he's your father?"

"Honestly?" She thought about it for a long moment. "Yes. But I wish I didn't."

"I'll leave you two alone." Stepping away, I retreated toward Dash waiting on his bike. Draven stepped up to Genevieve, giving her an awkward wave before tucking his hand in a pocket.

"I almost feel bad for him," Dash said when I reached his side.

"Will you ever forgive him?"

He shrugged. "Maybe. Maybe Nick was right. He's off

his pedestal now. Might give me a chance to see him as he is."

"He's trying to right his wrongs," I said, watching as Draven and Genevieve stood apart. They faced one another but she had her arms crossed over her chest, clearly indicating he was close enough. "Let's leave them be."

Dash nodded, driving us back to the garage after a quick detour at McDonald's to pick up some burgers and fries for the crew. We crossed the parking lot, each carrying paper bags dotted with grease.

"I almost asked Presley if she'd let me borrow her car so I could sneak away to meet Genevieve," I confessed. "But I thought you might have an aneurism."

He chuckled. "I would have. Do me a favor? Don't give me a heart attack before I get a chance to meet my kid."

I smiled. "I'll try."

"Fuck, but you make me crazy." He stopped walking and pulled me into his arms. "If anything happened to you, I—"

"It won't." I leaned back and cupped his cheek with my free hand. "I'll be careful. Promise."

Dash dropped a kiss on my lips, his touch firm but gentle.

My stomach growled, forcing us apart. We were almost at the office, more than ready to eat, when a familiar gray sedan pulled in behind us.

"Is that—"

"Genevieve?" I finished.

She parked by the office, directly in front of the staircase that led to Isaiah's apartment. Had Draven invited her here? He was nowhere in sight.

"What's she doing here?" Dash muttered.

"Maybe she wanted to meet you?"

He frowned. "Well, I don't much care to meet her."

I elbowed him in the side. "Be nice."

Genevieve got out of the car, her eyes glancing up the staircase before she moved in our direction. "Hey, again."

"Hi." I smiled. "Um, Genevieve, this is Dash. My boyfriend and your—"

"Half brother. Right."

Dash stood there, not saying a word. The silence grew thicker and thicker, until finally, I couldn't take it anymore and I elbowed him in the ribs. Again.

He frowned, shuffling paper bags to free a hand and extend it. "Hi."

As quickly as they touched, the shake was over. Dash jerked his chin to the garage and marched away, taking my french fries with him. "Got work to do."

At least I had the bags with all the burgers.

"Sorry," I told Genevieve.

"Two weeks ago, I was alone, trying to cope with losing Mom. Then I get kidnapped, find out I have a father in Montana who didn't know I existed and a half brother who hates me. I'm numb to it all at this point."

I opened my mouth to tell her she actually had *brothers*, plural, but decided it could wait for another day. "Dash doesn't hate you. He just hasn't had much time to wrap his head around it."

"It doesn't matter." She hung her head. "Nothing matters."

Before I could say anything, a pair of footsteps came down the stairs.

My eyes widened. "Isaiah? Where have you been? We thought you left."

"I did. Now I'm back."

He'd been gone a week, ever since the day of the mountain rescue. No note. No call. He'd just . . . disappeared. Did Dash know he was back?

Isaiah reached the bottom stair and looked at Genevieve. "Hey."

"Hi." She lifted her hand like she was going to shake his but then changed her mind and tucked a lock of hair behind her ear.

"Um, how was the trip?" Isaiah asked.

"Long."

The Colorado plates. I hadn't put it together at the cemetery, assuming she'd just rented a car, but this must be hers. Why would she drive to Montana? That had to be at least eight hours. Maybe more.

"I'll help haul up your stuff." Isaiah walked toward her car.

Stuff? Genevieve followed, her chin down, as Isaiah opened the back seat. It was filled with boxes and suitcases. Inside the trunk was more of the same.

"Are you staying?" I asked her.

Genevieve and Isaiah shared a look, one full of secrets. She nodded and Isaiah hefted out a suitcase and backpack, taking them up his stairs. She followed with a box.

Neither of them answered my question.

"What's goin' on?" Dash asked, coming to my side. "Was that Isaiah?"

"Yes. And I have no idea." Genevieve and Isaiah disappeared up the stairs. "But if I had to guess, I'd say Genevieve is moving into Isaiah's apartment."

He looked down at me, as confused as I was. "What the fuck happened on that mountain?"

CHAPTER TWENTY-EIGHT

BRYCE

"**M**orning." I shuffled into the kitchen in bare feet, wearing Dash's sweatshirt. It enveloped me, hanging thick on my shoulders. The sleeves draped past my fingertips and the hood bunched at the nape of my neck. Wearing it was like having my own personal Dash cocoon.

I'd be taking it with me whenever I went home.

Not that we'd talked about me leaving. In the three days since Genevieve had moved into Isaiah's apartment, I'd all but moved into Dash's home.

"Hey, baby." He crossed the kitchen from where he'd been standing next to the coffee pot. "How are you feeling?"

"Better." I yawned as he tugged me into his chest. "Thanks for letting me sleep in. I needed it."

"You were out."

"I know. I didn't even hear you snore last night."

He chuckled. "Didn't snore because I had my pillow."

"You have a special non-snoring pillow?" I leaned away to look at his face.

"Not a non-snoring pillow, just a decent pillow."

My eyes bulged. "You think my pillows are indecent?"

He grinned. "Admit it, my bed is better than yours."

"I don't want to." I smiled and fell back into his chest.

It was Friday, Dash's normal day off, but he planned to go to the garage later. Even though he had a ton of work to do, I'd begged him for a lazy morning. Some time to sleep in late and linger in the shower. I wanted to enjoy a few quiet moments, like this one, when the unanswered questions from the past six weeks got pushed aside.

"This is nice," I whispered.

He kissed my hair. "Agreed."

We stood like that, leaning into one another, until my stomach growled and forced us apart.

"Breakfast?" He went to the fridge. "What will it be today? More cereal? Or I can make fried eggs and bacon."

I scrunched up my nose. Just the thought of fried-egg-and-bacon-grease smell made my sensitive stomach turn. I needed bland. Carbs were my friends in the morning. "Cheerios, please."

"Cheerios," he grumbled but got out a bowl for me and one for himself.

We settled at a custom, farmhouse-style table in the dining room off the kitchen. It looked like a fancy picnic table with chairs instead of benches.

"Any word from your dad?" I asked.

He shook his head, swallowing a bite of cereal. "Nothing. But if something comes up, he'll call."

"Damn." We'd tried so hard to prove Draven was innocent. Now it looked like whoever had orchestrated this whole thing would win.

I hated losing.

Dash did too.

"Did Genevieve text you back?" he asked.

"Nope." I dropped my spoon into my cereal bowl. She was beginning to irritate me with her silence.

Whatever was going on between Isaiah and Genevieve, they weren't talking. She'd moved into his apartment, and rumor had it, he'd spent a night or two in the motel.

He'd asked Dash if he could keep his job, apologizing for skipping out without a word. Dash, of course, had cut him some slack and let him stay on because Isaiah was a good guy and a good mechanic. I'd hoped that Dash would have more luck with Isaiah than I had with Genevieve, but Isaiah was arguably worse when it came to opening up. He came to the garage every day, worked hard with as few words as possible, then left as soon as his shift was over.

Meanwhile, Genevieve was gone each morning when we got to the garage and didn't return until after we'd left for the evening. She also wasn't returning my calls or my texts.

I'd wear her down eventually. They couldn't keep their secret forever, could they? At some point, they'd have to tell us what had happened on that mountain, right?

But for today, I was pushing it from my mind.

I finished my cereal, then turned my gaze to the enormous bay window that overlooked Dash's backyard. The sun was shining. The grass was green. Under a bright blue sky, it was a peaceful corner of the world.

Dash had a sprawling deck with his hot tub off to one side. The lawn was wide and deep with a tall privacy fence to keep it cozy, even though he didn't have neighbors. An open field sat behind his yard. There was a small creek flowing through the middle and one lush grove of trees.

"How many acres do you own?" I asked Dash.

"Twenty. I wanted some space from the neighbors."

It was secluded but not remote. Close to town for convenience but away from the bustle. "Did you buy this house? Or have it built?"

"Had it built about three years ago."

I stood from the table, taking my bowl to the kitchen sink, then slowly wandered down the hallway that ran in the opposite direction from his bedroom. I'd explored some while I'd been here, but today I wanted more than a superficial glance to get my bearings.

The hallways were wide, the doors clean and white. The floors were a dark wood with rugs in a few rooms to soften them up.

"It's very . . . stylish," I told Dash as I walked, him trailing close behind. "Not what I would have expected from you."

"I shelled out a fucking fortune to get a designer in here to make it *stylish*. Mostly, I wanted nice shit that would last and was comfortable. Some of the stuff she picked I had to veto, but otherwise, it turned out just right." He came up behind me, wrapping his arms around my shoulders.

I traced my fingers along a tattoo on the inside of his wrist. It was the one tattoo I hadn't asked about yet, a date blocked in black letters. "What's this tattoo?"

"Mom's birthday. It was my first tattoo. Got it when I turned eighteen. I celebrate on that day every year. Make a chocolate cake. Candles."

"I bet she'd love that."

"Yeah." He pressed his cheek to the top of my head. "Glad you're here."

"Me too. I like your house."

"Good." He hugged me tighter, then let me go to turn me around. "Come check this out."

We turned and retreated down the hallway, making our

way toward his bedroom on the opposite end of the house. But instead of turning into his room like I'd expected, he opened a door to the office across the hall.

The desk in the corner was empty, nothing like the mess he had at the garage. The window on the side faced the front of the house. Outside the window was a bush full of white blooms.

Dash walked into the middle of the room. "How about this for a nursery?"

"Uh . . ." A nursery? *Did I hear that right?* I'd expected him to offer this room up for work, not a room for the baby.

We hadn't talked about the baby all week. I hadn't wanted to push it. I'd wanted to give him—both of us—some time for the concept to really sink deep. We had months to discuss a nursery. We didn't even know if we were having a boy or girl yet.

"I'll move the desk and stuff to one of the spare rooms. Or downstairs. I don't use it much anyway. We can get a crib or bassinette or whatever you want. It's right across the hall from our room. And—"

"Wait." I put a hand on the wall as the room began to spin. "Nursery? Our room? You want me to live here?"

"We're having a kid."

"Yes, but that doesn't dictate we move in together."

"Then how about you move in because I love you."

Seriously, my ears were not working right today. "You love me?"

"More every day." He came over and took my face in his hands. "Think how crazy I'll be about you when we're ninety."

A laugh escaped my lips. "Insane. I love you too."

"Good. That'll make it easier to be your roommate."

I smiled wider. "We're really doing this? Living together? Having a baby?"

"We're really doing this. Living together. Having a baby. Getting married."

"Married? Who are you and what have you done with Kingston Slater?" I'd gone to bed with Dash, a badass playboy, and woken up with a romantic. "Did you hit your head with a wrench yesterday? You're aware that you're asking me to marry you, right?"

"Well, yeah. You said you wanted to have a baby when you were married and settled. Way I see it, we've got about seven months to make that happen. Might as well get to it."

Oh. My heart sank. Dash wasn't doing this because he wanted to. He was doing it for me. "Dash, I appreciate it. But I don't want to get married because you feel like it's what I want."

"Then how about because it's what I want." His voice was low, smooth and silky. "Trust me, babe. I want to do this with you. Every day. Here until the end."

"Are you sure?"

"It's the best idea I've had in my life."

"Do you think we'll kill each other?"

"Probably." He dropped a kiss to my lips. "Is that a yes?"

I hesitated, making him sweat for it before I rescued him. "Yes."

"Hell yes." Dash tipped his head back and laughed. Then his hands fell from my face to wrap me in a hug. I giggled, clinging to him as he picked me up off my feet and spun me around the room.

For so long I'd wanted this. Never would I have imagined I'd find it, a home—love—with the man I'd set out to expose. The enemy. A criminal who'd stolen my heart.

All the foolish days and nights I'd spent wondering if I'd end up an old maid had been for nothing. The timing simply hadn't come together.

I'd been waiting for my Gypsy King.

"What about the baby?" I asked. "You didn't want kids."

Dash's smile softened but didn't disappear. "I'm scared. Never saw myself with a kid, but if there is anyone in the world I'd want to raise a baby with, it's you. Just keep me from fucking it up, okay?"

Oh, Dash. Why hadn't I realized this before? He wasn't scared *of* kids. He was scared of ruining his own. Again, timing was not on our side. Draven's drama had probably reinforced Dash's fears.

"I have faith in you. Blinding, unwavering faith. You'll be an amazing dad, Dash."

He dropped his forehead to mine. "Come on. I want to show you something else."

Dash took my hand and led me out of the office. We walked past his bedroom and through the living room, then around the kitchen and down another spacious hallway.

"This is a family house," I said. "If you didn't want a family, why build such a big house?"

He shrugged. "For the space. Not to feel crowded. I spent a lot of nights at the clubhouse and I lived above the garage for a while. When I was finally ready to buy, I wanted space. A home gym so I didn't have to go to town in the morning. An office. A theater room in the basement. Couldn't find anything to buy so I had it built instead."

"A sanctuary."

"Yeah, but there's one thing I hate about it out here." He shot me a heart-stopping smile over his shoulder. "It's too quiet. Figure you and our baby can fix that for me."

I laughed. Given his or her parents, there was no doubt our child would be loud and bold. "We'll do our best."

"Appreciated." Dash led me to the garage. He let go of my hand as he walked to the large, green gun safe on the far wall, spinning the combination on the dial until the door clicked open.

"Holy shit." My eyes widened at the small arsenal. "I guess we'll be safe after the apocalypse."

He took out a white envelope and shut the safe. The flap on the envelope wasn't sealed and he flipped it open, pulling out something from the corner.

No, not something.

A ring.

"This was Mom's." He held the ring in one hand as he reached for my left.

"It's beautiful." The gold band was thin and delicate because the solitaire in the center was the showpiece. It was a square-cut diamond—simple and flawless. The entire piece was classic, something I would have picked for myself.

"Dad gave this to me a few years ago. He'd bought it for her on their tenth wedding anniversary but she didn't wear it much. She preferred the chip he'd bought her when they were just two dirt-poor kids. He buried her with that one. Gave this to me since Nick was already married. Told me one day, I could give this to my old lady."

I was dumbfounded. I'd asked for a morning to rest and he'd changed the rules. But even in my shock, I hadn't missed those last two words.

"How about you never call me an old lady again?"

Dash laughed, the rich sound filling the garage. "Want me to get down on a knee? Do this right?"

"No." I smiled up at him, wiggling my finger so he'd slide

the ring into place. I didn't need the bended knee, the fancy words. "You already nailed it."

The moment the ring was settled onto my finger, Dash swooped down and captured me in a kiss. His tongue dove inside, demanding and delicious. Standing in a garage, the cement floor cool on my bare feet, we kissed until the heat was too much to stand. Then Dash scooped me up and carried me inside to his bed.

Our bed.

I'd admit, it was better than mine. The sweatshirt was stripped off. My panties dragged down my bare legs. Dash's jeans quickly disappeared along with the white T-shirt that stretched across his broad chest.

We moved together, my hips cradling his, like lovers who'd been together for years, not weeks. We came together, him bare and pulsing inside me, our hands linked and our mouths fused.

Together.

"I love you," I whispered into his ear as we clung to one another.

"Love you, baby." He leaned away, sweeping the hair from my forehead, and grinned. "Damn, but this life is going to be fun. And I promise, I'll do right by you."

He'd be the best husband and father I could have ever dreamed possible.

"You will." I smiled. "And you're right. This *is* going to be fun."

EPILOGUE

DASH

O *ne year later . . .*
　　"Hey, babe."

"Hi." Bryce smiled as she came into the living room, dropping her purse onto the couch before stealing Xander from my arms. She peppered his cheeks and forehead with kisses. "How's my guy?"

"He's good." I laced my hands behind my head. "Just slugged down eight ounces and had a hell of a burp."

"He's such a chunk." She smiled at our son, who was nearly comatose. "I love it."

Xander Lane Slater was four months old and his legs were fat roll upon fat roll. He had a pretty awesome double chin going too. We took extra care cleaning it during his nightly bath so it didn't smell like rotten formula.

I stood from my chair, going for her purse and the newspaper tucked inside. "How'd this morning go?"

"Perfect. Papers are out for delivery." She settled into the chair I'd vacated, rocking back and forth slightly. Xander would be out cold in thirty seconds or less.

368

Exactly as I'd planned. He was going in his crib and Bryce and I were going to have some fun in the bedroom.

But first, I had to read the paper.

I plopped down on the couch, opening the fold to read the front page. I'd never get sick of seeing my wife's name in print. It was a sense of pride I hoped would never fade.

Bryce had confessed not long after we'd gotten together that a part of her had felt like a failure when she'd moved to Clifton Forge. She'd had dreams of making it big, being the next nightly news anchor—not exactly the same as running a small-town paper. But then she'd realized that here, writing stories about our town and its people, was where she was meant to be. She reported on the good stuff that happened in Clifton Forge and occasionally the bad.

She'd embraced the birth and wedding announcements, even writing our own. We'd gotten married surrounded by our families and closest friends at dusk, along the bank of the river. Then we'd had a damn fine party at The Betsy—her idea, not mine. Her only request was that they scour the bathrooms first.

We'd gotten married a month after I'd proposed so she hadn't been showing. That was her only real request. She wanted to *hurry things along.*

Nick stood for me as best man. And Genevieve stood for Bryce.

I liked to think maybe Mom had a hand in Nick and me finding our wives. That wherever she was, she was looking down on her sons and had sent them the women they needed.

Including my sister.

"Did you take a copy to Genevieve?" I asked as I scanned the article on the front page.

"Yep."

"How'd she take it?"

"She cried," Bryce said, dropping her voice. Xander was completely zonked. "But she needed that closure. I think she's happy with how it turned out."

In today's paper, Bryce had written a memorial article for Amina, one she'd had drafted for over a year. Bryce had been ready to publish it weeks after Genevieve had moved to Clifton Forge, but my sister had asked her to delay it countless times.

She hadn't been ready to read that final farewell. After everything that had happened to us this past year, I didn't blame her.

I was proud that she'd finally found the courage to let it happen.

"Great piece, babe." I folded up the paper.

"Thanks. Though you should be congratulating yourself too. You practically read the whole thing while hovering over my shoulder as I wrote it."

"I don't hover."

Bryce rolled her eyes. "And I don't leave the laundry for you to fold."

Maybe I hovered.

In the past year, I'd kept a constant eye on Bryce. It was rare she went anywhere alone, and even then, I had someone watching. Today, that person was Lane. Bryce hadn't complained, not once all year, because she knew I needed it. I needed to make sure she was safe and she gave me that. But she needed freedom. To live without watching me worry myself in circles.

I'd be the first to admit that after Xander was born, I'd gone a little crazy with security. The system I'd installed at home was better than the one Emmett had put in at the clubhouse.

But I wasn't taking any chances with my family, not after the losses I'd suffered.

Maybe I'd loosen up eventually.

Maybe not.

I was taking things one day at a time, doing my best to become a decent dad. Bryce told me constantly I was good with Xander, but the fuck-ups were coming. I'd do something wrong and take a misstep here or there.

But what I could do was protect what was mine. I'd failed once when Bryce had been kidnapped. That had been the first and the last time.

"He's out." Bryce pushed herself up from the chair, nodding for me to follow her to the nursery.

I grinned, walking close behind her down the hallway. At the door to Xander's room, I placed my hands on her shoulders, bending down to drop a kiss on the bare skin of her neck. She'd worn her hair up in a ponytail today. Xander had just started to grab at things and her hair was his favorite thing to pull.

Maybe I'd wrap it around my fist too.

When she smiled over her shoulder, the blood rushed to my cock. We'd been working hard to make up for those six weeks postpartum when her body had been off-limits.

Bryce took Xander to the nursery, laying him in his crib. His arms immediately went above his head. Then she turned on his sound machine, the gentle sway of ocean waves filling the room. She tiptoed out, quietly closing the door.

I captured her hand, giving it a tug for the bedroom, but she stopped me.

"Wait. I need to ask you something."

"What's up?" My eyes scanned her from head to toe, making sure nothing was wrong. "You okay?"

She bit her bottom lip. "How would you feel about more kids?"

"Uh . . ." A deep conversation about our family wasn't exactly what I'd planned to have during naptime, but the question was out there now. *How would I feel?*

Having Xander was amazing. Even as a baby who ate and slept his way through the day, he was a blast. And when he got older, we could do stuff together like play ball in the yard or build a tree house or build a go-cart to race like the ones I did as a kid. That would be incredible.

"Good," I said, surprising us both. "Real good."

"Phew." Her frame relaxed and her smile was wide. "Great. I'm pregnant."

"Say what?" I stuck a finger in my ear, clearing it out. "You're pregnant? Already?"

"According to the tests I took this morning, yep. I mean, I stopped breastfeeding and didn't get on the pill. I have the pack to start next week but I didn't think it could happen so soon."

Pregnant. Was I still scared? Definitely. But this time around, I wasn't going to let the shock of her announcement chase me away. So I wrapped my arms around her, breathing in her hair. "Love you."

"Love you too." She melted into my chest, her arms snaking behind my back. "I was sure you'd freak."

I chuckled. "Not this time. We're going to kick ass with these kids."

Bryce leaned away, rising onto her toes for a kiss. "Hell yes, we are."

BONUS EPILOGUE
BRYCE

"Why did I think this would be a good idea?" I forced another smile as the photographer positioned herself behind the camera. Then, we waited. And waited.

"Take the fucking pic—"

Click.

Dash growled at my side, his body stiff.

"Oh, that looks so cute!" The photographer was a twenty-something-year-old woman with a ponytail pulled so tight, she had to be stretching brain cells. She'd come into our hospital room this morning, her smile irritatingly bright for eight o'clock.

I would have dismissed her for the smile alone, except then she'd whipped out this three-ring binder filled with newborn photos and I'd been suckered.

She'd given us a few hours to get up and move around a little. I'd fed Zeke and the nurses had come in to take him for a bath. Then I'd hopped into a lukewarm shower, swiping on the bare minimum makeup and blow-drying my hair, just in time for my parents, Genevieve, and Isaiah to drop by.

The photographer, of course, had chosen that moment to return, her camera ready.

Dash had stayed quiet for the first thirty photos. He'd sat by my side on the bed as she'd twisted and turned Zeke in a million different positions.

God bless that baby. He'd slept through it all.

Now he was in my arms, totally done—like his father—with the noise and chaos. His little face was turning red and angry. We'd asked for one family pose.

One.

And it had taken for-fucking-ever.

I was holding Zeke Draven Slater, a name I'd had to spell for her three times because she kept writing it wrong on the order form. Dash was wrestling with one-year-old Xander, who wanted to keep petting his new brother's matting of dark hair.

We kept smiling, the photographer going slower than any human on earth. My mother was in the corner, waving and jumping around like a lunatic to get Xander's attention for a picture.

"One more," the photographer said. "How about everyone?"

"Will we all fit?" I asked.

"Sure!" *God, she was loud.*

"Let's go. Get in here, people," Dash ordered.

Genevieve hurried over first, leaning in to whisper as she sat on the edge of the bed. "Sorry, we should have called first."

"It's okay."

Isaiah stood behind her, his hand resting on her shoulder. My parents crowded next to them. Dad stretched over us, tickling Xander's chin and making him laugh.

That was a sound I wish I could bottle, to stick in a seashell so I could press it against my ear when he was a teenager and remember how he'd sounded.

I smiled at my son, then looked up to find Dash's eyes waiting.

"Love you," we mouthed at the same time.

"Okay. One. Two. Three . . ." One would have expected a click after three. Not this lady.

Four. Five. Six.

Click.

The entire room sighed, ready to break. But then a knock came and two familiar little heads came bounding through the door.

"Hey." Nick and Emmeline followed their kids into the room. "Looks like we got a full house."

"Are you family?" the photographer asked, not waiting for an answer. "You should hop in the picture too."

"Uh . . ." Nick looked to me.

I sighed. "Come on in. Let's do this." The photographer wouldn't leave until she'd deemed this photo shoot a success.

Nick quickly ordered their son Draven and daughter Nora to hop up on the bed.

"Is that him?" Nora scooted my way, enamored with her new cousin. She'd been the same way when Xander was a baby. She squealed. "He's so cute!"

"Okay, guys. Turn around. Smile at the camera," Emmeline told her kids, taking up a place beside Dash. She gave him a wink, then reached over to squeeze my knee. "Hi."

"Hi." I smiled.

Somehow, I'd gotten lucky when it came to sisters-in-law. They were more than extended family. They were my best friends.

"Hey, Sis." Dash rose to kiss Emmeline's cheek, then shook hands with Nick. "Hey, brother. Glad you guys could make it."

Grins spread across both of their faces, their matching eyes full of joy. I hoped our boys would have that with each other too.

"Wouldn't miss it," Nick said, as he put his arm around Emmeline's shoulders. She flipped her long red hair free and smiled at her husband.

They were living their fairy tale.

So was I.

"Ready," Dash told the photographer.

"Okay. One second," she said, adjusting her tripod.

One second turned into three minutes. I know because I watched the clock tick the entire time.

"Jesus Christ," Nick muttered at the same time Dash said, "Fuck this."

"Ready." The photographer was going to be lucky to leave this room with her life. "One. Two. Three. Say—"

"Farts!"

That came from Draven who'd just turned eight.

The entire room erupted in laughter, Nora giggling next to her brother as they collapsed into hysteria on the foot of my bed. My parents hugged each other, Dad laughing into Mom's ear. Genevieve looked up at Isaiah as he smiled at her. Emmeline looked mortified. Nick beamed with pride, his chest shaking as a grin stretched across his face.

And Dash and I looked at one another, laughing as we held our sons.

Click.

ACKNOWLEDGMENTS

Thank you for reading *Steel King*! I am so grateful to have such amazing readers.

Special thanks to my editing and proofreading team: Elizabeth Nover, Marion Archer, Julie Deaton and Karen Lawson. To Jennifer Santa Ana for being my keeper of secrets. Thank you to Sarah Hansen for this beautiful cover.

I can't say thank you enough to all of the amazing bloggers who read and spread the word about my books. To Perry Street, thank you for loving my stories. Your excitement for them fills my heart!

And lastly, thank you to my friends and family, who never stop believing in me.

ABOUT THE AUTHOR

Devney is a *USA Today* bestselling author who lives in Washington with her husband and two sons. Born and raised in Montana, she loves writing books set in her treasured home state. After working in the technology industry for nearly a decade, she abandoned conference calls and project schedules to enjoy a slower pace at home with her family. Writing one book, let alone many, was not something she ever expected to do. But now that she's discovered her true passion for writing romance, she has no plans to ever stop.

Don't miss out on Devney's latest book news.
Subscribe to her newsletter!
www.devneyperry.com

Made in the USA
Middletown, DE
06 July 2023

34668644R00229